The yellowbacks… classics of popular fiction

The yellowjackets or yellowbacks were a great series of bestselling adventure and crime thrillers that had its origins in the mid to late 19th century following on from the 'penny dreadfuls'. They virtually began the mass market revolution of the early 20th century with a clear standard format and imprint/series livery (what would today be called branding). Hodder & Stoughton published the yellowjackets in two main series with series run dates of: 1923-1939 and later 1949-1957.

As the tagline ('where thrillers really began') on the back cover implies, the imprint and series focused on thrillers that were the bestsellers of their time. This current reissue or retro revival if you will, brings back many of these masterpieces, now classics in their own way and extends it further by including key titles from that period that were either great crime or thriller or even general commercial fiction (including sub-genres of noir, horror, gothic, romance, westerns, etc.) influences of their time. There are some perennial favourites and many rarities either lost or not easily available being revived in the current series. Writers and characters ranged from adventure heroes like Bulldog Drummond, Allan Quatermain, Richard Hannay or the Saint through thriller grandmasters Edgar Wallace and E. Phillips Oppenheim, crime and mystery maestros like Patricia Wentworth, GK Chesterton, Agatha Christie and the Detection club, to western and swashbucklers like Zane Grey, Max Brand, Captain Blood and even romance or general fiction classics like Hermina Black, Denise Robins, Marie Corelli or Stella Morton. These were books that had storytelling at their heart and always entertained.

The yellowbacks had both hardback (with varying design elements) and paperback (which built the series look) versions with the latter still carrying the imprint 'yellowjacket'. The current reissues pay tribute to both and use an amalgam of elements from both editions while retaining the complete yellow (or 'mustard-plaster') livery with the author's name in blue beveled type with a 'simulated emboss' effect and a white outer 'outline', and the book title in black. These reissues retain the distinctive size of the original mass market paperback and follow the three main category variations—the thrillers (crime, westerns, mystery, adventure) had blue lettering for the author's name, while Romance and softer general fiction had red; and other categories like humour had green.

For more detail and a full list of titles visit https://www.hachetteindia.com/home/yellowbacks

THE COMPLETE THINKING MACHINE

VOLUME 3

THE COMPLETE THINKING MACHINE

Jacques Heath Futrelle (9 April 1875 – 15 April 1912) was an American journalist and mystery writer who achieved fame for his detective stories featuring 'The Thinking Machine' which were originally published in *The Saturday Evening Post* and the *Boston American*. Futrelle died at age 37 on 15 April 1912, on the RMS Titanic. He refused to board a lifeboat, insisting that his wife board instead. Interestingly Futrelle was used as the lead character in Max Allan Collins' disaster series novel *The Titanic Murders* (1999), which was about two murders aboard the Titanic.

THE
COMPLETE
THINKING MACHINE

Jacques Futrelle

VOLUME 3

The Complete Thinking Machine
First published by Chapman & Hall, Limited, London in 1907

This Hodder Yellowback edition © Hachette India 2023
(Registered Name: Hachette Book Publishing India Pvt. Ltd.)
An Hachette UK Company www.hachetteindia.com

1

All rights reserved. No part of the publication may be reproduced, stored in a retrieval system (including but not limited to computers, disks, external drives, electronic or digital devices, e-readers, websites), or transmitted in any form or by any means (including but not limited to cyclostyling, photocopying, docutech or other reprographic reproductions, mechanical, recording, electronic, digital versions) without the prior written permission of the publisher, nor be otherwise circulated in any form of binding or cover other than that in which it is published and without a similar condition being imposed on the subsequent purchaser.

The texts in these editions in most cases have been reprinted as is, with minimal editorial changes and by and large no bowdlerizing for political correctness; though in some editions, a few words and phrases considered archaic, or those considered offensive now, along with archaic punctuation may have been modified in places to make the text more accessible to today's readers. The narratives, language, beliefs, social mores and/or cultural depictions, in these volumes are a reflection of their times and must be viewed as such. They may also contain certain cultural, racial and gender prejudices and stereotypes that may be outdated or clearly wrong then and wrong today; but their removal would be tantamount to claiming these prejudices never existed. The Publisher does not endorse or support those depictions or stereotypes; and these books have been made available for a discerning audience that will read it for entertainment value and a chronicle/record of popular fiction of past times.

Cover design by Priya Singh adapted from the original classic yellowjacket by Hodder & Stoughton.

Cover illustration by Ishan Trivedi.

Series note: Some of the books in the series (unless otherwise credited) may have cover or inside illustrations from the original yellowbacks or early editions, and while full restoration has been attempted, some images may be grainy or faded due to the condition of the original material. The end notes or bonus material or blurb details may have been sourced from the public domain or free use publications such as Wikipedia and attribution is hereby made also allowing similar free use reproduction from here. Sources requiring further specific attribution may write in and further detailing and/or corrections shall be made in subsequent printings/editions.

Reprint specifications may be subject to change including but not limited to finishes, paper, colour sections.

ISBN: 978-93-5731-074-1

Hachette Book Publishing India Pvt. Ltd.
4th & 5th Floors, Corporate Centre,
Plot No. 94, Sector 44, Gurugram – 122 003, India

Typeset in Electra LT STD 10/12.5 pt by Manipal Technologies Limited, Manipal

Printed and bound in India by Manipal Technologies Limited, Manipal

CONTENTS

1. Problem of the Stolen Rubens	1
2. Mystery of the Grip of Death	14
3. Problem of the Superfluous Finger	43
4. Problem of the Vanishing Man	62
5. The Case of the Scientific Murderer	80
6. The Great Auto Mystery	102
7. The Grinning God	145
8. The Mystery of Studio A	183
9. The Phantom Motor	214
10. The Problem of the Auto Cab	231
11. The Roswell Tiara	244
12. Problem of the Souvenir Cards	261
13. The Three Overcoats	274
14. Mystery of the Man Who Was Lost	287
15. Problem of Dressing Room A	322
16. The Leak	340
17. The Brown Coat	357

1

PROBLEM OF THE STOLEN RUBENS

Matthew Kale made fifty million dollars out of axle grease, after which he began to patronize the high arts. It was simple enough: he had the money, and Europe had the old masters. His method of buying was simplicity itself. There were five thousand square yards, more or less, in the huge gallery of his marble mansion which were to be covered, so he bought five thousand square yards, more or less, of art. Some of it was good, some of it fair, and much of it bad. The chief picture of the collection was a Rubens, which he had picked up in Rome for fifty thousand dollars.

Soon after acquiring his collection, Kale decided to make certain alterations in the vast room where the pictures hung. They were all taken down and stored in the ball room, equally vast, with their faces toward the wall. Meanwhile Kale and his family took refuge in a nearby hotel.

It was at this hotel that Kale met Jules de Lesseps. De Lesseps was distinctly French, the sort of Frenchman whose conversation resembles calisthenics. He was nervous, quick, and agile, and he told Kale in confidence that he was not only a painter himself, but was a connoisseur in the high arts. Pompous in the pride of possession, Kale went to a good deal of trouble to exhibit his private collection for de Lesseps' delectation. It happened in the ball room, and the true artist's delight shone in the Frenchman's eyes as he handled the pieces which were good. Some of the others made him smile, but it was an inoffensive sort of smile.

With his own hands Kale lifted the precious Rubens and held it before the Frenchman's eyes. It was a "Madonna and Child," one of those wonderful creations which have endured through the years with all the sparkle and color beauty of their pristine days. Kale seemed disappointed because de Lesseps was not particularly enthusiastic about this picture.

"Why, it's a Rubens!" he exclaimed.

"Yes, I see," replied de Lesseps.

"It cost me fifty thousand dollars."

"It is perhaps worth more than that," and the Frenchman shrugged his shoulders as he turned away.

Kale looked at him in chagrin. Could it be that de Lesseps did not understand that it was a Rubens, and that Rubens was a painter? Or was it that he had failed to hear him say that it cost him fifty thousand dollars. Kale was accustomed to seeing people bob their heads and open their eyes when he said fifty thousand dollars; therefore, "Don't you like it?" he asked.

"Very much indeed," replied de Lesseps; "but I have seen it before. I saw it in Rome just a week or so before you purchased it."

They rummaged on through the pictures, and at last a Whistler was turned up for their inspection. It was one of the famous Thames series, a water color. De Lesseps' face radiated excitement, and several times he glanced from the water color to the Rubens as if mentally comparing the exquisitely penciled and colored modern work with the bold, masterly technic of the old.

Kale misunderstood the silence. "I don't think much of this one myself," he explained apologetically. "It's a Whistler, and all that, and it cost me five thousand dollars, and I sort of had to have it, but still it isn't just the kind of thing that I like. What do you think of it?"

"I think it is perfectly wonderful!" replied the Frenchman enthusiastically. "It is the essence, the superlative, of modern work. I wonder if it would be possible," and he turned to face Kale, "for me to make a copy of that? I have some slight skill in painting myself, and dare say I could make a fairly creditable copy of it."

Kale was flattered. He was more and more impressed each moment with the picture. "Why, certainly," he replied. "I will have it sent up to the hotel, and you can—"

"No, no, no!" interrupted de Lesseps quickly. "I wouldn't care to accept the responsibility of having the picture in my charge. There is always a danger of fire. But if you would give me permission to come here – this room is large and airy and light, and besides it is quiet—"

"Just as you like," said Kale magnanimously. "I merely thought the other way would be most convenient for you."

De Lesseps drew near, and laid one hand on the millionaire's arm. "My dear friend," he said earnestly, "if these pictures were my pictures, I shouldn't try to accommodate anybody where they were concerned. I dare say the collection as it stands cost you—"

"Six hundred and eighty-seven thousand dollars," volunteered Kale proudly.

"And surely they must be well protected here in your house during your absence?"

"There are about twenty servants in the house while the workmen are making the alterations," said Kale, "and three of them don't do anything but watch this room. No one can go in or out except by the door we entered – the others are locked and barred – and then only with my permission, or a written order from me. No, sir, nobody can get away with anything in this room."

"Excellent-excellent!" said de Lesseps admiringly. He smiled a little bit. "I am afraid I did not give you credit for being the far-sighted businessman that you are." He turned and glanced over the collection of pictures abstractedly. "A clever thief, though," he ventured, "might cut a valuable painting, for instance the Rubens, out of the frame, roll it up, conceal it under his coat, and escape."

Kale laughed pleasantly and shook his head.

It was a couple of days later at the hotel that de Lesseps brought up the subject of copying the Whistler. He was profuse in his thanks when Kale volunteered to accompany him to the mansion and witness the preliminary stages of the work. They paused at the ball room door.

"Jennings," said Kale to the liveried servant there, "this is Mr de Lesseps. He is to come and go as he likes. He is going to do some work in the ball room here. See that he isn't disturbed."

De Lesseps noticed the Rubens leaning carelessly against some other pictures, with the holy face of the Madonna toward them. "Really, Mr Kale," he protested, "that picture is too valuable to be left about like that. If you will let your servants bring me some canvas, I shall wrap it and place it up on the table here off the floor. Suppose there were mice here!"

Kale thanked him. The necessary orders were given, and finally the picture was carefully wrapped and placed beyond harm's reach, whereupon de Lesseps adjusted himself, paper, easel, stool, and all, and began his work of copying. There Kale left him.

Three days later Kale just happened to drop in, and found the artist still at his labor.

"I just dropped by," he explained, "to see how the work in the gallery was getting along. It will be finished in another week. I hope I am not disturbing you?"

"Not at all," said de Lesseps; "I have nearly finished. See how I am getting along?" He turned the easel toward Kale.

The millionaire gazed from that toward the original which stood on a chair near by, and frank admiration for the artist's efforts was in his eyes. "Why, it's fine!" he exclaimed. "It's just as good as the other one, and I bet you don't want any five thousand dollars for it – eh?"

That was all that was said about it at the time. Kale wandered about the house for an hour or so, then dropped into the ball room where the artist was just getting his paraphernalia together, and they walked back to the hotel. The artist carried under one arm his copy of the Whistler, loosely rolled up.

Another week passed, and the workmen who had been engaged in refinishing and decorating the gallery had gone. De Lesseps volunteered to assist in the work of rehanging the pictures, and Kale gladly turned the matter over to him. It was in the afternoon of the day this work began that de Lesseps, chatting pleasantly with Kale, ripped loose the canvas which enshrouded the precious Rubens. Then he paused with an exclamation of dismay. The picture was gone; the frame which had held it was empty. A thin strip of canvas around the inside edge showed that a sharp penknife had been used to cut out the painting.

All of these facts came to the attention of Professor Augustus S. F. X. Van Dusen – The Thinking Machine. This was a day or so after Kale had rushed into Detective Mallory's office at police headquarters, with the statement that his Rubens had been stolen. He banged his fist down on the detective's desk and roared at him.

"It cost me fifty thousand dollars!" he declared violently. "Why don't you do something? What are you sitting there staring at me for?"

"Don't excite yourself, Mr Kale," the detective advised. "I will put my men at work right now to recover the – the – What is a Rubens, anyway?"

"It's a picture!" bellowed Mr Kale. "A piece of canvas with some paint on it, and it cost me fifty thousand dollars – don't you forget that!"

So the police machinery was set in motion to recover the painting. And in time the matter fell under the watchful eye of Hutchinson Hatch, reporter. He learned the facts preceding the disappearance of the picture, and then called on de Lesseps. He found the artist in a state of excitement bordering on hysteria; an intimation from the reporter of the object of his visit caused de Lesseps to burst into words.

"Mon Dieu! it is outrageous!" he exclaimed. "What can I do? I was the only one in the room for several days. I was the one who took such pains to protect the picture. And now it is gone! The loss is irreparable. What can I do?"

Hatch didn't have any very definite idea as to just what he could do, so he let him go on. "As I understand it, Mr de Lesseps," he interrupted at last, "no one else was in the room, except you and Mr Kale, all the time you were there?"

"No one else."

"And I think Mr Kale said that you were making a copy of some famous water color; weren't you?"

"Yes, a Thames scene, by Whistler," was the reply. "That is it, hanging over the mantel."

Hatch glanced at the picture admiringly. It was an exquisite copy, and showed the deft touch of a man who was himself an artist of great ability.

De Lesseps read the admiration in his face. "It is not bad," he said modestly. "I studied with Carolus Duran."

With all else that was known, and this little additional information, which seemed of no particular value to the reporter, the entire matter was laid before The Thinking Machine. That distinguished man listened from beginning to end without comment.

"Who had access to the room?" he asked finally.

"That is what the police are working on now," was the reply. "There are a couple of dozen servants in the house, and I suppose, in spite of Kale's rigid orders, there was a certain laxity in their enforcement."

"Of course that makes it more difficult," said The Thinking Machine in the perpetually irritated voice which was so distinctly a part of himself. "Perhaps it would be best for us to go to Mr Kale's home and personally investigate."

Kale received them with the reserve which all rich men show in the presence of representatives of the press. He stared frankly and somewhat curiously at the diminutive figure of the scientist, who explained the object of their visit.

"I guess you fellows can't do anything with this," the millionaire assured them. "I've got some regular detectives on it."

"Is Mr Mallory here now?" asked The Thinking Machine curtly.

"Yes, he is upstairs in the servants' quarters."

"May we see the room from which the picture was taken?" inquired the scientist, with a suave intonation which Hatch knew well.

Kale granted the permission with a wave of the hand, and ushered them into the ball room, where the pictures had been stored. From the relative center of this room The Thinking Machine surveyed it all. The windows were high. Half a dozen doors leading out into the hallways, to the conservatory, and quiet nooks of the mansion offered innumerable possibilities of access. After this one long comprehensive squint, The Thinking Machine went over and picked up the frame from which the Rubens had been cut. For a long time he examined it. Kale's impatience was painfully evident. Finally the scientist turned to him.

"How well do you know M. de Lesseps?" he asked.

"I've known him for only a month or so. Why?"

"Did he bring you letters of introduction, or did you meet him merely casually?"

Kale regarded him with evident displeasure. "My own personal affairs have nothing whatever to do with this matter," he said pointedly. "Mr de Lesseps is a gentleman of integrity, and certainly he is the last whom I would suspect of any connection with the disappearance of the picture."

"That is usually the case," remarked The Thinking Machine tartly. He turned to Hatch. "Just how good a copy was that he made of the Whistler picture?" he asked.

"I have never seen the original," Hatch replied; "but the workmanship was superb. Perhaps Mr Kale wouldn't object to us seeing—"

"Oh, of course not," said Kale resignedly. "Come in; it's in the gallery."

Hatch submitted the picture to a careful scrutiny. "I should say that the copy is well nigh perfect," was his verdict. "Of course, in its absence, I couldn't say exactly; but it is certainly a superb work."

The curtains of a wide door almost in front of them were thrown aside suddenly, and Detective Mallory entered. He carried something in his hand, but at the sight of them concealed it behind him. Unrepressed triumph was in his face.

"Ah, professor, we meet often; don't we?" he said.

"This reporter here and his friend seem to be trying to drag de Lesseps into this affair somehow," Kale complained to the detective. "I don't want anything like that to happen. He is liable to go out and print anything. They always do."

The Thinking Machine glared at him unwaveringly, straight in the eye for an instant, then extended his hand toward Mallory. "Where did you find it?" he asked.

"Sorry to disappoint you, professor," said the detective sarcastically, "but this is the time when you were a little late," and he produced the object which he held behind him. "Here is your picture, Mr Kale."

PROBLEM OF THE STOLEN RUBENS

Kale gasped a little in relief and astonishment, and held up the canvas with both hands to examine it. "Fine!" he told the detective. "I'll see that you don't lose anything by this. Why, that thing cost me fifty thousand dollars!" Kale didn't seem able to get over that.

The Thinking Machine leaned forward to squint at the upper right hand corner of the canvas. "Where did you find it?" he asked again.

"Rolled up tight, and concealed in the bottom of a trunk in the room of one of the servants," explained Mallory. "The servant's name is Jennings. He is now under arrest."

"Jennings!" exclaimed Kale. "Why, he has been with me for years."

"Did he confess?" asked the scientist imperturbably.

"Of course not," said Mallory. "He says some of the other servants must have hidden it there."

The Thinking Machine nodded at Hatch. "I think perhaps that is all," he remarked. "I congratulate you, Mr Mallory, upon bringing the matter to such a quick and satisfactory conclusion."

Ten minutes later they left the house and caught a car for the scientist's home. Hatch was a little chagrined at the unexpected termination of the affair, and was thoughtfully silent for a time.

"Mallory does show an occasional gleam of human intelligence; doesn't he?" he said at last quizzically.

"Not that I ever noticed," remarked The Thinking Machine crustily.

"But he found the picture," Hatch insisted.

"Of course he found it. It was put there for him to find."

"Put there for him to find!" repeated the reporter. "Didn't Jennings steal it?"

"If he did, he's a fool."

"Well, if he didn't steal it, who put it there?"

"De Lesseps."

"De Lesseps!" echoed Hatch. "Why the deuce did he steal a fifty thousand-dollar picture and put it in a servant's trunk to be found?"

The Thinking Machine twisted around in his seat and squinted at him coldly for a moment. "At times, Mr Hatch, I am absolutely amazed at your stupidity," he said frankly. "I can understand it in a man like Mallory, but I have always given you credit for being an astute, quickwitted man."

Hatch smiled at the reproach. It was not the first time he had heard of it. But nothing bearing on the problem in hand was said until they reached The Thinking Machine's apartments.

"The only real question in my mind, Mr Hatch," said the scientist then, "is whether or not I should take the trouble to restore Mr Kale's picture at all. He is perfectly satisfied, and will probably never know the difference. So—"

Suddenly Hatch saw something. "Great Scott!" he exclaimed. "Do you mean that the picture that Mallory found was—"

"A copy of the original," supplemented the scientist. "Personally I know nothing whatever about art; therefore, I could not say from observation that it is a copy, but I know it from the logic of the thing. When the original was cut from the frame, the knife swerved a little at the upper right hand corner. The canvas remaining in the frame told me that. The picture that Mr Mallory found did not correspond in this detail with the canvas in the frame. The conclusion is obvious."

"And de Lesseps has the original?"

"De Lesseps has the original. How did he get it? In any one of a dozen ways. He might have rolled it up and stuck it under his coat. He might have had a confederate. But I don't think that any ordinary method of theft would have appealed to him. I am giving him credit for being clever, as I must when we review the whole case.

"For instance, he asked for permission to copy the Whistler, which you saw was the same size as the Rubens. It was granted.

PROBLEM OF THE STOLEN RUBENS

He copied it practically under guard, always with the chance that Mr Kale himself would drop in. It took him three days to copy it, so he says. He was alone in the room all that time. He knew that Mr Kale had not the faintest idea of art. Taking advantage of that, what would have been simpler than to have copied the Rubens in oil? He could have removed it from the frame immediately after he canvased it over, and kept it in a position near him where it could be quickly concealed if he was interrupted. Remember, the picture is worth fifty thousand dollars; therefore, was worth the trouble.

"De Lesseps is an artist – we know that – and dealing with a man who knew nothing whatever of art, he had no fears. We may suppose his idea all along was to use the copy of the Rubens as a sort of decoy after he got away with the original. You saw that Mallory didn't know the difference, and it was safe for him to suppose that Mr Kale wouldn't. His only danger until he could get away gracefully was of some critic or connoisseur, perhaps, seeing the copy. His boldness we see readily in the fact that he permitted himself to discover the theft; that he discovered it after he had volunteered to assist Mr Kale in the general work of rehanging the pictures in the gallery. Just how he put the picture in Jenning's trunk I don't happen to know. We can imagine many ways." He lay back in his chair for a minute without speaking, eyes steadily turned upward, fingers placed precisely tip to tip.

"The only thing remaining is to go get the picture. It is in de Lesseps' room now – you told me that – and so we know it is safe. I dare say he knows that if he tried to run away it would inevitably put him under suspicion."

"But how did he take the picture from the Kale home?" asked Hatch.

"He took it with him probably under his arm the day he left the house with Mr Kale," was the astonishing reply.

Hatch was staring at him in amazement. After a moment the scientist arose and passed into the adjoining room, and the telephone bell there jingled. When he joined Hatch again he picked up his hat and they went out together.

De Lesseps was in when their cards went up, and received them. They conversed of the case generally for ten minutes, while the scientist's eyes were turned inquiringly here and there about the room. At last there came a knock on the door.

"It is Detective Mallory, Mr Hatch," remarked The Thinking Machine. "Open the door for him."

De Lesseps seemed startled for just one instant, then quickly recovered. Mallory's eyes were full of questions when he entered.

"I should like, Mr Mallory," began The Thinking Machine quietly, "to call your attention to this copy of Mr Kale's picture by Whistler – over the mantel here. Isn't it excellent? You have seen the original?"

Mallory grunted. De Lesseps' face, instead of expressing appreciation of the compliment, blanched suddenly, and his hands closed tightly. Again he recovered himself and smiled.

"The beauty of this picture lies not only in its faithfulness to the original," the scientist went on, "but also in the fact that it was painted under extraordinary circumstances. For instance, I don't know if you know, Mr Mallory, that it is possible so to combine glue and putty and a few other commonplace things into a paste which would effectually blot out an oil painting, and offer at the same time an excellent surface for water color work."

There was a moment's pause, during which the three men stared at him silently – with singularly conflicting emotions depicted on their faces.

"This water color – this copy of Whistler," continued the scientist evenly – "is painted on such a paste as I have described. That paste in turn covers the original Rubens picture. It can be removed with water without damage to the picture, which is in oil, so that instead of a copy of the Whistler painting, we have an original by Rubens, worth fifty thousand dollars. That is true; isn't it, M. de Lesseps?"

There was no reply to the question – none was needed. It was an hour later, after de Lesseps was safely in his cell, that Hatch called up The Thinking Machine on the telephone and asked one question.

"How did you know that the water color was painted over the Rubens?"

"Because it was the only absolutely safe way in which the Rubens could be hopelessly lost to those who were looking for it, and at the same time perfectly preserved," was the answer. "I told you de Lesseps was a clever man, and a little logic did the rest. Two and two always make four, Mr Hatch, not sometimes, but all the time."

2

MYSTERY OF THE GRIP OF DEATH

I

Deep silence, then a long shuddering wail of terror, a stifled, strangling cry for help, the sound of a body falling, and again deep silence. A pause, and after awhile the tramp, tramp of heavy shoes through a lower hall. A door slammed and a man staggered out into a deserted street, haggard, trembling and with lips hard set. He reeled down the street and turned the first corner, waving his trembling hands fantastically.

Another pause, and spears of light flashed through the black night from the second floor of a great six-story tenement in South Boston, then came the sound of stockinged feet hurrying along the hall. Half a dozen horror-stricken men and women gathered at the door of the room whence had come the cry, helplessly gazing into one another's eyes, waiting, waiting, listening.

Finally, from inside the room, they heard a faint whispering sound as of wind rustling through dead leaves, or the silken swish of skirts, or the gasp of a dying man. They listened with strained attention until the noise stopped.

At last one of the men rapped on the door lightly. There was no answer, no sound. Again he rapped, this time louder; then he beat his fists on the door and called out. Still a silence that was terrifying. Mute inquiry lay in the eyes of all.

"Break in the door," said some one at length, in an awed whisper.

"Send for the police," said another.

The police came. They smashed in the door, old and rotting from age, and two of them entered the dark room. One of them used his lantern and those who crowded the door heard an exclamation.

"He's dead!"

Peering curiously around the corner of the door the white-faced watchers in the hall saw a man, dressed for bed, lying still on the floor. Two chairs had been over-turned; the bed clothing was disarranged. One of the policemen was bending over the body, making a hurried examination. He finally arose.

"Strangled to death with a rope — but no rope here," he explained to the other. "This is a case for a medical examiner and detectives."

"What's his name?" asked one of the policemen of a man who stood looking in curiously.

"Fred Boyd," was the reply.

"Have a room-mate?"

"No."

The other policeman was fumbling about the table with his light. At last he turned and held up something in his hand.

"Look here," he said.

It was a new wedding ring. The bright gold glittered in the lantern light.

An hour later a man turned from a side street into the avenue where stood the big tenement house, and swung along in that direction. It was the man who had left the lower door soon after the cries were heard on the second floor. Then his face had been haggard, distorted; now it was calm. One might even trace a line of melancholy and regret there.

Around the street door of the tenement was gathered a crowd of half a hundred curious ones, half-clad and shivering in the chill of the night, all craning their necks to see into the hall over the broad shoulders of a policeman who barred the door.

From a score of windows the heads of other curious ones were thrust out; there was the hum of subdued conversation.

The stranger paused on the outskirts of the little knot and peered curiously into the hall, as others were doing. He saw nothing, and turned to a bystander.

"What is it?" he asked.

"Man murdered inside," was the short response.

"Murdered?" exclaimed the stranger, "who was it?"

"Fellow named Fred Boyd."

A flash of horror passed over the stranger's face and he made an involuntary motion with his hand toward his heart. Then he steadied himself with an effort.

"How was he-he murdered?" he asked.

"Choked to death," said the other. "Somebody heard him yell for help a little while ago, and when a policeman came he smashed in the door and found him dead. The body was still warm."

The stranger's face was white as death now and his lips moved nervously. His hands, thrust deep into his pockets, were clenched until the nails cut the flesh.

"What time did it happen?" he said.

"The cop says about fifteen minutes to eleven," was the reply. "One of the tenants who lived on the second floor, where Boyd had a room, looked at his clock when he got up after he heard Boyd shout, so they know just when it was."

Uncontrollable terror glittered in the stranger's eyes, but none noted it. All were intently looking into the hall waiting for something.

"Medical Examiner Barry and Detective Mallory are up there now," volunteered the bystander. "The body will be coming out in a minute."

Then an awed whisper went around: "It's coming."

The stranger stood peering on as the others did.

"Do they know who did it?" he asked. His voice was tense, and he fiercely repressed a quaver in it.

"No," said his informant. "I heard, though, that a fellow had been up in Boyd's room tonight, and the man who had the next room heard them talking very loud. They had been playing cards."

"Did the man go out?" asked the stranger.

"Nobody saw him if he did," was the reply. "I guess, though, the police know who he was, and they're probably looking for him by this time. If they don't know, Mallory'll find him out all right."

"Great God!" exclaimed the stranger between his tightly compressed lips.

The other man turned and looked at him curiously.

"What's the matter?" he asked.

"Nothing, nothing," said the stranger, hurriedly. "Look, there it comes – that's all. It's awful, awful, awful."

The big policeman in the door stepped to one side, and men came out bearing a litter, on which lay a grim, grisly something that had been a man. It was covered with a sheet. Beside it were Detective Mallory and Medical Examiner Barry. The little knot of onlookers was silent in the presence of death.

The stranger looked, looked as if fascinated by the horrid thing which lay there, watched them put the litter into the police ambulance, heard the Medical Examiner give some instructions and then Detective Mallory re-entered the house. The wagon drove away.

Turning suddenly, the stranger strode quickly down the avenue to the first corner. There he turned away and was swallowed up in the darkness. After a moment, from a distance, came the sound of a man's footsteps, running.

II

Several newspaper men, among them Hutchinson Hatch, went over the scene of the crime with Detective Mallory. It was a square, corner room on the second floor. The furniture consisted only of a bed, a table, a wash stand, chairs, there was no carpet to cover the gaping cracks in the floor, no curtains on the two windows.

The building was old and poorly constructed. Here a part of the cornice was sagging and broken, there the walls were mouldy; the ceiling was blotched with smoke, over by the steam radiator rats had gnawed a hole big enough to put one's fist in, the single-stemmed gas jet was grimy with dirt.

Of the two windows one was in the back wall and one in the side. Hutchinson Hatch trailed around the room with Detective Mallory. He saw that the two windows were securely fastened down with a sliding catch over the middle of the lower sash; there were no broken panes so that one leaving by the window might have reached in and fastened it after him.

Mr Mallory explored the closet, but found only the things that belong to a poor man: clothing, an old hat, a battered trunk. There was no opening, the walls were solid. Then Mr Mallory went to the door that had been smashed in. It was the only door except that of the closet. There was no transom.

Mr Mallory and the reporter looked at this door a long time. It had been fastened when the police came – barred with an iron rod from one side to the other – held in round, iron sockets, set in the door facing. Neither of the sockets was open at the top; the bar had to be pushed through one straight on across the door into the other.

Thus early in the investigation Hutchinson Hatch saw this problem. If the windows were fastened inside and the murderer could not have passed out that way; if the door was fastened inside with an iron bar in both sockets and the murderer could not have gone that way – What then?

Hatch thought instinctively of a certain scientist and logician of note. Professor Augustus S. F. X. Van Dusen, Ph.D., M.D., LL.D., etc., so-called The Thinking Machine, whom he had occasion to know well because of certain previous adventures in which the scientist had accomplished seemingly impossible things.

"And I think this would stump even him," Hatch said to himself with a grim smile.

Then he listened as Detective Mallory questioned the various tenants of the house. Briefly the detective brought out these facts:

A man, whose description the detective carefully noted, had called to see Boyd that evening about half past eight o'clock. He had been there many times before. Four persons had seen him this evening in Boyd's room, but no one of these knew his name. Some one passing had seen Boyd playing cards with him.

Shortly after 10 o'clock, when practically every one in the house had gone to bed, a man and woman in the next room heard Boyd's voice and that of his caller raised suddenly as if in argument. This continued for five minutes or so, then it quieted down. Such things were common in the tenement and the man and woman dropped off to sleep, thinking nothing of it.

Some time later, evidently only a few minutes, they were awakened by that pitiful, terror-stricken cry which made them shudder. With others in the house who had been aroused they dressed hurriedly. It was then they heard heavy foot steps in the hall below and the street door opened with a bang.

Both were of the opinion not five minutes could not have elapsed from the time they heard the cry until they stood outside the door where the man lay. They would have heard, they thought, anyone leave Boyd's room after they were awakened by the cry, yet there was no sound from there when they stood in the hall. Then they heard – what?

"It was a peculiar sound," the man explained. "It struck me first that it was the swish of silk skirt, then, of course, as no woman was in the room, it must have been the dying man breathing."

"Silk skirt! Woman! woman! wedding ring!" Hatch thought. Whose was it? How could a woman have escaped from the room when it seemed that it would have been impossible for a man to escape? The questionings concluded, Detective Mallory turned graciously to the representatives of the press who were waiting impatiently. It was after midnight, dangerously near the first edition time, and the reporters were anxious for the detective's comment.

He was about to begin when another reporter, one of Hatch's fellow workers, entered, called Hatch to one side and said something quickly. Hatch nodded his head and idly fingered a pack of playing cards he had taken from the table.

"Good," he said, "Go back to the office and write the story. I'll 'phone Mallory's statement and tell him that other thing. I want to do a little more work, but I'll be at the office by half-past 2 o'clock."

The reporter went out hurriedly.

"I suppose you boys want to know something about how all this happened?" the detective was saying. He lighted a cigar and spread his feet wide apart. "I'll tell you all I can – not all I know, mind you, because that wouldn't be wise, but how the murder happened, and you can put in the thrill and all that to suit yourself.

"About half-past 8 o'clock tonight a man called here to see Boyd. He knew Boyd very well – was probably a friend of several years' standing – and had called here frequently. We have an accurate description of him. He was seen by several persons who knew him by sight, therefore will be able to absolutely identify him when we arrest him.

"Now, those two men were together in this room for possibly two hours. They were playing cards. More than half the murders on record are committed in the heat of passion. These men quarrelled over their game, probably 'pitch' or 'casino'—"

"It's a pinochle pack," said Hatch.

"Then the crime was committed," the detective went on, not heeding the interruption, "the unknown man was sitting here," and Mallory indicated an overturned chair to his right.

"He leaped like this," and the detective, with a full eye for dramatic effect, illustrated, "seized Boyd by the throat, there was a struggle, notice the other overturned chair — and the unknown man bore Boyd down gripping his throat. He choked him to death."

"I thought the dead man was undressed when he was found?" asked Hatch. "The bed, too," and he indicated its disordered condition.

"He was, but — but it must have happened as I said," said the detective. He didn't like reporters who asked embarrassing questions. "His victim dead, the murderer went out by that door," and he pointed dramatically.

"Through the keyhole, I suppose?" said Hatch, quietly. "That door was fastened inside as no mere mortal could fasten it after he left the room."

"It's an old burglar's trick to fasten a door after you leave the room," said the detective, loftily.

"How about the wedding ring?"

"Ah!" and the detective looked wise. "There's nothing to be said of that now." He saw suddenly that he had made one mistake and he felt his prestige slipping away. The reporters turned a flood of questions upon him: "How did it happen Boyd was undressed?"

"Who put out the gas?"

"How would a burglar replace an iron bar like that?"

"Do you suspect a burglar?"

Mr Mallory raised his hand. "I will say absolutely nothing else about the case."

"Let's see if we understand you," said Hatch, and there was a mocking smile on his lips. "The police theory briefly is this: A man came here, there was a quarrel, a struggle; Boyd was killed, choked; then the murderer left this room by that door, possibly through the keyhole or a convenient crack. Then, being dead, Boyd got up, took off his clothes, turned out the gas, lay down on the floor, screamed for help and died again. Is that right?"

"Bah!" thundered Mr Mallory, on the verge of apoplexy. "Perhaps," he added scornfully, "you know more about it than I do."

"Well, yes, I'll confess that," said Hatch. "I know at least the name of the man who was here tonight, and these other reporters will know it when their outside men come in."

"You do, eh," demanded Mr Mallory. "Who is it?"

"His name is Frank Cunningham, a watchmaker of No. 213—Street."

"Then he is Boyd's murderer," Mr Mallory declared. "We'll have him under arrest in an hour."

"He has disappeared," said Hatch, and he left the room.

III

From the South Boston tenement house Hutchinson Hatch went to the undertaking establishment where the body of Fred Boyd lay, made a careful examination of the mark which showed that he had been throttled, and then went in a cab to the home of Professor Van Dusen, The Thinking Machine. As he drove up he noticed a bright light in the professor's laboratory. It was just fifteen minutes past 1 o'clock when he ascended the steps.

The Thinking Machine in person answered the door bell, the leonine head with its shock of yellow hair, the clean shaven face, and the perpetually squinted eyes behind thick glasses standing out boldly and grotesquely in the light from a nearby arc.

MYSTERY OF THE GRIP OF DEATH

"Who is it?" asked The Thinking Machine.

"Hutchinson Hatch," said the reporter. "I saw your light and I was particularly anxious for a little advise, so I thought—"

"Come in," said the scientist, and he extended his long, slender fingers cordially.

Hatch followed the thin, bowed figure of the scientist, which seemed that of a child, into the laboratory where he was motioned to a seat. Then Hatch told the story of the crime, so far as it was known, while the professor sat squinting steadily at him, his long taper fingers pressed together.

"Did you see the man?" asked The Thinking Machine.

"Yes."

"What kind of marks, exactly, were those on his neck?"

"They seemed to be such marks as would be made by a large rope drawn about the throat."

"Was the skin broken?"

"No, but whoever strangled him must have had tremendous strength," said the reporter. "The pressure seemed to have been all around."

The Thinking Machine sat silent for several minutes.

"Door fastened inside with iron bar," he mused, "and no transom, so the bar was not placed back in position. Both windows fastened inside."

"It would have been absolutely impossible for any person to leave that room after Boyd was dead," said the reporter, emphatically.

"Nothing is impossible, Mr Hatch," said The Thinking Machine, testily. "I thought I had demonstrated that clearly, once. The worst anything can be is extremely difficult – not impossible."

Hatch bowed gravely. He had walked over one of The Thinking Machine's pet hobbies.

"Man was undressed," went on The Thinking Machine. "Bed disordered, chairs overturned, gas out." He paused a moment, then asked: "You reason that the man must have gone to bed after putting out the light, and that his murderer came upon him unawares?"

"That seems to be the only possible thing to imagine," said Hatch.

"And in that case the other man – Cunningham – would not have been there?"

"Precisely."

"What sort of a wedding ring was it?"

"Perfectly new. It didn't seem to have ever been worn."

The Thinking Machine arose from his seat and took down a heavy volume, one of hundreds which lined his walls.

"You don't believe it probable that Cunningham left the room while angry and returned after Boyd was asleep and killed him?" asked The Thinking Machine as he fingered the leaves.

"He couldn't have come back if that door was fastened," said Hatch, doggedly.

"He could have, of course," said The Thinking Machine, "but it is hardly probable. Do you think it reasonable to suppose then that someone hidden in the closet waited until Cunningham was gone and then killed Boyd?"

"That sounds more plausible," said Hatch, after a moment's consideration. "But he couldn't have gone out of that room and fastened the door or window behind him."

"Of course he could have," said The Thinking Machine, irritably. "Don't keep saying he couldn't have done anything. It annoys me exceedingly."

Properly rebuked Hatch sat silent while The Thinking Machine sought something in the book.

"In the event, of course, that somebody was hidden in the room it would make it a premeditated murder, wouldn't it?" asked the scientist.

"Yes, unquestionably," replied the reporter.

"Here is something," said The Thinking Machine, as he squinted into the volume he held. "It is logic reduced to figures.

Criminologists agree, practically, that thirty and one-third per cent of all premeditated crimes are committed because of money, directly or indirectly; that two per cent are committed because of insanity; and that the others, sixty-seven and two-thirds per cent, are committed because of women."

Hatch nodded.

"We'll shut out for the time being the matter of insanity – it is only a remote chance; money would hardly enter into the case because of the fact that both men were poor. Therefore, there remains a woman. The wedding ring found in the room also indicates a woman, though in what connection is not clear.

"Now, Mr Hatch," he continued, glaring at the reporter almost fiercely, "find out all you can about the private life of this man Boyd – it will probably be like every other man of his class – and particularly his love affairs; find out also all you can about Cunningham and his love affairs. If the name of any woman appears in the case at all, find out all about her – and her love affairs. You understand?"

"Yes," was the reply.

"Don't delude yourself with the thought that it was impossible for anyone to leave that room after Boyd was dead," went on the scientist, with the stubborn persistence of a child. "Suppose this – I don't offer it as a solution – suppose that Boyd had been engaged to be married, that someone else loved the girl he was to marry, that that someone else had hidden in his room until Cunningham went away, then – you see?"

"By George!" exclaimed the reporter. "I never thought of that. But how did he get out?" he added helplessly.

"If a man did do such a thing he would have made every arrangement to leave that room in a manner calculated to puzzle anyone who came after. Mind, I don't say this is what happened at all – I merely suggest it as a possibility until I find more to work on."

Hatch arose, stretched his long legs and thanked The Thinking Machine as he pulled on his gloves.

"I'm sorry I could not have been of any more direct assistance," said the scientist. "When you do these things I ask come back to see me – I may be able to help you then. You see I'm at a tremendous disadvantage in not having seen the place where Boyd was killed. There is one thing, though, which I particularly would like for you to find out for me now – tonight."

"What is it?" asked Hatch.

"This tenement is an old building, I understand. I should like to know if the occupants have ever been annoyed by rats and mice, and if they are so annoyed now?"

"I don't quite see—" began the reporter in surprise.

"Of course not," said The Thinking Machine petulantly. "But I should like to know just the same."

"I'll find out for you."

Hutchinson Hatch had still nearly an hour, and he drove to the tenement in South Boston, to wake up its occupants and ask them – of all the silly questions in the world – "Are you annoyed by mice?" He set his teeth grimly and smiled.

When he reached the tenement he went straight on to the second floor. The steps ended within a few feet of the door where the crime had been committed. Hatch looked at the door curiously; the police had gone, the room was silent again, hiding its own mystery.

As he stood there he heard something which startled him. It came from the room where Boyd had been found dead. There was no question of that. It was a faint whispering sound as of wind rustling through dead leaves, or the silken swish of skirts, or the gasp of a dying man.

With blood tingling, Hatch rushed to the door and threw it open. He stepped inside, lighting a match as he did so. The room was empty save for the poor furniture. No sign of a living thing!

IV

Straining his ears to catch every sound, Hatch stood still, peering this way and that until the match burned his fingers. Then he lighted another and still another, but there was no repetition of the noise. At last the ghostly quiet of the room, its gloom and thoughts of the mystery which its walls had witnessed began to press on his nerves. He laughed shortly.

"A very pronounced case of enlargement of the imagination," he said to himself, and he passed out. "This thing is getting on my nerves."

Then, feeling very foolish, he aroused several persons and inquired solicitously as to whether or not they had ever been troubled with mice or rats, and when this annoyance had stopped, if it had stopped.

The concensus of opinion was that it was a silly thing to ask, but that up to a fortnight ago the rodents had been very bad. Since then no one had noticed particularly. These things, in so far as they related to rodents of any kind, were telephoned to The Thinking Machine.

"Uh, huh," he said over the 'phone. "Thanks. Goodnight."

From that point on every effort of the police and the press was directed to finding Frank Cunningham, who was openly charged with the murder of Fred Boyd. His disappearance had been complete. If there had been any doubt whatsoever of his guilt, this was convincing – to the police.

It was Hatch's personal efforts that uncovered the fact that Cunningham had had a bank account of $287 in a small institution, that on the morning following the mysterious crime in the South Boston tenement a check to "cash" had been presented for the full sum and that check had been honored. This began to look conclusive.

It was also due to Hatch's personal efforts that the police learned Cunningham was to have been married a week after his disappearance to Caroline Pierce, a working girl of the West End. Then Hatch discovered that Caroline Pierce had also disappeared; that she went away presumably to work on the morning after the murder of Boyd. Where had she gone? No one knew, not even Miss Jerrod, the girl who, with her, occupied a suite of three rooms in the West End. Why had she gone? No one knew that. When had she gone? Still no one knew. When would she return? Again the same answer.

To the reporter there seemed only one plausible explanation. This was that Cunningham had drawn his money from the bank – which he had saved to make a little home for the girl he loved – and they had gone away together. In the natural course of his duty Hatch printed this, and it came to the eyes of the police. Detective Mallory smiled.

But the wedding ring in Boyd's room?

There was no explanation of that. Boyd had had no love affair so far as any one knew. He had been a hard-working, steady-going man in his trade-electrician employed by a telephone company – and he and Cunningham had been friends since boyhood.

All these things, while interesting in themselves, still threw no light on the actual crime. Who killed Boyd, and why? How did the murderer get away? Hatch had put the question to himself time and again. There was no answer. Thus the intangible pall of mystery which lay over the happenings in the South Boston tenement was still impenetrable.

On the second day after the crime Hatch again consulted The Thinking Machine. The scientist listened patiently and carefully, but without any enthusiastic interest to the reporter's recital of what he had discovered.

"Have you a man watching the place where the girl lives?" he asked.

"No," Hatch replied. "I think she's gone for good."

"I don't think so," said The Thinking Machine. "I should send a man there to see if she returns."

"If you think best," said Hatch. "But don't you think now this man Cunningham must have been the criminal?"

The scientist squinted at the reporter a long time, seemingly having heard nothing of the question.

"It looks that way to me," Hatch went on, hesitatingly. "But frankly, I can't imagine a way that he might have left that room after Boyd was dead."

Still the scientist was silent, and the reporter nervously fingered his hat.

"That information you gave me about the rats was very interesting," said The Thinking Machine at last, irrelevantly.

"Perhaps, but I don't see how it applies."

"Looking out the windows of the room where Boyd was found, what did you see?" the scientist interrupted.

Hatch did not recall that he had ever looked out either of the windows; he had merely satisfied himself that neither had been used as a means of exit. Now he blushed guiltily.

"I'm afraid you haven't looked," said The Thinking Machine, testily. "I thought probably you wouldn't have. Suppose we go to South Boston this afternoon and see that room."

"If you only would," said Hatch, delightedly. Here was better luck than he dreamed of. "If you only would," he repeated.

"We'll go now," said The Thinking Machine. He left the room and returned a moment later dressed for the street. The slender, bent figure and the great head seemed more grotesque than ever.

"Before we go," he instructed, "telephone to your office and have a reliable man sent to watch the girl's house. Tell him under no circumstances to try to enter or speak with anyone there until he hears from us."

The Thinking Machine stood waiting impatiently while Hatch did this. Then they took a cab to the tenement in South Boston.

"Dear me, what an old, ramshackle affair it is!" commented the scientist as they climbed the stairs.

The door of Boyd's room was not locked. The furniture and the personal effects of the man had been moved out—taken in charge by the Medical Examiner for possible use at an inquest.

"Just how was this room fastened when Boyd was found?" asked the scientist.

Hatch showed him, at the door and windows. The Thinking Machine was interested for a moment and then looked out the side window. Straight down fifteen feet was a wilderness of ash barrels and boxes and papers – a typical refuse heap of a cheap tenement. Then The Thinking Machine squinted out the back window. There he saw an open space, a rough baseball diamond, intersected at two places by the trampled down rings of a circus.

Perfunctorily he peered into the closet, after which his eyes swept the room in one comprehensive squint. He noted the begrimed condition of the place; the drooping cornice, the smoky ceiling, the gaping cracks in the floor, the rat holes beside the radiator, the dirty gas pipe leading down to a single jet. He leaned against a wall and wrote for several minutes on a sheet of paper torn from his notebook.

"Have you an envelope?" he asked.

Hatch produced one. The Thinking Machine put what he had written into the envelope, sealed it and handed it back.

"There's something that may interest you some time," he said, "but don't open it until I give you permission to do so."

"Certainly not," said the reporter, puzzled but without question. "But may I ask—"

"What it is?" snapped the scientist. "No, I will tell you when to open it."

They descended the stairs together.

"Somewhere to a public telephone," were The Thinking Machine's instructions to the cabby. At a nearby drug store, he disappeared into a telephone booth and remained for five minutes. When he came out he asked for the envelope he had given Hatch and in a little crabbed hand wrote on it:

"November 9-10."

"Keep it," he commanded, as he returned it to the reporter. "Now we'll drive to the girl's place."

When the cab reached the West End address it was a little later than dusk. Caroline Pierce and her girl chum occupied a front apartment on the ground floor. As The Thinking Machine and Hatch were about to enter the building, Tom Manning, another reporter on Hatch's paper, approached them.

"The girl hasn't returned," he reported. "The other girl — Miss Jerrod — came back home from work just a few minutes ago."

"We'll see her," said The Thinking Machine. Then to Manning: "At the end of two minutes, by your watch, after I enter this apartment, ring the bell several times. Don't be afraid. Ring it! If any person runs out, man or woman, hold him. Mr Hatch, you go to the back entrance of this apartment. Stop any person, man or woman, coming from this suite."

"You believe then—" Hatch began.

"I'll give you two minutes to get to the back door," snapped The Thinking Machine.

Hatch disappeared hurriedly, and for just two minutes, not a second more, The Thinking Machine waited. Then he rang the bell of the apartment. Miss Jerrod appeared at the door. He followed her into the suite.

Manning at the front door waited, watch in hand. When the two minutes were up he rang the bell time after time, long, insistent rings. He could hear it tinkling furiously. Then he heard something else. It was the slamming of a door, a rush of feet and a struggle. Then The Thinking Machine appeared before him.

"Come in," he said, modestly. "We have Cunningham inside."

V

A little drama of human emotion was being enacted in the tiny front suite. Frank Cunningham, wanted for the murder of Fred Boyd, sat wearily resigned in the corner furthest from the door under the watchful eye of Hutchinson Hatch. The man was unshaven, haggard, and there lay in his eyes the restless, feverish look of one who lives his life in terror of the law. Caroline Pierce, who was to have been his wife, had flung herself on a couch, weeping hysterically.

Towering above the slender, shrinking figure of The Thinking Machine, Miss Jerrod was bitterly denouncing him for a trick which had given Cunningham into his hands. The scientist listened patiently, albeit unhappily. He couldn't help himself.

"You told me," stormed Miss Jerrod, "that you believed him innocent, and now this – this."

"Well?" said The Thinking Machine meekly.

Miss Jerrod was about to say something else when Cunningham stopped her with a gesture.

"I'm rather glad of it," he said, "or rather I would be if it were not for her," and he indicated Caroline Pierce. "I have never spent such hours of mortal fear as those since the murder of Fred Boyd. Now, somehow, it's a relief to know it must all come out."

"You know you were a fool to try to hide, anyway," said The Thinking Machine, frankly.

"I know I made a mistake – now," replied Cunningham. "But we were afraid – Caroline and I – and I couldn't help it."

"Well, go on with your story," commanded the scientist testily.

Manning, the other reporter, crossed the room and sat beside Hatch, while Cunningham moved over, took a seat beside the couch where the girl lay weeping and gently stroked her hair.

MYSTERY OF THE GRIP OF DEATH

"I'll tell what story I can," he said at last. "I don't know what you'll think of it, but—"

"Pardon me just a moment," said The Thinking Machine. He went to Cunningham and ran his long, slender fingers over the prisoner's head several times. Suddenly he leaned forward and squinted at Cunningham's head.

"What is this?" he asked.

"That is where a silver plate was put in," Cunningham replied. "I was badly injured by a fall when I was about fourteen years old."

"Yes, yes," said the scientist. "Go on with your story."

"I have known Boyd since we were boys together up in Vermont," Cunningham began, "and there, too, I knew Caroline. All three of us came from the same little town — Caroline only two years ago. Boyd and I had been in Boston for seven years when she came. Boyd lived for five years in that — that room in South Boston, where—"

"Never mind," said The Thinking Machine. "Go on."

"Well, Caroline came here two years ago as I said and I believe that Boyd loved her as well as I do," said Cunningham. "But she promised to be my wife and we were to be married next Wednesday—"

"But the night Boyd was killed," interrupted The Thinking Machine impatiently. "Come down to that."

"I went to Boyd's room that night at a few minutes after eight o'clock. We sat for an hour or more and talked of our work, our plans and various things as we played cards — pinochle it was. Neither of us was particularly interested in the game.

"Boyd didn't know of my coming marriage to Caroline and finally I happened to mention her name. I also showed him the wedding ring I had bought that day for her. He looked at it, and asked me what I intended to do with it. I then told him that Caroline and I were to be married.

"He was surprised. I think any man in his position would have been surprised, because I think it was his intention to ask her to marry him. Well, at any rate, he grew angry about it, and I tried to placate him.

"I guess he was pretty hard hit – worse than I thought – for several times between the deals he picked up the ring and looked at it, then he'd put it down each time on his side of the table.

"After awhile he threw down his hand with the remark that he didn't care to play. 'Now look here, Fred,' I said, 'I didn't think of the thing hitting you so hard.' He replied something about it not being fair to him, though just what he meant I didn't know.

"Then word led to word, until finally I was in a fury at a careless reference he made to Caroline – a thing he would never have thought of doing in his proper senses – and demanded an apology. He grew ugly and said still more, and then, somehow, I don't know quite what happened. I know that I had an insane desire to take hold of him – but—"

Cunningham paused and gently stroked the hand of the girl.

"And then?" asked The Thinking Machine.

"You know this hurt on my head was more serious than you may imagine," said Cunningham. "There are times, in moments of anger particularly, when things are not clear to me. I lose myself, I don't know what to do. A surgeon once explained to me why it was but I don't remember."

"I understand," said The Thinking Machine. "Go on."

"Well, from the moment the quarrel became really serious I would not swear to anything that happened," Cunningham resumed. "I know at last I found myself in the lower hall after what seemed a long time, and I remember leaving there, slamming the door behind me.

"I went down the avenue and was almost home when it occurred to me that the ring was in Boyd's room. By that time, too, I was seeing things more clearly. I wanted to go back and talk to Boyd more calmly and see if both of us hadn't said things we should not have said. It was with this double purpose of seeing him and getting the ring that I started back to the tenement.

"Outside, I found a crowd. I wondered why, and asked. One man told me Boyd had been murdered — choked to death; that the police knew who did it and were searching for him. I was terror-stricken, and after the body was taken out I walked away. The terror was on me, and after I turned into a side street I broke into a run. I knew myself, you see, and my own irresponsibility.

"Then, although it was midnight, I came straight here, aroused Caroline and Miss Jerrod and told them both what had happened so far as I knew. There seemed to be nothing else to do but hide; I did it. I remained here, as I thought safely enough. Two or three reporters came and asked questions, and once a detective was here, but Miss Jerrod answered their inquiries satisfactorily and that seemed to be all — until now. Tomorrow Caroline and I were going back to Vermont."

There was a long pause. Caroline pressed the hand of the man she loved to her cheek with a gesture of infinite confidence. The Thinking Machine sat silent with the tips of his long, slender fingers together.

"Mr Cunningham," he said at last, "you have not told us the one vital thing. Did you or did you not kill Fred Boyd?"

"I don't know," was the reply. "If I only could know!"

"Uh," grunted The Thinking Machine. "I was afraid you wouldn't know."

VI

Hutchinson Hatch and Manning, the other reporter, gazed at Cunningham thunderstruck, and from him to The Thinking Machine.

"Don't know whether or not you killed a man?" asked Hatch incredulously.

"It's perfectly possible, Mr Hatch," said The Thinking Machine, curtly. "I understand, Mr Cunningham," he explained. "I suppose you would be perfectly willing to go with me now?"

"No, no, no," exclaimed Caroline Pierce suddenly, in evident terror.

"Not to the police, Miss Pierce," said The Thinking Machine. He paused a moment and looked at the girl curiously. Of women he knew nothing, and knew he knew nothing. "Perhaps it would assure you, Miss Pierce, if I told you I know that Mr Cunningham did not kill Boyd."

"You believe he didn't, then?" she asked eagerly.

"I know he didn't," said The Thinking Machine tersely. "Two and two make four not some times, but all the time," he went on enigmatically. "If Mr Cunningham will come with me now we will establish beyond all doubt the cause of Boyd's death. Do you believe me?"

"Yes," said the girl slowly, and she looked steadily into the squint eyes of the scientist. "I – I have faith in you."

The Thinking Machine coughed, slightly embarrassed, and turned to Hatch with a faint color in his cheeks.

"Well, who did kill Boyd?" asked Hatch, amazed.

"That's what we will now demonstrate," was the reply. "Come on."

After Cunningham had himself assured the girl of his safety the four men passed out into the night – it was nearly 10 o'clock – entered a cab and were driven to the tenement in South Boston. There they passed up the one flight of stairs into the room where Boyd had been found, and after lighting the gas the scientist made one quick survey of the room.

"These walls are awfully thin," he commented petulantly. "If I should fire a pistol in here I might kill someone in another room. Yes, a knife would do better. Have any of you gentlemen a knife—one with a blade that won't break easily?"

"Will this do?" asked Cunningham, and he produced one.

The Thinking Machine examined it and nodded his satisfaction.

"Now a revolver," he said.

Manning went out to get one. While he was gone The Thinking Machine gave some formal instructions to Cunningham and Hatch.

"I'm going to put out this light and remain in this room alone," he said. "I may be here fifteen minutes or I may be here till daylight. I don't know. But I want you three to remain quietly outside the door and listen. When I need you I shall need you quickly. My life may be in danger, and I am not a strong man."

"What is it anyway?" asked Hatch curiously.

"After awhile you will hear something inside, I have no doubt," went on the scientist, paying no attention to the question. "But don't enter the room under any circumstances until I call out or you hear a struggle."

"But what is it?" asked Hatch again. "I don't understand at all."

"I'm going to find the murderer of Fred Boyd," said the scientist. "Please do not ask so many absurd questions. They annoy me exceedingly. I may have to kill him," he added reflectively.

"Kill him?" gasped Hatch. "Who, the murderer?" He couldn't help it.

"Yes, the murderer," was the tart reply.

Manning returned with the revolver, which The Thinking Machine examined and handed to Hatch.

"You will know what to do with it when you enter the room," he instructed. "You, Manning, come in with these other two and light this gas. Keep your matches in your hand."

Then the two reporters and Cunningham passed out of the room, closing the door, but not fastening it. Pressed close against the panels outside, listening, Hatch started to explain to Manning in a whisper when they heard the irritated voice of the scientist.

"Keep silent," was the sharp command.

Five minutes, ten minutes, half an hour of utter silence, save for a distant sound of some sort in the big tenement. But no one came up the stairs. The dim gas light fluttered weirdly down the hall.

A full hour passed, still nothing. Hatch could hear his heart beat, also he thought the regular breathing of The Thinking Machine. At last there came a slight sound, and Hatch started. The other men heard, too.

It was a faint whispering sound, as of the wind rustling through dead leaves, or the silken swish of skirts or the gasp of a dying man.

Hatch clutched the revolver more firmly and set his teeth hard together. He was going to face something – a deadly, terrible something – and had not the faintest idea of what it might be. Manning held a match ready for instant use.

Then, as they listened, there was another sound, still faint, as of something sliding over the floor. Suddenly there was a heavy thump, a half-strangled cry from The Thinking Machine and the sounds of a fearful struggle. Hatch rushed into the room with revolver raised; Manning was just behind him. A match flared up and they saw a struggling heap on the floor. The arm of the scientist rose and fell thrice, burying the knife each time in flesh.

In the light of the gas, which hissed into a brilliant light under the match, the reporter placed the revolver flat against the head of a writhing, twisting body and fired. For the second time he fired, and the struggling bodies lay still.

Then for the first time Hatch realized what had happened. A giant boa constrictor held The Thinking Machine in its coils and was in its death struggle almost crushing the life out of him. It required the combined efforts of the three men to release the scientist from the deadly folds. He lay still for a moment, but finally the life came back into his frail body with a rush. He raised up from Hatch's arms and looked curiously at the snake.

"Dear me, dear me," he commented. "What a brain would have been lost to scientific inquiry if that snake had killed me."

Occupants of the house, aroused by the two pistol shots, rushed again terror-stricken to the room, and after awhile the police came and rescued the four men from the besieging mob of questioners. All went to the police station, and there The Thinking Machine, with several caustic comments on the police in general, told his story. The body of the giant reptile lay full length on the floor.

"Mr Hatch here asked for my advice in the matter," he explained to the police captain, "and I did what I could to assist him. When he explained the condition of the body and the room when it was broken open – the fact the door and both windows were fastened securely inside – it instantly occurred to me that, with suicide removed as a possibility, the thing which had killed Boyd was still in the room or else had escaped only after the body was found.

"It was not unreasonable to suppose that any animal, a snake for instance, would have attempted to leave the room while a crowd of people blocked the door; in fact it was not unreasonable to suppose that such a snake, snuggly fixed in a large, tumble-down building, with the infinite possibility of feeding on rats and mice, would attempt to leave the building at all. It could get water easily from a dozen places.

"Therefore I presumed it was a snake, and I asked Mr Hatch to ascertain for me first if the people in the house had ever been greatly annoyed by rodents; if they were now, and if not, when they had noticed that they were not. He reported to me that they had been annoyed up to a fortnight preceding the crime, but since they had not noticed. Of course a boa constrictor can live on rodents, therefore they would leave the building or be eaten out of it gradually.

"A fortnight since they missed the rodents? That meant that the snake must have been in the building at least that long. All these conclusion I reached before I personally went over the scene. If it were a snake, as I thought possible, it must have come from somewhere. Where, then?"

The Thinking Machine paused and looked from one to another of his hearers. Each in turn shook his head, Hatch being the last to do so.

"And yet your own paper published a full solution of the mystery before it ever occurred," said the scientist sharply. "Looking from the back window of the room there, perfectly visible, were three banked rings, plainly where a circus had been. Possibly the snake escaped from that circus and crept into the house.

"I called up your office on the 'phone, Mr Hatch, and ascertained that there had been a circus on that place two weeks before, November 9 and 10, and further I found that a boa constrictor had escaped from that circus. You printed a column of it on the first page."

"Lord, and we really thought that was a press agent's yarn," remarked Hatch sadly.

"Tonight when we went to the room it was my intention to allow the snake to creep out of that large hole near the radiator – I suppose you noticed there was one there? – then to pass between the snake and the hole and call for Mr Hatch and these other gentlemen who were waiting outside the door. If the snake attacked me I had a knife and Mr Hatch had a revolver.

"But I'm afraid I didn't give the snake credit for quickness and such enormous strength," he went on ruefully. "I heard the snake come out of the hole, and then instantly almost I felt its folds crushing me. Then these gentlemen rushed in. I can readily understand how it choked Boyd, he having no way to defend himself, and then crawled away when those people knocked on the door. It nearly crushed the life out of me."

That seemed to be all, and The Thinking Machine stopped.

"But Frank Cunningham?" asked the police captain. "Why did he run away, and where is he now?"

"Cunningham?" repeated the scientist, puzzled.

"Yes," said the captain. "Where is he?"

"Why here he is," and The Thinking Machine indicated the accused man. "Mr Cunningham permit me to introduce you to Captain-er-er. I don't know his name."

The captain was not surprised; he was nonplussed. It had never occurred to him to ask the name of the fourth member of the party; he knew the two newspaper men.

"How-where-when did you—" he began.

"Not knowing whether or not he had killed his friend Boyd," explained the scientist, "he was hiding in the suite of Miss Caroline Pierce, his fiancé. His lack of knowledge was due entirely to a queer mental condition. He was badly hurt at one time and wears a silver plate in his head. That accounts for many things."

"How did you get him?" asked the captain, amazed.

"I walked into Miss Pierce's suite after I had put a man at the back and front to stop any one who ran out, and told Miss Pierce's friend, Miss Jerrod, that I believed – in fact knew – that Cunningham was innocent, and that I had come merely to warn him," said The Thinking Machine.

"I told her then that three policemen were at the front door, and then Mr Manning here rang the bell violently, as I had instructed him, and Cunningham dashed out of a rear room and started out the back way. Mr Hatch got him there. It was perfectly simple — that part of it. Of course, there was a chance that he wasn't there at all — but he was."

The Thinking Machine arose.

"Is that all?" he asked.

"Why did you examine Cunningham's head before he told us his story?" asked Hatch.

"I have some idea of the cranial formation of criminals and I merely wanted to satisfy myself," said the scientist. "It was then that I discovered the silver plate in his head."

"And this?" asked Hatch. He took from his pocket the sealed envelope which The Thinking Machine had given him in the tenement room immediately after he had inspected the room. On this envelope was written "November 9-10", this being the date the circus was in South Boston.

"Oh, that?" said Professor Van Dusen a little impatiently, "that is merely a solution to the mystery."

Hatch opened the envelope and looked at it. There were only a few words:

"Snake. Came through hole near radiator. Lived in walls. Escaped from circus. Cunningham innocent."

"That all?" again asked The Thinking Machine.

There was no answer, and the scientist and the two newspaper men left the police station, followed by Cunningham.

3

PROBLEM OF THE SUPERFLUOUS FINGER

She drew off her left glove, a delicate, crinkled suede affair, and offered her bare hand to the surgeon. An artist would have called it beautiful, perfect, even; the surgeon, professionally enough, set it down as an excellent structural specimen. From the polished pink nails of the tapering fingers to the firm, well moulded wrist, it was distinctly the hand of a woman of ease—one that had never known labour, a pampered hand Dr Prescott told himself.

"The fore-finger," she explained calmly. "I should like to have it amputated at the first joint, please."

"Amputated?" gasped Dr Prescott. He stared into the pretty face of his caller. It was flushed softly, and the red lips were parted in a slight smile. It seemed quite an ordinary affair to her. The surgeon bent over the hand with quick interest. "Amputated!" he repeated.

"I came to you," she went on with a nod, "because I have been informed that you are one of the most skilful men of your profession, and the cost of the operation is quite immaterial."

Dr Prescott pressed the pink nail of the fore-finger then permitted the blood to rush back into it. Several times he did this, then he turned the hand over and scrutinized it closely inside from the delicately lined palm to the tips of the fingers.

When he looked up at last there was an expression of frank bewilderment on his face.

"What's the matter with it?" he asked.

"Nothing," the woman replied pleasantly. "I merely want it off from the first joint."

The surgeon leaned back in his chair with a frown of perplexity on his brow, and his visitor was subjected to a sharp, professional stare. She bore it unflinchingly and even smiled a little at his obvious perturbation.

"Why do you want it off?" he demanded.

The woman shrugged her shoulders a little impatiently.

"I can't tell you that," she replied. "It really is not necessary that you should know. You are a surgeon, I want an operation performed. That is all."

There was a long pause; the mutual stare didn't waver.

"You must understand, Miss-Miss-er—" began Dr Prescott at last. "By the way, you have not introduced yourself?" She was silent. "May I ask your name?"

"My name is of no consequence," she replied calmly. "I might, of course, give you a name, but it would not be mine, therefore any name would be superfluous."

Again the surgeon stared.

"When do you want the operation performed?" he inquired.

"Now," she replied. "I am ready."

"You must understand," he said severely, "that surgery is a profession for the relief of human suffering, not for mutilation—wilful mutilation I might say."

"I understand that perfectly," she said. "But where a person submits of her own desire to – to mutilation as you call it I can see no valid objection on your part."

"It would be criminal to remove a finger where there is no necessity for it," continued the surgeon bluntly. "No good end could be served."

A trace of disappointment showed in the young woman's face, and again she shrugged her shoulders.

PROBLEM OF THE SUPERFLUOUS FINGER

"The question after all," she said finally, "is not one of ethics but is simply whether or not you will perform the operation. Would you do it for, say, a thousand dollars?"

"Not for five thousand dollars," blurted the surgeon,

"Well, for ten thousand then?" she asked, quiet casually.

All sorts of questions were pounding in Dr Prescott's mind. Why did a young and beautiful woman desire – why was she anxious even – to sacrifice a perfectly healthy finger? What possible purpose would it serve to mar a hand which was as nearly perfect as any he had ever seen? Was it some insane caprice? Staring deeply into her steady, quiet eyes he could only be convinced of her sanity. Then what?

"No, madam," he said at last, vehemently, "I would not perform the operation for any sum you might mention, unless I was first convinced that the removal of that finger was absolutely necessary. That, I think, is all."

He arose as if to end the consultation. The woman remained seated and continued thoughtful for a minute.

"As I understand it," she said, "you would perform the operation if I could convince you that it was absolutely necessary?"

"Certainly," he replied promptly, almost eagerly. His curiosity was aroused. "Then it would come well within the range of my professional duties."

"Won't you take my word that it is necessary, and that it is impossible for me to explain why?"

"No. I must know why."

The woman arose and stood facing him. The disappointment had gone from her face now.

"Very well," she remarked steadily. "You will perform the operation if it is necessary, therefore if I should shoot the finger off, perhaps—?"

"Shoot it off?" exclaimed Dr Prescott in amazement. "Shoot it off?"

"That is what I said," she replied calmly. "If I should shoot the finger off you would consent to dress the wound? You would make any necessary amputation?"

She held up the finger under discussion and looked at it curiously. Dr Prescott himself stared at it with a sudden new interest.

"Shoot it off?" he repeated. "Why you must be mad to contemplate such a thing," he exploded, and his face flushed in sheer anger. "I – I will have nothing whatever to do with the affair, madam. Goodday."

"I should have to be very careful of course," she mused, "but I think perhaps one shot would be sufficient, then I should come to you and demand that you dress it?"

There was a question in the tone. Dr Prescott stared at her for a full minute then walked over and opened the door.

"In my profession, madam," he said coldly, "there is too much possibility of doing good and relieving actual suffering for me to consider this matter or discuss it further with you. There are three persons now waiting in the ante-room who need my services. I shall be compelled to ask you to excuse me."

"But you will dress the wound?" the woman insisted, undaunted by his forbidding tone and manner.

"I shall have nothing whatever to do with it," declared the surgeon, positively, finally. "If you need the services of any medical man permit me to suggest that it is an alienist and not a surgeon."

The woman didn't appear to take offence.

"Someone would have to dress it," she continued insistently. "I should much prefer that it be a man of undisputed skill – you I mean, therefore I shall call again. Goodday."

There was a rustle of silken skirts and she was gone. Dr Prescott stood for an instant gazing after her with frank wonder and annoyance in his eyes, his attitude, then he went back and

PROBLEM OF THE SUPERFLUOUS FINGER 47

sat down at the desk. The crinkled suede glove still lay where she had left it. He examined it gingerly then with a final shake of his head dismissed the affair and turned to other things.

Early next afternoon Dr Prescott was sitting in his office writing when the door from the ante-room where patients awaited his leisure was thrown open and the young man in attendance rushed in.

"A lady has fainted, sir," he said hurriedly. "She seems to be hurt."

Dr Prescott arose quickly and strode out. There, lying helplessly back in her chair with white face and closed eyes, was his visitor of the day before. He stepped toward her quickly then hesitated as he recalled their conversation. Finally, however, professional instinct, the desire to relieve suffering, and perhaps curiosity too, caused him to go to her. The left hand was wrapped in an improvised bandage through which there was a trickle of blood. He glared at it with incredulous eyes.

"Hanged if she didn't do it," he blurted angrily.

The fainting spell, Dr Prescott saw, was due only to loss of blood and physical pain, and he busied himself trying to restore her to consciousness. Meanwhile he gave some hurried instructions to the young man who was in attendance in the ante-room.

"Call up Professor Van Dusen on the 'phone," he directed his assistant, "and ask him if he can assist me in a minor operation. Tell him it's rather a curious case and I am sure it will interest him."

It was in this manner that the problem of the superfluous finger first came to the attention of The Thinking Machine. He arrived just as the mysterious woman was opening her eyes to consciousness from the fainting spell. She stared at him glassily, unrecognizingly; then her glance wandered to Dr Prescott. She smiled.

"I knew you'd have to do it," she murmured weakly.

After the ether had been administered for the operation, a simple and an easy one, Dr Prescott stated the circumstances of the case to The Thinking Machine. The scientist stood with his long, slender fingers resting lightly on the young woman's pulse, listening in silence.

"What do you make of it?" demanded the surgeon.

The Thinking Machine didn't say. At the moment he was leaning over the unconscious woman squinting at her forehead. With his disengaged hand he stroked the delicately pencilled eye-brows several times the wrong way, and again at close range squinted at them. Dr Prescott saw and seeing, understood.

"No, it isn't that," he said and he shuddered a little. "I thought of it myself. Her bodily condition is excellent, splendid."

It was some time later when the young woman was sleeping lightly, placidly under the influence of a soothing potion, that The Thinking Machine spoke of the peculiar events which had preceded the operation. Then he was sitting in Dr Prescott's private office. He had picked up a woman's glove from the desk.

"This is the glove she left when she first called, isn't it?" he inquired.

"Yes."

"Did you happen to see her remove it?"

"Yes."

The Thinking Machine curiously examined the dainty, perfumed trifle, then, arising suddenly, went into the adjoining room where the woman lay asleep. He stood for an instant gazing down admiringly at the exquisite, slender figure; then, bending over, he looked closely at her left hand. When at last he straightened up it seemed that some unspoken question in his mind had been answered. He rejoined Dr Prescott.

"It's difficult to say what motive is back of her desire to have the finger amputated," he said musingly. "I could perhaps venture a conjecture but if the matter is of no importance to

PROBLEM OF THE SUPERFLUOUS FINGER

you beyond mere curiosity I should not like to do so. Within a few months from now, I daresay, important developments will result and I should like to find out something more about her. That I can do when she returns to wherever she is stopping in the city. I'll 'phone to Mr Hatch and have him ascertain for me where she goes, her name and other things which may throw a light on the matter."

"He will follow her?"

"Yes, precisely. Now we only seem to know two facts in connection with her. First, she is English."

"Yes," Dr Prescott agreed. "Her accent, her appearance, everything about her suggests that."

"And the second fact is of no consequence at the moment," resumed The Thinking Machine. "Let me use your 'phone please."

Hutchinson Hatch, reporter, was talking.

"When the young woman left Dr Prescott's she took the cab which had been ordered for her and told the driver to go ahead until she stopped him. I got a good look at her, by the way. I managed to pass just as she entered the cab and walking on down got into another cab which was waiting for me. Her cab drove for three or four blocks aimlessly, and finally stopped. The driver stooped down as if to listen to someone inside, and my cab passed. Then the other cab turned across a side street and after going eight or ten blocks pulled up in front of an apartment house. The young woman got out and went inside. Her cab went away. Inside I found out that she was Mrs Frederick Chevedon Morey. She came there last Tuesday – this is Friday – with her husband, and they engaged—"

"Yes, I knew she had a husband," interrupted The Thinking Machine.

"– engaged apartments for three months. When I had learned this much I remembered your instructions as to steamers from Europe landing on the day they took apartments or possibly a day or so before. I was just going out when Mrs Morey stepped out of the elevator and preceded me to the door. She had changed her clothing and wore a different hat.

"It didn't seem to be necessary then to find out where she was going for I knew I could find her when I wanted to, so I went down and made inquiries at the steamship offices. I found, after a great deal of work, that no one of the three steamers which arrived the day they took apartments brought a Mr and Mrs Morey, but one steamer on the day before brought a Mr and Mrs David Girardeau from Liverpool. Mrs Girardeau answered Mrs Morey's description to the minutest detail even to the gown she wore when she left the steamer – that is the same she wore when she left Dr Prescott's after the operation."

That was all. The Thinking Machine sat with his enormous yellow head pillowed against a high-backed chair and his long slender fingers pressed tip to tip. He asked no questions and made no comment for a long time, then:

"About how many minutes was it from the time she entered the house until she came out again?"

"Not more than ten or fifteen," was the reply. "I was still talking casually to the people downstairs trying to find out something about them."

"What do they pay for their apartment?" asked the scientist, irrelevantly.

"Three hundred dollars a month."

The Thinking Machine's squint eyes were fixed immovably on a small discoloured spot on the ceiling of his laboratory.

"Whatever else may develop in this matter, Mr Hatch," he said after a time, "we must admit that we have met a woman with extraordinary courage – nerve, I daresay you'd call it. When Mrs Morey left Dr Prescott's operating room she was so ill and weak from the shock that she could hardly stand, and now you tell me she changed her dress and went out immediately after she returned home."

"Well, of course —" Hatch said, apologetically.

"In that event," resumed the scientist, "we must assume also that the matter is one of the utmost importance to her, and yet the nature of the case had led me to believe that it might be months, perhaps, before there would be any particular development in it."

"What? How?" asked the reporter.

"The final development doesn't seem, from what I know, to belong on this side of the ocean at all," explained The Thinking Machine. "I imagine it is a case for Scotland Yard. The problem of course is: What made it necessary for her to get rid of that finger? If we admit her sanity we can count the possible answers to this question on one hand, and at least three of these answers take the case back to England." He paused. "By the way, was Mrs Morey's hand bound up in the same way when you saw her the second time?"

"Her left hand was in a muff," explained the reporter. "I couldn't see but it seems to me that she wouldn't have had time to change the manner of its dressing."

"It's extraordinary," commented the scientist. He arose and paced back and forth across the room. "Extraordinary," he repeated. "One can't help but admire the fortitude of women under certain circumstances, Mr Hatch. I think perhaps this particular case had better be called to the attention of Scotland Yard, but first I think it would be best for you to call on the Moreys tomorrow – you can find some pretext – and see what you can learn about them. You are an ingenious young man – I'll leave it all to you."

Hatch did call at the Morey apartments on the morrow but under circumstances which were not at all what he expected. He went there with Detective Mallory, and Detective Mallory went there in a cab at full speed because the manager of the apartment house had 'phoned that Mrs Frederick Chevedon Morey had been found murdered in her apartments. The detective ran up two flights of stairs and blundered, heavy-footed into the rooms, and there he paused in the presence of death.

The body of the woman lay on the floor and some one had mercifully covered it with a cloth from the bed. Detective Mallory drew the covering down from over the face and Hatch stared with a feeling of awe at the beautiful countenance which had, on the day before, been so radiant with life. Now it was distorted into an expression of awful agony and the limbs were drawn up convulsively. The mark of the murderer was at the white, exquisitely rounded throat – great black bruises where powerful, merciless fingers had sunk deeply into the soft flesh.

A physician in the house had preceded the police. After one glance at the woman and a swift, comprehensive look about the room Detective Mallory turned to him inquiringly.

"She has been dead for several hours," the doctor volunteered, "possibly since early last night. It appears that some virulent, burning poison was administered and then she was choked. I gather this from an examination of her mouth."

These things were readily to be seen; also it was plainly evident for many reasons that the finger marks at the throat were those of a man, but each step beyond these obvious facts only served to further bewilder the investigators. First was the statement of the night elevator boy.

"Mr and Mrs Morey left here last night about eleven o'clock," he said. "I know because I telephoned for a cab, and later brought them down from the third floor. They went into the manager's office leaving two suit cases in the hall. When they came out I took the suit cases to a cab that was waiting. They got in it and drove away."

"When did they return?" inquired the detective.

"They didn't return, sir," responded the boy. "I was on duty until six o'clock this morning. It just happened that no one came in after they went out until I was off duty at six."

The detective turned to the physician again.

"Then she couldn't have been dead since early last night," he said.

"She has been dead for several hours – at least twelve, possibly longer," said the physician firmly. "There's no possible argument about that."

The detective stared at him scornfully for an instant, then looked at the manager of the house.

"What was said when Mr and Mrs Morey entered your office last night?" he asked. "Were you there?"

"I was there, yes," was the reply. "Mr Morey explained that they had been called away for a few days unexpectedly, and left the keys of the apartment with me. That was all that was said; I saw the elevator boy take the suit cases out for them as they went to the cab."

"How did it come, then, if you knew they were away that some one entered here this morning, and so found the body?"

"I discovered the body myself," replied the manager. "There was some electric wiring to be done in here and I thought their absence would be a good time for it. I came up to see about it and saw – that."

He glanced at the covered body with a little shiver and a grimace. Detective Mallory was deeply thoughtful for several minutes.

"The woman is here and she's dead," he said finally. "If she is here she came back here, dead or alive last night between the time she went out with her husband and the time her body was found this morning. Now that's an absolute fact. But how did she come here?"

Of the three employees of the apartment house only the elevator boy on duty had not spoken. Now he spoke because the detective glared at him fiercely.

"I didn't see either Mr or Mrs Morey come in this morning," he explained hastily. "Nobody had come in at all except the postman and some delivery wagon drivers up to the time the body was found."

Again Detective Mallory turned on the manager.

"Does any window of this apartment open on a fire escape?" he demanded.

"Yes – this way."

They passed through the short hallway to the back. Both the windows were locked on the inside, so instantly it appeared that even if the woman had been brought into the room that way the windows would not have been fastened unless her murderer went out of the house the front way. When Detective Mallory reached this stage of the investigation he sat down and stared from one to the other of the silent little party as if he considered the entire matter some affair which they had perpetrated to annoy him.

Hutchinson Hatch started to say something, then thought better of it, and turning, went to the telephone below. Within a few minutes The Thinking Machine stepped out of a cab in front and paused in the lower hall long enough to listen to the facts developed. There was a perfect network of wrinkles in the dome-like brow when the reporter concluded.

"It's merely a transfer of the final development in the affair from England to this country," he said enigmatically. "Please 'phone for Dr Prescott to come here immediately."

He went on to the Morey apartments. With only a curt nod for Detective Mallory, the only one of the small party who knew him, he proceeded to the body of the dead woman and squinted down without a trace of emotion into the white, pallid face. After a moment he dropped on his knees beside the inert body and examined the mouth and the finger marks about the white throat.

"Carbolic acid and strangulation," he remarked tersely to Detective Mallory who was leaning over watching him with something of hopeful eagerness in his stolid face. The Thinking

Machine glanced past him to the manager of the house. "Mr Morey is a powerful, athletic man in appearance?" he asked.

"Oh no," was the reply. "He's short and slight, only a little larger than you are."

The scientist squinted aggressively at the manager as if the description were not quite what he expected. Then the slightly puzzled expression passed.

"Oh, I see," he remarked. "Played the piano." This was not a question; it was a statement.

"Yes, a great deal," was the reply, "so much so in fact that twice we had complaints from other persons in the house despite the fact that they had been here only a few days."

"Of course," mused the scientist abstractedly. "Of course. Perhaps Mrs Morey did not play at all?"

"I believe she told me she did not."

The Thinking Machine drew down the thin cloth which had been thrown over the body and glanced at the left hand.

"Dear me! Dear me!" he exclaimed suddenly, and he arose. "Dear me!" he repeated. "That's the—" He turned to the manager and the two elevator boys. "This is Mrs Morey beyond any question?"

The answer was a chorus of affirmation accompanied by some startling facial expressions.

"Did Mr and Mrs Morey employ any servants?"

"No," was the reply. "They had their meals in the cafe below most of the time. There is no housekeeping in these apartments at all."

"How many persons live in the building?"

"A hundred I should say."

"There is a great deal of passing to and fro, then?"

"Certainly. It was rather unusual that so few persons passed in and out last night and this morning, and certainly Mrs Morey and her husband were not among them if that's what you're trying to find out."

The Thinking Machine glanced at the physician who was standing by silently.

"How long do you make it that she's been dead?" he asked.

"At least twelve hours," replied the physician. "Possibly longer."

"Yes, nearer fourteen, I imagine."

Abruptly he left the group and walked through the apartment and back again slowly. As he re-entered the room where the body lay, the door from the hall opened and Dr Prescott entered, followed by Hutchinson Hatch. The Thinking Machine led the surgeon straight to the body and drew the cloth down from the face. Dr Prescott started back with an exclamation of astonishment, recognition.

"There's no doubt about it at all in your mind?" inquired the scientist.

"Not the slightest," replied Dr Prescott positively. "It's the same woman."

"Yet, look here!"

With a quick movement The Thinking Machine drew down the cloth still more. Dr Prescott, together with those who had no idea of what to expect, peered down at the body. After one glance the surgeon dropped on his knees and examined closely the dead left hand. The fore-finger was off at the first joint. Dr Prescott stared, stared incredulously. After a moment his eyes left the maimed hand and settled again on her face.

"I have never seen-never dreamed – of such a startling—" he began.

"That settles it all, of course," interrupted The Thinking Machine. "It solves and proves the problem at once. Now, Mr Mallory, if we can go to your office or some place where we will be undisturbed I will—"

"But who killed her?" demanded the detective abruptly.

"I have the photograph of her murderer in my pocket," returned The Thinking Machine. "Also a photograph of an accomplice."

PROBLEM OF THE SUPERFLUOUS FINGER

Detective Mallory, Dr Prescott, The Thinking Machine, Hutchinson Hatch, and the apartment house physician were seated in the front room of the Morey apartments with all doors closed against prying, inquisitive eyes. At the scientist's request Dr Prescott repeated the circumstances leading up to the removal of a woman's left fore-finger, and there The Thinking Machine took up the story.

"Suppose, Mr Mallory," and the scientist turned to the detective, "a woman should walk into your office and say she must have a finger cut off, what would you think?"

"I'd think she was crazy," was the prompt reply.

"Naturally, in your position," The Thinking Machine went on, "you are acquainted with many strange happenings. Wouldn't this one instantly suggest something to you. Something that was to happen months off."

Detective Mallory considered it wisely, but was silent.

"Well here," declared The Thinking Machine. "A woman whom we now know to be Mrs Morey wanted her finger cut off. It instantly suggested three, four, five, a dozen possibilities. Of course only one, or possibly two in combination, could be true. Therefore which one? A little logic now to prove that two and two always make four – not some times but all the time.

"Naturally the first supposition was insanity. We pass that as absurd on its face. Then disease – a taint of leprosy perhaps which had been visible on the left fore-finger. I tested for that, and that was eliminated. Three strong reasons for desiring the finger off, either of which is strongly probable, remained. The fact that the woman was English unmistakably was obvious. From the mark of a wedding ring on her glove and a corresponding mark on her finger – she wore no such ring – we could safely surmise that she was married. These were the two first facts I learned. Substantiative evidence that she was married and not a widow came partly from her extreme youth and the lack of mourning in her attire.

"Then Mr Hatch followed her, learned her name, where she lived, and later the fact that she had arrived with her husband on a steamer a day or so before they took apartments here. This was proof that she was English, and proof that she had a husband. They came over on the steamer as Mr and Mrs David Girardeau – here they were Mr and Mrs Frederick Chevedon Morey. Why this difference in name? The circumstance in itself pointed to irregularity – crime committed or contemplated. Other things made me think it was merely contemplated and that it could be prevented; for then the absence of every fact gave me no intimation that there would be murder. Then came the murder presumably of – Mrs Morey?"

"Isn't it Mrs Morey?" demanded the detective.

"Mr Hatch recognized the woman as the one he had followed, I recognized her as the one on whom there had been an operation, Dr Prescott also recognized her," continued the Thinking Machine. "To convince myself, after I had found the manner of death, that it was the woman, I looked at her left hand. I found that the fore-finger was gone – it had been removed by a skilled surgeon at the first joint. And this fact instantly showed me that the dead woman was not Mrs Morey at all, but somebody else; and incidentally cleared up the entire affair."

"How?" demanded the detective. "I thought you just said that you had helped cut off her fore-finger."

"Dr Prescott and I cut off that finger yesterday," replied The Thinking Machine calmly. "The finger of the dead woman had been cut off months, perhaps years, ago."

There was blank amazement on Detective Mallory's face, and Hatch was staring straight into the squint eyes of the scientist. Vaguely, as through a mist, he was beginning to account for many things which had been hitherto inexplicable.

"The perfectly healed wound on the hand eliminated every possibility but one," The Thinking Machine resumed.

"Previously I had been informed that Mrs Morey did not – or said she did not – play the piano. I had seen the bare possibility of an immense insurance on her hands, and some trick to defraud an insurance company by marring one. Of course against this was the fact that she had offered to pay a large sum for the operation; that their expenses here must have been enormous, so I was beginning to doubt the tenability of this supposition. The fact that the dead woman's finger was off removed that possibility completely, as it also removed the possibility of a crime of some sort in which there might have been left behind a tell-tale print of that fore-finger. If there had been a serious crime with the trace of the finger as evidence, its removal would have been necessary to her.

"Then the one thing remained – that is that Mrs Morey or whatever her name is – was in a conspiracy with her husband to get possession of certain properties, perhaps a title – remember she is English – by sacrificing that finger so that identification might be in accordance with the description of an heir whom she was to impersonate. We may well believe that she was provided with the necessary documentary evidence, and we know conclusively – we don't conjecture but we know – that the dead woman in there is the woman whose rights were to have been stolen by the so-called Mrs Morey."

"But that is Mrs Morey, isn't it?" demanded the detective again.

"No," was the sharp retort. "The perfect resemblance to Mrs Morey and the finger removed long ago makes that clear. There is, I imagine, a relationship between them—perhaps they are cousins. I can hardly believe they are twins because the necessity, then of one impersonating the other to obtain either money or a title, would not have existed so palpably although it is possible that Mrs Morey, if disinherited or disowned, would have resorted to such a course. This dead woman is Miss – Miss – " and he glanced at the back of a photograph, "Miss Evelyn Rossmore, and she has evidently been living in this city for some time. This is her picture, and it was made at least a year ago by Harkinson here. Perhaps he can give you her address as well."

There was silence for several minutes. Each member of the little group was turning over the stated facts mentally, and Detective Mallory was staring at the photograph, studying the handwriting on the back.

"But how did she come here – like this?" Hatch inquired.

"You remember, Mr Hatch, when you followed Mrs Morey here you told me she dressed again and went out?" asked the scientist in turn. "It was not Mrs Morey you saw then – she was ill and I knew it from the operation – it was Miss Rossmore. The manager says a hundred persons live in this house – that there is a great deal of passing in and out. Can't you see that when there is such a startling resemblance Miss Rossmore could pass in and out at will and always be mistaken for Mrs Morey? That no one would ever notice the difference?"

"But who killed her?" asked Detective Mallory, curiously. "How? Why?"

"Morey killed her," said The Thinking Machine flatly and he produced two other photographs from his pocket. "There's his picture and his wife's picture for identification purposes. How did he kill her? We can fairly presume that first he tricked her into drinking the acid, then perhaps she was screaming with the pain of it, and he choked her to death. I imagined first he was a large, powerful man because his grip on her throat was so powerful that he ruptured the jugular inside; but instead of that he plays the piano a great deal, which would give him the hand-power to choke her. And why? We can suppose only that it was because she had in some way learned of their purpose. That would have established the motive. The crowning delicacy of the affair was Morey's act in leaving his keys with the manager here. He did not anticipate that the apartments would be entered for several days – after they were safely away –

while there was a chance that if neither of them had been seen here and their disappearance was unexplained the rooms would have been opened to ascertain why. That is all, I think."

"Except to catch Morey and his wife," said the detective grimly.

"Easily done with those photographs," said The Thinking Machine. "I imagine, if this murder is kept out of the newspapers for a couple of hours you can find them about to sail for Europe. Suppose you try the line they came over on?"

It was just three hours later that the accused man and wife were taken prisoner. They had just engaged passage on the steamer which sailed at half-past four o'clock. Their trial was a famous one and resulted in conviction after an astonishing story of an attempt to seize an estate and title belonging rightfully to Miss Evelyn Rossmore who had mysteriously disappeared years before.

4

PROBLEM OF THE VANISHING MAN

There was a feverish restlessness in the merciless gray eyes, an unpleasant frown on his brow, as Charles Duer Carroll paused on the curb in front of a tall down town office building and stared moodily across the busy street into nothingness. Carroll was a remarkable looking young man in many ways. He was young, – only thirty, – and physically every line of his body expressed power, sturdiness rather than youth, force rather than grace. He was blessed too with an indomitable, uncompromising jaw, the jaw of a fighting man. The chin was square, the lips thin, avaricious perhaps, the nose slightly hooked, the cheek bones high. In general his appearance was that of a keenly alert man who is never surprised; who chooses his way and pursues it aggressively without haste, without mercy, and without mistakes.

Despite his youth, – it may have been because of it, – Carroll was president and active head of the great brokerage concern, the Carroll-Swayne-McPartland Company, with general offices on the fourth floor of this huge building behind him. He held that responsible position by right of being the grandson of its founder, old Nick Carroll. Upon his retirement from active business a year previously the old man, a wrinkled, venomous image of the young, had banged his desk with lusty fist and so declared it – Charlie Carroll was to be his successor. There had been heartburnings, objections, violent protests even; but the old man owned five thousand of the ten thousand shares of the company, and – Charles Duer Carroll was president.

Financially the young man was interested in the company only to the extent of owning twenty-five shares, this being a gift from old Nick and a necessary qualification for an office holder. Beyond this rather meager possession, – meager at least in comparison with the holdings of other officers and stockholders of the company, – young Carroll had only his salary of twenty thousand dollars a year, – nothing else, for he had been exalted to this from a salary of eighteen hundred and a clerk's desk in the general office. Here for six years old Nick Carroll had drilled the business into him, warp and woof; then had come the exaltation.

Thus it came about that a pauper, from the viewpoint of financial circles, directed the affairs of a company whose business ran into millions and tens of millions annually. If young Carroll felt that he needed advice, he did not hesitate to disregard his fellows and go straight to the fountainhead, old Carroll. And when he asked for that advice he regarded it scrupulously, minutely. At other times – in fact, as a general thing – young Carroll sailed on his own course, – took the bit in his teeth and did as he pleased, – leaving accrued profits to inform the various stockholders of his actions. At such times old Nick was wont to rub his skinny hands together and smile.

For months after young Carroll assumed the reins of government there had been fear of a misstep and consequent wreck in the conservative hearts of officers and stockholders, except in the case of old Carroll; then this apprehension was dissipated, leaving a residue of rankling envy. Not one man in authority would have said it was not for the best that old Nick had thrust this infusion of aggressive young blood into the staid old company; but half a dozen persons at interest could have enumerated a thousand reasons why a youth of thirty should not hold the position of president, when some older man – one of themselves – knew the business better and had been in the office longer.

Be that as it may, Charles Duer Carroll, the pauper, was president of the company. When he stepped into that position he brought with him new vigor and virility and vitality and a surly, curt, merciless method which had enabled him to achieve things. This was the young man – this Charles Duer Carroll – who stood on the curb one morning staring, glaring, across the busy street. At last he dropped a half smoked cigar, ground it to shreds on the pavement beneath a vigorous heel, and turning stared up at the building. There was a window of his office in the corner straight above him, and there was work that called. But Carroll wasn't thinking of that particularly; he was thinking of—

He snapped his fingers impatiently and entered the building. An elevator whirled him up to the fourth floor, and he entered the large outer office of the company. The forbidding frown was still on his brow, the steeliness still in his gray eyes. Several clerks nodded respectfully as he entered; but there was no greeting in return, not even a curt time of day. He strode straight across the room to his private office without a glance either to right or left, banging the door behind him.

Over in a corner of the outer office Gordon Swayne, secretary and treasurer, was dictating letters. He glanced round with an expression of annoyance on his face at the sudden noise. "Who did that?" he demanded of his stenographer.

"It was Mr Carroll, sir."

"Oh!" and he resumed his dictation.

For an hour or more he continued dictating; then a letter which required the attention of President Carroll came to hand and he went into the private office. He came out after a moment and spoke to his stenographer again.

"Did Mr Carroll go into his office this morning?"

"Yes, sir."

Swayne turned and glanced round the outer office inquiringly. "Did you see him come out?" he inquired.

"No, sir."

That was all. Swayne laid the letter aside for the moment and continued with the other correspondence. From time to time he glanced impatiently at the clock, thence to the door from the hall. At ten minutes past eleven the stenographer returned to her own desk, and with a worried countenance Swayne went over and spoke to a bookkeeper near the door.

"Did you see Mr Carroll go out?" he asked. "Or do you know where he went?"

"He hasn't gone out, sir," replied the bookkeeper. "I saw him go into his office a couple of hours ago."

Swayne went straight toward the private office with the evident intention of leaving the letter on the president's desk. The door of the room was still closed. He was reaching out his hand to open it, when it was opened from within and Carroll started out. Swayne stared at him a moment in a manner nearly approaching amazement.

"Well, what is it?" demanded Carroll curtly.

"I-er-here's something I wanted to ask you about," Swayne explained haltingly.

Carroll glanced over the extended letter. His brows contracted and he quickly looked up at the clock.

"Did this come in the morning mail?" he demanded impatiently.

"Yes. I knew—"

"You should have called it to my attention two hours ago," said Carroll sharply. "Answer by wire that we'll accept the proposition."

Swayne's face flamed suddenly at the tone and manner. "I tried to call it to your attention two hours ago," he explained; "but you were not in your office, nor were you out here."

"I've been in my office right along," said Carroll sharply, and he glared straight into Swayne's eyes. "Wire immediately that we'll accept the proposition."

The two men stood thus face to face, eyes challenging eyes, for an instant, then simultaneously turned away. Swayne's countenance showed not only anger but bewilderment; whatever Carroll felt was not evident. Perhaps there was more color in his face than was usually there; but it had been that way when he came out of the private office, therefore was not due to any feeling aroused by the scene with Swayne.

That afternoon Carroll caused a neat placard to be placed on the door of his private office. It said briefly:

Do not enter this room without knocking. If Mr Carroll does not answer a knock, it is to be understood that he is not to be disturbed under any circumstances.

Swayne read it and wondered, feeling somehow that it was a direct rebuke to him; the dozen or more clerks read it and wondered, and commented upon it varyingly; two office boys read it and added their opinions. On the following day the incident was repeated with slight variations. Swayne saw Carroll enter the front door, pass through the main office, and go into the private office, closing the door behind him. Half an hour later Swayne spoke to the bookkeeper Black, to whom he had spoken the day before.

"Please hand that to Mr Carroll in his private office," he directed.

The bookkeeper took the slip of paper which the secretary offered, crossed the office, and rapped on Carroll's door. After a minute he returned to Swayne, who was apparently adding a column of figures.

"Mr Carroll doesn't answer, sir," explained the bookkeeper.

"You know he's in there, don't you?" asked Swayne blandly.

"I saw him go in a few minutes ago, yes, sir; but I didn't intrude because of the notice on the door."

"Oh, that's of no consequence," exclaimed Swayne impatiently. "This is a matter of importance. Take it into him anyway, whether he answers or not."

Again the bookkeeper went away, and again he returned. "Mr Carroll wasn't in there, sir," he explained; "and I had to leave the paper on his desk."

"I thought you said you saw him go in?" demanded Swayne.

"I did, sir."

"Well, he must be in there; he hasn't come out," insisted Swayne. "Are you sure he isn't there?"

"Why, positive, yes, sir," replied the bewildered bookkeeper.

Swayne was bending over the high desk intently studying the figures before him. The bookkeeper stood for a little while as if awaiting another order, then resumed his work.

"We'll go in there together and see if he isn't to be found," said Swayne at last in a most matter of fact tone.

"But I just—" the bookkeeper began.

"Never mind, come along," directed Swayne; "and don't talk too loud," he added in a lower tone.

Wonderingly the bookkeeper followed the secretary. Swayne himself rapped on the door. There was no answer, and finally he pushed the door open quietly. Carroll was sitting at his desk going over the morning mail. He apparently was not aware that the door had been opened, and Swayne started to close it as he and the bookkeeper withdrew.

"You were mistaken, Black," Swayne remarked casually.

"Come in, Mr Swayne, you and Black," called Carroll just as the door was closing.

Swayne warned the bookkeeper to silence with one quick, comprehensive glance, then reopened the door, and they entered the private office, closing the door behind them. Swayne faced his superior calmly, defiantly almost; the bookkeeper twiddled his fingers nervously.

"Since when is it customary for employees here to disobey my orders?" demanded Carroll coldly.

"Mr Black told me you were not here, and I came to see myself," replied Swayne with a singular emphasis on every word.

"You see that he was mistaken, then?" demanded Carroll. "Mr Black, we shall not require your services any longer. Mr Swayne will give you a check immediately for what is due you. And you, Mr Swayne, understand that if my orders are not obeyed to the letter in this office I shall be compelled to make other changes. From this time forward the door will be locked when I am in my office. That's all."

"But I was obeying orders when—" Black began in trepidation.

"I put my order on the door for you to obey," interrupted Carroll. "Go write him a check, Mr Swayne."

Swayne and Black went out, and Swayne closed the door. Carroll had been seated as they went out; but the door had no sooner closed now than they heard the lock snap inside.

"What does it mean, Black?" Swayne inquired quietly.

"I don't know, sir," replied the astonished bookkeeper. "He certainly was not in that room when I was in there. And as for discharging me—"

"You are not discharged," Swayne said impatiently, with a new note in his voice. "You are going to take a vacation of a couple of weeks, though, on full salary. Meanwhile have luncheon with me today."

Professor Augustus S. F. X. Van Dusen – The Thinking Machine – straightened up in his chair suddenly and turned his squinting, belligerent eyes full upon his two visitors.

"Never mind your personal opinion or prejudices, Mr Swayne," he rebuked sharply. "If you want my assistance in this matter, I must insist that you relate the facts, and only the facts, freed of all colouring which may have been infused into them by your ill feeling toward Mr Carroll. I understand readily enough the cause of this—this ill feeling. You are his

PROBLEM OF THE VANISHING MAN

senior in the office, and he was promoted over your head to be the president of the company, while you remained secretary and treasurer. Now give me the remainder of the facts, please."

There was a considerable pause. A flush had slowly mounted Swayne's face, and it was only with an obvious effort that he controlled himself. Once he looked toward Black, who had been a silent witness of the interview.

"Well, after those first two incidents," Swayne went on at last, "the door of Mr Carroll's private office was always locked on the inside the moment he was left alone. Now I am not a fool, Professor Van Dusen. In my mind it stands to reason that if Mr Carroll disappeared from that room twice when the door was left unlocked, he is gone from it practically all the time when the door is locked; therefore—"

"Opinion again," interrupted The Thinking Machine curtly. "Facts, Mr Swayne, facts!"

"If he isn't gone, why does he keep the door locked?"

"Perhaps," and the crabbed little scientist regarded him coldly, – "perhaps it's really because he is busy and doesn't want to be interrupted. That is always possible, you know. I'm that way myself sometimes."

"And where does he go? How does he go? And why does he go?"

"If I had to diagnose this case," remarked The Thinking Machine almost pleasantly, "I should say it was a severe attack of idle curiosity, complicated with prejudice and suspicion." Suddenly his whole tone, his whole manner, changed. "Has the conduct of the business of the company been all it should have been since Mr Carroll has been in charge?" he demanded.

"Well, yes," admitted Swayne.

"He has made money for the company?"

"Yes."

"Perhaps increased its earnings, if anything?"

Swayne nodded reluctantly.

"Nothing is stolen?" the scientist demanded. "Nothing is missing? Nothing has gone wrong?"

Three times Swayne shook his head.

The Thinking Machine arose impatiently. "If there had been anything wrong, of course you would have gone to the police," The Thinking Machine went on. "There being nothing wrong, you came to me. I don't mind giving what assistance I can in instances where it works for good; but my time is valuable to the world of science, Mr Swayne, and really I can't be disturbed by such a trivial affair as this. If anything does go wrong, if anything does happen, you are at liberty to call again. Goodday."

The two men arose, stood staring blankly at each other for a moment, then turned to go out. Swayne's face was crimson with anger, chagrin, at his abrupt dismissal. But at the door he turned back for one final question.

"Would you mind informing us how Mr Carroll disappeared from his office on the two occasions when we know he did disappear, before he locked his door against us?"

"You saw him go in one door; he went out another, I suppose," replied The Thinking Machine.

"There is only one other door," retorted Swayne with something like triumph in his voice. "That is blocked in his office by his desk and also blocked in the stockholders' meeting room, to which it leads, by a long couch. The offices are fifty feet from the ground; so he couldn't jump from a window. He didn't go through the stockholders' room, either, because that has only one door, and that opens into the outer office within two or three feet of the door to his private office. There are no fire escapes at either of his windows, I may add. Now, how did he get out—if he got out?"

The face was flushed and angry again, the voice raised stridently. The Thinking Machine stared for half a minute, then opened the door to the street.

"I don't know if you know it," he said calmly at last; "but you are almost convincing me that there is something wrong there, and that you are responsible for it. Goodday."

The steel gray eyes of Charles Duer Carroll were blazing as he flung open the outside door of the offices of Carroll-Swayne-McPartland Company and entered the large general office. Was it anger? Not one of the dozen clerks who raised half timid eyes as he appeared could have answered the question. Was it excitement? Still there would have been no answer. He went straight to his private office, without a look or word for his subordinates then wheeled suddenly on his heel there and called:

"Mr Swayne!"

The secretary and treasurer started a little at the imperative command, and Carroll motioned for him to approach. Then he led the way into his office, Swayne following, and the clerks outside heard the lock click. Swayne, inside, stood waiting the president's pleasure. A vague sense of physical danger oppressed him.

"Sit down!" commanded Carroll. The secretary obeyed. "You are the secretary and treasurer of this company, are you not?" demanded Carroll brutally.

"Certainly. Why?"

"Then you know, or are supposed to know, exactly what securities this company holds in trust for its customers to protect margins, don't you?" Carroll went on. His eyes were blazing as the secretary met them.

"Certainly I know," Swayne responded after a moment.

"You know that in the round three million dollars worth of securities in our vaults and safety deposit vaults over the city there is one lot of four hundred thousand dollars' worth of United States gold bonds, and that these include the numbers 0043917 to 0044120?"

Swayne disregarded the urgent demand for an immediate answer which lay behind the tone, and stopped to consider the matter carefully. Was it a trap of some sort? He couldn't tell.

"Do you or do you not know that this consignment of bonds includes those numbers?" demanded Carroll hotly.

"Yes" was the reply, "I know that those numbers are included in the Mason-Hackett trust lot. Further I know that I locked them myself in the vault in the office here."

Carroll's eyes were contracted to pin points, and all the latent power of the man seemed aroused as he turned savagely in his chair.

"If you know that to be true, then what does that mean?" and he flung down a sheet of paper violently under the eyes of the secretary and treasurer.

Swayne, with a vague sense of terror which he could not fathom at the moment, picked up the paper and glanced over it. It was an affidavit signed by E. C. Morgan & Co., brokers, and dated the day before. It was in the usual form, and attested, with innumerable reiterations, that United States Government gold bonds, numbers 0043917 to 0043940 inclusive, were in the possession of E. C. Morgan & Co., having been bought in the open market three days previously.

Swayne stared unbelievingly at the affidavit, and slowly, slowly, the colour deserted his face until it was chalk white. Twice he raised his eyes from the affidavit to the strangely working face of Carroll, and twice he lowered them under the baleful glare they met. When he raised them the third time there was mystification, wonder, utter helplessness, in them.

"Well?" blazed out Carroll. "Well?" he repeated.

Swayne started to his feet.

"Just a moment, Mr Swayne," warned the president in a voice which had become suddenly and strangely quiet. "You had better remain here for a few minutes until we look into this." He arose and went to the door, and spoke to some one outside.

"Please bring me all the securities of all kinds in our vaults," he directed, "and send messengers to bring those which are in safety deposit vaults elsewhere. Bring them all to me personally – not to Mr Swayne."

He closed the door and turned back toward the secretary. The colour came back into Swayne's face with a rush under the impetus of some powerful emotion, and he stood swaying a little, closing and unclosing his hands spasmodically. At length he found tongue, and now his voice was as steady and quiet as was the others.

"Do I understand you accuse me of-of stealing those bonds?" he demanded.

"The bonds are missing," was the reply. "They were in your care. It really is of no concern whether they were misappropriated or lost. The result is the same. Bonds were intrusted to us to protect our customers. We are responsible for them; you are responsible to us."

Swayne dropped back into a chair with his head in his hands. Utterly at a loss for words, he sat thus until there came a respectful rap on the door. Carroll opened it, and a clerk entered with a package of the securities.

"Is this all of them?" inquired Carroll.

"All except about six hundred thousand dollars' worth which were in a safety deposit vault farther up town," was the reply. "A messenger is on his way with them now."

Carroll dismissed him with a curt nod and spilled the securities on the table before him. Then he spoke to Swayne again. There was a singular softening of his tone – Swayne chose to read it as mocking.

"Really I'm very sorry, Mr Swayne," the president said soothingly. "I had trusted you to the utmost: indeed, I dare say every stockholder in the company did, and whether you are at fault or not now remains to be seen. We know if those bonds are missing, as the affidavit asserts, there may be others missing, and the entire amount will have to be verified. I shall do that personally."

Still Swayne didn't speak. There seemed to be nothing to say. Once he glanced up into the steady gaze which was directed toward him, and relapsed immediately into his former position, with his head resting in his hands.

"Don't misunderstand me, please," said Carroll. "You are not a prisoner. This is a matter that will not go to the police – as yet anyway. It would not be safe for our office force to know what has happened. It might precipitate disaster. Meanwhile go on about your duties as if nothing has happened."

"My God, Charlie! you don't believe I stole them, do you?" Swayne burst out at last piteously as he rose to his feet.

"That's the first time you have called me by that name since I have been president of this company," Carroll remarked irrelevantly. "I want to like you, – I've always wanted to like you, – but of late you have wilfully antagonized me. Now, my first duty is here," and he indicated the heap of securities on his desk. "I must not be interrupted until I have finished. It is as necessary to you as to me; so go on about your work. Afterward we'll see what we can do."

For an hour, perhaps, Swayne sat at his desk gazing dreamily across the office. Half a dozen questions were asked; he didn't answer. But slowly there came a subtle change in his face; slowly some strong determination seized upon him, and at last it brought him to his feet, with staring eyes. For only an instant he hesitated over this idea which had come to him, and then spoke to the girl in charge of the office telephone exchange.

"Connect booth 3 with Central," he commanded sharply, "then leave the exchange there and don't answer a ring under any circumstances!"

Within less than a minute Swayne was talking to The Thinking Machine over the wire.

"This is Gordon Swayne," he began abruptly. "Something has happened, I don't know what. You told me I might call on you if something did happen. Can you come to the office at once?"

"What happened?" demanded The Thinking Machine irritably.

"I'm afraid it's a huge defalcation," was the instant response. "Carroll has locked himself in the room from which he had disappeared previously, with millions of dollars in securities which came into his possession by a trick, and I believe as firmly as I believe I'm living that he has run away with them. It's the only thing to account for his strange actions. He went into the room an hour ago – I'd wager my life he isn't there now."

"Why don't you rap on the door and ask for him?" came an imperturbable question.

"Can you come at once?" demanded Swayne abruptly.

"I'll be there in fifteen minutes," was the reply. "Don't do anything absurd until I get there; and don't call the police, because you are probably only suffering from another manifestation of that complaint with which I found you suffering before. Goodbye."

Swayne forced himself to calmness again, and after a few minutes' wait rapped quietly on the door of the private office. There was no response from inside. He tried the door. It was locked. It was just then that the door from the hall opened, and The Thinking Machine entered, peering about his curiously. In tones subdued by sheer force, Swayne related the incidents of the morning in detail.

"I believe – I know – Carroll has stolen those securities!" Swayne burst out at last. "What shall I do?"

For a minute or more The Thinking Machine sat silently squinting upward with white fingers at rest tip to tip, then he arose and readjusted his glasses.

"I believe," he said quietly, "I'd smash in the door. It might be something worse than you think."

Swayne called to two of the clerks as he went, and the four men paused for an instant at the entrance to the private office.

"Well, do it!" commanded The Thinking Machine irritably.

Swayne and the clerks placed their shoulders against the door; then from inside there came a sharp click. It was the key turning in the lock. They drew back and waited. The door swung open, and Carroll in person appeared before them, with both hands behind his back. There was an instant's pause, then in the strained, harsh voice of Swayne came the question – an accusation:

"Where are those securities?"

"Here," responded Carroll, and he produced them from behind his back. "Swayne, you are a childish idiot!" he added sharply.

The Thinking Machine nearly smiled.

The explanation of the problem of the vanishing man, as The Thinking Machine stated it, was ludicrously simple. After Carroll had so mercilessly smashed Swayne's hypothesis of a defalcation, by appearing in person with the bonds and other securities, the secretary had stalked out moodily, and now he was in The Thinking Machine's small reception room, staring gloomily at the floor.

"My first diagnosis fits the case," remarked the diminutive scientist; "idle curiosity with complications. You see, Mr Swayne, you businessmen are too practical, if I may say so. You in this instance could not or would not see beyond the obvious. A little imagination would have aided you – imagination coupled with a knowledge of the rudimentary rules of logic. Logic doesn't make mistakes – it is as certainly infallible as that two and two make four, not sometimes but all the time.

"Briefly I knew from your first statement of the case that Mr Carroll was comparatively poor, despite the fact that he is the head of this great company. In ninety-nine cases out of a hundred every man wants to get rich. Mr Carroll had increased the earnings of his company; but he had not increased his own, therefore let us credit him with a desire to get rich. If he did not have such a desire, he would not be in the position he now holds. The moment we allow for this, and also allow for the fact that the securities were returned intact, we have the solution of the entire affair. I am admitting that not only did Mr Carroll disappear from his private office at the times you specify; but that he was also gone from that office practically all the time he kept the door locked.

"In the stock markets (I have just enough acquaintance with them to know that money begets money) it is possible to make or lose millions in an hour. Therefore if Mr Carroll could get all the securities of the company into his possession for an hour, and cared to do so, he could work wonders in the open market. This is precisely what he did. By a trick, we'll say, he got them together in a way which could not arouse even your suspicions, and used them on the market. The inference is that he made money by the use of those securities for that hour – the fact that he brought them back shows that he did not lose money, or he would not have had them. So, that's all of it: Mr Carroll used the firm's money to make money for himself. Technically he has committed a crime; but—"

"It is a crime then?" demanded Swayne. "He was the criminal then, when he accused me of-of stealing the United States bonds?"

"By accusing you of appropriating or misplacing those bonds he did the necessary thing," replied The Thinking Machine; "that is, distracted your attention and gave himself, even in your eyes, the best possible excuse for getting all the securities together, without even a glimmer of light as to his purpose when he got them. Mr Carroll is a very remarkable and very able man; he knows what he wants, and he knows how to get it. In other words, he is tremendously resourceful."

"But how-how did he leave that private office to use the securities, say in a market transaction?" Swayne insisted.

"Simply enough," was the reply. "I don't know; but I dare say through a window. It is a simple matter to stand on a window sill and swing yourself to the sill of the next window, particularly when a man has the steady nerve and strength of this man. If perchance the next room was unoccupied, you see how simple it would have been for Mr Carroll to leave his office and remain away for hours, with the door of his private office locked behind him. There is really no mystery about the affair at all. It is simply a question of how much the transaction netted Mr Carroll."

An hour later the board of directors of the Carroll-Swayne-McPartland Company met in the room adjoining Carroll's private office. The call had been issued by Swayne without consulting President Carroll. The secretary stated the case pithily, violently even. Carroll listened to the end.

"I am very glad that the directors have met," he said then as he arose. "I have committed a crime technically, as Mr Swayne says. By that crime I have made a little more than two million dollars. The tremendous power which the millions of securities of this company gave me allowed me to turn the market upside down, to manipulate it at will, then to withdraw. This company is old; it's conservative. If this thing becomes known outside, it will hurt. But this company has its securities again, intact; I have made a fortune. If the company chooses to accept one-half of what I made, I to hold the other half, it is agreeable to me. I had intended to make this proposition anyway."

There was a long argument, a great many words, and finally acquiescence.

"And now shall I resign?" inquired Carroll finally.

"No," returned old Nick Carroll. "You young scoundrel, if you even think about resigning, why-why, confound it, we'll fire you! A man who can do such a thing as that—Why, Charlie, you're a wonder! You'll stay! do you understand?"

He arose and glared defiantly about the room. There was not even a head shake—nothing.

"You stay on the job, Charlie," said the old man. "That's all."

5

THE CASE OF THE SCIENTIFIC MURDERER

Certainly no problem that ever came to the attention of The Thinking Machine required in a greater degree subtlety of mind, exquisite analytical sense, and precise knowledge of the marvels of science than did that singular series of events which began with the death of the Honorable Violet Danbury, only daughter and sole heir of the late Sir Duval Danbury, of Leamington, England. In this case The Thinking Machine – more properly, Professor Augustus S. F. X. Van Dusen, Ph. D., M. D., F. R. S., et cetera, et cetera – brought to bear upon an extraordinary mystery of crime that intangible genius of logic which had made him the court of last appeal in his profession. "Logic is inexorable," he has said; and no greater proof of his assertion was possible than in this instance where literally he seemed to pluck a solution of the riddle from the void.

Shortly after eleven o'clock on the morning of Thursday, May 4, Miss Danbury was found dead, sitting in the drawing-room of apartments she was temporarily occupying in a big family hotel on Beacon Street. She was richly gowned, just as she had come from the opera the night before; her marble-white bosom and arms aglitter with jewels. On her face, dark in death as are the faces of those who die of strangulation, was an expression of unspeakable terror. Her parted lips were

THE CASE OF THE SCIENTIFIC MURDERER

slightly bruised, as if from a light blow; in her left cheek was an insignificant, bloodless wound. On the floor at her feet was a shattered goblet. There was nothing else unusual, no disorder, no sign of a struggle. Obviously she had been dead for several hours.

All these things considered, the snap judgement of the police – specifically, the snap judgement of Detective Mallory, of the bureau of criminal investigation – was suicide by poison. Miss Danbury had poured some deadly drug into a goblet, sat down, drained it off, and died. Simple and obvious enough. But the darkness in her face? Oh, that! Probably some effect of a poison he didn't happen to be acquainted with. But it looked as if she might have been strangled! Pooh! Pooh! There were no marks on her neck, of fingers or anything else. Suicide, that's what it was – the autopsy would disclose the nature of the poison.

Cursory questions of the usual nature were asked and answered. Had Miss Danbury lived alone? No; she had a companion upon whom, too, devolved the duties of chaperon – a Mrs Cecelia Montgomery. Where was she? She'd left the city the day before to visit friends in Concord; the manager of the hotel had telegraphed the facts to her. No servants? No. She had availed herself of the service in the hotel. Who had last seen Miss Danbury alive? The elevator attendant the night before, when she had returned form the opera, about half past eleven o'clock. Had she gone alone? No. She had been accompanied by Professor Charles Meredith, of the university. He had returned with her, and left her at the elevator.

"How did she come to know Professor Meredith?" Mallory inquired. "Friend, relative—"

"I don't know," said the hotel manager. "She knew a great many people here. She'd only been in the city two months this time, but once, three years ago, she spent six months here."

"Any particular reason for her coming over? Business, for instance, or merely a visit?"

"Merely a visit, I imagine."

The front door swung open, and there entered at the moment a middle-aged man, sharp-featured, rather spare, brisk in his movements, and distinctly well groomed. He went straight to the inquiry desk.

"Will you please phone to Miss Danbury, and ask her if she will join Mr Herbert Willing for luncheon at the country club?" he requested. "Tell her I am below with my motor."

At mention of Miss Danbury's name both Mallory and the house manager turned. The boy behind the inquiry desk glanced at the detective blankly. Mr Willing rapped upon the desk sharply.

"Well, well?" he demanded impatiently. "Are you asleep?"

"Goodmorning, Mr Willing," Mallory greeted him.

"Hello, Mallory," and Mr Willing turned to face him. "What are you doing here?"

"You don't know that Miss Danbury is" – the detective paused a little — "is dead?"

"Dead!" Mr Willing gasped. "Dead!" he repeated incredulously. "What are you talking about?" He seized Mallory by the arm, and shook him. "Miss Danbury is—"

"Dead," the detective assured him again. "She probably committed suicide. She was found in her apartments two hours ago."

For half a minute Mr Willing continued to stare at him as if without comprehension, then he dropped weakly into a chair, with his head in his hands. When he glanced up again there was deep grief in his keen face.

"It's my fault," he said simply. "I feel like a murderer. I gave her some bad news yesterday, but I didn't dream she would—" He stopped.

"Bad news?" Mallory urged.

"I've been doing some legal work for her," Mr Willing explained. "She's been trying to sell a huge estate in England,

and just at the moment the deal seemed assured it fell through. I – I suppose it was a mistake to tell her. This morning I received another offer from an unexpected quarter, and I came by to inform her of it." He stared tensely into Mallory's face for a moment without speaking. "I feel like her murderer!" he said again.

"But I don't understand why the failure of the deal—" the detective began; then: "She was rich, wasn't she? What did it matter particularly if the deal did fail?"

"Rich, yes; but land poor," the lawyer elucidated. "The estates to which she held title were frightfully involved. She had jewels and all those things, but see how simply she lived. She was actually in need of money. It would take me an hour to make you understand. How did she die? When? What was the manner of her death?"

Detective Mallory placed before him those facts he had, and finally went away with him in his motor car to see Professor Meredith at the university. Nothing bearing on the case developed as the result of that interview. Mr Meredith seemed greatly shocked, and explained that his acquaintance with Miss Danbury dated some weeks back, and friendship had grown out of it through a mutual love of music. He had accompanied her to the opera half a dozen times.

"Suicide!" the detective declared, as he came away. "Obviously suicide by poison."

On the following day he discovered for the first time that the obvious is not necessarily true. The autopsy revealed absolutely no trace of poison, either in the body or clinging to the shattered goblet, carefully gathered up and examined. The heart was normal, showing neither constriction nor dilation, as would have been the case had poison been swallowed, or even inhaled.

"It's the small wound in her cheek, then," Mallory asserted. "Maybe she didn't swallow or inhale poison—she injected it directly into her blood through that wound."

"No," one of the examining physicians pointed out. "Even that way the heart would have shown constriction or dilation."

"Oh, maybe not," Mallory argued hopefully.

"Besides," the physician went on, "that wound was made after death. That is proven by the fact that it did not bleed." His brow clouded in perplexity. "There doesn't seem to be the slightest reason for that wound, anyway. It's really a hole, you know. It goes straight through her cheek. It looks as if it might have been made with a large hatpin."

The detective was staring at him. If that wound had been made after death, certainly Miss Danbury didn't make it – she had been murdered! And not murdered for robbery, since her jewels had been undisturbed.

"Straight through her cheek!" he repeated blankly. "By George! Say, if it wasn't poison, what killed her?"

The three examining physicians exchanged glances.

"I don't know that I can make you understand," said one. "She died of absence of air in her lungs, if you follow me."

"Absence of air—well, that's illuminating!" the detective sneered heavily. "You mean she was strangled, or choked to death?"

"I mean precisely what I say," was the reply. "She was not strangled – there is no mark on her throat; or choked – there is no obstruction in her throat. Literally she died of absence of air in her lungs."

Mallory stood silently glowering at them. A fine lot of physicians, these!

"Let's understand one another," he said at last. "Miss Danbury did not die a natural death?"

"No!" emphatically.

"She wasn't poisoned? Or strangled? Or shot? Or stabbed? Or run over by a truck? Or blown up by dynamite? Or kicked by a mule? Nor," he concluded, "did she fall from an aeroplane?"

"No."

"In other words, she just quit living?"

"Something like that," the physician admitted. He seemed to be seeking a means of making himself more explicit. "You know the old nursery theory that a cat will suck a sleeping baby's breath?" he asked. "Well, the death of Miss Danbury was like that, if you understand. It is as if some great animal or-or thing had—" He stopped.

Detective Mallory was an able man, the ablest, perhaps, in the bureau of criminal investigation, but a yellow primrose by the river's brim was to him a yellow primrose, nothing more. He lacked imagination, a common fault of that type of sleuth who combines, more or less happily, a number eleven shoe and a number six hat. The only vital thing he had to go on was the fact that Miss Danbury was dead—murdered, in some mysterious, uncanny way. Vampires were something like that, weren't they? He shuddered a little.

"Regular vampire sort of thing," the youngest of the three physicians remarked, echoing the thought in the detective's mind. "They're supposed to make a slight wound, and—"

Detective Mallory didn't hear the remainder of it. He turned abruptly, and left the room.

On the following Monday morning, one Henry Sumner, a longshoreman in Atlantic Avenue, was found dead sitting in his squalid room. On his face, dark in death, as are the faces of those who die of strangulation, was an expression of unspeakable terror. His parted lips were slightly bruised, as if from a light blow; in his left cheek was an insignificant, bloodless wound. On the floor at his feet was a shattered drinking glass!

'Twas Hutchinson Hatch, newspaper reporter, long, lean, and rather prepossessing in appearance, who brought this double mystery to the attention of The Thinking Machine. Martha, the eminent scientist's one servant, admitted the newspaper man, and he went straight to the laboratory. As he opened the door The Thinking Machine turned testily from his worktable.

"Oh, it's you, Mr Hatch. Glad to see you. Sit down. What is it?" That was his idea of extreme cordiality.

"If you can spare me five minutes?" the reporter began apologetically.

"What is it?" repeated The Thinking Machine, without raising his eyes.

"I wish I knew," the reporter said ruefully. "Two persons are dead — two persons as widely apart as the poles, at least in social position, have been murdered in precisely the same manner, and it seems impossible that —"

"Nothing is impossible," The Thinking Machine interrupted, in the tone of perpetual irritation which seemed to be a part of him. "You annoy me when you say it."

"It seems highly improbable," Hatch corrected himself, "that there can be the remotest connection between the crimes, yet—"

"You're wasting words," the crabbed little scientist declared impatiently. "Begin at the beginning. Who was murdered? When? How? Why? What was the manner of death?"

"Taking the last question first," the reporter explained, "we have the most singular part of the problem. No one can say the manner of death, not even the physicians."

"Oh!" For the first time The Thinking Machine lifted his petulant, squinting, narrowed eyes, and stared into the face of the newspaper man. "Oh!" he said again. "Go on."

As Hatch talked, the lure of a material problem laid hold of the master mind, and after a little The Thinking Machine dropped into a chair. With his great, grotesque head tilted back, his eyes turned steadily upward, and slender fingers placed precisely tip to tip, he listened in silence to the end.

"We come now," said the newspaper man, "to the inexplicable after developments. We have proven that Mrs Cecelia Montgomery, Miss Danbury's companion, did not go to Concord to visit friends; as a matter of fact, she is missing.

THE CASE OF THE SCIENTIFIC MURDERER 87

The police have been able to find no trace of her, and today are sending out a general alarm. Naturally, her absence at this particular moment is suspicious. It is possible to conjecture her connection with the death of Miss Danbury, but what about—"

"Never mind conjecture," the scientist broke in curtly. "Facts, facts!"

"Further," and Hatch's bewilderment was evident on his face, "mysterious things have been happening in the rooms where Miss Danbury and this man Henry Sumner were found dead. Miss Danbury was found dead last Thursday. Immediately after the body was removed, Detective Mallory ordered her room locked, his idea being that nothing should be disturbed at least for the present, because of the strange circumstances surrounding her death. When the nature of the Henry Sumner affair became known, and the similarity of the cases recognized, he gave the same order regarding Sumner's room."

Hatch stopped, and stared vainly into the pallid, wizened face of the scientist. A curious little chill ran down his spinal column.

"Some time Tuesday night," he continued, after a moment, "Miss Danbury's room was entered and ransacked; and some time that same night Henry Sumner's room was entered and ransacked. This morning, Wednesday, a clearly defined hand print in blood was found in Miss Danbury's room. It was on the wooden top of a dressing table. It seemed to be a woman's hand. Also, an indistinguishable smudge of blood, which may have been a hand print, was found in Sumner's room!" He paused; The Thinking Machine's countenance was inscrutable. "What possible connection can there be between this young woman of the aristocracy, and this-this longshoreman? Why should—"

"What chair," questioned The Thinking Machine, "does Professor Meredith hold in the university?"

"Greek," was the reply.

"Who is Mr Willing?"

"One of the leading lawyers of the city."

"Did you see Miss Danbury's body?"

"Yes."

"Did she have a large mouth, or a small mouth?"

The irrelevancy of the questions, to say nothing of their disjointedness, brought a look of astonishment to Hatch's face; and he was a young man who was rarely astonished by the curious methods of The Thinking Machine. Always he had found that the scientist approached a problem from a new angle.

"I should say a small mouth," he ventured. "Her lips were bruised as if – as if something round, say the size of a twenty-five-cent piece, had been crushed against them. There was a queer, drawn, caved-in look to her mouth and cheeks."

"Naturally," commented The Thinking Machine enigmatically. "And Sumner's was the same?"

"Precisely. You say 'naturally.' Do you mean—" There was eagerness in the reporter's question.

It passed unanswered. For half a minute The Thinking Machine continued to stare into nothingness. Finally:

"I dare say Sumner was of the English type? His name is English?"

"Yes; a splendid physical man, a hard drinker, I hear, as well as a hard worker."

Again a pause.

"You don't happen to know if Professor Meredith is now or ever has been particularly interested in physics – that is, in natural philosophy?"

"I do not."

"Please find out immediately," the scientist directed tersely. "Willing has handled some legal business for Miss Danbury. Learn what you can from him to the general end of establishing some connection, a relationship possibly, between

Henry Sumner and the Honorable Violet Danbury. That, at the moment, is the most important thing to do. Neither of them may have been aware of the relationship, if relationship it was, yet it may have existed. If it doesn't exist, there's only one answer to the problem."

"And that is?" Hatch asked.

"The murders are the work of a madman," was the tart rejoinder. "There's no mystery, of course, in the manner of the deaths of these two."

"No mystery?" the reporter echoed blankly. "Do you mean you know how they—"

"Certainly I know, and you know. The examining physicians know, only they don't know that they know." Suddenly his tone became didactic. "Knowledge that can't be applied is utterly useless," he said. "The real difference between a great mind and a mediocre mind is only that the great mind applies its knowledge." He was silent a moment. "The only problem remaining here is to find the person who was aware of the many advantages of this method of murder."

"Advantages?" Hatch was puzzled.

"From the viewpoint of the murderer there is always a good way and a bad way to kill a person," the scientist told him. "This particular murderer chose a way that was swift, silent, simple, and sure as the march of time. There was no scream, no struggle, no pistol shot, no poison to be traced, nothing to be seen except—"

"The hole in the left cheek, perhaps?"

"Quite right, and that leaves no clew. As a matter of fact, the only clew we have at all is the certainty that the murderer, man or woman, is well acquainted with physics, or natural philosophy."

"Then you think," the newspaper man's eyes were about to start from his head, "that Professor Meredith—"

"I think nothing," The Thinking Machine declared briefly. "I want to know what he knows of physics, as I said; also I want to know if there is any connection between Miss Danbury and the longshoreman. If you'll attend to—"

Abruptly the laboratory door opened and Martha entered, pallid, frightened, her hands shaking.

"Something most peculiar, sir," she stammered in her excitement.

"Well?" the little scientist questioned.

"I do believe," said Martha, "that I'm a – going to faint!"

And as an evidence of good faith she did, crumpling up in a little heap before their astonished eyes.

"Dear me! Dear me!" exclaimed The Thinking Machine petulantly. "Of all the inconsiderate things! Why couldn't she have told us before she did that?"

It was a labor of fifteen minutes to bring Martha around, and then weakly she explained what had happened. She had answered a ring of the telephone, and some one had asked for Professor Van Dusen. She inquired the name of the person talking.

"Never mind that," came the reply. "Is he there? Can I see him?"

"You'll have to explain what you want, sir," Martha had told him. "He always has to know."

"Tell him I know who murdered Miss Danbury and Henry Sumner," came over the wire. "If he'll receive me I'll be right up."

"And then, sir," Martha explained to The Thinking Machine, "something must have happened at the other end, sir. I heard another man's voice, then a sort of a choking sound, sir, and then they cursed me, sir. I didn't hear any more. They hung up the receiver or something, sir." She paused indignantly. "Think of him, sir, a – swearing at me!"

For a moment the eyes of the two men met; the same thought had come to them both. The Thinking Machine voiced it.

"Another one!" he said. "The third!"

With no other word he turned and went out; Martha followed him grumblingly. Hatch shuddered a little. The hand of the clock went on to half past seven, to eight. At twenty minutes past eight the scientist reëntered the laboratory.

"That fifteen minutes Martha was unconscious probably cost a man's life, and certainly lost to us an immediate solution of the riddle," he declared peevishly. "If she had told us before she fainted there is a chance that the operator would have remembered the number. As it is, there have been fifty calls since, and there's no record." He spread his slender hands helplessly. "The manager is trying to find the calling number. Anyway, we'll know tomorrow. Meanwhile, try to see Mr Willing tonight, and find out about what relationship, if any, exists between Miss Danbury and Sumner; also, see Professor Meredith."

The newspaper man telephoned to Mr Willing's home in Melrose to see if he was in; he was not. On a chance he telephoned to his office. He hardly expected an answer, and he got none. So it was not until four o'clock in the morning that the third tragedy in the series came to light.

The scrubwomen employed in the great building where Mr Willing had his law offices entered the suite to clean up. They found Mr Willing there, gagged, bound hand and foot, and securely lashed to a chair. He was alive, but apparently unconscious from exhaustion. Directly facing him his secretary, Maxwell Pittman, sat dead in his chair. On his face, dark in death, as are the faces of those who die of strangulation, was an expression of unspeakable terror. His parted lips were slightly bruised, as if from a light blow; in his left cheek was an insignificant, bloodless wound!

Within an hour Detective Mallory was on the scene. By that time Mr Willing, under the influence of stimulants, was able to talk.

"I have no idea what happened," he explained. "It was after six o'clock, and my secretary and I were alone in the offices, finishing up some work. He had stepped into another room for a moment, and I was at my desk. Some one crept up behind me, and held a drugged cloth to my nostrils. I tried to shout, and struggled, but everything grew black, and that's all I know. When I came to myself poor Pittman was there, just as you see him."

Snooping about the offices, Mallory came upon a small lace handkerchief. He seized upon it tensely, and as he raised it to examine it he became conscious of a strong odor of drugs. In one corner of the handkerchief there was a monogram.

"'C. M.,'" he read; his eyes blazed. "Cecelia Montgomery!"

In the grip of an uncontrollable excitement Hutchinson Hatch bulged in upon The Thinking Machine in his laboratory.

"There was another," he announced.

"I know it," said The Thinking Machine, still bent over his worktable. "Who was it?"

"Maxwell Pittman," and Hatch related the story.

"There may be two more," the scientist remarked. "Be good enough to call a cab."

"Two more?" Hatch gasped in horror. "Already dead?"

"There may be, I said. One, Cecelia Montgomery, the other the unknown who called on the telephone last night." He started away, then returned to his worktable. "Here's rather an interesting experiment," he said. "See this tube," and he held aloft a heavy glass vessel, closed at one end, and with a stopcock at the other. "Observe. I'll place this heavy piece of rubber over the mouth of the tube, and then turn the stopcock." He suited the action to the word. "Now take it off."

The reporter tugged at it until the blood rushed to his face, but was unable to move it. He glanced up at the scientist in perplexity.

"What hold it there?"

"Vacuum," was the reply. "You may tear it to pieces, but no human power can pull it away whole." He picked up a steel bodkin, and thrust it through the rubber into the mouth of the tube. As he withdrew it, came a sharp, prolonged, hissing sound. Half a minute later the rubber fell off. "The vacuum is practically perfect – something like one-millionth of an atmosphere. The pin hole permits the air to fill the tube, the tremendous pressure against the rubber is removed, and—" He waved his slender hands.

In that instant a germ of comprehension was born in Hatch's brain; he was remembering some college experiments.

"If I should place that tube to your lips," The Thinking Machine resumed, "and turn the stopcock, you would never speak again, never scream, never struggle. It would jerk every particle of air out of your body, paralyze you; within two minutes you would be dead. To remove the tube I should thrust the bodkin through your cheek, say your left, and withdraw it—"

Hatch gasped as the full horror of the thing burst upon him. "Absence of air in the lungs," the examining physicians had said.

"You see, there was no mystery in the manner of the deaths of these three," The Thinking Machine pointed out. "You knew what I have shown you, the physicians knew it, but neither of you knew you knew it. Genius is the ability to apply the knowledge you may have, not the ability to acquire it." His manner changed abruptly. "Please call a cab," he said again.

Together they were driven straight to the university, and shown into Professor Meredith's study. Professor Meredith showed his astonishment plainly at the visit, and astonishment became indignant amazement at the first question.

"Mr Meredith, can you account for every moment of your time from mid-afternoon yesterday until four o'clock this morning?" The Thinking Machine queried flatly. "Don't misunderstand me – I mean every moment covering the time in which it is possible that Maxwell Pittman was murdered?"

"Why, it's a most outrageous—" Professor Meredith exploded.

"I'm trying to save you from arrest," the scientist explained curtly. "If you can account for all that time, and prove your statement, believe me, you had better prepare to do so. Now, if you could give me any information as to—"

"Who the devil are you?" demanded Professor Meredith belligerently. "What do you mean by daring to suggest—"

"My name is Van Dusen," said The Thinking Machine, "Augustus S. F. X. Van Dusen. Long before your time I held the chair of philosophy in this university. I vacated it by request. Later the university honored me with a degree of LL.D."

The result of the self-introduction was astonishing. Professor Meredith, in the presence of the master mind in the sciences, was a different man.

"I beg you pardon," he began.

"I'm curious to know if you are at all acquainted with Miss Danbury's family history," the scientist went on. "Meanwhile, Mr Hatch, take the cab, and go straight and measure the precise width of the bruise on Pittman's lips; also, see Mr Willing, if he is able to receive you, and ask him what he can give you as to Miss Danbury's history – I mean her family, her property, her connections, all about everything. Meet me at my house in a couple of hours."

Hatch went out, leaving them together. When he reached the scientist's home The Thinking Machine was just coming out.

"I'm on my way to see Mr George Parsons, the so-called copper king," he volunteered. "Come along."

From that moment came several developments so curious, and bizarre, and so widely disassociated that Hatch could make nothing of them at all. Nothing seemed to fit into anything else. For instance, The Thinking Machine's visit to Mr Parsons' office.

"Please ask Mr Parsons if he will see Mr Van Dusen?" he requested of an attendant.

"What about?" the query came from Mr Parsons.

"It is a matter of life and death," the answer went back.

"Whose?" Mr Parsons wanted to know.

"His!" The scientist's answer was equally short.

Immediately afterward The Thinking Machine disappeared inside. Ten minutes later he came out, and he and Hatch went off together, stopping at a toy shop to buy a small, high-grade, hard-rubber ball; and later at a department store to purchase a vicious-looking hatpin.

"You failed to inform me, Mr Hatch, of the measurement of the bruise?"

"Precisely one and a quarter inches."

"Thanks! And what did Mr Willing say?"

"I didn't see him as yet. I have an appointment to see him in an hour from now."

"Very well," and The Thinking Machine nodded his satisfaction. "When you see him, will you be good enough to tell him, please, that I know – I know, do you understand? – who killed Miss Danbury, and Sumner, and Pittman. You can't make it too strong. I know – do you understand?"

"Do you know?" Hatch demanded quickly.

"No," frankly. "But convince him that I do, and add that tomorrow at noon I shall place the extraordinary facts I have gathered in possession of the police. At noon, understand; and I know!" He was thoughtful a moment. "You might add that I have informed you that the guilty person is a person of high position, whose name has been in no way connected with the crimes – that is, unpleasantly. You don't know that name; no one knows it except myself. I shall give it to the police at noon tomorrow."

"Anything else?"

"Drop in on me early tomorrow morning, and bring Mr Mallory."

Events were cyclonic on that last morning. Mallory and Hatch had hardly arrived when there came a telephone message for the detective from police headquarters. Mrs Cecelia Montgomery was there. She had come in voluntarily, and asked for Mr Mallory.

"Don't rush off now," requested The Thinking Machine, who was pottering around among the retorts, and microscopes and what not on his worktable. "Ask them to detain her until you get there. Also, ask her just what relationship existed between Miss Danbury and Henry Sumner." The detective went out; the scientist turned to Hatch. "Here is a hatpin," he said. "Some time this morning we shall have another caller. If, during the presence of that person in this room, I voluntarily put anything to my lips, a bottle, say, or anything is forced upon me, and I do not remove it in just thirty seconds, you will thrust this hatpin through my cheek. Don't hesitate."

"Thrust it through?" the reporter repeated. An uncanny chill ran over him as he realized the scientist's meaning. "Is it absolutely necessary to take such a chance to—"

"I say if I don't remove it!" The Thinking Machine interrupted shortly. "You and Mallory will be watching from another room; I shall demonstrate the exact manner of the murders." There was a troubled look in the reporter's face. "I shall be in no danger," the scientist said simply. "The hatpin is merely a precaution if anything should go wrong."

After a little Mallory entered, with clouded countenance.

"She denies the murders," he announced, "but admits that the hand prints in blood are hers. According to her yarn, she searched Miss Danbury's room and Sumner's room after the murders to find some family papers which were necessary to establish claims to some estate – I don't quite understand. She hurt her hand in Miss Danbury's room, and it bled a lot, hence the hand print. From there she went straight to Sumner's room, and presumably left the smudge there. It seems that Sumner was a distant cousin of Miss Danbury's – the only son of a younger brother who ran away years ago after some wild escapade, and came to this country. George Parsons, the copper king, is the only other relative in this country. She advises us to warn him to be on his guard – seems to think he will be the next victim."

"He's already warned," said The Thinking Machine, "and he has gone West on important business."

Mallory stared.

"You seem to know more about this case than I do," he sneered.

"I do," asserted the scientist, "quite a lot more."

"I think the third degree will change Mrs Montgomery's story some," the detective declared. "Perhaps she will remember better—"

"She is telling the truth."

"Then why did she run away? How was it we found her handkerchief in Mr Willing's office after the Pittman affair? How was it—"

The Thinking Machine shrugged his shoulders, and was silent. A moment later the door opened, and Martha appeared, her eyes blazing with indignation.

"That man who swore at me over the telephone," she announced distinctly, "wants to see you, sir."

Mallory's keen eyes swept the faces of the scientist and the reporter, trying to fathom the strange change that came over them.

"You are sure, Martha?" asked The Thinking Machine.

"Indeed I am, sir." She was positive about it. "I'd never forget his voice, sir."

For an instant her master merely stared at her, then dismissed her with a curt, "Show him in," after which he turned to the detective and Hatch.

"You will wait in the next room," he said tersely. "If anything happens, Mr Hatch, remember."

The Thinking Machine was sitting when the visitor entered — a middle-aged man, sharp-featured, rather spare, brisk in his movements, and distinctly well groomed. It was Herbert Willing, attorney. In one hand he carried a small bag. He paused an instant, and gazed at the diminutive scientist curiously.

"Come in, Mr Willing," The Thinking Machine greeted. "You want to see me about—" He paused questioningly.

"I understand," said the lawyer suavely, "that you have interested yourself in these recent-er-remarkable murders, and there are some points I should like to discuss with you. I have some papers in my bag here, which" – he opened it – "maybe of interest. Some er-newspaper man informed me that you have certain information indicating the person–"

"I know the name of the murderer," said The Thinking Machine.

"Indeed! May I ask who it is?"

"You may. His name is Herbert Willing."

Watching tensely Hatch saw The Thinking Machine pass his hand slowly across his mouth as if to stifle a yawn; saw Willing leap forward suddenly with what seemed to be a bottle in his hand; saw him force the scientist back into his chair, and thrust the bottle against his lips. Instantly came a sharp click, and some hideous change came over the scientist's wizened face. His eyes opened wide in terror, his cheeks seemed to collapse. Instinctively he grasped the bottle with both hands.

For a scant second Willing stared at him, his countenance grown demoniacal; then he swiftly took something else from the small bag, and smashed it on the floor. It was a drinking glass!

After which the scientist calmly removed the bottle from his lips.

"The broken drinking glass," he said quietly, "completes the evidence."

Hutchinson Hatch was lean and wiry, and hard as nails; Detective Mallory's bulk concealed muscles of steel, but it took both of them to overpower the attorney. Heedless of the struggling trio The Thinking Machine was curiously scrutinizing the black bottle. The mouth was blocked by a small rubber ball, which he had thrust against it with his tongue a fraction of an instant before the dreaded power the bottle held had been released by pressure upon a cunningly concealed spring. When he raised his squinting eyes at last, Willing, manacled, was glaring at him in impotent rage. Fifteen minute later the four were at police headquarters; Mrs Montgomery was awaiting them.

"Mrs Montgomery, why," – and the petulant pale-blue eyes of The Thinking Machine were fixed upon her face– "why didn't you go to Concord, as you had said?"

"I did go there," she replied. "It was simply that when news came of Miss Danbury's terrible death I was frightened, I lost my head; I pleaded with my friends not to let it be known that I was there, and they agreed. If any one had searched their house I would have been found; no one did. At last I could stand it no longer. I came to the city, and straight here to explain everything I knew in connection with the affair."

"And the search you made of Miss Danbury's room? And of Sumner's room?"

"I've explained that," she said. "I knew of the relationship between poor Harry Sumner and Violet Danbury, and I knew each of them had certain papers which were of value as establishing their claims to a great estate in England now in litigation. I was sure those papers would be valuable to the only other claimant, who was—"

"Mr George Parsons, the copper king," interposed the scientist. "You didn't find the papers you sought because Willing had taken them. That estate was the thing he wanted, and I dare say by some legal jugglery he would have gotten it."

Again he turned to face Mrs Montgomery. "Living with Miss Danbury, as you did, you probably held a key to her apartment? Yes. You had only the difficulty then, of entering the hotel late at night, unseen, and that seemed to be simple. Willing did it the night he killed Miss Danbury, and left it unseen, as you did. Now, how did you enter Sumner's room?"

"It was a terrible place," and she shuddered slightly. "I went in alone, and entered his room through a window from a fire escape. The newspapers, you will remember, described its location precisely, and – "

"I see," The Thinking Machine interrupted. He was silent a moment. "You're a shrewd man, Willing, and your knowledge of natural philosophy is exact if not extensive. Of course, I knew if you thought I knew too much about the murders you would come to me. You did. It was a trap, if that's any consolation to you. You fell into it. And, curiously enough, I wasn't afraid of a knife or a shot; I knew the instrument of death you had been using was too satisfactory and silent for you to change. However, I was prepared for it, and – I think that's all." He arose.

"All?" Hatch and Mallory echoed the word. "We don't understand—"

"Oh!" and The Thinking Machine sat down again. "It's logic. Miss Danbury was dead—neither shot, stabbed, poisoned, nor choked; 'absence of air in her lungs,' the physicians said. Instantly the vacuum bottle suggested itself. That murder, as was the murder of Sumner, was planned to counterfeit suicide, hence the broken goblet on the floor. Incidentally the murder of Sumner informed me that the crimes were the work of a madman, else there was an underlying purpose which might have arisen through a relationship. Ultimately I established that relationship through Professor Meredith, in whom Miss Danbury had confided to a certain extent; at the same time he convinced me of his innocence in the affair.

THE CASE OF THE SCIENTIFIC MURDERER 101

"Now," he continued, after a moment, "we come to the murder of Pittman. Pittman learned, and tried to phone me, who the murderer was. Willing heard that message. He killed Pittman, then bound and gagged himself, and waited. It was a clever ruse. His story of being overpowered and drugged is absurd on the face of it, yet he asked us to believe that by leaving a handkerchief of Mrs Montgomery's on the floor. That was reeking with drugs. Mr Hatch can give you more of these details." He glanced at his watch. "I'm due at a luncheon, where I am to make an address to the Society of Psychical Research. If you'll excuse me—"

He went out; the others sat staring after him.

6

THE GREAT AUTO MYSTERY

I

With a little laugh of sheer light-heartedness on her lips and a twinkle in her blue eyes, Marguerite Melrose bound on a grotesque automobile mask, and stuffed the last strand of her recalcitrant hair beneath her veil. The pretty face was hidden from mouth to brow; and her curls were ruthlessly imprisoned under a cap held in place by the tightly tied veil.

"It's perfectly hideous, isn't it?" she demanded of her companions.

Jack Curtis laughed.

"Well," he remarked, quizzically, "it's just as well that we know you are pretty."

"We could never discover it as you are now," added Charles Reid. "Can't see enough of your face to tell whether you are white or black."

The girl's red lips were pursed into a pout, which ungraciously hid her white teeth, as she considered the matter seriously.

"I think I'll take it off," she said at last.

"Don't," Curtis warned her. "On a good road The Green Dragon only hits the tall places."

"Tear your hair off," supplemented Reid. "When Jack lets her loose it's just a pszzzzt! – and wherever you're going you're there."

"Not on a night as dark as this?" protested the girl, quickly.

"I've got lights like twin locomotives," Curtis assured her, smilingly. "It's perfectly safe. Don't get nervous."

He tied on his own mask with its bleary goggles, while Reid did the same. The Green Dragon, a low, gasoline car of racing build, stood panting impatiently, awaiting them at a side door of the hotel. Curtis assisted Miss Melrose into the front seat and climbed in beside her, while Reid sat behind in the tonneau. There was a preparatory quiver, the car jerked a little and then began to move.

The three persons in it were Marguerite Melrose, an actress who had attracted attention in the West five years before by her great beauty and had afterwards, by her art, achieved a distinct place; Jack Curtis, a friend since childhood, when both lived in San Francisco and attended the same school, and Charles Reid, his chum, son of a mine owner at Denver.

The unexpected meeting of the three in Boston had been a source of mutual pleasure. It had been two years since they had seen one another in Denver, where Miss Melrose was playing. Now she was in Boston, pursuing certain vocal studies before returning West for her next season.

Reid was in Boston to lay siege to the heart of a young woman of society, Miss Elizabeth Dow, whom he first met in San Francisco. She was only nineteen years old, but despite this he had begun a siege and his ardor had never cooled, even after Miss Dow returned East. In Boston, he had heard, she looked with favor upon another man, Morgan Mason, poor but of excellent family, and frantically Reid had rushed, like Lochinvar out of the West, to find the rumor true.

Curtis was one who never had anything to do save seek excitement in a new and novel way. He had come East with

Reid. They had been together constantly since their arrival in Boston. He was of a different type from Reid in that his wealth was distinctly a burden, a thing which left him with nothing to do, and opened illimitable possibilities of dissipation. The pace he led was one which caused other young men to pause and think.

Warm-hearted and perfectly at home with both Curtis and Reid, Miss Melrose, the actress, frequently took occasion to scold them. It was charming to be scolded by Miss Melrose, so much so in fact that it was worth while sinning again. Since she had appeared on the horizon Curtis had devoted a great deal of time to her; Reid had his own difficulties trying to make Miss Dow change her mind.

The Green Dragon with its three passengers ran slowly down from the Hotel Yarmouth, where Miss Melrose was stopping, toward the Common, twisting and winding tortuously through the crowd of vehicles. It was half-past six o'clock in the evening.

"Cut across here to Commonwealth Avenue," Miss Melrose suggested. She remembered something and her bright blue eyes sparkled beneath the disfiguring mask. "I know a delightful old-fashioned inn out this way. It would be an ideal place to stop for supper. I was there once five years ago when I was in Boston."

"How far?" asked Reid.

"Fifteen or twenty miles," was the reply.

"Right," said Curtis. "Here we go."

Soon after they were skimming along Commonwealth Avenue, which at that time of day is practically given over to automobilists, past the Vendome, the Somerset and on over the flat, smooth road. It was perfectly light now, because the electric lights were about them; but there was no moon above, and once in the country it would be dark going.

Curtis was intent on his machine; Reid was thoughtful for a time, but after awhile leaned over and talked to Miss Melrose.

"I heard something today that might interest you," he remarked.

"What is it?" she asked.

"Don MacLean is in Boston."

"I heard that," she replied, casually.

"Who is he?" asked Curtis.

"A man who is frantically in love with Marguerite," said Reid, with a smile.

"Charlie," the girl reproved, and a flush crept into her face. "It was never anything very serious."

Curtis looked at her curiously for a moment, then his eyes turned again to the road ahead.

"I don't suppose it's very serious if a man proposes to a girl seven times, is it?" Reid asked, banteringly.

"Did he do that?" asked Curtis, quickly.

"He merely made a fool of himself and me," replied the actress, with spirit, speaking to Curtis. "He was – in love with me, I suppose, but his family objected because I was on the stage and threatened to disinherit him, and all that sort of thing. So – it ended it. Not that I ever considered the matter seriously anyway," she added.

There was silence again as The Green Dragon plunged into the darkness of the country, the two brilliant lights ahead showing every dip and rise in the road. After awhile Curtis spoke again.

"He's now in Boston?"

"Yes," said the girl. "At least, I've heard so," she added, quickly.

Then the conversation ran into other channels, and Curtis, busy with the great machine and the innumerable levers which made it do this or do that or do the other, dropped out of it. Reid and Miss Melrose talked on, but the whirr of the car as it gained speed made talking unsatisfactory and finally the girl gave herself up to the pure delight of high speed; a dangerous pleasure which sets the nerves atingle and makes one greedy for more.

"Do you smell gasoline?" Curtis asked suddenly, turning to the others.

"Believe I do," said Reid.

"Confound it! If I've sprung a leak in my tank it will be the deuce," Curtis growled amiably.

"Do you think you've got enough to get to the inn?" asked Miss Melrose. "It can't be more than five or six miles now."

"I'll run on until we stop," said Curtis. "We might be able to stir up some along here somewhere. I suppose they are prepared for autos."

At last lights showed ahead, many lights glimmering through the trees.

"I suppose that's the inn now," said Curtis. "Is it?" he asked of the girl.

"Really, I don't know, but I have an impression that it isn't. The one I mean seems farther out than this and it seems to me we passed one on the way. However, I don't remember very well."

"We'll stop and get some gasoline, anyhow," said Curtis.

Puffing and snorting odorously The Green Dragon came to a standstill in front of an old house which stood back twenty feet or more from the road. It was lighted up, and from inside they could hear the cheery rattle of dishes and see white-aproned waiters moving about. Above the door was a sign, "Monarch Inn."

"Is this the place?" asked Reid.

"Oh, no," replied Miss Melrose. "The inn I spoke of was back from the road three or four hundred feet through a grove."

Curtis leaped out, and evidently dropped something from his pocket as he did so, for he stopped and felt around for a moment. Then he examined his tank.

"It's a leak," he said, in irritation. "I haven't more than half a gallon left. These people must have some gasoline. Wait a few minutes."

Miss Melrose and Reid still sat in the car as he started away toward the house. Almost at the veranda he turned and called back:

"Charlie, I dropped something there when I jumped out. Get down and strike a match and see if you can find it. Don't go near that gasoline tank with the match."

He disappeared inside the house. Reid climbed out and struck several matches. Finally he found what was lost and thrust it into an outside pocket. Miss Melrose was gazing away down the road at two brilliant lights coming toward them rapidly.

"Rather chilly," Reid said, as he straightened up. "Want a cup of coffee or something?"

"Thanks, no," the girl replied.

"I think I'll run in and scare up some sort of a hot drink, if you'll excuse me?"

"Now, Charlie, don't," the girl asked, suddenly. "I don't like it."

"Oh, one won't hurt," he replied, lightly.

"I shan't speak to you when you come out," she insisted, half banteringly.

"Oh, yes, you will." He laughed, and passed into the house.

Miss Melrose tossed her pretty head impatiently and turned to watch the approaching lights. They were blinding as they drew nearer, clearly revealing her figure, in its tan auto coat, to the occupant of the other car. The newcomer stopped and then she heard whoever was in it – she couldn't see – speaking to her.

"Would you mind turning your car a little so I can run in off the road?"

"I don't know how," she replied, helplessly.

There was a little pause. The occupant of the other car was leaning forward, looking at her closely.

"Is that you, Marguerite?" he asked finally.

"Yes," she replied. "Who is that? Don?"

"Yes."

A man's figure leaped out of the other machine and came toward her.

Curtis appeared beside the Green Dragon with a huge can of gasoline twenty minutes later. The two occupants of the car were clearly silhouetted against the sky, and Reid, leaning back in the tonneau, was smoking.

"Find it?" he asked.

"Yes," growled Curtis. And he began the work of repairing the leak and refilling his tank. It took only five minutes or so, and then he climbed up into the car.

"Cold, Marguerite?" he asked.

"She won't speak," said Reid, leaning forward a little. "She's angry because I went inside to get a hot Scotch."

"Wish I had one myself," said Curtis.

"Let's wait till we get to the next place," Reid interposed. "A little supper and trimmings will put all of us in a better humor."

Without answering, Curtis threw a lever, and the car pulled out. Two automobiles which had been standing when they arrived were still waiting for their owners. Annoyed at the delay, Curtis put on full speed. Finally Reid leaned forward and spoke to the girl.

"In a good humor?" he asked.

She gave no sign of having heard, and Reid placed his hand on her shoulder as he repeated the question. Still there was no answer. "Make her talk to you, Jack," he suggested to Curtis.

"What's the matter, Marguerite?" asked Curtis, as he glanced around.

Still there was no answer, and he slowed up the car a little. Then he took her arm and shook it gently. There was no response.

"What is the matter with her?" he demanded. "Has she fainted?"

Again he shook her, this time more vigorously than before.

"Marguerite," he called.

Then his hand sought her face; it was deathly cold, clammy even about the chin. The upper part was still covered by the mask. For the third time he shook her, then, really frightened, apparently, he caught at her gloved wrist and brought the car to a standstill. There was no trace of a pulse; the wrist was cold as death.

"She must be ill – very ill," he said in some agitation. "Is there a doctor near here?"

Reid was leaning over the senseless body now, having raised up in the tonneau, and when he spoke there seemed to be fear in his tone.

"Better run on as fast as you can to the inn ahead," he instructed Curtis. "It's nearer than the one we just left. There may be a doctor there."

Curtis grabbed frantically at the lever and the car shot ahead suddenly through the dark. In three minutes the lights of the second inn were in sight. The two men leaped from the car simultaneously and raced for the house.

"A doctor, quick," Curtis breathlessly demanded of a waiter.

"Next door."

Without waiting for further instructions, Curtis and Reid ran to the auto, lifted the girl in their arms and took her to a house which stood just a few feet away. There, after much clamoring, they aroused some one. Was the doctor in? Yes. Would he hurry? Yes.

The door opened and the men laid the girl's body on a couch in the hall. Dr Leonard appeared. He was an old fellow, grizzled, with keen, kindly eyes and rigid mouth.

"What's the matter?" he asked.

"Think she's dead," replied Curtis.

The doctor adjusted his glasses rather hurriedly.

"Who is she?" he asked, as he bent over the still figure and fumbled about the throat and breast.

"Miss Marguerite Melrose, an actress," explained Curtis, hurriedly.

"What's the matter with her?" demanded Reid, fiercely.

The doctor still bent over the figure. In the dim lamplight Curtis and Reid stood waiting anxiously, impatiently, with white faces. At last the doctor straightened up.

"What is it?" demanded Curtis.

"She's dead," was the reply.

"Great God!" exclaimed Reid. "How?" Curtis seemed speechless.

"This," said the doctor, and he exhibited a long knife, damp with blood. "Stabbed through the heart."

Curtis stared at him, at the knife, then at the inert figure, and lastly at the dead white of her face where it showed beneath the mask.

"Look, Jack!" exclaimed Reid, suddenly. "The knife!"

Curtis looked again, then sank down on the couch beside the body.

"Oh, my God! It's horrible!" he said.

II

To Hutchinson Hatch and half a dozen other reporters, Dr Leonard, at his home late that night, told the story of the arrival of Jack Curtis and Charles Reid with the body of the girl, and the succeeding events so far as he knew them. The police and Medical Examiner Francis had preceded the newspaper men, and the body had been removed to a nearby village.

"They came here in great excitement," Dr Leonard explained. "They brought the body in with them, the man Curtis lifting her by the shoulders and the man Reid at the feet. They placed the body on this couch. I asked them who she was, and they told me she was Marguerite Melrose, an actress. That's all that was said of her identity.

"Then I made an examination of the body, seeking a trace of life. There was none, although the body was not then entirely cold. In examining her heart my hand struck the knife which had killed her — a heavy weapon, evidently used for rough work, with a blade of six or seven inches. I drew the knife out. Of course, knowing that it had pierced her heart, any idea of doing anything to save her was beyond question.

"One of the men, Curtis, seemed greatly excited about this knife after Reid called his attention to it. Curtis took the knife out of my hand and examined it closely, then asked if he might keep it. I told him it would have to be turned over to the medical examiner. He argued about it, and finally, to settle the argument, I took it out of his hand. Reid explained to Curtis that it was necessary for me to keep the knife, and finally Curtis seemed to agree to it.

"Then I suggested that the police be notified. I did this myself by telephone, the men remaining with me all the time. I asked if they could throw any light on the tragedy, but neither could. Curtis said he had been out searching for a man who had the keys to a shed where some gasoline was locked up, and it took fifteen or twenty minutes to find him. As soon as he got the gasoline he returned to the auto.

"Reid and Miss Melrose were at this time in the auto, he said. What had happened while he had been away Curtis didn't know. Reid said he, too, had stepped out of the automobile, and after exchanging a few words with Miss Melrose went into the inn. There he remained fifteen minutes or so, because inside he saw a woman he knew and spoke to her. He declared that any one of three waiters could verify his statement that he was in the Monarch Inn.

"After I had notified the police Curtis grew very uneasy in his actions — it didn't occur to me at the moment, but now

I recall that it was so – and suggested to Reid that they go on to Boston and send out detectives – special Pinkerton men. I tried to dissuade them, but they went away. I couldn't stop them. They gave me their cards, however. They are at the Hotel Teutonic, and told me they could be seen there at any time. The medical examiner and the police came afterwards. I told them, and one of the detectives started immediately for Boston. They have probably told their story to him by this time."

"What did the young woman look like?" asked Hatch.

"Really, I couldn't say," said the doctor. "She wore an automobile mask which covered all her face except the chin, and there was a veil tied over her cap, concealing her hair. I didn't remove these; I left the body just as it was for the medical examiner."

"How was she dressed?" Hatch went on.

"She wore a long tan automobile dust coat of what seemed to be rich material, and beneath this a handsome – not a fancy – gown. I believe it was tailor-made. She was a woman of superb figure."

That was all that could be learned from Dr Leonard, and Hatch and the other men raced back to Boston. The next day the newspapers flamed with the mystery of the murder of Miss Melrose, a beautiful Western actress who was visiting Boston. Each newspaper watched the other greedily to see if there was a picture of Miss Melrose; neither had one.

The newspapers also carried the stories of Jack Curtis and Charles Reid in connection with the murder. The stories were in substance just what Dr Leonard had said, but were given in more detail. It was the general presumption, almost a foregone conclusion, that some one had killed Miss Melrose while the two men were away from the auto.

Who was this some one? Man or woman? No one could answer. Reid's story of being inside the Monarch Inn, where he spoke to a lady he knew – but whose name he refused to give – was verified by Hatch's paper. Three waiters had seen him.

The medical examiner had made only a brief statement, in which he had said, in answer to a question, that the person who killed Miss Melrose might have been either at her right, in the position Curtis would have occupied while driving the car, or might have leaned forward from behind and stabbed her. Thus it was not impossible that one of the men in the car with her had killed her, yet against this possibility was the fact that each of the men was one whom one could not readily associate with such a crime.

The fact that the fatal blow was delivered from the right was proven, said the astute medical examiner, by the fact that the knife slanted as a knife could not have been slanted conveniently by a person on her other side — her left. There were many dark, underlying intimations behind what the medical man said; but he refused to say any more. Meanwhile the body remained in the village where it had been taken. Efforts to get a photograph were unavailing; pleas of newspaper artists for permission to sketch her fell upon deaf ears.

Curtis and Reid, after their first statements, remained in seclusion at the Teutonic. They were not arrested because this did not seem necessary. Both had offered to do anything in their power to solve the riddle, had even employed Pinkerton men who were now on the case; but they would say nothing nor see anyone except the police. The police encouraged them in this attitude, and hinted darkly and mysteriously at clews which "would lead to an arrest within twenty-four hours."

Hatch read these intimations and smiled grimly. Then he went out to try what a little patience and perseverance and human intelligence would do. He learned something of Reid's little romance in Boston. Yet not all of it. It was a fact, however, that Reid had called at the home of Miss Elizabeth Dow on Beacon Hill just after noon and inquired for her.

"She is not in," the maid had replied.

"I'll leave my card for her," said Reid.

"I don't think she'll be back," the girl answered.

"Not be back?" Reid repeated "Why?"

"Haven't you seen the afternoon papers?" asked the girl. "They will explain. Mrs Dow, her mother, told me not to tell to anyone."

Reid left the house with a wrinkle in his brow and walked on toward the Common. There he halted a newsboy and bought an afternoon paper – many afternoon papers. The first pages were loaded with details of the murder of Miss Melrose, theories, conjectures, a thousand little things, with long dispatches of her history and her stage career from San Francisco.

Reid passed these over impatiently with a slight shiver and looked inside the paper. There he found the thing to which the maid had referred.

"By George!" he exclaimed.

It was a story of the elopement of Elizabeth Dow with Morgan Mason, Reid's rival. It seemed that Miss Dow and Mason met by appointment at the Monarch Inn and went from there in an automobile. The bride had written to her parents before she started, saying she preferred Mason despite his poverty. The family refused to talk of the matter. But there in facsimile was the marriage license.

Reid's face was a study as he walked back to the hotel. In a private room off the café he found Curtis, who had been drinking heavily, yet who, with the strange mood of some men, was not visibly intoxicated. Reid threw the paper down, open at the elopement announcement.

"See that," he said shortly.

Curtis read it – or glanced at it – but did not make a remark until he came to the name, the Monarch Inn. Then he looked up.

"That's where the other thing happened, isn't it?" he asked, rather thickly.

"Yes."

Curtis rambled off into something else; studiously he avoided any reference to the tragedy, yet that was the one thing which was in his mind. It was in a futile effort to forget it that he was drinking now. He talked on as a drunken man will for a time, then turned suddenly to Reid.

"I loved her," he declared suddenly, passionately. "My God!"

"Try not to think of it," Reid advised.

"You'll never say anything about that other thing – the knife – will you?" pleaded Curtis.

"Of course not," said Reid, impatiently. "They couldn't drag it out of me. But you're drinking too much – you want to quit it. First thing you know you'll be saying more than – get up and go out and take a walk."

Curtis stared at Reid vacantly for a moment, as if not understanding, then arose. He had regained possession of himself to a certain extent, but his face was pale.

"I think I will go out," he said.

After a time he passed through the café door into a side street and, refreshed a little by the cool air, started to walk along Tremont Street toward the shopping district. It was two o'clock in the afternoon and the streets were thronged.

Half a dozen reporters were idling in the lobby of the hotel, waiting vainly for either Reid or Curtis. The newspapers were shouting for another story from the only two men who could know a great deal of the circumstances attending the tragedy. Reid, on his return, had marched boldly through the crowd of reporters, paying no attention to their questions. They had not seen Curtis.

As Curtis, now free of the reporters, crossed a side street on Tremont on his way toward the shopping district he met Hutchinson Hatch, who was bound for the hotel to see his man there. Hatch instantly recognized him and fell in behind, curious to see where he would go. At a favorable opportunity, safe beyond reach of the other men, he intended to ask a few questions.

Curtis turned into Winter Street and strolled along through the crowd of women. Half way down Winter Street Hatch followed, and then for a moment he lost sight of him. He had gone into a store, he imagined. As he stood at a door waiting, Curtis came out, rushed through the crowd of women, slinging his arms like a madman, with frenzy in his face. He ran twenty steps, then stumbled and fell.

Hatch immediately ran to his assistance, lifted him up and gazed into the staring, terror-stricken eyes and an ashen face.

"What is it?" asked Hatch, quickly.

"I-I'm very ill. I – I think I need a doctor," gasped Curtis. "Take me somewhere, please."

He fell back limply, half fainting, into Hatch's arms. A cab came worming through the crowd; Hatch climbed into it, assisting Curtis, and gave some directions to the cabby.

"And hurry," he added. "This gentleman is ill."

The cabby applied the whip and drove out into Tremont, then over toward Park Street. Curtis aroused a little.

"Where're we going?" he demanded.

"To a doctor," replied Hatch.

Curtis sank back with eyes closed and his face white – so white that Hatch felt of the pulse to assure himself that the heart was still beating. After a few minutes the cab stopped and, still assisting Curtis, Hatch went to the door. An aged woman answered the bell.

"Professor Van Dusen here?" asked the reporter.

"Yes."

"Please tell him that Mr Hatch is here with a gentleman who needs immediate attention," Hatch directed, hurriedly.

He knew his way here and, still supporting Curtis, walked in. The woman disappeared. Curtis sank down on a couch in the little reception room, looked at Hatch glassily for a moment, then without a sound dropped back on the couch unconscious.

After a moment the door opened and there came in Professor Augustus S. F. X. Van Dusen, The Thinking Machine. He squinted inquiringly at Hatch, and Hatch waved his head toward Curtis.

"Dear me, dear me," exclaimed The Thinking Machine.

He leaned over the prostrate figure a moment, then disappeared into another room, returning with a hypodermic. After a few anxious minutes Curtis sat up straight. He stared at the two men with unseeing eyes, and in them was unutterable terror.

"I saw her! I saw her!" he screamed. "There was a dagger in her heart. Marguerite!"

Again he fell back unconscious. The Thinking Machine squinted at Hatch.

"The man's got delirium tremens," he snapped impatiently.

III

For fifteen minutes Hatch silently looked on as The Thinking Machine worked over the unconscious man. Once or twice Curtis moved uneasily and moaned slightly. Hatch had started to explain the situation to The Thinking Machine, but the irascible scientist glared at him and the reporter became silent. After ten or fifteen minutes The Thinking Machine turned to Hatch more genially.

"He'll be all right in a little while now," he said. "What is it?"

"Well, it's a murder," Hatch began. "Marguerite Melrose, an actress, was stabbed through the heart last night, and—"

"Murder?" interrupted The Thinking Machine. "Might it not have been suicide?"

"Might have been; yes," said the reporter, after a moment's pause. "But it appears to be murder."

"When you say it is murder," said The Thinking Machine, "you immediately give the impression that you were there and saw it. Go on."

From the beginning, then, Hatch told the story as he knew it; of the stopping of The Green Dragon at the Monarch Inn, of the events there, of the whereabouts of Curtis and Reid at the time the girl received the knife thrust and of the confirmation of Reid's story. Then he detailed those incidents of the arrival of the men with the girl at Dr Leonard's house, of what had transpired there, of the effort Curtis had made to get possession of the knife.

With finger tips pressed together and squinting steadily upward, The Thinking Machine listened. At its end, which bore on the actions of Curtis just preceding his appearance in the room with them, The Thinking Machine arose and walked over to the couch where Curtis lay. He ran his slender fingers idly through the unconscious man's thick hair several times.

"Doesn't it strike you as perfectly possible, Mr Hatch," he asked finally, "that Miss Melrose did kill herself?"

"It may be perfectly possible, but it doesn't appear so," said Hatch. "There was no motive."

"And certainly you've shown no motive for anything else," said the other, crustily. "Still," he mused, "I really can't say anything until I talk to him."

He again turned to his patient, and as he looked saw the red blood surge back into the face.

"Ah, now we're all right," he announced.

Thus it happened, for after another ten minutes the patient sat up suddenly on the couch and looked at the two men before him, bewildered.

"What's the matter?" he asked. The thickness was gone from his speech; he was himself again, although a little shaky.

Briefly, Hatch explained to him what had happened, and he listened silently. Finally he turned to The Thinking Machine.

"And this gentleman?" he asked. He noted the queer appearance of the scientist, and stared into the squint eyes frankly.

"Professor Van Dusen, a distinguished scientist and physician," Hatch introduced. "I brought you here. He has been working with you for an hour."

"And now, Mr Curtis," said The Thinking Machine, "if you will tell us all you know about the murder of Miss Melrose—"

Curtis paled suddenly.

"Why do you ask me?" he demanded.

"You said a great deal while you were unconscious," remarked The Thinking Machine, as he dreamily stared at the ceiling. "I know that worry over that and too much alcohol have put you in a condition bordering on nervous collapse. I think it would be better if you told it all."

Hatch instantly saw the trend of the scientist's remarks, and remained discreetly silent. Curtis stared at both for a moment, then paced nervously across the room. He did not know what he might have said, what chance word might have been dropped. Then, apparently, he made up his mind, for he stopped suddenly in front of The Thinking Machine.

"Do I look like a man who would commit murder?" he asked.

"No, you do not," was the prompt response.

His recital of the story was similar to that of Hatch, but the scientist listened carefully.

"Details! details!" he interrupted once.

The story was complete from the moment Curtis jumped out of the car until the return to the hotel of Curtis and Reid. There the narrator stopped.

"Mr Curtis, why did you try to induce Dr Leonard to give up the knife to you?" asked The Thinking Machine, finally.

"Because—well, because—" He faltered, flushed and stopped.

"Because you were afraid it would bring the crime home to you?" asked the scientist.

"I didn't know what might happen," was the response.

"Is it your knife?"

Again the tell-tale flush overspread Curtis's face.

"No," he said, flatly.

"Is it Reid's knife?"

"Oh, no," he said, quickly.

"You were in love with Miss Melrose?"

"Yes," was the steady reply.

"Had she ever refused to marry you?"

"I had never asked her."

"Why?"

"Is this a third degree?" demanded Curtis, angrily, and he arose. "Am I a prisoner?"

"Not at all," said The Thinking Machine, quietly. "You maybe made a prisoner, though, on what you said while unconscious. I am merely trying to help you."

Curtis sank down in a chair with his head in his hands and remained motionless for several minutes. At last he looked up.

"I'll answer your questions," he said.

"Why did you never ask Miss Melrose to marry you?"

"Because – well, because I understood another man, Donald MacLean, was as in love with her, and she might have loved him. I understood she would have married him had it not been that by doing so she would have caused his disinheritance. MacLean is now in Boston."

"Ah!" exclaimed The Thinking Machine.

"Your friend Reid didn't happen to be in love with her, too, did he?"

"Oh, no," was the reply. "Reid came here hoping to win the love of Miss Dow, a society girl. I came with him."

"Miss Dow?" asked Hatch, quickly. "The girl who eloped last night with Morgan Mason?"

"Yes," replied Curtis. "That elopement and this crime have put Reid almost in as bad a condition as I am."

"What elopement?" asked The Thinking Machine.

Hatch explained how Mason had procured a marriage license, how Miss Dow and Mason had met at the Monarch

Inn—where Miss Melrose must have been killed according to all stories – how Miss Dow had written to her parents from there of the elopement and then of their disappearance. The Thinking Machine listened, but without apparent interest.

"Have you such a knife as was used to kill Miss Melrose?" he asked at the end.

"No."

"Did you ever have such a knife?"

"Well, once."

"Where did you carry it when it was not in your auto kit?"

"In my lower coat pocket."

"By the way, what kind of looking woman was Miss Melrose?"

"One of the most beautiful women I ever met," said Curtis with a certain enthusiasm. "Of ordinary height, superb figure – a woman who would attract attention anywhere."

"I believe she wore a veil and an automobile mask at the time she was killed?"

"Yes. They covered all her face except her chin."

"Could she, wearing an automobile mask, see either side of herself without turning?" asked The Thinking Machine, pointedly. "Had you intended to stab her, say while the car was in motion and had the knife in your hand, even in daylight, could she have seen it without turning her head? Or, if she had had the knife, could you have seen it?"

Curtis shuddered a little.

"No, I don't believe so."

"Was she blonde or brunette?"

"Blonde, with great clouds of golden hair," said Curtis, and again there was admiration in his tone.

"Golden hair?" Hatch repeated. "I understood Medical Examiner Francis to say she had dark hair?"

"No, golden hair," was the positive reply.

"Did you see the body, Mr Hatch?" asked the scientist.

"No. None of us saw it. Dr Francis makes that a rule."

The Thinking Machine arose, excused himself and passed into another room. They heard the telephone bell ring and then some one closed the door connecting the two rooms. When the scientist returned he went straight to a point which Hatch had impatiently awaited.

"What happened to you this afternoon in Winter Street?"

Curtis had retained his composure well up to this point; now he became uneasy again. Quick pallor on his face was succeeded by a flush which crept up to the roots of his hair.

"I've been drinking too much," he said at last. "That and this thing have completely unnerved me. I am afraid I was not myself."

"What did you think you saw?" insisted The Thinking Machine.

"I went into a store for something. I've forgotten what now. I know there was a great crowd of women – they were all about me. There I saw—" He stopped and was silent for a moment. "There I saw," he went on with an effort, "a woman – just a glimpse of her, over the heads of the others in the store—and—"

"And what?" insisted The Thinking Machine.

"At the moment I would have sworn it was Marguerite Melrose," was the reply.

"Of course you know you were mistaken?"

"I know it now," said Curtis. "It was a chance resemblance, but the effect on me was awful. I ran out of there shrieking – it seemed to me. Then I found myself here."

"And you don't know what you said or did from that time until the present?" asked the scientist, curiously.

"No, except in a hazy sort of way."

After awhile Martha, the scientist's aged servant, appeared in the doorway. "Mr Mallory and a gentleman, sir."

"Let them come in," said The Thinking Machine. "Mr Curtis," and he turned to him gravely, "Mr Reid is here. I sent for him as if at your request to ask him two questions. If he answers those questions, as I believe he will, I can demonstrate that you are not guilty of and have no connection with the murder of Miss Melrose. Let me ask these questions, without any hint or remark from you as to what the answer must be. Are you willing?"

"I am," replied Curtis. His face was white, but his voice was firm.

Detective Mallory, whom Curtis didn't know, and Charles Reid entered the room. Both looked about curiously. Mallory nodded brusquely at Hatch. Reid looked at Curtis and Curtis looked away.

"Mr Reid," said The Thinking Machine without any preliminary, "Mr Curtis tells me that the knife used to kill Miss Melrose was your property. Is that so?" he demanded quickly, as Curtis faced about wonderingly.

"No," thundered Reid fiercely.

"Is it Mr Curtis's knife?" asked The Thinking Machine.

"Yes," flashed Reid. "It's a part of his auto."

Curtis started to speak; The Thinking Machine waved his hand toward him. Detective Mallory caught the gesture and understood that Jack Curtis was his prisoner for murder.

IV

Curtis was led away and locked up. He raved and bitterly denounced Reid for the information he had given, but he did not deny it. Indeed, after the first burst of fury he said nothing.

Once he was under lock and key the police, led by Detective Mallory, searched his rooms at the Hotel Teutonic and there they found a handkerchief stained with blood. It was slight, still it was a stain. This was immediately placed in the hands of an expert, who pronounced it human blood. Then the case against Curtis seemed complete; it was his knife, he had been in love with Miss Melrose, therefore probably jealous of her, and here was the tell-tale blood-stain.

Meanwhile Reid was permitted to go his way. He seemed crushed by the rapid sequence of events, and read eagerly every line he could find in the public prints concerning both the murder and the elopement of Miss Dow. This latter affair, indeed, seemed to have greater sway over his mind than the murder, or that a lifetime friend was now held as the murderer.

Meanwhile The Thinking Machine had signified to Hatch his desire to visit the scene of the crime and see what might be done there. Late in the afternoon, therefore, they started, taking a train for a village nearest the Monarch Inn.

"It's a most extraordinary ease," The Thinking Machine said, "much more extraordinary than you can imagine."

"In what respect?" asked the reporter.

"In motive, in the actual manner of the girl meeting her death and in a dozen other details which I can't state now because I haven't all the facts."

"You don't doubt but what it was murder?"

"It doesn't necessarily follow," said The Thinking Machine, evasively. "Suppose we were seeking a motive for Miss Melrose's suicide, what would we have? We would have her love affair with this man MacLean whom she refused to marry because she knew he would be disinherited. Suppose she had not seen him for a couple of years – suppose she had made up her mind to give him up – that he had suddenly appeared when she sat alone in the automobile in front of the Monarch Inn—suppose, then, finding all her love reawakened, she had decided to end it all?"

"But Curtis's knife and the blood on his handkerchief?"

"Suppose, having made up her mind to kill herself, she had sought a weapon?" went on The Thinking Machine, as if there had been no interruption. "What is more natural than she should have sought something – the knife, say – in the tool bag or kit, which must have been near her? Suppose she stabbed herself while the men were away from the automobile, or even after they had started on again in the darkness?"

Hatch looked a little crestfallen.

"You believe, then, that she did kill herself?" he asked.

"Certainly not," was the prompt response. "I don't believe Miss Melrose killed herself – but as yet I know nothing to the contrary. As for the blood on Curtis's handkerchief, remember he helped carry the body to Dr Leonard; it might have come from that – it might have come from a slight spattering of blood."

"But circumstances certainly implicate Curtis."

"I wouldn't convict any man of any crime on any circumstantial evidence," was the response. "It's worthless unless a man is forced to confess."

The reporter was puzzled, bewildered, and his face showed it. There were many things he did not understand, but the principal question in his mind took form:

"Why did you turn Curtis over to the police, then?"

"Because he is the man who owned the knife," was the reply. "I knew he was lying to me from the first about the knife. Men have been executed on less evidence than that."

The train stopped and they proceeded to the office of the medical examiner, where the body of the woman lay. Professor Van Dusen was readily permitted to see the body, even to offer his expert assistance in an autopsy which was then being performed; but the reporter was stopped at the door. After an hour The Thinking Machine came out.

"She was stabbed from the right," he said answer to Hatch's inquiring look, "either by some one sitting at her right, by some one leaning over her right shoulder, or she might have done it herself."

Then they went on to Monarch Inn, five miles way. Here, after a comprehensive squint at the landscape, The

Thinking Machine entered and for an hour questioned three waiters there.

Did these waiters see Mr Reid? Yes. They identified his published picture as a gentleman who had come in and taken a hot Scotch at the bar. Any one with him? No. Speak to anyone in the inn? Yes, a lady.

"What did she look like?" asked The Thinking Machine.

"Couldn't say, sir," the waiter replied. "She came in an automobile and wore a mask, with a veil tied about her head and a long tan automobile coat."

"With the mask on you couldn't see her face?"

"Only her chin, sir."

"No glimpse of her hair?"

"No, sir. It was covered by the veil."

Then The Thinking Machine turned loose a flood of questions. He learned that the woman had been waiting at the inn for nearly an hour when Reid entered; that she had come there alone and at her request had been shown into a private parlor – "to wait for a gentleman," she had told the waiter.

She had opened the door when she heard Reid enter and had glanced out, but he had disappeared into the bar before she saw him. When he started away she looked out again. Then she saw him and he saw her. She seemed surprised and started to close the door, when he spoke to her. No one heard what was said, but he went in and the door was closed.

No one knew just when either Reid or the woman left the inn. Some half an hour or so after Reid entered the room a waiter rapped on the door. There was no answer. He opened the door and went in, but there was no one there. It was presumed then that the gentleman she had been waiting for had appeared and they had gone out together. It was a fact that an automobile had come up meanwhile – in addition to that in which Curtis, Miss Melrose and Reid had come – and had gone away again.

When all this questioning had come to an end and these facts were in possession of The Thinking Machine, the reporter advanced a theory.

"That woman was unquestionably Miss Dow, who knew Reid and who eloped that night with Morgan Mason."

The Thinking Machine looked at him a moment without speaking, then led the way into the private room where the lady had been waiting. Hatch followed. They remained there five or ten minutes, then The Thinking Machine came out and started toward the front door, only eight or ten feet from this room. The road was twenty feet away.

"Let's go," he said, finally.

"Where?" asked Hatch.

"Don't you see?" asked The Thinking Machine, irrelevantly, "that it would have been perfectly possible for Miss Melrose herself to have left the automobile and gone inside the inn for a few minutes?"

Following previously received directions The Thinking Machine now set out to find the man who had charge of the gasoline tank. They went away together and remained half an hour.

On the scientist's return to where Hatch had been waiting impatiently they climbed into the car which had brought them to the inn.

"Two miles down this road, then the first road to your right until I tell you to stop," was the order to the chauffeur.

"Where are you going?" asked Hatch, curiously.

"Don't know yet," was the enigmatic reply.

The car ran on through the night, with great, unblinking lights staring straight out ahead on a road as smooth as asphalt. The turn was made, then more slowly the car proceeded along the cross road. At the second house, dimly discernible through the night, The Thinking Machine gave the signal to stop.

Hatch leaped out, and The Thinking Machine followed. Together they approached the house, a small cottage some distance back from the road. As they went up the path they came upon another automobile, but it had no lights and the engine was still. Even in the darkness they could see that one of the forward wheels was gone, and the front of the car was demolished.

"That fellow had a bad accident," Hatch remarked.

An old woman and a boy appeared at the door in answer to their rap.

"I am looking for a gentleman who was injured last night in an automobile accident," said The Thinking Machine. "Is he still here?"

"Yes. Come in."

They stepped inside as a man's voice called from another room:

"Who is it?"

"Two gentlemen to see the man who was hurt," the woman called.

"Do you know his name?" asked The Thinking Machine.

"No, sir," the woman replied. Then the man who had spoken appeared.

"Would it be possible for us to see the gentleman who was hurt?" asked The Thinking Machine.

"Well, the doctor said we would have to keep folks away from him," was the reply. "Is there anything I could tell you?"

"We would like to know who he is," said The Thinking Machine. "It may be that we can take him off your hands."

"I don't know his name," the man explained; "but here are the things we took off him. He was hurt on the head, and hasn't been able to speak since he was brought here."

The Thinking Machine took a gold watch, a small notebook, two or three cards of various business concerns, two railroad tickets to New York and one thousand dollars in large bills. He merely glanced at the papers. No name appeared anywhere on them; the same with the railroad tickets. The business cards meant nothing at the moment. It was the gold watch on which the scientist concentrated his attention. He looked on both sides, then inside, carefully. Finally he handed it back.

"What time did this gentleman come here?" he asked.

"We brought him in from the road about nine o'clock," was the reply. "We heard his automobile smash into something and found him there beside it a moment later. He was unconscious. His car had struck a stone on the curve and he was thrown out head first."

"And where is his wife?"

"His wife?" The man looked from The Thinking Machine to the woman. "His wife? We didn't see anybody else."

"Nobody ran away from the machine as you went out?" insisted the scientist.

"No, sir," was the positive reply.

"And no woman has been here to inquire for him?"

"No, sir."

"Has anybody?"

"No, sir."

"What direction was the car going when it struck?"

"I couldn't tell you, sir. It had turned entirely over and was in the middle of the road when we found it."

"What's the number of the car?"

"It didn't have any."

"This gentleman has good medical attention, I suppose?"

"Yes, sir. Dr Leonard is attending him. He says his condition isn't dangerous, and meanwhile we're letting him stay here, because we suppose he'll make it all right with us when he gets well."

"Thank you – that's all," said The Thinking Machine. "Goodnight."

With Hatch he turned and left the house.

"What is all this?" asked Hatch, bewildered.

"That man is Morgan Mason," said The Thinking Machine.

"The man who eloped with Miss Dow?" asked Hatch, breathlessly.

"Now, where is Miss Dow?" asked The Thinking Machine, in turn.

"You mean—"

The Thinking Machine waved his hand off into the vague night; it was a gesture which Hatch understood perfectly.

V

Hutchinson Hatch was deeply thoughtful on the swift run back to the village. There he and The Thinking Machine took train to Boston. Hatch was turning over possibilities. Had Miss Dow eloped with some one besides Mason? There had been no other name mentioned. Was it possible that she killed Miss Melrose? Vaguely his mind clutched for a motive for this, yet none appeared, and he dismissed the idea with a laugh at its absurdity. Then, What? Where? How? Why?

"I suppose the story of an actress having been murdered in an automobile under mysterious circumstances would have been telegraphed all over the country, Mr Hatch?" asked The Thinking Machine.

"Yes," said Hatch. "If you mean this story, there's not a city in the country that doesn't know of it by this time."

"It's perfectly wonderful, the resources of the press," the scientist mused.

Hatch nodded his acquiescence. He had hoped for a moment that The Thinking Machine had asked the question as a preliminary to something else, but that was apparently all. After awhile the train jerked a little and The Thinking Machine spoke again.

"I think, Mr Hatch I wouldn't yet print anything about the disappearance of Miss Dow," he said. "It might be unwise at present. No one else will find it out, so—"

"I understand," said Hatch. It was a command.

"By the way," the other went on, "do you happen to remember the name of that Winter Street store that Curtis went in?"

"Yes," and he named it.

It was nearly midnight when The Thinking Machine and Hatch reached Boston. The reporter was dismissed with a curt:

"Come up at noon tomorrow."

Hatch went his way. Next day at noon promptly he was waiting in the reception room of The Thinking Machine's home. The scientist was out-down in Winter Street, Martha explained – and Hatch waited impatiently for his return. He came in finally.

"Well?" inquired the reporter.

"Impossible to say anything until day after tomorrow," said The Thinking Machine.

"And then?" asked Hatch.

"The solution," replied the scientist positively. "Now I'm waiting for some one."

"Miss Dow?"

"Meanwhile you might see Reid and find out in some way if he ever happened to make a gift of any little thing, a thing that a woman would wear on the outside of her coat, for instance, to Miss Dow."

"Lord, I don't think he'll say anything."

"Find out, too, when he intends to go back West."

It took Hatch three hours, and required a vast deal of patience and skill, to find out that on a recent birthday Miss Dow had received a present of a monogram belt buckle from Reid. That was all; and that was not what The Thinking Machine meant. Hatch had the word of Miss Dow's maid for it that while

Miss Dow wore this belt at the time of her elopement, it was underneath the automobile coat.

"Have you heard anything more from Miss Dow?" asked Hatch.

"Yes," responded the maid. "Her father received a letter from her this morning. It was from Chicago, and said that she and her husband were on their way to San Francisco and that the family might not hear from them again until after the honeymoon."

"How? What?" gasped Hatch. His brain was in a muddle. "She in Chicago, with – her husband?"

"Yes, sir."

"Is there any question about the letter being in her handwriting?"

"Not at all," replied the maid, positively. "It's perfectly natural," she concluded.

"But—" Hatch began, then he stopped.

For one fleeting instant he was tempted to tell the maid that the man whom the family had supposed was Miss Dow's husband was lying unconscious at a farmhouse not a great way from the Monarch Inn, and that there was no trace of Miss Dow. Now this letter! His head whirled when he thought of it.

"Is there any question but that Miss Dow did elope with Mr Mason and not some other man?" he asked.

"It was Mr Mason all right," the girl responded. "I knew there was to be an elopement and helped arrange for Miss Dow to go," she added, confidently. "It was Mr Mason, I know."

Then Hatch rushed away and telephoned to The Thinking Machine. He simply couldn't hold this latest development until he saw him again.

"We've made a mistake," he bellowed through the 'phone.

"What's that?" demanded The Thinking Machine, aggressively.

"Miss Dow is in Chicago with her husband—family has received a letter from her – that man out there with the smashed head can't be Mason." The reporter explained hurriedly.

"Dear me, dear me!" said The Thinking Machine over the wire. And again: "Dear me!"

"Her maid told me all about it," Hatch rushed on, "that is, all about her aiding Miss Dow to elope, and all that. Must be some mistake."

"Dear me!" again came in the voice of The Thinking Machine. Then: "Is Miss Dow a blonde or brunette?"

The irrelevancy of the question caused Hatch to smile in spite of himself.

"A brunette," he answered. "A pronounced brunette."

"Then," said The Thinking Machine, as if this were merely dependent upon or a part of the blonde or brunette proposition, "get immediately a picture of Mason somewhere – I suppose you can – go out and see that man with the smashed head and see if it is Mason. Let me know by 'phone."

"All right," said Hatch, rather hopelessly. "But it is impossible—"

"Don't say that," snapped The Thinking Machine. "Don't say that," he repeated, angrily. "It annoys me exceedingly."

It was nearly ten o'clock that night when Hatch again 'phoned to The Thinking Machine. He had found a photograph, he had seen the man with the smashed head. They were the same. He so informed The Thinking Machine.

"Ah," said that individual, quietly. "Did you find out about any gift that Reid might have made to Miss Dow?" he asked.

"Yes, a monogram belt buckle of gold," was the reply.

Hatch was over his head and knew it. He was finding out things and answering questions which, by the wildest stretch of his imagination, he could not bring to bear on the matter in hand – the mystery surrounding the murder of Marguerite Melrose, an actress.

"Meet me at my place here at one o'clock day after tomorrow," instructed The Thinking Machine. "Publish as little as you can of this matter until you see me. It's extraordinary – perfectly extraordinary. Goodbye."

That was all. Hatch groped hopelessly through the tangle, seeking one fact that he could grasp. Then it occurred to him that he had never ascertained when Reid intended to return West, and he went to the Hotel Teutonic for this purpose. The clerk informed him that Reid was to start in a couple of days. Reid had hardly left his room since Curtis was locked up.

Precisely at one o'clock on the second day following, as directed by The Thinking Machine, Hatch appeared and was ushered in. The Thinking Machine was bowed over a retort in his laboratory, and he looked up at the reporter with a question in his eyes.

"Oh, yes," he said, as if recollecting for the first time the purpose of the visit. "Oh, yes."

He led the way to the reception room and gave instructions to Martha to admit whoever inquired for him; then he sat down and leaned back in his chair. After awhile the bell rang and two men were shown in. One was Charles Reid; the other a detective whom Hatch knew.

"Ah! Mr Reid," said The Thinking Machine. "I'm sorry to have troubled you, but there were some questions I wanted to ask before you went away. If you'll wait just a moment."

Reid bowed and took a seat.

"Is he under arrest?" Hatch inquired of the detective, aside.

"Oh, no," was the reply. "Oh, no. Detective Mallory told me to ask him to come up. I don't know what for."

After awhile the bell rang again. Then Hatch heard Detective Mallory's voice in the hall and the rustle of skirts; then the voice of another man. Mallory appeared at the door after a moment; behind him came two veiled women and a man who was a stranger to Hatch.

"I'm going to make a request, Mr Mallory," said The Thinking Machine. "I know it will be a cause of pleasure to Mr Reid. It is that you release Mr Curtis, who is charged with the murder of Miss Melrose."

"Why?" demanded Mallory, quickly. Hatch and Reid stared at the scientist curiously.

"This," said The Thinking Machine.

The two women simultaneously removed their veils.

One was Miss Marguerite Melrose.

VI

"Miss Melrose that was," explained The Thinking Machine, "now Mrs Donald MacLean. This, gentlemen, is her husband. This other young woman is Miss Dow's maid. Together I believe we will be able to throw some light on the death of the young woman who was found in Mr Curtis's automobile."

Stupefied with amazement, Hatch stared at the woman whose reported murder had startled and puzzled the entire country. Reid had shown only slight emotion – an emotion of a kind hard to read. Finally he advanced to Miss Melrose, or Mrs MacLean, with outstretched hand.

"Marguerite," he said.

The girl looked deeply into his eyes, then took the proffered hand.

"And Jack Curtis?" she asked.

"If Detective Mallory will have him brought here we can immediately end his connection with this case so far as your murder is concerned," said The Thinking Machine.

"Who-who was murdered then?" asked Hatch.

"A little circumstantial development is necessary to show," replied The Thinking Machine.

Detective Mallory retired into another room and 'phoned to have Curtis brought up. On his assurance that there had been a mistake which he would explain later, Curtis set out from his cell with a detective and within a few minutes appeared in the room, wonderingly.

One look at Marguerite and he was beside her, gripping her hand. For a time he didn't speak; it was not necessary. Then the actress, with flushed face, indicated MacLean, who had stood quietly by, an interested but silent spectator.

"My husband, Jack," she said.

Quick comprehension swept over Curtis and he looked from one to another. Then he approached MacLean with outstretched hand.

"I congratulate you," he said, with deep feeling. "Make her happy."

Reid had stood unobserved meanwhile. Hatch's glance traveled from one to another of the persons in the room. He was seeking to explain that expression on Reid's face, vainly thus far. There was a little pause as Reid and Curtis came face to face, but neither spoke.

"Now, please, what does it all mean?" asked MacLean, who up to this time had been silent.

"It's a strange study of the human brain," said The Thinking Machine, "and incidentally a little proof that circumstantial evidence is absolutely worthless. For instance, here it was proven that Miss Melrose was dead, that Mr Curtis was jealous of her, that while drinking he had threatened her—this I learned at the Hotel Yarmouth, but now it is unimportant — that his knife killed her, and finally that there was blood on one of his handkerchiefs. This is the complete circumstantial chain; and Miss Melrose appears, alive.

"Suppose we take the case from the point where I entered it. It will be interesting as showing the methods of a brain which reduces all things to tangible strands which may be woven into a whole, then fitting them together. My knowledge of the affair began when Mr Curtis was brought to these apartments by Mr Hatch. Mr Curtis was ill. I gave him a stimulant; he aroused suddenly and shrieked: 'I saw her. There was a dagger in her heart. Marguerite!'

"My first impression was that he was insane; my next that he had delirium tremens, because I saw he had been drinking heavily. Later I saw it was temporary mental collapse due to excessive drinking and a tremendous strain. Instantly I associated Marguerite with this – 'a dagger in her heart.' Therefore, Marguerite dead or wounded. 'I saw her.' Dead or alive? These, then, were my first impressions.

"I asked Mr Hatch what had happened. He told me Miss Melrose, an actress, had been murdered the night before. I suggested suicide, because suicide is always the first possibility in considering a case of violent death which is not obviously accidental. He insisted that he believed it was murder, and told me why. It was all he knew of the story.

"There was the stopping of The Green Dragon at the Monarch Inn for gasoline; the disappearance of Mr Curtis, as he told the police, to hunt for gasoline – partly proven by the fact that he brought it back; the statement of Mr Reid to the police that he had gone into the inn for a hot Scotch, and confirmation of this. Above all, here was the opportunity for the crime — if it were committed by any person other than Curtis or Reid.

"Then Mr Hatch repeated to me the statement made to him by Dr Leonard. The first thing that impressed me here was the fact that Curtis had, in taking the girl into the house, carried her by the shoulders. Instantly I saw, knowing that the girl had been stabbed through the heart, how it would be possible for blood to get on Mr Curtis's hands, thence on his handkerchief or clothing. This was before I knew or considered his connection with the death at all.

"Curtis told Dr Leonard that the girl was Miss Melrose. The body wasn't yet cold, therefore death must have come just before it reached the doctor. Then the knife was discovered. Here was the first tangible working clew – a rough knife, with a blade six or seven inches long. Obviously not the sort of knife a woman would carry about with her. Therefore, where did it come from?

"Curtis tried to induce the doctor to let him have the knife; probably Curtis's knife, possibly Reid's. Why Curtis's? The nature of the knife, a blade six or seven inches long, indicated a knife used for heavy work, not for a penknife. Under ordinary circumstances such a knife would not have been carried by Reid; therefore it may have belonged to Curtis's auto kit. He might have carried it in his pocket.

"Thus, considering that it was Miss Melrose who was dead, we had these facts: Dead only a few minutes, possibly stabbed while the two men were away from the car; Curtis's knife used – not a knife from any other auto kit, mind you, because Curtis recognized this knife. Two and two make four, not sometimes, but all the time."

Every person in the room was leaning forward, eagerly listening; Reid's face was perfectly white. The Thinking Machine finally arose, walked over and ran his fingers through Reid's hair, then sat again squinting at the ceiling. He spoke as if to himself.

"Then Mr Hatch told me another important thing," he went on. "At the moment it appeared a coincidence, later it assumed its complete importance. This was that Dr Leonard did not actually see the face of the girl – only the chin; that the hair was covered by a veil and the mask covered the remainder of the face. Here for the first time I saw that it was wholly possible that the woman was not Miss Melrose at all. I saw it as a possibility; not that I believed it. I had no reason to, then.

"The dress of the young woman meant nothing; it was that of thousands of other young women who go automobiling – handsome tailor-made gown, tan dust coat. Then I tricked Mr Curtis – I suppose it is only fair to use the proper word – into telling me his story by making him believe he made compromising admissions while unconscious. I had, I may say, too, examined his head minutely. I have always maintained that the head of a murderer will show a certain indentation. Mr Curtis's head did not show this indentation, neither does Mr Reid's.

"Mr Curtis told me the first thing to show that the knife which killed the girl – I still believed her Miss Melrose then – could have passed out of his hands. He said when he leaped from the automobile he thought he dropped something, searched for it a moment, failed to find it, then, being in a hurry, went on. He called back to Mr Reid to search for what he had lost. That is when Mr Curtis lost the knife; that is when it passed into the possession of Mr Reid. He found it."

Every eye was turned on Reid. He sat as if fascinated, staring into the upward turned face of the scientist.

"There we had a girl – presumably Miss Melrose – dead, by a knife owned by Mr Curtis, last in the possession of Mr Reid. Mr Hatch had previously told me that the medical examiner said the wound which killed the girl came from her right, in a general direction. Therefore here was a possibility that Mr Reid did it in the automobile – a possibility, I say.

"I asked Mr Curtis why he tried to recover the knife from Dr Leonard. He stammered and faltered, but really it was because, having recognized the knife, he was afraid the crime would come home to him. Mr Curtis denied flatly that the knife was his, and in denying told me that it was. It was not Mr Reid's I was assured. Mr Curtis also told me of his love for Miss Melrose, but there was nothing there, as it appeared, strong enough to suggest a motive for murder. He mentioned you, Mr MacLean, then.

"Then Mr Curtis named Miss Dow as one whose hand had been sought by Mr Reid. Mr Hatch told me this girl – Miss Dow – had eloped the night before with Morgan Mason from Monarch Inn – or, to be exact, that her family had received a letter from her stating that she was eloping; that Mason had taken out a marriage license. Remember this was the girl that Reid was in love with; it was singular that there should have been a Monarch Inn end to that elopement as well as to this tragedy.

"This meant nothing as bearing on the abstract problem before me until Mr Curtis described Miss Melrose as having golden hair. With another minor scrap of information Mr Hatch again opened up vast possibilities by stating that the medical examiner, a careful man, had said Miss Melrose had dark hair. I asked him if he had seen the body; he had not. But the medical examiner told him that. Instantly in my mind the question was aroused: Was it Miss Melrose who was killed? This was merely a possibility; it still had no great weight with me.

"I asked Mr Curtis as to the circumstances which caused his collapse in Winter Street. He explained it was because he had seen a woman whom he would have sworn was Miss Melrose if he had not known that she was dead. This, following the dark hair and blonde hair puzzle, instantly caused this point to stand forth sharply in my mind. Was Miss Melrose dead at all? I had good reason then to believe that she was not.

"Previously, with the idea of fixing for all time the ownership of the knife – yet knowing in my own mind it was Mr Curtis's – I had sent for Mr Reid. I told him Mr Curtis had said it was his knife. Mr Reid fell into the trap and did the very thing I expected. He declared angrily the knife was Mr Curtis's, thinking Curtis had tried to saddle the crime on him. Then I turned Mr Curtis over to the police. When he was locked up I was reasonably certain that he did not commit any crime, because I had traced the knife from him to Mr Reid."

There was a glitter in Reid's eyes now. It was not fear, only a nervous battle to restrain himself. The Thinking Machine went on:

"I saw the body of the dead woman – indeed, assisted at her autopsy. She was a pronounced brunette – Miss Melrose was a blonde. The mistake in identity was not an impossible one in view of the fact that each wore a mask and had her hair tied up under a veil. That woman was stabbed from the right — still a possibility of suicide."

"Who was the woman?" demanded Curtis. He seemed utterly unable to control himself longer.

"Miss Elizabeth Dow, who was supposed to have eloped with Morgan Mason," was the quiet reply.

Instant amazement was reflected on every face save Reid's, and again every eye was turned to him. Miss Dow's maid burst into tears.

"Mr Reid knew who the woman was all the time," said The Thinking Machine. "Knowing then that Miss Dow was the dead woman — this belief being confirmed by a monogram gold belt buckle, 'E. D.,' on the body — I proceeded to find out all I could in this direction. The waiters had seen Mr Reid in the inn; had seen him talking to a masked and veiled lady who had been waiting for nearly an hour; had seen him go into a room with her, but had not seen them leave the inn. Mr Reid had recognized the lady — not she him. How? By a glimpse of the monogram belt buckle which he knew because he probably gave it to her."

"He did," interposed Hatch.

"I did," said Reid, calmly. It was the first time he had spoken.

"Now, Mr Reid went into the room and closed the door, carrying with him Mr Curtis's knife," went on The Thinking Machine. "I can't tell you from personal observation what happened in that room, but I know. Mr Reid learned in some way that Miss Dow was going to elope; he learned that she had been waiting long past the time when Mason was due there; that she believed he had humiliated her by giving up the idea at the last minute. Being in a highly nervous condition, she lost faith in Mason and in herself, and perhaps mentioned suicide?"

"She did," said Reid, calmly.

"Go on, Mr Reid," suggested The Thinking Machine.

"I believed, too, that Mason had changed his mind," the young man continued, with steady voice. "I pleaded with Miss Dow to give up the idea of eloping, because, remember, I loved her, too. She finally consented to go on with our party, as her automobile had gone. We came out of the inn together. When we reached the automobile – The Green Dragon, I mean – I saw Miss Melrose getting into Mr MacLean's automobile, which had come up meanwhile. Instantly I saw, or imagined, the circumstances, and said nothing to Miss Dow about it, particularly as Mr MacLean's car dashed away at full speed.

"Now, in taking Miss Dow to The Green Dragon it had been my purpose to introduce her to Miss Melrose. She knew Mr Curtis. When I saw Miss Melrose was gone I knew Curtis would wonder why. I couldn't explain, because every moment I was afraid Mason would appear to claim Miss Dow and I was anxious to get her as far away as possible. Therefore I requested her not to speak until we reached the next inn, and there I would explain to Curtis.

"Somewhere between the Monarch Inn and the inn we had started for Miss Dow changed her mind; probably was overcome by the humiliation of her position, and she used the knife. She had seen me take the knife from my pocket and throw it into the tool kit on the floor beside her. It was comparatively a trifling matter for her to stoop and pick it up, almost from under her feet, and—"

"Under all these circumstances, as stated by Mr Reid," interrupted The Thinking Machine, "we understand why, after he found the girl dead, he didn't tell all the truth, even to Curtis. Any jury on earth would have convicted him of murder on circumstantial evidence. Then, when he saw Miss Dow dead, mistaken for Miss Melrose, he could not correct the impression without giving himself away. He was forced to silence.

"I realized these things – not in exact detail as Mr Reid has told them, but in a general way – after my talk with the waiters. Then I set out to find out why Mason had not appeared. It was possibly due to accident. On a chance entirely I asked the man in charge of the gasoline tank at the Monarch if he had heard of an accident nearby on the night of the tragedy. He had.

"With Mr Hatch I found the injured man. A monogram, 'M.M.,' on his watch, told me it was Morgan Mason. Mr Mason had a serious accident and still lies unconscious. He was going to meet Miss Dow when this happened. He had two railroad tickets to New York – for himself and bride – in his pocket."

Reid still sat staring at The Thinking Machine, waiting. The others were awed into silence by the story of the tragedy.

"Having located both Mason and Miss Dow to my satisfaction, I then sought to find what had become of Miss Melrose. Mr Reid could have told me this, but he wouldn't have, because it would have turned the light on the very thing which he was trying to keep hidden. With Miss Melrose alive, it was perfectly possible that Curtis had seen her in the Winter Street store.

"I asked Mr Hatch if he remembered what store it was. He did. I also asked Mr Hatch if such a story as the murder of Miss Melrose would be telegraphed all over the country. He said it would. It did not stand to reason that if Miss Melrose were in any city, or even on a train, she could have failed to hear of her own murder, which would instantly have called forth a denial.

"Therefore, where was she? On the water, out of reach of newspapers? I went to the store in Winter Street and asked if any purchases had been sent from there to any steamer about to sail on the day following the tragedy. There had been several purchases made by a woman who answered Miss Melrose's description as I had it, and these had been sent to a steamer which sailed for Halifax.

"Miss Melrose and Mr MacLean, married then, were on that steamer. I wired to Halifax to ascertain if they were coming back immediately. They were. I waited for them. Otherwise, Mr Hatch, I should have given you the solution of the mystery two days ago. As it was, I waited until Miss Melrose, or Mrs MacLean, returned. I think that's all."

"The letter from Miss Dow in Chicago?" Hatch reminded him.

"Oh, yes," said The Thinking Machine. "That was sent to a friend in her confidence, and mailed on a specified date. As a matter of fact, she and Mason were going to New York and thence to Europe. Of course, as matters happened, the two letters – the other being the one mailed from the Monarch Inn – were sent and could not be recalled."

This strange story was one of the most astonishing news features the American newspapers ever handled. Charles Reid was arrested, established his story beyond question, and was released. His principal witnesses were Professor Augustus S. F. X. Van Dusen, Jack Curtis and Mrs Donald MacLean.

7

THE GRINNING GOD

This story is the result of an unusual method of collaboration between Mrs Jacques Futrelle, and Jacques Futrelle, creator of The Thinking Machine, – unusual in that the first installment, "Wraiths of the Storm," which presents a remarkable, even an intangible, problem, is entirely the work of Mrs Futrelle, and the second installment, "The House That Was," is a legitimate attempt by Mr Futrelle to solve the problem on the stated facts with the aid of The Thinking Machine.

PART I. WRAITHS OF THE STORM

By Mrs Jacques Futrelle

Professor Augustus S. F. X. Van Dusen – The Thinking Machine – readjusted his thick spectacles, dropped back into the depths of the huge chair, manuscript in hand, and read:

"Something less than three months ago I had a photograph taken. As I look upon it now I see a man of about thirty years, clean shaven, full faced, and vigorous with health; eyes which are clear and calm and placid, almost phlegmatic; a brow upon which sits the serenity of perfect physical and mental poise; a pleasant mouth with quizzical lines about the corners; a chin with determination and assurance in every line; hair brown and unmarked with age. I was red blooded then, lusty, buoyant with life and animalism, while now—

"Here is a hand mirror. It reflects back at me the gaunt, haggard face of a man who might be any age; furtive, shifting eyes in which lies perpetual, hideous fear; a brow ruffled over into spidery lines of suffering; a drooping, flabby mouth; a chin weak and utterly devoid of the assurances of manhood; hair dead white over the temples, with strange grey streaks through it. My blood is become water; youth is frozen into senility; all things worth while are gone.

"Fear, Webster says, is apprehension, dread, alarm – and it is more than that. It is a loss of the sense of proportion, an unseating of mental power, a phantasmagoria of perverted imagination; a vampire which saps hope and courage and common sense, and leaves a quivering shell of what was once a man. I know what fear is – no man better. I knew it that night in the forest, and I know it now, when I find myself sitting up in bed staring into nothingness with the echo of screams in my ears; I knew it when that grim, silent old man moved about me, and I know it now when without conscious effort my imagination conjures up those dead, glassy eyes; I knew it when vicious little tongues of flames lapped at me that night, and I know it now when at times I seem to feel their heat.

"I know what fear is! It is typified by a little ivory god which squats upon my mantel as I write, grinning hideously. Perhaps there is some explanation of the event of that night, some single hidden fact which, if revealed, would make it all clear; but seeking that explanation I have grown like this. When it will end, I don't know – I can only wait and listen, always, always!

"Impatient, half famished, and wholly disgusted at a sudden failure of my gasolene supply, I ran my automobile off the main roadway and brought it to a standstill in a small open space before a little country store. I had barely been able to make out the outlines of the building through the utter darkness of the night, – a darkness which was momentarily growing more dense. Black, threatening clouds swooped across the face of the heavens, first obscuring, then obliterating, the brilliant star points.

"I knew where I was perfectly, although I had never been over the road before. Behind me lay Pelham, a quiet little village which had been sound asleep when I rushed through, and somewhere vaguely in front was Millen. I had been due there about seven o'clock; but, thanks to some trouble with a crank, it was now about ten. I was well nigh exhausted from hours at the steering wheel, and nothing to eat since luncheon. I would spend the night in Millen, store up a few hours' sleep, after the insistent demands of my appetite had been appeased, then on the morrow proceed comfortably on my way.

"This was what I had intended to do. The sudden shortage of motive power brought me to a stop in front of the forbidding little store, and a little maneuvering back and forth cleared the road's fairway of the bulk of my machine. No light showed in the house, but as I had not passed another building in two or three miles back, it seemed not improbable that the keeper of the store slept on the premises. I put this hypothesis to a test by a loud halloing, which in the course of time brought a nightcapped head to a window just above the door. I hailed the appearance of the head as a good omen.

" 'Got any gasolene?' I asked.

" 'I calculate as how I might have a little,' came the answer in a man's voice.

" 'Well, will you please let me have enough to get me to Millen?'

" 'It's ag'in' the law to draw gasolene at night,' said the man placidly. 'Cal'late as how you'll have to wait till mornin'.'

" 'Wait till morning?' I complained. 'Why man, there's a storm coming! I've got to get to Millen.'

" 'Can't help that,' was the reply. 'Law's law, you know. I'd be sorter skeered, anyway, to draw gasolene now.'

"Here was another dilemma, unexpected as it was annoying. The tone of the voice left no room for argument, and I knew the obstinacy of this man's type. I was prepared, therefore, to accept the inevitable.

" 'Well, if you can't draw any gasolene tonight, can you give me a bite to eat and put me up till morning?' I asked. 'I can't stay out in this storm.'

" 'Ain't got no room,' explained the man. 'Jus' enough space up here for me an' the dog, an' he kinder crowds.'

" 'Well, something must be done,' I insisted. 'What is the price of your gasolene?' I added by way of suggestion.

" 'Twenty-five cents a gallon in day time.'

" 'Well, how is fifty cents a gallon at night?' I went on.

"The whitecapped head was withdrawn, and the window banged down suddenly. For a moment I thought I had hopelessly offended some puritanical old man of the woods; but then a light glowed inside the store, and the front door opened. I stepped inside. The light came from a safety lantern in the hands of a shrunken shanked, little old man, who proceeded to draw the gasolene.

" 'How far is it to Millen?' I inquired casually.

" 'Calculate as how it's about five miles.'

" 'Straight roads?'

" 'Straight 'cept where it bends,' he replied. 'They ain't no turnout nor nothin'. You can't go wrong 'less you climb a fence.'

"The gasolene was drawn and paid for, after which the old man accompanied me to the automobile with his safety lantern. He stood looking on curiously as I filled the tank.

" ' 'Pears to be a right smart storm comin' up,' he remarked consolingly.

"I glanced upward. Every star point was lost now behind an impenetrable veil of black; there was a whispering, sighing sound of wind in the trees.

" 'I think I can beat it into Millen,' I replied hopefully.

" 'I cal'late as how you oughter,' responded the old man. 'Ain't no thunder an' lightnin' yet, an' I cal'late as how they'll be a pile of it before it rains.'

"I handed back the empty gasolene can, cranked up, then climbed aboard my car. There was a whir as I touched the power lever, and the machine trembled beneath me.

" 'If I should get caught before I get to Millen, is there any place I might stop,' I inquired.

" 'I cal'late as how you might stop anywhere,' the old man chuckled; 'but they ain't no houses nor nothin'. They ain't even a dog kennel 'tween here an' Millen. But they ain't no turnouts, an' you can hit it up as fast as you want to. You'll be all right.'

"A sudden gust of wind brought a whirling cloud of dust upon us, and the thinly clad old man scampered off into the house.

" 'Goodnight,' I called.

" 'Goodnight,' he answered, and the door slammed.

"I backed my car, then straightened out into the road, a wide yellow stretch, as smooth as asphalt, where the swirling, eddying winds awoke little dust devils to play. Then I kicked loose the speed gear, pulled the lever far back, and went plunging off into the night.

"It might have been only my imagination, or it might have been that, as the car swept on, I heard some one calling me; I'll never know which. But the lowering clouds and a quickened rush of wind did not make a stop inviting; so the car sped on.

"I knew a capital little all night restaurant in Millen, and was speculating pleasantly as to whether it should be a chop and a mug of ale, or a more substantial steak and potatoes. I was aroused from this anticipatory mood by the fact that the glittering lamps of my car showed me straight ahead two roads instead of one. Two roads! Here was another unexpected annoyance. I brought the automobile to a stop, in doubt and perplexity.

"To the right the road ran off into the thickening forest, as far as the steady light gleams showed; to the left it seemed a little more marked, as if more travelled, and where the light melted into the enveloping blackness it appeared to widen. I leaped out of the car and went forward, seeking a guide post or something to show my way. There was nothing.

"Then I remembered that I had a road map in my pocket. Of course that would tell me. A grumble of thunder came from far off as I drew near the car to examine the map in the light. Here was Pelham, and here was Millen; here even the little store where I stopped, marked with a star, which meant that gasolene was to be procured there. Now I was somewhere between that store and Millen. The map was a large one. It should show not only the main road, but every little bypath that cut athwart it. Yet from the little store to Millen the road was an unbroken line. There was no branch road on the map; and yet here was one.

"I was perplexed, impatient, and incidentally starving; so hastily made up my mind which road to take: the left and more beaten one. Heaping maledictions upon the head of the man who drew that particular map, I started to climb into the car again, when the veil of night was cleft by a vivid zigzag flash of lightning. It startled me, blinded me almost, and was followed instantly by the crash and roar of thunder.

"Then came another sound, – a curdling, nerve racking scream, – a scream of agony, of pain, of fear, – a hideous, awful thing which seemed to stop my heart for one fearful instant, then was lost in the thunder of the approaching storm. Suddenly all was silent again, save for the wind as it whipped its way through the forest.

"I was not a nervous man; so after the first shock the blood rushed back to my heart, my head cleared, and I was perfectly calm. But I stood waiting with my foot on the step – waiting and listening. I argued calmly. Some one was evidently in distress.

But where? In what direction? The singing wind, the whirling dust, left me no guess. And then again came that scream, this time a series of quick, sharp shrieks ending in a wail which made me clench my hands until the nails bit into the flesh, and left me weak and trembling absurdly.

"But now I had the direction. The cries had come apparently from the road, somewhere behind me. I walked to the rear of the car where the tail light shot out a feeble ray, and stood peering off into the blackness in the direction whence I had come. At first I could distinguish nothing, then a white, intangible something slowly grew out of the night, – something hazy, floating, indistinct, yet unmistakably something. Fascinated, I stood still and continued to stare. The floating white figure seemed to grow sensibly larger and clearer. It was coming toward me; it would cross the path of the light in another moment. I caught my breath and waited.

"Suddenly again came the reverberating crash of thunder, nearer and louder, but unaccompanied by lightning. Instantly, as if in echo, came that scream again. Obviously it was some one in distress, – a woman perhaps, lost in the woods and in terror of the approaching storm. If this was true then there was only one thing to do; go to her relief.

"I stopped and tugged at the tail lamp to release it from its fastenings. A ragged edge cut my hand cruelly; but I hardly felt the sting. At last the light was free in my hand, and I started with it back along the road to where I had seen the figure. With the lamp thrust straight out in front of me at arm's length I ran back ten yards, twenty, fifty, and saw – nothing. I screened the light with my hand, and peered about through the gloom, and saw—nothing.

"A panic was growing upon me. I flashed the light to the right, to the left, and it showed only the gaunt, silent trees, straight ahead of me along the yellow road, and behind me toward the panting automobile. There was nothing – absolutely nothing!

I rushed back to the car; but no one was there. I called aloud; but the grim forest gave me back only the sound of my own voice, mingled with the swishing of the wind.

"Then I stopped still in silence and awe, and listened. For a long time I stood there, light in hand, until the silence grew more terrifying than the screams had been. I wanted to hear that scream again now, to bring relief to my bursting heart and shaking nerves, to tell me that it was real and not some trick of overwrought fancy. But the silence was unbroken save for the freshening gusts of air which stirred the dry leaves and rained them down in a gentle patter.

"Finally I turned and walked back to where the car stood throbbing like a living, breathing thing. It gave me confidence. I struck the tonneau with my open palm, and laughed suddenly at my unreasoning terror. It was absurd, a school boy running from his shadow, and here I was a man – a sound, healthy, hungry man. I had heard the screams, I knew; I had seen the floating white figure. There was nothing very remarkable about it; it was a thing to be explained, of course.

"So now, deliberately I searched the road again, this time with the light turned toward the ground. I went along, stooping, seeking footprints. I found none; but I could explain even that; the wind gusts had covered them with dust, obliterated them.

"I straightened up suddenly. Something had sounded, something louder than the rustling of the leaves, something louder even than the creaking of the trees. It was a crackling sound – a sound that might have been a foot pressure upon dry twigs. It seemed to be to the left, and I turned the light in that direction. Grotesque shadows danced and swayed as the trees reeled about me. Then high up where the light straggled through the branches I saw something white – dead white!

"I cleared the road at a stride and plunged into the forest with the light turned upward. I stumbled over rocks half buried in the leaves; I slipped once into a ditch which I couldn't see. Finally my foot struck a fallen tree, and I went forward sprawling on my hands and knees. The lamp rolled beyond my reach, and utter blackness swooped down as the light was smothered in the underbrush. As I groped for it I heard again that crackling sound as of breaking twigs. Perhaps it was coming toward me – and I couldn't see!

"At last my frantic fingers closed on the lamp, and I shot the light high above my head, seeking that white something up among the trees. It was gone! I paused to wipe the perspiration from my brow, and tore my collar loose. A sudden shower of leaves came down upon my head; there was another zigzag flash of lightning, a nearby roll of thunder, and the sinister patter of raindrops falling about me like leaden bullets. The storm had burst.

"Heedless of all the intangible horrors of that lonely spot in the forest, maddened by terror at the inexplicable things which had befallen me, I stumbled back to the pulsating automobile, clambered in, and sent it forward headlong on the road to the left, – the well-beaten road, – the road which bore evidence of constant travel. The pace was furious; for somewhere behind me I felt was a misty, floating figure of white, and somewhere a woman screaming. The rain beat me in the face steadily; the lightning burst forth in livid, flaming tongues; the thunder crashed about me, – and my only haven was Millen.

"Suddenly the road widened where a path cut through the dense wood, and was lost in a perspective of gloom. A single sidelong glance at it as I rushed past told me it was wider than would be naturally worn by persons passing, and yet not wide enough for my car, nor even for a narrow wagon. Here that road map was at fault again. I remembered that grimly, even as the automobile went splashing along through growing pools of water and invisible ruts in the wagonway. I clung grimly to the steering wheel with only one idea in mind: to get to Millen. Already I was wet through from the terrific downpour, and a chilling numbness was seizing upon my limbs.

"Gradually the road turned toward the left, or so it seemed to me. But that too might have been the effect of an overwrought brain. The road did not look so much travelled now, despite the deceptive ruts into which my wheels sank with maddening frequency. Yet beneath its sheet of water the steadily gleaming lights showed that there was a road, plainly marked. For a minute or more, I suppose, I went straight on, desperately, recklessly; then an illuminating flash across the sky showed me that I was plunging into open country, and that the forest was gradually receding.

"Finally, through the swirling, drenching rain, I saw a faint rosy point in the distance. Whatever it was, a lantern I supposed, it at least indicated the presence of some fellow human being. I drove straight toward it. The gleam did not falter or fade. Another dazzling burst of lightning answered my question as to the nature of the light. It was in a farm house, – a farm house out here where there weren't any farm houses, squatting in an open field, a ramshackle, two-storied affair. But at least it would serve to shelter me from the fury of the storm. I took in all of it at one glance, even to a small shed in the rear where I might store my machine.

"I didn't pause to call as I drew near, but drove to the shed and ran my car in. Then, guided by the constant lightning flashes, I walked round to the front of the farm house, passing through the stream of light from the window as I went. It cheered me, that light. It offered an unexpected haven, that physical refreshment of which I was so much in need, possible companionship, and above all a refuge.

"I knocked on the front door loudly, the thunder was rolling incessantly now, then shook the water from my dripping garments. I waited – waited patiently enough for half a minute, I suppose. There was no answering sound of any sort, and again I knocked, this time insistently, even clamorously. Still no answer. It was not difficult to imagine that the continuous roar of the elements had drowned the feeble knock, and I repeated the performance with several thumping, banging variations. Still no answer.

"Even in this desperate strait I did not care to enter the house as a thief might, by forcing my way, and run the risk too of being received as a thief, possibly with a bullet. So I stepped down from the veranda, and went to the lighted window, intending to attract attention by rapping on the glass. My first glimpse told me no one was there; but the room gave every evidence of occupancy. A big cheerful log fire was burning, and its flickering light showed books strewn about here and there, inviting chairs, a table, and all the little knickknacks that make a comfortable sitting room. There beside that brightly blazing fire was comfort, and here the penetrating chill of the storm.

"I had no further scruples about it. I was going into that room! I ran up the steps, and was just reaching out my hand to try the knob, when the latch clicked, and slowly, silently, the door swung open. Naturally I expected to meet some one, – some one who had anticipated me in lifting the latch, – but I saw no one. The door had merely opened, revealing a rather long, broad hallway, with a stair in the distance, and unlighted save for the reflection from the sitting room. I took just two steps across the threshold, enough to get out of the swirling rain, then stopped and called. No one answered. I called a second time. For a wonder the thunders were silent just then, and there was no sound save that of my own voice. I ventured along the hall to the sitting room door and looked in. It was cozy, warm, comfortable, more so even than I had imagined when I looked in through the window.

"All at once I was overcome by a guilty sense of intrusion. What right had I to enter a strange house at this time of night in this manner, even to get out of a storm? My personal safety seemed at stake, somehow. I turned and started back for the door by which I had entered, with the intention of remaining there till in someway I could attract the attention of the occupants of the house.

"But I didn't reach the door; for directly in front of me stood a man. He was tall, angular, aged, and a little bent. A straggling gray beard almost covered his face, and thick gray hair hung down limply from beneath the brim of an old slouch hat. He was beside me, almost within reach of my hand, almost treading upon my toes with his great boots, and yet I had not heard one sound, except when the door clicked as I entered. It all came to me at once, and I shivered involuntarily.

"'I must apologize—' I began; but I got no further. He had not heard me, had not even seen me, if I might judge by the manner in which he walked slowly past me with his chin upon his breast, and his hands clasped behind his back. I stepped back to avoid a collision.

"'I beg your pardon—' I began again; but he had disappeared into the sitting room, stalked away noiselessly without even a glance in my direction, leaving me dripping, chilly, and overcome by the indefinable sense of impending danger.

"I paused there in the hall and pondered the situation. Surely the old man had seen me. But I had spoken! Of course, it was possible that he had neither seen nor heard me; yet-yet—

"'I'm going in there, and I am going to stay until the storm moderates!' I told myself. 'Perhaps it is just a peculiar old man's way.'

"I removed my automobile coat, hung it upon a peg, walked along the hallway with a firm tread, and stepped into the sitting room. It was deserted!

"There are moments in every man's life when the weight of a revolver in his hand is tremendously reassuring. This was mine. I drew the weapon from my hip pocket, examined it, and thrust it into my coat within easy reach of my right hand. Then I stood by the table, drumming my fingers upon it idly,

THE GRINNING GOD 157

and debating with myself as to what I should do. I was looking toward the door by which I had entered. No one came in, and yet—Suddenly the gray bearded old man was throwing a log on the fire. The flames shot up and the sparks flew; but there was not the crackle of fresh burning wood as there should have been – just this silent old man. My heart was in my throat, and I laughed sheepishly.

" 'You startled me,' I explained foolishly in apology.

"He did not look at me; but busied himself about the room for a moment, and laid his hat upon a couch. Then he went out by the door into the hallway.

" 'Well, upon my soul!' I ejaculated.

"I sat down and deliberately waited for the old man to return. The uncanniness of it all was growing upon me, the silence of his great boots as he walked, the fire which didn't crackle as it burned, the lack of any sign or movement to indicate that he had recognized my presence. Was the old man real? I came to my feet with an exclamation. Or was it – was it some weird continuation of that horrible thing in the forest?

"I put out a cold, clammy hand to the fire. That seemed real – at least a warmth came to me, and gradually my fingers lost their numbness, and looking upon my own hand I fell to remembering the hands of my strange host. They were knotted, toil worn, and the left forefinger was missing. That fact struck sharply upon my memory, and I remembered too a scar over one eye when he removed his hat. That all seemed real too, as did these things upon the mantel here in front of me: an empty spool, an alabaster cat, glaring red and white, a piece of crystal of peculiar shape upon the farthermost corner. And near it, so close that at first it seemed a part of it, was a queer little ivory god sitting upon his haunches, grinning hideously.

"I lifted the ivory image and examined it curiously. It was real enough. I had stepped back from the mantel a pace to let the firelight fall upon it, when suddenly I knew that the old man had returned. I didn't hear him, I hadn't seen him, – I merely knew he was there. I felt it. I slipped the little image into my pocket involuntarily as I turned; for all my interest was instantly transferred to a tray of food which the old man carried. I remembered I was hungry.

"He placed the things upon the table in the same ghostly silence. There was a jug of milk, some jelly, a little pat of butter, and several biscuits. I went forward and thanked him. He was absolutely impassive, seeing nothing, hearing nothing, and seeming to have no connection with the things around him. He didn't invite me to eat, – I assumed that privilege and gingerly poked a finger into a biscuit. It felt like a biscuit. I bit it; it tasted like a biscuit. In fact, I am convinced to this day that it was a biscuit. And against the reality of that biscuit was the silent old man and his ghostly tread.

"Real, or unreal, the food was refreshing and good, and I fell to with a will. The old man sat down in a rocker by the fire and folded his hands in his lap. I ventured a remark about the storm. He didn't answer. I really had not expected that he would. The modest supper brought a tingle to my blood again. My rioting nerves were calmed, the room cozy, the fire comfortable. I was beginning to enjoy this singular experience; but an occasional glance at the swaying rocker where the old man sat by the fire kept expectation on the *qui vive*. The rocker swayed dismally, but without the slightest sound.

"The warmth, the food, and my utter exhaustion conspired to make me a little drowsy, and I think once I must have closed my eyes. I opened them with a start. From somewhere above me, below me, or outside where the storm still growled, came that awful, heart tearing scream again, ending in a wail that brought me to my feet. The old man did not heed the quick movement by the slightest sign, – he was still comfortably rocking.

" 'What is it?' I demanded. 'What is it?'

"Revolver in hand, I rushed toward the door leading into the hallway. The old man was there ahead of me. He didn't touch me, and yet imperceptibly I was forced aside. He crossed the hall and went up the stairs. After a moment I heard a door open and shut.

"Except for the noise of the storm, the scream, and my own voice, it was the only sound I had heard since I entered the house.

"I went up those stairs; why I cannot say, except that something, a vague, undefined curiosity, seemed to impel me. And with this impulse came again, stronger than ever, that sense of personal danger to myself – the feeling that had possessed me ever since I entered the house.

"I groped my way through the darkness to the top of the stairs; then my hand ran along a wall till I came to an open door. I stood there a moment undecided whether to investigate further or to retrace my steps. I was on the point of going back down the stairs; but the flare of a candle almost in my face stopped me. The old man held the candle, shading it with his left hand, from which the forefinger was missing. The wavering light gave the withered old face a strangely drawn expression.

"He was within three feet of me, gazing straight into my face, and yet I felt, I knew, he didn't see me. It occurred to me even then that it was the first time I had seen his eyes. They were white and glassy. Blind? I do not know. For one moment he stood there staring, then passing me entered the room beyond, where he put down the candle. I followed him into the room as a moth follows a flame. It was the light, I think, that lured me in. Here once for all I would make an end of the thing. The old man, still noiselessly, went out the door by which he had entered, off through the darkness – somewhere. The door swung to. Like a madman I sprang forward and shot the bolt. I don't know why.

"I felt caged. Whatever was to come, was to come here! It was an intuition more strongly upon me than the sense of danger.

I sat down on a clean little bed and stared thoughtfully at the single door, – that only way out save one of two small windows which I imagined overlooked the yard. I examined my revolver carefully. Every chamber was loaded, and the cylinder whirled easily. Well and good. I waited. What for? I don't know.

"The candle burned with a straight, unwavering flame, while I crouched there on the bed for a long time. The grumble of thunder was growing faint and far away; but the rain swished against the windows in sheets. Here was a vigil, it seemed, and a long one; for sleep seemed hopelessly out of the question despite the insistent drowsiness of exhaustion. I wondered if the candle would last throughout the night. It was not yet half burned. I gazed at it with a certain returning sense of assurance; and as I gazed it flickered, flared up suddenly, and went out.

"I don't know what happened then. It might have been ten minutes later, or it might have been half a dozen hours, when strangling, choking fumes of smoke aroused me. My lungs were bursting for air. I struggled up on the bed, and was instantly conscious of the crackling sound of burning wood—of fire. The house was on fire! I rushed toward the bolted door, to find the flames already eating through the thin panels, and little red tongues shot out at me. I was cut off from the stairs.

"From there to one of the little windows! The glow far out through the rain told me instantly that the structure was aflame. I glanced downward. Sinuous forks were below me, on each side of me, above me. There was nothing to do but jump. I had only a moment to decide. I drew in my breath and pulled myself upon the ledge.

"And then again I heard that scream. Far across the open field where the glow from the blaze dimmed off into the shadows, I saw faintly a misty white figure with outstretched arms fleeing toward the forest. A little behind the floating white figure, and nearer to me, well within the range of the firelight, the old man was following. Even at the distance I could see that his chin drooped upon his chest and his hands clasped behind his back. That was all I saw.

"The next instant I had jumped.

"I found myself in my automobile skimming along a smooth, hard road that led through a forest. It was not familiar, and I don't know in what direction I was headed, nor did it matter then so long as I got away from those things behind. My ankle was broken, my clothing torn and burned in spots, and my head was throbbing with pain.

"Then I found myself in what seemed to be a street in a small city. A faint, rosy line was just tinging the eastern sky. Houses to right and left of me were closed forbiddingly; but just ahead was the solitary figure of a man, walking slowly along, swinging a stick. I ran the automobile alongside him, shouting some senseless question, then fell forward fainting. My last recollection was of shutting off power.

"When I recovered consciousness it was to find myself upon a cot in a strange room, perhaps a hospital. A physician was bandaging my ankle. A thousand questions leaped to my lips; and some of them burst forth in a torrent.

" 'Don't talk!' commanded the physician brusquely.

" 'But where am I?' I insisted.

" 'Millen,' he responded tersely. 'Don't talk!'

"It struck me curiously that I should be here, – that I should have reached the point for which I was bound even after all that had happened to me. It seemed centuries since I had left Pelham somewhere behind. Perhaps it was all a dream. But those screams! That silent old man! This broken ankle! I dropped into agonizing slumber after awhile, – the sleep of sheer exhaustion, – but asleep I lived again those awful moments which had almost driven me mad.

"On the following day I was calmer. The physician asked me some questions, and I answered them to the best of my ability. He did not smile at my fright; only shook his head and gave me something which made me sleep again. And so for a week I lay there, helpless, half asleep, and half awake. But one day I awoke to clear consciousness, comparatively free of the torture of the broken ankle, and myself again. Then the physician and I discussed the matter at length.

"He listened respectfully as I repeated it all, and at the end shook his head.

" 'There is no intersecting road between the small store of which you speak and the outskirts of Millen,' he said positively.

" 'But, man, I was there!' I protested. 'I turned into the other road, and ran along till I saw the house in the open field. I tell you —'

"But he let me go no further. I knew why. He thought it was some mental vagary; for after awhile he gave me a pill and went away. So I resolved to solve the matter for myself. I would go back along that road by day, and find that silent old man, and, if not the house itself, the charred spot where it had stood. I would know that intersection; I would know even the path which led from the mysterious road off into the wood. When I found these I knew the maze would fade into some simple, plain explanation – perhaps even an absurd one.

"So I bided my time. In the course of another week I was able to leave my cot and hobble about with the aid of crutches. It was then that I took the physician in my car, and we went back along the highway toward Pelham. It was all unfamiliar ground to me; there was no road, and suddenly there ahead of me was the little store where I had bought the gasolene that night. I would question the old man I had seen there; but there was no old man. The little store was unoccupied; it seemed to have been unoccupied for weeks.

"I turned back and traversed the road toward Millen again. I recognized nothing; I couldn't find a trace of a bypath from the highway in any direction. And once more I went over the ground at night. Nothing! After that the physician, a singularly patient man, accompanied me as I hobbled through the forest on each side of the road seeking that house, or its ashes. I never saw anything to lead me, to even suggest, a single incident of that awful night.

" 'I know the country, every inch of it,' the physician told me. 'There isn't any such place as you mention.'

"And — well, that's all. I know his opinion was that my story was some sort of delusion — a dream. But how he accounts for the broken ankle I don't know. Then the condition of my clothing! I had been compelled to discard everything I wore for garments sent down from the city. And so in time I came to believe the experience a dream. I was growing content with this story, even knowing it to be wrong, because it brought mental rest, and was beginning to be myself again.

"Then one day I had occasion to search the coat I had worn that night for some papers which had been misplaced. In the course of the search I thrust my hand into an outside pocket, and drew out — a little ivory god, sitting on his haunches, grinning hideously!

"Now I am like this — and the little god sits up laughing at me. He knows!"

When he had finished reading, The Thinking Machine dropped back into the chair, with squint eyes turned steadily upward, and long slender fingers pressed tip to tip. Hutchinson Hatch, reporter, sat staring in silence at the drawn, inscrutable face of the scientist.

"And the writer of this?" demanded The Thinking Machine at last.

"His name is Harold Fairbanks," the reporter explained. "He was removed to an asylum yesterday, hopelessly insane."

PART II. THE HOUSE THAT WAS

By Jacques Futrelle

   Editor's Note. – Mrs Futrelle undertook to set up a problem which The Thinking Machine could not solve. "Wraiths of the Storm," presented what she thought to be a mystery story impossible of solution. Printer's proofs of the story were submitted to Mr Futrelle, who, after frequent consultations with Professor Van Dusen, – The Thinking Machine, – evolved "The House that Was" as the perfect solution.

The Thinking Machine lowered his squint eyes and favored Hutchinson Hatch with a long, steady stare which for the moment seemed totally to obliterate him as a personality. Gradually, under the continued unseeing but tense gaze, there grew upon the newspaper man a singular sense of utter transparency, a complete invisibility, an uncomfortable feeling of not being present. He laughed a little finally, and lighted a cigarette.

"As I was saying," Hatch began, "this Harold Fairbanks is hopelessly insane, and—"

"I imagine," interrupted the eminent man of science, – "I imagine that this insanity of Fairbanks's is rather a maniacal condition?"

"Yes," Hatch told him. "I was going to say—"

"And that possibly it took a homicidal turn?" The Thinking Machine continued.

"Yes," the reporter assented. "He tried to—"

"Against a woman, perhaps?"

"Precisely. The direct cause of his—"

"Please don't interrupt, Mr Hatch!" snapped The Thinking Machine. He was silent for a time; Hatch smiled whimsically. "The object of his homicidal mania," the scientist continued slowly, as if feeling his way, "was–was his mother?"

"Yes."

Hatch dropped back into his chair and met the squint blue eyes fairly. He was not surprised at this statement of the case, thus far correct, because he was accustomed to the unerring accuracy of the master mind behind those eyes; but he was curious to know just how far that logical brain would follow a circumstantial thread which it had developed of itself out of an apparent nothingness. Nothing in the manuscript, nothing he had said, had even indicated, to his mind, the more recent developments.

The leaves of the manuscript fluttered through the slender white fingers of The Thinking Machine, and the straight line of the thin lips was drawn down a little as he glanced over a page or so.

"He shot at her?" he queried at last.

"Three times," the reporter informed him. The Thinking Machine raised his eyes quickly, inquiringly, to those of the newspaper man. "She was not wounded," the reporter hastened to say. "The shots went wild."

"That happened in Fairbanks's own room?"

"Yes."

"At night?"

"Yes; about one o'clock."

"Of course!" exclaimed the little scientist crabbedly. "I know that." Again there was a pause. "Mrs Fairbanks has a room near that of her son—perhaps on the same floor?"

"Just across the hall."

"And she was awakened by some unusual noise in his room?"

"She hadn't been to sleep." The reporter smiled.

"Oh!" and again The Thinking Machine's squint eyes were turned toward the ceiling. "Some unusual noise attracted her attention, then?"

"Yes," the reporter agreed.

"Screams?"

"Yes."

The Thinking Machine nodded. "So she ran to her son's room just as she was – in a white night robe, I imagine?"

"Precisely."

The reporter was leaning forward in his chair now, staring into the impassive face before him. Still he wasn't surprised – he was merely curious and interested in the workings of that mind which laid before him in order these incidents which were not known to it by any tangible method.

"And as she entered her son's room," the scientist resumed, "he shot at her?"

"Three times – yes."

The Thinking Machine was silent for a long time. "That's all?" he remarked inquiringly at last.

"Well, Fairbanks was raving, of course," and Hatch dropped back in his chair. "He was over-powered by two servants, and—"

"Yes, I know," broke in The Thinking Machine. "He is now in a padded cell in a private asylum somewhere." This was not a question; it was a statement. "And this manuscript was found in his room after he had gone?"

"It lay open on his table. That is his handwriting," explained the newspaper reporter.

The Thinking Machine arose and walked the length of the room three times. Finally he stopped before the newspaper man. "And is there really such a thing as this grinning god that he describes?" he demanded.

"Certainly," Hatch responded, and his tone indicated surprise.

"Not necessarily certain," said the scientist sharply. "Do you know there is a grinning god?"

"Yes," replied the newspaper man emphatically. "It was taken away from Fairbanks when he was locked up. He fought like a fiend for it."

"Naturally," was the terse comment. "You have seen it, have you?"

"Yes, I saw it. It's about six inches tall, seems to be cut from a solid piece of ivory, and—"

"And has shiny eyes?" interrupted the other.

"Yes. The eyes seem to be of amethyst, highly polished."

Again The Thinking Machine walked the length of the room three times. "Do you know anything about self hypnotism, Mr Hatch?" he inquired at last.

"Only that there is such a thing," replied the reporter, wondering at the abrupt change in the trend of the conversation. "Why?"

The Thinking Machine didn't say why. "You came to me, of course, to see if it was possible, by throwing light on this affair, to restore Fairbanks's mind?" he inquired instead.

"Well, that was the idea," Hatch agreed. "Fairbanks was evidently driven to his present condition by the haunting mystery of this thing, by brooding over it, and by the tangible existence in his hands of that ivory god which established a definite connection with an experience which might otherwise have been only a nightmare, and it occurred to me that if he could be made to see just what had happened and the underlying causes for its happening, he might be brought back to a normal condition." The reporter was silent for a moment, with eyes set on the drawn, inscrutable face of The Thinking Machine. "Of course," he added, "I am presuming that if it was not a diseased mental condition the things as he set them down did happen, and if they did happen I know you won't believe that they were due to other than natural causes."

"I don't disbelieve in anything, Mr Hatch," and The Thinking Machine regarded the newspaper man quietly. "I don't even disbelieve in what is broadly termed the supernatural — I merely don't know. It is necessary, in the solution of material problems, to work from a material basis, and then the things which are conjured up by fear and – and failure to understand may be dissipated. That is done by logic, Mr Hatch. Disregard the supernatural, so called, in our material problems, and logic is as inevitable as that two and two make four, not sometimes, but all the time."

"You don't deny the possibility of the so called supernatural, then?" Hatch asked, and again there was a note of surprise in his voice.

"I don't deny anything until I know," was the response. "I don't know that there is a supernatural force; therefore," and he shrugged his slender, stooping shoulders, "I work only from a material basis. If this manuscript states facts, then Fairbanks saw an old man, not a spook; he saw a woman, not a wraith; he jumped to escape a real fire, not a ghost fire. When we disregard the supernatural, we must admit that everything was real, unless it was pure invention, and the broken ankle and burned clothing are against that. If these were real people, we can find them – that's all there is to that. Yet there is a chance that the whole tale is a fiction, or the product of a disordered brain. But even that being true, it interferes in no way with the inevitable logic of the affair. When we know that this manuscript is in existence, and when we know that the man who produced it has since become a raving maniac, the sheer logic of the thing reveals clearly the intermediate steps."

"How, for instance?" Hatch inquired curiously.

"Well, we have this," and The Thinking Machine rattled the sheets of the manuscript impatiently; "and while we'll admit it was written by a sane man, we know that that man has since become a maniac. I stated the incidents which led to his incarceration as logic unfolded them to me. First I knew that insanity from fear and failure to understand nearly always takes the maniacal turn; therefore I saw that instead of being insane, as you stated first, Fairbanks was probably a maniac. There is a difference."

The reporter nodded.

"Next, one of the first manifestations of a maniacal condition is a homicidal tendency. Did Fairbanks attempt homicide? Yes.

"Now the problem grew a little more complex, rather intricately – psychological, if I may say it that way," The Thinking Machine explained precisely. "However, it goes back generally to the broad grounds that a woman in a flowing white night robe typifies the popular conception of the ghostly, and when we know that this supposed wraith, or one of them, was a woman in white, we see that in Fairbanks's condition at the moment the appearance of such a figure would have instantly aroused him to the frenzy which led to the subsequent events."

"I understand, so far," Hatch remarked.

"Now the only woman – the most likely woman, I should say – to go to his room in a white night robe was his mother." He paused for a moment. "Therefore, his mother was in all probability the object of his attack. Remember, he was mad with fear, and, appearing suddenly as she did, perhaps in a dim light, she was to his disordered brain the incarnation of that thing he most feared."

Hatch seemed to be perfectly fascinated. His cigarette burned up until the fire touched his fingers; and he barely noticed it.

"In this manuscript," The Thinking Machine resumed after a moment, "Fairbanks tells me that he had a revolver, and shows a distinct weakness for the weapon. Therefore, wouldn't he shoot at this incarnation of the thing which was responsible for his condition. He did shoot. The fact that the incidents happened in Fairbanks's own room at night was an assumption based upon the fact that his mother figured in it, and the further fact that she was dressed for bed when she appeared in his room. Of course, if her room was near, her attention would be attracted by some unusual noise. If these noises were due to a maniac, they were in all probability screams."

"Well, by George!" Hatch remarked fervently. "It's —"

"Now the first thing to do is to see Fairbanks in person," interrupted The Thinking Machine, with a sudden change to a most business like tone. "I think, if he can comprehend at all, that I may be able to do something for him."

The Thinking Machine – Professor Augustus S. F. X. Van Dusen, scientist – was cordially, even deferentially, received by Dr Pollock, physician in charge of the Westbrook Sanatorium.

"I should like to spend ten minutes in the padded cell with Fairbanks," he announced tersely.

Dr Pollock regarded him curiously, but without surprise. "It's dangerous," he remarked doubtfully. "I have no objection, of course; but I should advise that a couple of keepers go in with you."

"I'll go alone," announced the diminutive man of science. "It may be that I can quiet him." Dr Pollock merely stared. "By the way," The Thinking Machine added, "you have that little ivory god here, haven't you? Well, let me see it, please."

It was produced and subjected to a searching scrutiny, after which the scientist set it up on a table, dropped into a seat facing it, leaned forward on his elbows, and sat staring straight into the amethyst eyes for a long time. A curious silence fell upon the watchers as he sat there immovable, minute after minute, staring, staring. Hatch absently glanced at his watch and went over and looked out the window. The thing was getting on his nerves.

At last the scientist arose and thrust the grinning god into his pocket. "Now, please," he directed curtly, "I shall go into the cell with Fairbanks alone. I want the door closed behind me, and I want that door to remain closed for ten minutes. Under no circumstances must there be any interruption." He turned upon Dr Pollock. "Don't have any fears for me. I'm not a fool."

Dr Pollock led the way along the corridor, down some stairs, and paused before a door.

"Just ten minutes – no more, no less," directed the scientist.

THE GRINNING GOD

The key was inserted in the lock, and the door swung on its hinges. Instantly the ears of the three men outside were assailed by a torrent of screams, of blasphemy, hideous imprecations. The maniac rushed for the door, and Hatch for an instant gazed straight into a distorted, pallid face in which there was no trace of intelligence, or even of humanity. He turned away with a shudder. Dr Pollock thrust his arm forward to stay the swaying figure, and glanced round at The Thinking Machine doubtfully.

"Look at me! Look at me!" commanded the scientist sharply, and the squint blue eyes fearlessly met the glitter of madness in the eyes of Fairbanks. He raised his right hand suddenly in front of his face, and instantly the incoherent ravings stopped, while some strange, sudden change came over the maniacal face. In the scientist's right hand was the grinning god. That was the magic which had stilled the ravings. Slowly, slowly, with his eyes fixed upon those of the maniac, the scientist edged his way into the cell, Fairbanks retreating almost imperceptibly. Never for an instant did the maniacal eyes leave the ivory image; yet he made no attempt to seize it, he seemed merely fascinated.

"Close the door," directed The Thinking Machine quietly, without so much as a glance back. "Ten minutes!"

Dr Pollock closed the door and turned the key in the lock, after which he looked at the newspaper man with an expression of frank bewilderment on his face. Hatch said nothing, only glanced at his watch and went over to the window, where he stood staring out moodily, with every nerve strained to catch any sound which might by chance penetrate the heavy, padded walls.

One minute, two minutes, three minutes! The second hand of Hatch's watch moved at a snail's pace! Four minutes, five minutes, six minutes! Then through the well nigh impenetrable wall came faintly the sound of hoarse cries, of screams, and finally the crash of something falling. Dr Pollock's face paled a little and he turned the key in the lock.

"No!" and Hatch sprang forward to seize the physician's hand.

"But he's in danger," declared the doctor emphatically; "maybe even killed!" Again he tugged at the door.

"No!" said Hatch again, and he shoved the physician aside. "He said ten minutes, and – and I know the man!"

Eight minutes! Listening tensely, they knew that the screaming had stopped; there was dead silence. Nine minutes! Still they stood there, Hatch guarding the door, and his eyes unflinchingly fixed on the physician's face. Ten minutes! And Hatch opened the door.

Professor Augustus S. F. X. Van Dusen – The Thinking Machine – was sitting calmly on a padded seat beside Harold Fairbanks, with one slender hand resting on his pulse. Fairbanks himself sat with his ivory image held close up to his eyes, babbling and mumbling at it incoherently. An overturned table lay in the middle of the cell. So great had been the power used to upset it that an iron bolt which held it fast to the floor had been broken short off. The scientist arose and came toward them; and Hatch drew a deep breath of relief.

"I would advise that this man be placed in another cell," said the little scientist quietly. "There is no further need to keep him in a padded cell. Put him somewhere where he can see out and find something to attract his attention. Meanwhile let him keep that ivory image, and there'll be no more raving."

"What – what did you do to him?" demanded the physician in deep perplexity.

"Nothing – yet," was the enigmatic response. "I'd like for him to stay here a couple of days longer, under constant watch as to his physical condition, – never mind his mental condition now, – and then with your permission I'll make a little experiment which I believe will restore him to a normal condition. Meanwhile he needs the best of physical care. Let him babble, – he will, anyway, – that doesn't matter just now."

Harold Fairbanks sat beside The Thinking Machine in the second seat of a huge touring car, with the slender hand of the scientist resting lightly on his wrist. In front of them the chauffeur was busy with the multiple levers of the great machine; and behind them sat Hutchinson Hatch and Dr Pollock. They were scudding along a smooth road, with the wind beating in their faces, guided by the ribbons of light which shot out ahead from their forward lamps. The night was perfectly black, with not a light point visible save those carried by their own car.

Behind them lay the quiet little village of Pelham, and miles away in front was the town of Millen. From time to time as the car rushed on The Thinking Machine peered inquisitively through the darkness into the face of the man beside him; but he could barely make out its general shape, – a pallid splotch in the darkness. The hand lay quietly beside his own, and a senile voice mumbled and babbled – that was all. The newspaper man and the physician in the rear seat had nothing to say; they too were peering vainly at Fairbanks.

At last through the gloom the outlines of a small building loomed dimly in front of them, just off the road to the left. The Thinking Machine leaned forward and touched the chauffeur on the arm.

"We'll stop here for gasolene," he said distinctly.

"Gasolene – stop here for gasolene!" babbled a senseless voice beside him.

The Thinking Machine felt the hand he held move spasmodically as the huge car ran off the main roadway and maneuvered back and forth to clear the fairway of its bulk. Finally it stopped, with its tonneau, end on, within a few feet of the door of the building. The scientist's fingers closed more tightly on the wrist; and after a moment the incoherent mumbling began again.

Hutchinson Hatch and Dr Pollock arose and got out. Hatch went straight to the little building and rapped sharply. The sound caused Fairbanks to turn vacant, wavering eyes in that direction. After a moment a nightcapped head appeared at the window above. The Thinking Machine shot an electric flashlight into Fairbanks's face. The eyes, now fixed on the nightcapped head, were wide open, and a glint of childish curiosity lay in them. The babblings were silent for a moment,—somewhere in a recess of the maddened brain a germ of intelligence was struggling. Then, as the scientist regarded him steadily, the expression of the face changed again, the eyes grew vacant, the mouth flabby, the senile mumblings began again.

Hatch began and concluded negotiations for five gallons of gasolene. A shrunken shanked old man brought it out in a can, delivered it, and scuttled back into the house with his safety lantern. Dr Pollock and Hatch took their seats again, while The Thinking Machine clambered out and went round to the back, where he spoke to the chauffeur, who was busy at the tank. The chauffeur nodded as if he understood, and followed the scientist to his seat.

"Now for Millen," directed the scientist quietly.

"Millen!" Fairbanks repeated meaninglessly.

The chauffeur twisted his wheel, backed a little, caught the forward clutch, whirled his car straight to the road again, and shot out through the darkness. For two or three minutes there was utter silence, save for the chug and whir of the engine and the clanking rattle of the car; then The Thinking Machine spoke over his shoulder to Hatch and Dr Pollock.

"Did either of you notice anything peculiar?" he inquired.

"No," was the simultaneous response. "Why?"

"Mr Hatch, you have that automobile map," the scientist continued without heeding the question. "Take this electric light and examine it once more, to satisfy us that there is no road between the little store and Millen."

"I know there isn't," Hatch told him.

"Do as I say!" directed the other crabbedly. "We can't afford to make mistakes."

Obediently enough Hatch and Dr Pollock studied the map. There was the road, straight away from the star, to Millen. There was not a bypath or deviation of any kind marked on it.

"Straight as a string," Hatch announced.

"Now look!" directed The Thinking Machine.

The huge car slowed up and came to a standstill. The glittering lamps of the car showed two roads instead of one — two roads, here where there were not two roads! Hatch glared at them for a moment, then fumbled with the automobile map.

"Why, hang it! there can't be two roads!" he declared.

"But there they are," replied The Thinking Machine.

He felt Fairbanks's hand flutter, and then it was raised suddenly. Again he threw the light on the pallid face. A strange expression was there; a set, incredible, vague expression which might have meant anything. The eyes were turned ahead to where the road was split by a small clump of trees.

"Keep on to your left," The Thinking Machine directed the chauffeur, without, however, removing his eyes from the face of the man beside him. "A little more slowly."

The car started up again and swung off to the left, sharply. Every eye, save the squint, blue ones of the scientist, was turned ahead; he was still staring into the face of his patient. His light still showed realization struggling feebly there. Perhaps only the chauffeur realized what a steady turn to the left the car made; but he said nothing, only felt his way along till suddenly the road widened a little where a path cut through the dense forest, and was lost in the perspective of gloom. The car slowed up.

"Don't stop!" commanded the scientist sharply. "Go ahead!"

With a sudden spurt the car rushed forward, skimming along easily for a time, and then the heavy jolting told them all that the road was growing rougher, and here, dimly ahead of them, they saw an open patch of sky. It was evidently the edge of the forest. The car went steadily on and out into the open, clear of the forest; then the chauffeur slowed down.

"There isn't any road here," he remarked.

"Go on!" commanded The Thinking Machine tensely. "Road or no road – straight ahead!"

The chauffeur took a new grip on his wheel and went straight ahead, over plowed ground, apparently, for the bumping and jolting were terrific, and the steering gear tore at the sockets of his arms viciously. For two or three minutes they proceeded this way, while the scientist's light still played on Fairbanks's face and the squint eyes unwaveringly watched every tiny change in it.

"There!" shrieked Fairbanks suddenly, and he came to his feet. "There!"

Hatch and Dr Pollock saw it at the same instant, – a faint, rosy point in the distance; The Thinking Machine didn't alter the direction of his gaze.

"Straight for the light!" he commanded.

...the room showed every evidence of occupancy... log fire was burning, and its flickering light showed books strewn about here and there... directly in front of them stood a man, tall, angular, aged, and a little bent... hands were knotted, toil worn; and the left forefinger was missing... eyes white and glassy!

With a choking, gutteral exclamation of some sort, Fairbanks darted forward and placed the grinning god upon the mantel beside a piece of crystal, then turned back to The Thinking Machine and seized him by the arm, as a child might have sought protection. The Thinking Machine nodded at him, and a grin of foolish delight overspread the pallid face.

Meanwhile, the strange old man, who seemed utterly oblivious of their presence, stood beside the fire gazing into it with sightless eyes. The scientist moved toward him slowly,

Fairbanks staring as if fascinated. Finally the scientist extended his hand, which held that of Fairbanks, and touched the old man on the shoulder. He started violently and stretched out both hands instinctively.

Then, while Hatch and Dr Pollock looked on silently, The Thinking Machine stood motionless, while the strange old man's hands ran up his arm, and the fingers touched his face. The right fore-finger paused for an instant at the eyes, then was laid lightly across the thin lips. It remained there.

"You are blind?" asked the scientist.

The strange old man nodded.

"You are deaf?"

Again the old man nodded. His forefinger still rested lightly on The Thinking Machine's lips.

"You are dumb?" the scientist went on. Again the nod.

"Deafness, dumbness, blindness, result of disease?"

The nod again.

The Thinking Machine turned and lifted Fairbanks's hand till it rested on the old man's shoulder, then slowly down the arm, while his eyes studied the changed expression on the pallid face.

"Real, real!" said The Thinking Machine slowly to Fairbanks. "A man – you understand?"

Fairbanks merely started back; but it was evident that some great struggle was going on in his mind. There was a growing interest in his face, the mouth was no longer flabby, the eyes were fixed.

...then there came another sound... a curdling, nerve-racking scream... a scream of agony, of pain, of fear... a hideous, awful thing... suddenly all was silent again.

At the first sound Fairbanks straightened up, then slowly he started forward. Three steps, and he fell. Hatch and Dr Pollock turned him over and found on his face an expression of utter, cringing fear. The eyes were roving, glittering, and he was babbling again. Only his weakness had prevented flight.

"Stay there!" commanded The Thinking Machine hurriedly, and ran out of the room.

Hatch heard him as he went up the steps; then after a moment there came more screams, rather a sharp, intermittent wailing. Fairbanks struggled feebly, then lay still, flat on his back. A minute more, and The Thinking Machine reentered the room, leading a woman by the hand – a woman in a gingham apron and with her hair flying loose about her face. He went straight to the old man, who had stood motionless through it all, and raised the toilworn finger to his lips.

"A woman is here – your wife?" he asked.

The old man shook his head.

"Your sister?"

The old man nodded.

"She is insane?"

Again a nod.

The woman stood for an instant with roving eyes, then rushed toward the mantel with a peculiar sobbing cry. In another instant she had clasped the ugly ivory image to her withered breast, and was crooning to it softly as a mother to her babe. Fairbanks raised himself from the floor, stared at her dully for a moment, then fell back into the arms of Dr Pollock and Hatch with a sigh. He had fainted.

"I think, gentlemen, this is all," remarked The Thinking Machine.

It was more than a month later that The Thinking Machine called upon Harold Fairbanks at his home. The young man was sitting up in bed, weak but intelligently cognizant of everything about him. There was still an occasional restless roving of his eyes; but that was all.

"You remember me, Mr Fairbanks?" began the scientist.

"Yes," was the reply.

"You remember the events of the night we were together?"

"Everything, from the time the automobile left the road and the light appeared in the distance," said Fairbanks. "I remember seeing the old man again, and the woman appearing. I know now that he was deaf and dumb and blind, and that she was insane. That seems to clear the situation a great deal." He passed a wasted hand across his brow. "But where is the place. I couldn't find it."

"Listen for just a moment now, please," said The Thinking Machine soothingly. "You don't remember shooting at your mother? No. Don't excite yourself; she was not wounded. Immediately after that you were placed in a sanatorium. I saw you there. The ivory image had been taken away from you. I went into the room where you were confined and gave it back to you. It acted as I thought it would, – quieted you. To make certain that it was this and nothing else that had that effect, I took it away from you again, and you grew violent – as a matter of fact, your condition was such that you overturned a heavy table that was bolted to the floor – broke the bolt. You don't remember that?"

"No."

"I left the image with you. That really was the tangible cause of your condition. If it hadn't been for that, and the brooding over the mystery which it constantly caused, the events of that first night would have passed out of your mind in time. You superinduced self hypnotism with that little image; that is, you must understand that self hypnotism is possible to persons of a certain temperament in a mechanical way, when the object employed is highly polished – shiny, I might say.

"Although that image brought you to the condition you were in, I restored it to you to quiet you physically. That was necessary before I could reproduce for you the events of the first night. You went with us in an automobile, from Pelham to the little store where you had stopped that first night for gasolene. We stopped there for gasolene, and saw the man you saw that first night. As a matter of fact, he had gone away only for a few months, and is now installed in the little store again.

This was all done, you understand, to arouse you, if possible, to what was passing around you. In a way it succeeded.

"Well, from the little store we went as you went the night of your first trouble, until we came to the two roads, one leading by sharp turns to the left. Then we went straight to the farm house where the old man and the woman were. There I wanted to convince you that they were real people, – that there was nothing of the ghostly about them. As a matter of fact, that old man and the woman never knew you were in the house that night. The man had no means of knowing it so long as you never touched him nor he you. You say he brought in something to eat. In all probability that was intended for the woman. You assumed it was for yourself. The fire which compelled you to jump and which resulted in the broken ankle for you, did not destroy the house. There were still marks of it there but the heavy rain extinguished it, and carpenters made the necessary repairs. Now all that is clear, isn't it?"

"Perfectly," was the reply; "but the white thing in the road – the screaming I heard there?"

"There is no mystery whatever about that," continued the scientist calmly. "That road that turns to the left turns more sharply than you imagine. After a little distance it goes almost parallel with the main road, so that following it at night you would, without any knowledge of it, pass within a few hundred feet of a point on the main road. Now the house where these people live is say five hundred feet from the road that turns to the left therefore not more than eight hundred feet, we'll say, from the main road. Thus the screaming you heard in the main road was the woman who lived in that house; the figure you saw was that woman. Just why she had left the house and was wandering around through the wood does not appear; it is certain that she was there, and was frightened by the storm. I can only say that she might have known she was pursued by you and taken refuge on an overhanging limb, and thus gave

THE GRINNING GOD

you the impression of her figure rising above the ground and moving about among the trees.

"It followed naturally that by the time you had taken the roundabout way with your automobile and reached the house she had reached it by going straight ahead through the wood-say for eight hundred feet, and again you heard her screams there. Many things happened in that house that night of no consequence in themselves, but which to your excited imagination were mysterious. One of these was the candle going out. It is obvious that a gust of wind did that, or else a single drop of water from a leak in the roof. Do you follow me?"

Fairbanks was silent for several minutes as he lay back with his eyes closed. "But the vital thing, the real thing that bewildered me most of all," he said slowly, "you haven't touched. That is, Why was it that after all my searching for the road to the left and the farm house, I didn't find them, if they were there?"

"Of course you don't remember," explained The Thinking Machine; "but the night our party went over the route I asked Dr Pollock and Mr Hatch just after we left the little store whether they had noticed anything peculiar. They replied in the negative. As a matter of fact," and the scientist was speaking very quietly, "our automobile went the same way yours had gone — not toward Millen, as you supposed and they supposed, but back toward Pelham. You didn't find the road to the left and the farm house when you were searching, for the reason that they were beyond the little store toward Pelham, eight or ten miles away."

A great wave of relief swept over the young man, and he leaned forward eagerly. "But wouldn't I have known when I turned the wrong way?" he demanded.

The Thinking Machine shrugged his shoulders. "You would have known in daylight, yes," was the reply, "but at night, in a hurry and somewhat confused by the flying dust, you turned the wrong way – toward Pelham, not toward Millen. You see that is possible when I tell you that Dr Pollock and Mr Hatch didn't notice that we had turned the wrong way, when there was no storm, and when I asked them if they had noticed anything peculiar."

There was a long silence. Fairbanks dropped back in the bed and lay silent.

"In your manuscript," resumed The Thinking Machine at last, "you mentioned that you seemed to hear some one calling you as you started away from the little store. This you attributed vaguely to imagination. As a matter of fact, you did hear some one call—it was the man who sold you the gasolene. He knew you intended going to Millen, saw that you had turned the wrong way, and called to tell you so. You didn't wait to hear."

And that was all of it.

8

THE MYSTERY OF STUDIO A

I

Where the light slants down softly into one corner of a noted art museum in Boston there hangs a large picture. Its title is "Fulfillment." Discriminating art critics have alternately raved at it and praised it; from the day it appeared there it has been a fruitful source of acrimonious discussion. As for the public, it accepts the picture as a startling, amazing thing of beauty, and there is always a crowd around it.

"Fulfillment" is typified by a woman. She stands boldly forth against a languorous background of deep tones. Flesh tints are daringly laid on the semi-nude figure, diaphanous draperies hide, yet, reveal, the exquisite lines of the body. Her arms are outstretched straight toward the spectator, the black hair ripples down over her shoulders, the red lips are slightly parted. The mysteries of complete achievement and perfect life lie in her eyes.

Into this picture the artist wove the spiritual and the worldly; here he placed on canvas an elusive portrayal of success in its fullest and widest meaning. One's first impression of the picture is that it is sensual; another glance shows the underlying typification of success, and love and life are there. One by one the qualities stand forth.

The artist was Constans St. George. After the first flurry of excitement which the picture caused there came a whirlwind of criticism. Then the artist, who had labored for months on the work which he had intended and which proved to be his masterpiece, collapsed. Some said it was overwork—they were partly right; others that it was grief at the attacks of critics who did not see beyond the surface of the painting. Perhaps they, too, were partly right.

However that may be, it is a fact that for several months after the picture was exhibited St. George was in a sanitarium. The physicians said it was nervous collapse—a total breaking-down, and there were fears for his sanity. At length there came an improvement in his condition, and he returned to the world. Since then he had lived quietly in his studio, one of many in a large office building. From time to time he had been approached with offers for the picture, but always he refused to sell. A New York millionaire made a flat proposition of fifty thousand dollars, which was as flatly refused.

The artist loved the picture as a child of his own brain; every day he visited the museum where it was exhibited and stood looking at it with something almost like adoration in his eyes. Then he went away quietly, tugging at his straggling beard and with the dim blindness of tears in his eyes. He never spoke to anyone; and always avoided that moment when a crowd was about.

Whatever the verdict of the critics or of the public on "Fulfillment," it was an admitted fact that the artist had placed on canvas a representation of a wonderfully beautiful woman. Therefore, after awhile the question of who had been the model for "Fulfillment" was aroused. No one knew, apparently. Artists who knew St. George could give no idea—they only knew that the woman who had posed was not a professional model.

This led to speculation, in which the names of some of the most beautiful women in the United States were mentioned. Then a romance was woven. This was that the artist was in love with the original and that his collapse was partly due to her refusal to wed him. This story, as it went, was elaborated until the artist was said to be pining away for love of one whom he had immortalized in oils.

As the story grew it gained credence, and a search was still made occasionally for the model. Half a dozen times Hutchinson Hatch, a newspaper reporter of more than usual astuteness, had been on the story without success; he had seen and studied the picture until every line of it was firmly in his mind. He had seen and talked to St. George twice. The artist would answer no questions as to the identity of the model.

This, then, was the situation on the morning of Friday, November 27, when Hatch entered the reportorial rooms of his newspaper. At sight of him the City Editor removed his cigar, placed it carefully on the "official block" which adorned his flat-topped desk, and called to the reporter.

"Girl reported missing," he said, brusquely. "Name is Grace Field, and she lived at No. 195 – Street, Dorchester. Employed in the photographic department of the Star, a big department store. Report of her disappearance made to the police early today by Ellen Stanford, her roommate, also employed at the Star. Jump out on it and get all you can. Here is the official police description."

Hatch took a slip of paper and read:

"Grace Field, twenty-one years, five feet seven inches tall, weight 151 pounds, profuse black hair, dark-brown eyes, superb figure, oval face, said to be beautiful."

Then the description went into details of her dress and other things which the police note in their minute records for a search. Hatch absorbed all these things and left his office. He went first to the department store, where he was told Miss

Stanford had not appeared that day, sending a note that she was ill.

From the store Hatch went at once to the address given in Dorchester. Miss Stanford was in. Would she see a reporter? Yes. So Hatch was ushered into the modest little parlor of a boarding-house, and after awhile Miss Stanford entered. She was as a petite blonde, with pink cheeks and blue eyes, now reddened by weeping.

Briefly Hatch explained the purpose of his visit—an effort to find Grace Field, and Miss Stanford eagerly and tearfully expressed herself as willing to tell him all she knew.

"I have known Grace for five months," she explained; "that is, from the time she came to work at the Star. Her counter is next to mine. A friendship grew up between us, and we began rooming together. Each of us is alone in the East. She comes from the West, somewhere in Nevada, and I come from Quebec.

"Grace has never said much about herself, but I know that she had been in Boston a year or so before I met her. She lived somewhere in Brookline, I believe, but it seems that she had some funds and did not go to work until she came to the Star. This is as I understand it.

"Three days ago, on Tuesday it was, there was a letter for Grace when we came in from work. It seemed to agitate her, although she said nothing to me about what was in it, and I did not ask. She did not sleep well that night, but next morning, when we started to work, she seemed all right. That is, she was all right until we got to the subway station, and then she told me to go on to the store, saying she would be there after awhile.

"I left her, and at her request explained to the manager of our floor that she would be late. From that time to this no one has seen her or heard of her. I don't know where she could have gone," and the girl burst into tears. "I'm sure something dreadful has happened to her."

"Possibly an elopement?" Hatch suggested.

"No," said the girl, quickly. "No. She was in love, but the man she was in love with has not heard of her either. I saw him the night after she disappeared. He called here and asked for her, and seemed surprised that she had not returned home, or had not been at work."

"What's his name?" asked Hatch.

"He's a clerk in a bank," said Miss Stanford. "His name is Willis—Victor Willis. If she had eloped with him I would not have been surprised, but I am positive she did not, and if she did not, where is she?"

"Were there any other admirers you know of?" Hatch asked.

"No," said the girl, stoutly. "There may have been others who admired her, but none she cared for. She has told me too much-I-I know," she faltered.

"How long have you known Mr Willis?" asked Hatch.

The girl's face flamed scarlet instantly.

"Only since I've known Grace," she replied. "She introduced us."

"Has Mr Willis ever shown you any attention?"

"Certainly not," Miss Stanford flashed, angrily. "All his attention was for Grace."

There was the least trace of bitterness in the tone, and Hatch imagined he read it aright. Willis was a man whom both perhaps loved; it might be in that event that Miss Stanford knew more than she had said of the whereabouts of Grace Field. The next step was to see Willis.

"I suppose you'll do everything possible to find Miss Field?" he asked.

"Certainly," said the girl.

"Have you her photograph?"

"I have one, yes, but I don't think-I don't believe Grace—"

"Would like to have it published?" asked Hatch. "Possibly not, under ordinary circumstances—but now that she is missing it is the surest way of getting a trace of her. Will you give it to me?"

Miss Stanford was silent for a time. Then apparently she made up her mind, for she arose.

"It might be well, too," Hatch suggested, "to see if you can find the letter you mentioned."

The girl nodded and went out. When she returned she had a photograph in her hand; a glimpse of it told Hatch it was a bust picture of a woman in evening dress. The girl was studying a scrap of paper.

"What is it?" asked Hatch, quickly.

"I don't know," she responded. "I was searching for the letter when I remembered she frequently tore them up and dropped them into the waste-basket. It had been emptied every day, but I looked and found this clinging to the bottom, caught between the cane."

"May I see it?" asked the reporter.

The girl handed it to him. It was evidently a piece of a letter torn from the outer edge just where the paper was folded to put it into the envelope. On it were these words and detached letters, written in a bold hand:

> sday
> ill you
> to the
> ho

Hatch's eyes opened wide.

"Do you know the handwriting?" he asked.

The girl faltered an instant.

"No," she answered, finally.

Hatch studied her face a moment with cold eyes, then turned the scrap of paper over. The other side was blank. Staring down at it he veiled a glitter of anxious interest.

THE MYSTERY OF STUDIO A

"And the picture?" he asked, quietly.

The girl handed him the photograph. Hatch took it and as he looked it was with difficulty he restrained an exclamation of astonishment—triumphant astonishment. Finally, with his brain teeming with possibilities, he left the house, taking the photograph and the scrap of paper. Ten minutes later he was talking to his City Editor over the 'phone.

"It's a great story," he explained, briefly. "The missing girl is the mysterious model of St. George's picture, 'Fulfillment.'"

"Great," came the voice of the City Editor.

II

Having laid his story before his City Editor, Hatch sat down to consider the fragmentary writing. Obviously "sday" represented a day of the week—either Tuesday, Wednesday, or Thursday, these being the only days where the letter "s" preceded the "day." This seemed to be a definite fact, but still it meant nothing. True, Miss Field had last been seen on Wednesday, but then?—nothing.

To the next part of the fragment Hatch attached the greatest importance. It was the possibility of a threat, – "ill you." Did it mean "kill you" or "will you" or "till you" or-or what? There might be dozens of other words ending in "ill" which he did not recall at the moment. His imagination hammered the phrase into his brain as "kill you." The "to the" – the next words – were clear, but meant nothing at all. The last letters were distinctly "ho," possibly "hope."

Then Hatch began real work on the story. First he saw the bank clerk, Victor Willis, who Miss Stanford had said loved Grace Field, and whom Hatch suspected Miss Stanford loved. He found Willis a grim, sullen-faced young man of twenty-eight years, who would say nothing.

From that point Hatch worked vigorously for several hours. At the end of that time he had found out that on Wednesday, the day of Miss Field's disappearance, a veiled woman – probably Grace Field – had called at the bank and inquired for Willis. Later, Willis, urging necessity, had asked to be allowed the day off and left the bank. He did not appear again until next morning. His actions did not impress any of his associates with the idea that he was a bridegroom; in fact, Hatch himself had given up the idea that Miss Field had eloped. There seemed no reason for an elopement.

When Hatch called at the studio, and home, of Constans St. George, to inform him of the disappearance of the model whose identity had been so long guarded, he was told that Mr St. George was not in; that is, St. George refused to answer knocks at the door, and had not been seen for a day or so. He frequently disappeared this way, his informant said.

With these facts – and lack of facts – in his possession on Friday evening, Hatch called on Professor S. F. X. Van Dusen. The Thinking Machine received him as cordially as he ever received anybody.

"Well, what is it?" he asked.

"I don't believe this is really worth your while Professor," Hatch said, finally. "It's just a case of a girl who disappeared. There are some things about it which are puzzling, but I'm afraid it's only an elopement."

The Thinking Machine dragged up a footstool, planted his small feet on it comfortably and leaned back in his chair.

"Go on," he directed.

Then Hatch told the story, beginning at the time when the picture was placed in the art museum, and continuing up to the point where he had seen Willis after finding the photograph and the scrap of paper. He had always found that it saved time to begin at the beginning with The Thinking Machine; he did it now as a matter of course.

"And the scrap of paper?" asked The Thinking Machine.

"I have it here," replied the reporter.

For several minutes the scientist examined the fragment and then handed it back to the reporter.

"If one could establish some clear connection between that and the disappearance of the girl it might be valuable," he said. "As it is now, it means nothing. Any number of letters might be thrown into the waste-basket in the room the two girls occupied, therefore dismiss this for the moment."

"But isn't it possible–" Hatch began.

"Anything is possible. Mr Hatch," retorted the other, belligerently. "You might take occasion to see the handwriting of St. George, the artist, and see if that is his—also look at Willis's. Even if it were Willis's, however, it may mean nothing in connection with this."

"But what could have happened to Miss Field?"

"Any of fifty things," responded the other. "She might have fallen dead in the street and been removed to a hospital or undertaking establishment; she might have been arrested for shoplifting and given a wrong name; she might have gone mad and gone away; she might have eloped with another man; she might have committed suicide; she might have been murdered. The question is not what could have happened, but what did happen."

"Yes, I thoroughly understand that," Hatch replied, with a slight smile. "But still I don't see–"

"Probably you don't," snapped the other. "We'll take it for granted that she did none of these things, with the possible exception of eloping, killing herself, or was murdered. You are convinced that she did not elope. Yet you have only run down one possible end of this—that is, the possibility of her elopement with Willis. You don't believe she did elope with him. Well, why not with St. George?"

"St. George?" gasped Hatch. "A great artist elope with a shop-girl?"

"She was his ideal in a picture which you say is one of the greatest in the world," replied the other, testily. "That being true, it is perfectly possible that she was his ideal for a wife, isn't it?"

The matter had not occurred to Hatch in just that light. He nodded his head, with a feeling of having been weighed and found wanting.

"Now, you say, too, that St. George has not been seen around his studio for a couple of days," said the scientist. "What is more possible than that they are together somewhere?"

"I see," said the reporter.

"It was understood, too, as I understand it, that St. George was in love with her," went on The Thinking Machine. "So, I should imagine a solution of the mystery might be reached by taking St. George as the center of the affair. Suicide may be passed by for the moment, because she had no known motive for suicide—rather, if she loved Willis, she had every reason to live. Murder, too, may be passed for the moment—although there is a possibility that we might come back to that. Question St. George. He will listen if you make him, and then he must answer."

"But his place is all closed up," said Hatch. "It is supposed he is half crazy."

"Possibly he might be," said The Thinking Machine. "Or it is possible that he is keeping to his studio at work – or he might even be married to Miss Field and she might be there with him."

"Well, I see no way to ascertain definitely that he is there," said the reporter, and a puzzled wrinkle came into his face. "Of course I might remain on watch night and day to see if he comes out for food, or if anything to eat is sent in."

"That would take too long, and besides it might not happen at all," said The Thinking Machine. He arose and went into the adjoining room. He returned after a moment, and glanced at the clock on the mantel. "It is just nine o'clock now," he commented. "How long would it take you to get to the studio?"

"Half an hour."

"Well, go there now," directed the scientist. "If Mr St. George is in his studio he will come out of it tonight at thirty-two minutes past nine. He will be running, and may not wear either a hat or coat."

"What?" and Hatch grinned, a weak, puzzled grin.

"You wait where he can't see you when he comes out," the scientist went on. "When he goes he may leave the door open. If he does go on see if you find any trace of Miss Field, and then, on his return, meet him at the outer door, ask him what you please, and come to see me to-morrow morning. He will be out of his studio about twenty minutes."

Vaguely Hatch felt that the scientist was talking rot, but he had seen this strange mind bring so many odd things to pass that he could not doubt this, even if it were absurd on its face.

"At thirty-two minutes past nine tonight," said the reporter, and he glanced at his watch.

"Come to see me tomorrow after you see the handwriting of Willis and St. George," directed the scientist. "Then you may also tell me just what happens tonight."

Hatch was feeling like a fool. He was waiting in a darkened corner, just a few feet from St. George's studio. It was precisely half-past nine o'clock. He had been there for seven minutes. What strange power was to bring St. George, who for two days had denied himself to everyone, out of that studio, if, indeed, he were there?

For the twentieth time Hatch glanced at his watch, which he had set with the little clock in The Thinking Machine's home.

Slowly the minute hand crept around, to 9:31, 9:311/2, and he heard the door of the studio rattle. Then suddenly it was thrown open and St. George appeared.

Without a glance to right or left, hatless and coatless, he rushed out of the building. Hatch got only a glimpse of his face; his lips were pressed tightly together; there was a glint of madness in his eyes. He jerked at the door once, then ran through the hall and disappeared down the stairs leading to the street. The studio door stood open behind him.

III

When the clatter of the running footsteps had died away and Hatch heard the outer door slam, he entered the studio, closing the door behind him. It was close here, and there was a breath of Chinese incense which was almost stifling. One quick glance by the light of an incandescent told Hatch that he stood in the reception-room. Typically, from floor to ceiling, the place was the abode of an artist; there was a rich gradation of color and everywhere were scraps of art and half-finished studies.

The reporter had given up the idea of solving the mystery of why St. George had so suddenly left his apartments; now he devoted himself to a quick, minute search of the place. He found nothing to interest him in the reception-room, and went on into the studio where the artist did his work.

Hatch glanced around quickly, his eyes taking in all the details, then went to a little table which stood, half-covered with newspapers. He turned these over, then bent forward suddenly and picked up—a woman's glove. Beside it lay its mate. He stuffed them into his pocket.

Eagerly he sought now for anything that might come to hand. At last he reached another door, leading into the bedroom. Here on a large table was a chafing dish, many dishes which had not been washed, and all the other evidences of a careless man who did a great deal of his own cooking. There was a dresser here, too, a gorgeous, mahogany affair. Hatch didn't stop to admire this because his eye was attracted by a woman's veil which lay on it. He thrust it into his pocket.

"Quite a haul I'm making," he mused, grimly.

From this room a door, half open, led into a bath-room. Hatch merely glanced in, then looked at his watch. Fifteen minutes had elapsed. He must get out, and he started for the outer door. As he opened it quietly and stepped into the hall he heard the street door open one flight below, and started down the steps. There, half way, he met St. George.

"Mr St. George?" he asked.

"No," was the reply.

Hatch knew his man perfectly, because he had seen him half a dozen times and had talked to him twice. The denial of identity therefore was futile.

"I came to tell you that Grace Field, the model for your 'Fulfillment,' has disappeared," Hatch went on, as the other glared at him.

"I don't care," snapped the other. He darted up the steps. Hatch listened until he heard the door of the studio close.

It was ten minutes to ten o'clock when Hatch left the building. Now he would see Miss Stanford and have her identify the gloves and the veil. He boarded a car and drew out and closely examined the gloves and veil. The gloves were tan, rather heavy, but small, and the veil was of some light, cobwebby material which he didn't know by name.

"If these are Grace Field's," the reporter argued, to himself, "it means something. If they are not, I'm simply a burglar."

There was a light in the Dorchester house where Miss Stanford lived, and the reporter rang the bell. A servant appeared.

"Would it be possible for me to see Miss Stanford for just a moment?" he asked.

"If she has not gone to bed."

He was ushered into the little parlor again. The servant disappeared, and after a moment Miss Stanford came in.

"I hated to trouble you so late," said the reporter, and she smiled at him frankly, "but I would like to ask if you have ever seen these?"

He laid in her hands the gloves and the veil. Miss Stanford studied them carefully and her hands trembled.

"The gloves, I know, are Grace's — the veil I am not so positive about," she replied.

Hatch felt a great wave of exultation sweep over him, and it stopped his tongue for an instant.

"Did you-did you find them in Mr Willis's possession?" asked the girl.

"I am not at liberty to tell just where I found them," Hatch replied. "If they are Miss Field's — and you can swear to that, I suppose — it may mean that we have a clew."

"Oh, I was afraid it would be this way," gasped the girl, and she sank down weeping on a couch.

"Knew what would be which way?" asked Hatch, puzzled.

"I knew it! I knew it!" she sobbed. "Is there anything to connect Mr Willis directly with the-the murder?"

The reporter started to say something, then paused. He wasn't quite sure of himself. He had uncovered something, he didn't know what yet.

"It would be better, Miss Stanford," he explained, gently, "if you would tell me all you know about this affair. The things which are now in my possession are fragmentary — if you could give me any new detail it would be only serving the ends of justice."

For a little while the girl was silent, then she arose and faced him.

"Is Mr Willis yet under arrest?" she asked, calmly now.

"Not yet," said the reporter.

"Then I will say nothing else," she declared, and her lips closed in a straight line.

"What was the motive for murder?" Hatch, insisted.

"I will say nothing else," she replied, firmly.

"And what makes you positive there was murder?"

"Goodnight. You need not come again, for I will not see you."

Miss Stanford turned and left the room. Hatch, sadly puzzled, bewildered, stood staring after her a moment, then went out, his brain alive with possibilities, with intangible ends which would not be connected. He was eager to lay the new facts before The Thinking Machine.

From Dorchester the reporter took a car for his home. In his room, with the tangible threads of the mystery spread out on a table, he thought and surmised far into the night, and when he finally replaced them all in his pocket and turned down the light it was with a hopeless shake of his head.

On the following morning when Hatch arose he picked up a paper and went to breakfast. He spread the paper before him and there—the first thing he saw—was a huge headline, stating that a burglar had entered the room of Constans St. George and had tried to kill Mr St. George. A shot had been fired at him and had passed through his left arm.

Mr St. George had been asleep when the door of his apartments was burst in by the thief. The artist arose at the noise, and as he stepped into the reception-room had been shot. The wound was trivial. The burglar escaped; there was no clew.

IV

It was a long story of seemingly hopeless complications that Hatch told The Thinking Machine that morning. Nothing connected with anything, and yet here was a series of happenings, all apparently growing out of the disappearance of Miss Field, and which must have some relation one to the other. At the conclusion of the story, Hatch passed over the newspaper containing the account of the burglary in the studio. The artist had been removed to a hospital.

The Thinking Machine read the newspaper account and turned to the reporter with a question:

"Did you see Willis's handwriting?"

"Not yet," replied the reporter.

"See it at once," instructed the other. "If possible, bring me a sample of it. Did you see St. George's handwriting?"

"No," the reporter confessed.

"See that and bring me a sample if you can. Find out first if Willis has a revolver now or has ever had. If so, see it and see if it is loaded or empty—its exact condition. Find out also if St. George has a revolver—and if he has one, get possession of it if it is in your power."

The scientist twisted the two gloves and the veil which Hatch had given to him in his fingers idly, then passed them to the reporter again.

Hatch arose and stood waiting, hat in hand.

"Also find out," The Thinking Machine went on, "the exact condition of St. George—his mental condition particularly. Find out if Willis is at his office in the bank today, and, if possible, where and how he spent last night. That's all."

"And Miss Stanford?" asked Hatch.

"Never mind her," replied The Thinking Machine. "I may see her myself. These other things are of immediate consequence. The minute you satisfy yourself come back to me. Quickness on your part may prevent a tragedy."

The reporter went away hurriedly. At four o'clock that afternoon he returned. The Thinking Machine greeted him; he held a piece of letter-paper in his hand.

"Well?" he asked.

"The handwriting is Willis's," said Hatch, without hesitation. "I saw a sample—it is identical, and the paper on which he writes is identical."

The scientist grunted.

"I also saw some of St. George's writing," the reporter went on, as if he were reciting a lesson. "It is wholly dissimilar."

The Thinking Machine nodded.

"Willis has no revolver that anyone ever heard of," Hatch continued. "He was at dinner with several of his fellow employees last night, and left the restaurant at eight o'clock."

"Been drinking?"

"Might have had a few drinks," responded the reporter. "He is not a drinking man."

"Has St. George a revolver?"

"I was unable to find that out or do anything except get a sample of his writing from another artist," the reporter explained. "He is in a hospital, raving crazy. It seems to be a return of the trouble he had once before, except it is worse. The wound itself is not bad."

The scientist was studying the sheet of paper.

"Have you that scrap?" he asked.

Hatch produced it, and the scientist placed it on the sheet; Hatch could only conjecture that he was fitting it to something else already there. He was engaged in this work when Martha entered.

"The young lady who was here earlier today wants to see you again," she announced.

"Show her in," directed The Thinking Machine, without raising his eyes.

Martha disappeared, and after a moment Miss Stanford entered. Hatch, himself unnoticed, stared at her curiously, and arose, as did the scientist. The girl's face was flushed a little, and there was an eager expression in her eyes.

"I know he didn't do it," she began. "I've just gotten a letter from Springfield stating that he was there on the day Grace went away—and—"

"Know who didn't do what?" asked the scientist.

"That Mr Willis didn't kill Grace," replied the girl, her enthusiasm suddenly checked. "See here."

The scientist read a letter which she offered, and the girl sank into a chair. Then for the first time she saw Hatch and her eyes expressed her surprise. She stared at him a moment, then nodded a greeting, after which she fell to watching The Thinking Machine.

"Miss Stanford," he said, at length, "you made several mistakes when you were here before in not telling me the truth—all of it. If you will tell me all you know of this case I may be able to see it more clearly."

The girl reddened and stammered a little, then her lips trembled.

"Do you know – not conjecture, but know – whether or not Miss Field, or Grace, as you call her, was engaged to Willis?" the irritated voice asked.

"I-I know it, yes," she stammered.

"And you were in love with Mr Willis—you are in love with him?"

Again the tell-tale blush swept over her face. She glanced at Hatch; it was the nervousness of a girl who is driven to a confession of love.

"I regard Mr Willis very highly," she said, finally, her voice low.

"Well," and the scientist arose and crossed to where the girl sat, "don't you see that a very grave charge might be brought home to you if you don't tell all of this? The girl has disappeared. There might be even a hint of murder in which your name would be mentioned. Don't you see?"

There was a long pause, and the girl stared steadily into the squint eyes above her. Finally her eyes fell.

"I think I understand. Just what is it you want me to answer?"

"Did or did you not ever hear Mr Willis threaten Miss Field?"

"I did once, yes."

"Did or did you not know that Miss Field was the original of the painting?"

"I did not."

"It is a semi-nude picture, isn't it?"

Again there was a flush in the girl's face.

"I have heard it was," she said. "I have never seen it. I suggested to Grace several times that we go to see it, but she never would. I understand why now."

"Did Willis know she was the original of that painting? That is, knowing it yourself now, do you have any reason to suppose that he previously knew?"

"I don't know," she said, frankly. "I know that there was something which was always causing friction between them—something they quarreled about. It might have been that. That was when I heard Mr Willis threaten her—it was something about shooting her if she ever did something—I don't know what."

"Miss Field knew him before you did, I think you said?"

"She introduced me to him."

The Thinking Machine fingered the sheet of paper he held.

"Did you know what those scraps of paper you brought me contained?"

"Yes, in a way," said the girl.

"Why did you bring them, then?"

"Because you told me you knew I had them, and I was afraid it might make more trouble for me and for Mr Willis if I did not."

The Thinking Machine passed the sheet to Hatch.

"This will interest you, Mr Hatch," he explained. "Those words and letters in parentheses are what I have supplied to complete the full text of the note, of which you had a mere scrap. You will notice how the scrap you had fitted into it."

The reporter read this:

"If you go to th(at stud)io Wednesday to see that artist, (I will k)ill you bec(ause I w)on't have it known to the world that(t you a)re a model. I hope you will heed this warning. V. W."

The reporter stared at the patched-up letter, pasted together with infinite care, and then glanced at The Thinking Machine, who settled himself again comfortably in the chair.

"And now, Miss Stanford," asked the scientist, in a most matter-of-fact tone, "where is the body of Miss Field?"

V

The blunt question aroused the girl, and she arose suddenly, staring at The Thinking Machine. He did not move. She stood as if transfixed, and Hatch saw her bosom rise and fall rapidly with the emotion she was seeking to repress.

"Well?" asked The Thinking Machine.

"I don't know," flamed Miss Stanford, suddenly, almost fiercely. "I don't even know she is dead. I know that Mr Willis did not kill her, because, as that letter I gave you shows, he was in Springfield. I won't be tricked into saying anything further."

The outburst had no appreciable effect on The Thinking Machine beyond causing him to raise his eyebrows slightly as he looked at the defiant little figure.

"When did you last see Mr Willis have a revolver?"

"I know nothing of any revolver. I know only that Victor Willis is innocent as you are, and that I love him. Whatever has become of Grace Field I don't know."

Tears leaped suddenly to her eyes, and, turning, she left the room. After a moment they heard the outer door slam as she passed out. Hatch turned to the scientist with a question in his eyes.

"Did you smell anything like chloroform or ether when you were in St. George's apartments?" asked The Thinking Machine as he arose.

"No," said Hatch. "I only noticed that the place seemed close, and there was an odor of Chinese incense — joss sticks — which was almost stifling."

The Thinking Machine looked at the reporter quickly, but said nothing. Instead, he passed out of the room, to return a few minutes later with his hat and coat on.

"Where are we going?" asked Hatch.

"To St. George's studio," was the answer.

Just then the telephone bell in the next room rang. The scientist answered it in person.

"Your City Editor," he called to Hatch.

Hatch went to the 'phone and remained there several minutes. When he came back there was a new excitement in his face.

"What is it?" asked the scientist.

"Another queer thing my City Editor told me," Hatch responded. "Constans St. George, raving mad, has escaped from the hospital and disappeared."

"Dear me, dear me!" exclaimed the scientist, quickly. It was as near surprise as he ever showed. "Then there is danger."

With quick steps he went to the telephone and called up Police Headquarters.

"Detective Mallory," Hatch heard him ask for. "Yes. This is Professor Van Dusen. Please meet me immediately here at my house. Be here in ten minutes? Good. I'll wait. It's a matter of great importance. Goodbye."

Then impatiently The Thinking Machine moved about, waiting. The reporter, whose acquaintance with the logician was an extended one, had never seen him in just such a state. It started when he heard St. George had escaped.

At last they left the house and stood waiting on the steps until Detective Mallory appeared in a cab. Into that Hatch and The Thinking Machine climbed, after the latter had given some direction, and the cabby drove rapidly away. It was all a mystery to Hatch, and he was rather glad of it when Detective Mallory asked what it meant.

"Means that there is danger of a tragedy," said The Thinking Machine, crustily. "We may be in time to avert it. There is just a chance. If I'd only known this an hour ago – even half an hour ago – it might have been stopped."

The Thinking Machine was the first man out of the cab when it stopped, and Hatch and the detective followed quickly.

"Is Mr St. George in his apartments?" asked the scientist of the elevator boy.

"No, sir," said the boy. "He's in hospital, shot."

"Is there a key to his place? Quick."

"I think so, sir, but I can't give it to you."

"Here, give it to me, then!" exclaimed the detective. He flashed a badge in the boy's eyes, and the youth immediately lost a deal of his coolness.

"Gee, a detective! Yes, sir."

"How many rooms has Mr St. George?" asked the scientist.

"Three and a bath," the boy responded.

Two minutes later the three men stood in the reception-room of the apartments. There came to them from somewhere inside a deadly, stifling odor of chloroform. After one glance around The Thinking Machine rushed into the next room, the studio.

"Dear me, dear me!" he exclaimed.

There on the floor lay huddled the figure of a man. Blood had run from several wounds on his head. The Thinking

Machine stooped a moment, and his slender fingers fumbled over the heart.

"Unconscious, that's all," he said, and he raised the man up.

"Victor Willis!" exclaimed Hatch.

"Victor Willis!" repeated The Thinking Machine, as if puzzled. "Are you sure?"

"Certain," said Hatch, positively. "It's the bank clerk."

"Then we are too late," declared the scientist.

He arose and looked about the room. A door to his right attracted his attention. He jerked it open and peered in. It was a clothes press. Another small door on the other side of the room was also thrown open. Here was as a kitchenette, with a great quantity of canned stuffs.

The Thinking Machine went on into the little bedroom which Hatch had searched. He flung open the bathroom and peered in, only to shut it immediately. Then he tried the handle of another door, a closet. It was fastened.

"Ah!" he exclaimed.

Then on his hands and knees he sniffed at the crack between the door and the flooring. Suddenly, as if satisfied, he arose and stepped away from the door.

"Smash that door in," he directed.

Detective Mallory looked at him stupefied. There was a similar expression on Hatch's face.

"What's-what's in there?" the detective asked.

"Smash it," said the other, tartly. "Smash it, or God knows what you'll find in there."

The detective, a powerful man, and Hatch threw their weight against the door; it stood rigid. They pulled at the handle; it refused to yield.

"Lend me your revolver?" asked The Thinking Machine.

The weapon was in his hand almost before the detective was aware of it, and, placing the barrel to the keyhole, The Thinking Machine pulled the trigger. There was a resonant report, the lock was smashed and the detective put out his hand to open the door.

"Look out for a shot," warned The Thinking Machine, sharply.

VI

The Thinking Machine drew Detective Mallory and Hatch to one side, out of immediate range of any person who might rush out, then pulled the closet door open. A cloud of suffocating fumes – the sweet, sickening odor of chloroform – gushed out, but there was no sound from inside. The detective looked at The Thinking Machine inquiringly.

Carefully, almost gingerly, the scientist peered around the edge of the door. What he saw did not startle him, because it was what he expected. It was Constans St. George lying prone on the floor as if dead, with a blood-spattered revolver clasped loosely in one hand; the other hand grasped the throat of a woman, a woman of superb physical beauty, who also lay with face upturned, staring glassily.

"Open the windows—all of them, then help me," commanded the scientist.

As Detective Mallory and Hatch turned to obey the instructions, The Thinking Machine took the revolver from the inert fingers of the artist. Then Hatch and Mallory returned and together they lifted the unconscious forms toward a window.

"It's Grace Field," said the reporter.

In silence for half an hour the scientist labored over the unconscious forms of his three patients. The detective and reporter stood by, doing only what they were told to do. The wind, cold and stinging, came pouring through the windows, and it was only a few minutes until the chloroform odor was dissipated. The first of the three unconscious ones to show any sign of returning comprehension was Victor Willis, whose

THE MYSTERY OF STUDIO A

presence at all in the apartments furnished one of the mysteries which Hatch could not fathom.

It was evident that his condition was primarily due to the wounds on his head—two of which bled profusely. The chloroform had merely served to further deaden his mentality. The wounds were made with the butt of the revolver, evidently in the hands of the artist. Willis's eyes opened finally and he stared at the faces bending over him with uncomprehending eyes.

"What happened?" he asked.

"You're all right now," was the scientist's assuring answer. "This man is your prisoner, Detective Mallory, for breaking and entering and for the attempted murder of Mr St. George."

Detective Mallory was delighted. Here was something he could readily understand; a human being given over to his care; a tangible thing to put handcuffs on and hold. He immediately proceeded to put the handcuffs on.

"Any need of an ambulance?" he asked.

"No," replied The Thinking Machine. "He'll be all right in half an hour."

Gradually as reason came back Willis remembered. He turned his head at last and saw the inert bodies of St. George and Grace Field, the girl whom he had loved.

"She was here, then!" he exclaimed suddenly, violently. "I knew it. Is she dead?"

"Shut up that young fool's mouth, Mr Mallory," commanded the scientist, sharply. "Take him in the other room or send him away."

Obediently Mallory did as directed; there was that in the voice of this cold, calm being, The Thinking Machine, which compelled obedience. Mallory never questioned motives or orders.

Willis was able to walk to the other room with help. Miss Field and St. George lay side by side in the cold wind from the open window. The Thinking Machine had forced a little whiskey down their throats, and after a time St. George opened his eyes.

The artist was instantly alert and tried to rise. He was weak, however, and even a strength given to him by the madness which blazed in his eyes did not avail. At last he lay raving, cursing, shrieking. The Thinking Machine regarded him closely.

"Hopeless," he said, at last.

Again for many minutes the scientist worked with the girl. Finally he asked that an ambulance be sent for. The detective called up the City Hospital on the telephone in the apartments and made the request. The Thinking Machine stared alternately at the girl and at the artist.

"Hopeless," he said again. "St. George, I mean."

"Will the girl recover?" asked Hatch.

"I don't know," was the frank reply. "She's been partly stupefied for days—ever since she disappeared, as a matter of fact. If her physical condition was as good as her appearance indicates she may recover. Now the hospital is the best place for her."

It was only a few minutes before two ambulances came and the three persons were taken away; Willis a prisoner, and a sullen, defiant prisoner, who refused to speak or answer questions; St. George raving hideously and cursing frightfully; the woman, beautiful as a marble statue, and colorless as death.

When they had all gone, The Thinking Machine went back into the bedroom and examined more carefully the little closet in which he had found the artist and Grace Field. It was practically a padded cell, relatively six feet each way. Heavy cushions of felt two or three inches thick covered the interior of the little room closely. In the top of it there was a small aperture, which had permitted some of the fumes of the chloroform to escape. The place was saturated with the poison.

"Let's go," he said, finally.

Detective Mallory and Hatch followed him out and a few minutes later sat opposite him in his little laboratory. Hatch had told a story over the telephone that made his City Editor rejoice madly; it was news, great, big, vital news.

"Now, Mr Hatch, I suppose you want some details," said The Thinking Machine, as he relapsed into his accustomed attitude. "And you, too, Mr Mallory, since you are holding Willis a prisoner on my say-so. Would you like to know why?"

"Sure," said the detective.

"Let's go back a little—begin at the beginning, where Mr Hatch called on me," said The Thinking Machine. "I can make the matter clearer that way. And I believe the cause of justice, Mr Mallory, requires absolute accuracy and clarity in all things, does it not?"

"Sure," said the detective again.

"Well, Mr Hatch told me at some length of the preliminaries of this case," explained The Thinking Machine. "He told me the history of the picture; the mystery as to the identity of the model; her great beauty; how he found her to be Grace Field, a shop-girl. He also told me of the mental condition of the artist, St. George, and repeated the rumor as he knew it about the artist being heartbroken because the girl—his model—would not marry him.

"All this brought the artist into the matter of the girl's disappearance. She represented to him, physically, the highest ideal of which he could conceive—hope, success, life itself. Therefore it was not astonishing that he should fall in love with her; and it is not difficult to imagine that the girl did not fall in love with him. She is a beautiful woman, but not necessarily a woman of mentality; he is a great artist, eccentric, childish even in certain things. They were two natures totally opposed.

"These things I could see instantly. Mr Hatch showed me the photograph and also the scrap of paper. At the time the scrap of paper meant nothing. As I pointed out, it might have no bearing at all, yet it made it necessary for me to know whose handwriting it was. If Willis's, it still might mean nothing; if St. George's, a great deal, because it showed a direct thread to him. There was reason to believe that any friendship between them had ended when the picture was exhibited.

"It was necessary, therefore, even that early in the work of reducing the mystery to logic to center it about St. George. This I explained to Mr Hatch and pointed out the fact that the girl and the artist might have eloped—were possibly together somewhere. First it was necessary to get to the artist; Mr Hatch had not been able to do so.

"A childishly simple trick, which seemed to amaze Mr Hatch considerably, brought the artist out of his rooms after he had been there closely for two days. I told Mr Hatch that the artist would leave his rooms, if he were there, one night at 9:32, and told him to wait in the hall, then if he left the door open to enter the apartments and search for some trace of the girl. Mr St. George did leave his apartments at the time I mentioned, and—"

"But why, how?" asked Hatch.

"There was one thing in the world that St. George loved with all his heart," explained the scientist. "That was his picture. Every act of his life has demonstrated that. I looked at a telephone book; I found he had a 'phone. If he were in his rooms, locked in, it was a bit of common sense that his telephone was the best means of reaching him. He answered the 'phone; I told him, just at 9:30, that the Art Museum was on fire and his picture in danger.

"St. George left his apartments to go and see, just as I knew he would, hatless and coatless, and leaving the door open. Mr Hatch went inside and found two gloves and a veil, all belonging to Miss Field. Miss Stanford identified them and asked if he had gotten them from Willis, and if Willis had been arrested. Why did she ask these questions? Obviously because she knew, or thought she knew, that Willis had some connection with the affair.

"Mr Hatch detailed all his discoveries and the conversation with Miss Stanford to me on the day after I 'phoned to St. George, who, of course, had found no fire. It showed that Miss Stanford suspected Willis, whom she loved, of the murder of Miss Field. Why? Because she had heard him threaten. He's a hare-brained young fool, anyway. What motive? Jealousy. Jealousy of what? He knew in some way that she had posed for a semi-nude picture, and that the man who painted it loved her. There is your jealousy. It explains Willis's every act."

The Thinking Machine paused a moment, then went on:

"This conversation with Mr Hatch made me believe Miss Stanford knew more than she was willing to tell. In what way? By a letter? Possibly. She had given Mr Hatch a scrap of a letter; perhaps she had found another letter, or more of this one. I sent her a note, telling her I knew she had these scraps of letters, and she promptly brought them to me. She had found them after Mr Hatch saw her first somewhere in the house — in a bureau drawer she said, I think.

"Meanwhile, Mr Hatch had called my attention to the burglary of St. George's apartments. One reading of that convinced me that it was Willis who did this. Why? Because burglars don't burst in doors when they think anyone is inside; they pick the lock. Knowing, too, Willis's insane jealousy, I figured that he would be the type of man who would go there to kill St. George if he could, particularly if he thought the girl was there.

"Thus it happened that I was not the only one to think that St. George knew where the girl was. Willis, the one most interested, thought she was there. I questioned Miss Stanford mercilessly, trying to get more facts about the young man from her which would bear on this, trying to trick her into some statement, but she was loyal to the last.

"All these things indicated several things. First, that Willis didn't actually know where the girl was, as he would have known had he killed her; second, that if she had disappeared with a man, it was St. George, as there was no other apparent possibility; third, that St. George would be with her or near her, even if he had killed her; fourth, the pistol shot through the arm had brought on again a mental condition which threatened his entire future, and now as it happens has blighted it.

"Thus, Miss Field and St. George were together. She loved Willis devotedly, therefore she was with St. George against her will, or she was dead. Where? In his rooms? Possibly. I determined to search there. I had just reached this determination when I heard St. George, violently insane, had escaped from the hospital. He had only one purpose then—to get to the woman. Then she was in danger.

"I reasoned along these lines, rushed to the artist's apartments, found Willis there wounded. He had evidently been there searching when St. George returned, and St. George had attacked him, as a madman will, and with the greater strength of a madman. Then I knew the madman's first step. It would be the end of everything for him; therefore the death of the girl and his own. How? By poison preferably, because he would not shoot her—he loved beauty too much. Where? Possibly in the place where she had been all along, the closet, carefully padded and prepared to withstand noises. It is really a padded cell. I have an idea that the artist, sometimes overcome by his insane fits, and knowing when they would come, prepared this closet and used it himself occasionally. Here the girl could have been kept and her shrieks would never have been heard. You know the rest."

The Thinking Machine stopped and arose, as if to end the matter. The others arose, too.

"I took you, Mr Mallory, because you were a detective, and I knew I could force a way into the apartments which I imagined would be locked. I think that's all."

"But how did the girl get there?" asked Hatch.

"St. George evidently asked her to come, possibly to pose again. It was a gratification to the girl to do this—a little touch of vanity caused her to pose in the first place. It was this vanity that Willis was fighting so hard, and which led to his threats and his efforts to kill St. George. Of course the artist was insane when she came; his frantic love for her led him to make her a prisoner and hold her against her will. You saw how well he did it."

There was an awed pause. Hatch was rubbing the nap of his hat against his sleeve, thoughtfully. Detective Mallory had nothing to say; it was all said. Both turned as if to go, but the reporter had two more questions.

"I suppose St. George's case is hopeless?"

"Absolutely. It will end in a few months with his death."

"And Miss Field?"

"If she is not dead by this time she will recover. Wait a minute." He went into the next room and they heard the telephone bell jingle. After a time he came out. "She will recover," he said. "Goodafternoon."

Wonderingly, Hutchinson Hatch, reporter, and Detective Mallory passed down the street together.

9

THE PHANTOM MOTOR

Two dazzling white eyes bulged through the night as an automobile swept suddenly around a curve in the wide road and laid a smooth, glaring pathway ahead. Even at the distance the rhythmical crackling-chug informed Special Constable Baker that it was a gasoline car, and the headlong swoop of the unblinking lights toward him made him instantly aware of the fact that the speed ordinance of Yarborough County was being a little more than broken — it was being obliterated.

Now the County of Yarborough was a wide expanse of summer estates and superbly kept roads, level as a floor and offered distracting temptations to the dangerous pastime of speeding. But against this was the fact that the county was particular about its speed laws, so particular in fact that had stationed half a hundred men upon its highways to abate the nuisance. Incidentally it had found that keeping record of the infractions of the law was an excellent source of income.

'Forty miles an hour if an inch,' remarked Baker to himself.

He arose from a camp-stool where he was wont to make himself comfortable from six o'clock until midnight on watch, picked up his lantern, turned up the light and stepped down to the edge of the road. He always remained on watch at the same place — at one end of a long stretch which autoists had unanimously dubbed The Trap. The Trap was singularly tempting – perfectly macadamized road bed lying between two tall stone walls with only enough of a sinuous twist in it to make each end invisible from the other. Another man, Special Constable Bowman, was stationed at the other end of The Trap and there was telephonic communication between the points, enabling the men to check each other and incidentally, if one failed to stop a car or get its number, the other would. That at least was the theory.

So now, with the utmost confidence, Baker waited beside the road. The approaching lights were only a couple of hundred yards away. At the proper instant he would raise his lantern, the car would stop, its occupants would protest and then the county would add a mite to its general fund for making the roads even better and tempting autoists still more. Or sometimes the cars didn't stop. In that event it was part of the Special Constables' duties to get the number as it flew past, and reference to the monthly automobile register would give the name of the owner. An extra fine was always imposed in such cases.

Without the slightest diminution of speed the car came hurtling on toward him and swung wide so as to take the straight path of The Trap at full speed. At the psychological instant Baker stepped out into the road and waved his lantern.

'Stop!' he commanded.

The crackling-chug came on, heedless of the cry. The auto was almost upon him before he leaped out of the road – a feat at which he was particularly expert – then it flashed by and plunged into The Trap. Baker was, at the instant, so busily engaged in getting out of the way that he couldn't read the number, but he was not disconcerted because he knew there was no escape from The Trap. On the one side a solid stone wall eight feet high marked the eastern boundary of the John Phelps Stocker country estate, and on the other side a stone fence nine feet high marked the western boundary of the

Thomas Q. Rogers country estate. There was no turnout, no place, no possible way for an auto to get out of The Trap except at one of the two ends guarded by the special constables. So Baker, perfectly confident of results, seized the phone.

'Car coming through sixty miles an hour,' he bawled. 'It won't stop. I missed the number. Look out.'

'All right,' answered Special Constable Bowman.

For ten, fifteen, twenty minutes Baker waited expecting a call from Bowman at the other end. It didn't come and finally he picked up the phone again. No answer. He rang several times, battered the box and did some tricks with the receiver. Still no answer. Finally he began to feel worried. He remembered that at that same post one Special Constable had been badly hurt by a reckless chauffeur who refused to stop or turn his car when the officer stepped out into the road. In his mind's eye he saw Bowman now lying helpless, perhaps badly injured. If the car held the pace at which it passed him it would be certain death to whoever might be unlucky enough to get in its path.

With these thoughts running through his head and with genuine solicitude for Bowman, Baker at last walked on along the road of The Trap toward the other end. The feeble rays of the lantern showed the unbroken line of the cold, stone walls on each side. There was no shrubbery of any sort, only a narrow strip of grass close to the wall. The more Baker considered the matter the more anxious he became and he increased his pace a little. As he turned a gentle curve he saw a lantern in the distance coming slowly toward him. It was evidently being carried by someone who was looking carefully along each side of the road.

'Hello!' called Baker, when the lantern came within distance. 'That you, Bowman?'

'Yes,' came the hallooed response.

The lanterns moved on and met. Baker's solicitude for the other constable was quickly changed to curiosity.

THE PHANTOM MOTOR

'What're you looking for?' he asked.

'That auto,' replied Bowman. 'It didn't come through my end and I thought perhaps there had been an accident so I walked along looking for it. Haven't seen anything.'

'Didn't come through your end?' repeated Baker in amazement. 'Why it must have. It didn't come back my way and I haven't passed it so it must have gone through.'

'Well, it didn't,' declared Bowman conclusively. 'I was on the lookout for it, too, standing beside the road. There hasn't been a car through my end in an hour.'

Special Constable Baker raised his lantern until the rays fell full upon the face of Special Constable Bowman and for an instant they stared each at the other. Suspicion glowed from the keen, avaricious eyes of Baker.

'How much did they give you to let em' by?' he asked.

'Give me?' exclaimed Bowman, in righteous indignation. 'Give me nothing. I haven't seen a car.'

A slight sneer curled the lips of Special Constable Baker.

'Of course that's all right to report at headquarters,' he said, 'but I happen to know that the auto came in here, that it didn't go back my way, that it couldn't get out except at the ends, therefore it went your way.' He was silent for a moment. 'And whatever you got, Jim, seems to me I ought to get half.'

Then the worm – i.e., Bowman – turned. A polite curl appeared about his lips and was permitted to show through the grizzled mustache.

'I guess,' he said deliberately, 'you think because you do that, everybody else does. I haven't seen any autos.'

'Don't I always give you half, Jim?' Baker demanded, almost pleadingly.

'Well I haven't seen any car and that's all there is to it. If it didn't go back your way there wasn't any car.' There was a pause; Bowman was framing up something particularly unpleasant. 'You're seeing things, that's what's the matter.'

So was sown discord between two officers of the County of Yarborough. After awhile they separated with mutual sneers and open derision and went back to their respective posts. Each was thoughtful in his own way. At five minutes of midnight when they went off duty Baker called Bowman on the phone again.

'I've been thinking this thing over, Jim, and I guess it would be just as well if we didn't report it or say anything about it when we go in,' said Baker slowly. 'It seems foolish and if we did say anything about it it would give the boys the laugh on us.'

'Just as you say,' responded Bowman.

Relations between Special Constable Baker and Special Constable Bowman were strained on the morrow. But they walked along side by side to their respective posts. Baker stopped at his end of The Trap; Bowman didn't even look around.

You'd better keep your eyes open tonight, Jim,' Baker called as a last word.

'I had 'em open last night,' was the disgusted retort.

Seven, eight, nine o'clock passed. Two or three cars had gone through The Trap at moderate speed and one had been warned by Baker. At a few minutes past nine he was staring down the road which led into The Trap when he saw something that brought him quickly to his feet. It was a pair of dazzling white eyes, far away. He recognized them – the mysterious car of the night before.

'I'll get it this time,' he muttered grimly, between closed teeth.

Then when the onrushing car was a full two hundred yards away Baker planted himself in the middle of the road and began to swing the lantern. The auto seemed, if anything, to be travelling even faster than on the previous night. At a hundred yards Baker began to shout. Still the car didn't lessen speed, merely rushed on. Again at the psychological instant Baker jumped. The auto whisked by as the chauffeur gave it a dextrous twist to prevent running down the Special Constable.

Safely out of its way Baker turned and stared after it, trying to read the number. He could see there was a number because a white board swung from the tail axle, but he could not make out the figures. Dust and a swaying car conspired to defeat him. But he did see that there were four persons in the car dimly silhouetted against the light reflected from the road. It was useless, of course, to conjecture as to sex for even as he looked, the fast receding car swerved around the turn and was lost to sight.

Again he rushed to the telephone; Bowman responded promptly.

'That car's gone in again,' Baker called. 'Ninety miles an hour. Look out!'

'I'm looking,' responded Bowman.

'Let me know what happens,' Baker shouted.

With the receiver to his ear he stood for ten or fifteen minutes, then Bowman hallooed from the other end.

'Well?' Baker responded. 'Get 'em?'

'No car passed through and there's none in sight,' said Bowman.

'But it went in,' insisted Baker.

'Well it didn't come out here,' declared Bowman. 'Walk along the road till I meet you and look out for it.'

Then was repeated the search of the night before. When the two men met in the middle of The Trap their faces were blank – blank as the high stone walls which stared at them from each side.

'Nothing!' said Bowman.

'Nothing!' echoed Baker.

Special Constable Bowman perched his head on one side and scratched his grizzly chin.

'You're not trying to put up a job on me?' he inquired coldly. 'You did see a car?'

'I certainly did,' declared Baker, and a belligerent tone underlay his manner. 'I certainly saw it, Jim, and if it didn't come out your end, why – why –'

He paused and glanced quickly behind him. The action inspired a sudden similar caution on Bowman's part.

"Maybe – maybe –' said Bowman after a minute, 'maybe it's a – a spook auto?'

'Well it must be,' mused Baker. 'You know as well as I do that no car can get out of this trap except at the ends. That car came in here, it isn't here now and it didn't go out your end. Now where is it?'

Bowman stared at him a minute, picked up his lantern, shook his head solemnly and wandered along the road back to his post. On his way he glanced around quickly, apprehensively, three times – Baker did the same thing four times.

On the third night the phantom car appeared and disappeared precisely as it had done previously. Again Baker and Bowman met half way between posts and talked it over.

'I'll tell you what, Baker,' said Bowman in conclusion, 'maybe you're just imagining that you see a car. Maybe if I was at your end I couldn't see it.'

Special Constable Baker was distinctly hurt at the insinuation.

'All right, Jim,' he said at last, 'if you think that way about it we'll swap posts tomorrow night. We won't have to say anything about it when we report.'

'Now that's the talk,' exclaimed Bowman with an air approaching enthusiasm. 'I'll bet I don't see it.'

On the following night Special Constable Bowman made himself comfortable on Special Constable Baker's camp-stool. And he saw the phantom auto. It came upon him with a rush and a crackling-chug of engine and then sped on leaving him nerveless. He called Baker over the wire and Baker watched half an hour for the phantom. It didn't appear.

Ultimately all things reach the newspapers. So with the story of the phantom auto. Hutchinson Hatch, reporter, smiled incredulously when his City Editor laid aside an inevitable cigar and tersely stated the known facts. The known facts in this instance were meager almost to the disappearing point. They consisted merely of a corroborated statement that an automobile, solid and tangible enough to all appearances, rushed into The Trap each night and totally disappeared.

But there was enough of the bizarre about it to pique the curiosity, to make one wonder, so Hatch journeyed down to Yarborough County, an hour's ride from the city, met and talked to Baker and Bowman and then, in broad daylight strolled along The Trap twice. It was a leisurely, thorough investigation with the end in view of finding out how an automobile once inside might get out again without going out either end.

On the first trip through Hatch paid particular attention to the Thomas Q. Rogers side of the road. The wall, nine feet high, was an unbroken line of stone with not the slightest indication of a secret wagon-way through it anywhere. Secret wagon-way! Hatch smiled at the phrase. But when he reached the other end – Bowman's end – of The Trap he was perfectly convinced of one thing – that no automobile had left the hard, macadamized road to go over, under or through the Thomas Q. Rogers wall. Returning, still leisurely, he paid strict attention to the John Phelps Stocker side, and when he reached the other end – Baker's end – he was convinced of another thing – that no automobile had left the road to go over, under or through the John Phelps Stocker wall. The only opening of any sort was a narrow footpath, not more than 16 inches wide.

Hatch saw no shrubbery along the road, nothing but a strip of scrupulously cared for grass, therefore the phantom auto could not be hidden any time, night or day. Hatch failed, too, to find any holes in the road so the automobile didn't go down through the earth. At this point he involuntarily glanced up at the blue sky above. Perhaps, he thought whimsically, the automobile was a strange sort of bird, or – or – and he stopped suddenly.

'By George!' he exclaimed. 'I wonder if –'

And the remainder of the afternoon he spent systematically making inquiries. He went from house to house, the Stocker house, the Rogers house, both of which were at the time unoccupied, then to cottage, cabin and hut in turn. But he didn't seem overladen with information when he joined Special Constable Baker at his end of The Trap that evening about seven o'clock.

Together they rehearsed the strange points of the mystery as the shadows grew about them until finally the darkness was so dense that Baker's lantern was the only bright spot in sight. As the chill of the evening closed in a certain awed tone crept into their voices. Occasionally an auto bowled along and each time as it hove in sight Hatch glanced at Baker questioningly. And each time Baker shook his head. And each time, too, he called Bowman, in this manner accounting for every car that went into The Trap.

'It'll come all right,' said Baker after a long silence, 'and I'll know it the minute it rounds the curve coming toward us. I'd know its two lights in a thousand.'

They sat still and smoked. After awhile two dazzling white lights burst into view far down the road and Baker, in excitement, dropped his pipe.

'That's her,' he declared. 'Look at her coming!'

And Hatch did look at her coming. The speed of the mysterious car was such as to make one look. Like the eyes of a giant the two lights came on toward them, and Baker perfunctorily went through the motions of attempting to stop it. The car fairly whizzed past them and the rush of air which tugged at their coats was convincing enough proof of its solidity. Hatch strained his eyes to read the number as the auto flashed past. But it was hopeless. The tail of the car was lost in an eddying whirl of dust.

'She certainly does travel,' commented Baker, softly.

'She does,' Hatch assented.

Then, for the benefit of the newspaper man, Baker called Bowman on the wire.

'Car's coming again,' he shouted. 'Look out and let me know!'

Bowman, at his end, waited twenty minutes, then made the usual report – the car had not passed. Hutchinson Hatch was a calm, cold, dispassionate young man but now a queer, creepy sensation stole along his spinal column. He lighted a cigarette and pulled himself together with a jerk.

'There's one way to find out where it goes,' he declared at last, emphatically, 'and that's to place a man in the middle just beyond the bend of The Trap and let him wait and see. If the car goes up, down, or evaporates he'll see and can tell us.'

Baker looked at him curiously.

'I'd hate to be the man in the middle,' he declared. There was something of uneasiness in his manner.

'I rather think I would, too,' responded Hatch.

On the following evening, consequent upon the appearance of the story of the phantom auto in Hatch's paper, there were twelve other reporters on hand. Most of them were openly, flagrantly sceptical; they even insinuated that no one had seen an auto. Hatch smiled wisely.

'Wait!' he advised with deep conviction.

So when the darkness fell that evening the newspaper men of a great city had entered into a conspiracy to capture the phantom auto. Thirteen of them, making a total of fifteen men with Baker and Bowman, were on hand and they agreed to a suggestion for all to take positions along the road of The Trap from Baker's post to Bowman's, watch for the auto, see what happened to it and compare notes afterwards. So they scattered themselves along a few hundred feet apart and waited. That night the phantom auto didn't appear at all and twelve reporters jeered at Hutchinson Hatch and told him to light his pipe with the story. And next night when Hatch and Baker and Bowman alone were watching the phantom auto reappeared.

Like a child with a troublesome problem, Hatch took the entire matter and laid it before Professor Augustus S. F. X. Van Dusen, the master brain. The Thinking Machine, with squint eyes turned steadily upward and long, slender fingers pressed tip to tip, listened to the end.

'Now I know of course that automobiles don't fly,' Hatch burst out savagely in conclusion, 'and if this one doesn't fly, there is no earthly way for it to get out of The Trap, as they call it. I went over the thing carefully – I even went so far as to examine the ground and the tops of the walls to see if a runway had been let down for the auto to go over.'

The Thinking Machine squinted at him inquiringly.

'Are you sure you saw an automobile?' he demanded irritably.

'Certainly I saw it,' blurted the reporter. 'I not only saw it – I smelled it. Just to convince myself that it was real I tossed my cane in front of the thing and it smashed it to toothpicks.'

'Perhaps, then, if everything is as you say, the auto actually does fly,' remarked the scientist.

The reporter stared into the calm, inscrutable face of The Thinking Machine, fearing first that he had not heard a right. Then he concluded that he had.

'You mean,' he inquired eagerly, 'that the phantom may be an auto-aeroplane affair, and that it actually does fly?'

'It's not at all impossible,' commented the scientist.

'I had an idea something like that myself,' Hatch explained, 'and questioned every soul within a mile or so but I didn't get anything.'

The perfect stretch of road there might be the very place for some daring experimenter to get up sufficient speed to soar a short distance in a light machine,' continued the scientist.

'Light machine?' Hatch repeated. 'Did I tell you that this car had four people in it?'

'Four people!' exclaimed the scientist. 'Dear me! Dear me! That makes it very different. Of course four people would be too great a lift for an – '

'For ten minutes he sat silent, and tiny, cobwebby lines appeared in his dome-like brow. Then he arose and passed into the adjoining room. After a moment Hatch heard the telephone bell jingle. Five minutes later The Thinking Machine appeared, and scowled upon him unpleasantly.

'I suppose what you really want to learn is if the car is a – a material one and to whom it belongs?' he queried.

'That's it,' agreed the reporter, 'and of course, why it does what it does, and how it gets out of The Trap.'

'Do you happen to know a fast, long-distance bicycle rider?' demanded the scientist abruptly.

'A dozen of them,' replied the reporter promptly. 'I think I see the idea, but – '

'You haven't the faintest inkling of the idea,' declared The Thinking Machine positively. 'If you can arrange with a fast rider who can go a distance – it might be thirty, forty, fifty miles – we may end this little affair without difficulty.'

Under these circumstances Professor Augustus S. F. X. Van Dusen, Ph.D., LL.D., F.R.S., M.D., etc., etc., scientist and logician, met the famous Jimmie Thalhauer, the world's champion long distance bicyclist. He held every record from five miles up to and including six hours, had twice won the six-day race and was, altogether, a master in his field. He came in chewing a toothpick. There were introductions.

'You ride the bicycle?' inquired the crusty little scientist.

'Well, some,' confessed the champion modestly with a wink at Hatch.

'Can you keep up with an automobile for a distance of, say, thirty or forty miles?'

'I can keep up with anything that ain't got wings,' was the response.

'Well, to tell you the truth,' volunteered The Thinking Machine, 'there is a growing belief that this particular automobile has wings. However, if you can keep up with it –'

'Ah, quit your kiddin,' said the champion, easily. 'I can ride rings around anything on wheels. I'll start behind it and beat it where it's going.'

The Thinking Machine examined the champion, Jimmie Thalhauer, as a curiosity. In the seclusion of his laboratory he had never had an opportunity of meeting just such another worldly young person.

'How fast can you ride, Mr Thalhauer?' he asked at last.

'I'm ashamed to tell you,' confided the champion in a hushed voice. 'I can ride so fast that I scare myself.' He paused a moment. 'But it seems to me,' he said, 'if there's thirty or forty miles to do I ought to do it on a motorcycle.'

'Now that's just the point,' explained The Thinking Machine. 'A motorcycle makes noise and if it could have been used we would have hired a fast automobile. This proposition briefly is: I want you to ride without lights behind an automobile which may also run without lights and find out where it goes. No occupant of the car must suspect that it is followed.'

'Without lights?' repeated the champion. 'Gee! Rubber shoe, eh?'

The Thinking Machine looked his bewilderment.

'Yes, that's it,' Hatch answered for him.

'I guess it's good for a four column head? Hunh?' inquired the champion. 'Special pictures posed by the champion? Hunh?'

'Yes,' Hatch replied.

'"Tracked on a Bicycle" sounds good to me. Hunh?'

Hatch nodded.

So arrangements were concluded and then and there The Thinking Machine gave definite and conclusive instructions to the champion. While these apparently bore broadly on the problem in hand they conveyed absolutely no inkling of his plan to the reporter. At the end the champion arose to go.

'You're a most extraordinary young man, Mr Thalhauer,' commented The Thinking Machine, not without admiration for the sturdy, powerful figure.

And as Hatch accompanied the champion out the door and down the steps Jimmie smiled with easy grace.

'Nutty old guy, ain't he? Hunh?'

Night! Utter blackness, relieved only by a white, ribbon-like road which winds away mistily under a starless sky. Shadowy hedges line either side and occasionally a tree thrusts itself upward out of the sombreness. The murmur of human voices in the shadows, then the crackling-chug of an engine and an automobile moves slowly, without lights, into the road. There is the sudden clatter of an engine at high speed and the car rushes away.

From the hedge comes the faint rustle of leaves as of wind stirring, then a figure moves impalpably. A moment and it becomes a separate entity; a quick movement and the creak of a leather bicycle saddle. Silently the single figure, bent low over the handlebars, moves after the car with ever increasing momentum.

Then a long, desperate race. For mile after mile, mile after mile the auto goes on. The silent cyclist has crept up almost to the rear axle and hangs there doggedly as a racer to his pace. On and on they rush together through the darkness, the chauffeur moving with a perfect knowledge of his road, the single rider behind clinging on grimly with set teeth. The powerful, piston-like legs move up and down to the beat of the engine.

At last, with dust-dry throat and stinging, aching eyes the cyclist feels the pace slacken and instantly he drops back out of sight. It is only by sound that he follows now. The car stops; the cyclist is lost in the shadows.

For two or three hours the auto stands deserted and silent. At last the voices are heard again, the car stirs, moves away and the cyclist drops in behind. Another race which leads off in another direction. Finally, from a knoll, the lights of a city are seen. Ten minutes elapse, the auto stops, the headlights flare up and more leisurely it proceeds on its way.

On the following evening The Thinking Machine and Hutchinson Hatch called upon Fielding Stanwood, President of the Fordyce National Bank. Mr Stanwood looked at them with interrogative eyes.

'We called to inform you, Mr Stanwood,' explained The Thinking Machine, 'that a box of securities, probably United States bonds, is missing from your bank.'

'What?' exclaimed Mr Stanwood, and his face paled. 'Robbery?'

'I only know the bonds were taken out of the vault tonight by Joseph Marsh, your assistant cashier,' said the scientist, 'and that he, together with three other men, left the bank with the box and are now at a place I can name.'

Mr Stanwood was staring at him in amazement.

'You know where they are?' he demanded.

'I said I did,' replied the scientist, shortly.

'Then we must inform the police at once, and –'

'I don't know that there has been an actual crime,' interrupted the scientist. 'I do know that every night for a week these bonds have been taken out through the connivance of your watchman and in each instance have been returned, intact, before morning. They will be returned tonight. Therefore

I would advise, if you act, not to do so until the four men return with the bonds.'

It was a singular party which met in the private office of President Stanwood at the bank just after midnight. Marsh and three companions, formally under arrest, were present as were President Stanwood, The Thinking Machine and Hatch, besides detectives. Marsh had the bonds under his arms when he was taken. He talked freely when questioned.

'I will admit,' he said without hesitating, 'that I have acted beyond my rights in removing the bonds from the vault here, but there is no ground for prosecution. I am a responsible officer of this bank and have violated no trust. Nothing is missing, nothing is stolen. Every bond that went out of the bank is here.'

'But why – why did you take the bonds?' demanded Mr Stanwood.

Marsh shrugged his shoulders.

'It's what has been called a get-rich-quick scheme,' said The Thinking Machine. 'Mr Hatch and I made some investigations today. Mr Marsh and these other three are interested in a business venture which is ethically dishonest but which is within the law. They have sought backing for the scheme amounting to about a million dollars. Those four or five men of means with whom they have discussed the matter have called each night for a week at Marsh's country place. It was necessary to make them believe that there was already a million or so in the scheme, so these bonds were borrowed and represented to be owned by themselves. They were taken to and fro between the bank and his home in a kind of an automobile. This is really what happened, based on knowledge which Mr Hatch has gathered and what I myself developed by the use of a little logic.'

And his statement of the affair proved to be correct. Marsh and the others admitted the statement to be true. It was while The Thinking Machine was homeward bound that he explained the phantom auto affair to Hatch.

'The phantom auto, as you call it,' he said, 'is the vehicle in which the bonds were moved about. The phantom idea came merely by chance. On the night the vehicle was first noticed it was rushing along – we'll say to reach Marsh's house in time for an appointment. A road map will show you that the most direct line from the bank to Marsh's was through The Trap. If an automobile should go half way through there, then out across the Stocker estate to the other road, distance would be lessened by a good five miles. This saving at first was of course valuable, so the car in which they rushed into The Trap was merely taken across the Stocker estate to the road in front.'

'But how?' demanded Hatch. 'There's no road there.'

'I learned by phone from Mr Stocker that there is a narrow walk from a very narrow foot-gate in Stocker's wall on The Trap leading through the grounds to the other road. The phantom auto wasn't really an auto at all – it was merely two motor cycles arranged with seats and a steering apparatus. The French Army has been experimenting with them. The motor cycles are, of course, separate machines and as such it was easy to trundle them through a narrow gate and across to the other road. The seats are light; they can be carried under the arm.'

'Oh!' exclaimed Hatch suddenly, then after a minute: 'But what did Jimmie Thalhauer do for you?' 'He waited in the road at the other end of the foot-path from The Trap,' the scientist explained. 'When the auto was brought through and put together he followed it to Marsh's home and from there to the bank. The rest of it you and I worked out today. It's merely logic, Mr Hatch, logic.'

There was a pause. 'That Mr Thalhauer is really a marvelous young man, Mr Hatch, don't you think?'

10

THE PROBLEM OF THE AUTO CAB

Hutchinson Hatch gathered up his overcoat and took the steps coming down two at a time. There was no car in sight, nothing on wheels in fact, until – yes, here was an automobile turning the corner, an automobile cab drifting along apparently without purpose. Hatch hailed it.

"Get me out to Commonwealth Avenue and Arden Street in a hurry!" he instructed. "Take a chance with the speed law, and I'll make it worth while. It's important."

He yanked open the door, stepped in, and closed it with a slam. The chauffeur gave a twist to his lever, turned the car almost within its length, and went scuttling off up street.

Safely inside, Hatch became suddenly aware that he had a fellow passenger. Through the gloom he felt, rather than saw, two inquisitive eyes staring out at him, and there was the faintest odor of violets.

"Hello!" Hatch demanded. "Am I in your way?"

"Not in the slightest," came the voice of a woman. "Am I in yours?"

"Why – I beg your pardon," Hatch stammered. "I thought I had the cab alone – didn't know there was a passenger. Perhaps I'd better get out?"

"No, no!" protested the woman quickly. "Don't think of it."

Then from outside came the bellowing voice of a policeman. "Hey, there! I'll report you!"

Glancing back, Hatch saw him standing in the middle of the street jotting down something in a notebook. The chauffeur made a few uncomplimentary remarks about bluecoats in general, swished round a corner, and sped on. With a half smile of appreciation on his lips, Hatch turned back to his unknown companion.

"If you will tell me where you are going," he suggested, "I'll have the chauffeur set you down."

"It's of no consequence," replied the woman a little wearily. "I am going no place particularly – just riding about to collect my thoughts."

A woman unattended, riding about in an automobile at fifteen minutes of eleven o'clock at night to collect her thoughts! And the chauffeur didn't know he had a passenger! The reporter sat oblivious of the bumping, grinding, of the automobile, trying to consider this unexpected incident calmly.

"You are a reporter?" inquired the woman.

"Yes," Hatch replied. "How did you guess it?"

"From seeing you rush out of a newspaper office in such a hurry at this time of night," she replied. "Something important, I dare say?"

"Well, yes," Hatch agreed. "A jewel robbery at a ball. Don't know much about it yet. Just got a police bulletin stating that Mrs Windsor Dillingham had been robbed of a necklace worth thirty thousand dollars at a big affair she is giving tonight."

The inside of the cab was lighted brilliantly by the electric arc outside, and Hatch had an opportunity of seeing the woman face to face at close range. She was pretty; she was young; and she was well dressed. From her shoulders she was enveloped in some loose cloak of dark material; but it was not drawn together at her throat, and her bare neck gleamed.

THE PROBLEM OF THE AUTO CAB

There being nothing whatever to say, Hatch sat silently staring out of the window as the automobile whirled into Commonwealth Avenue and slowed up as it approached Arden Street.

"Will you do me one favor, please?" asked the woman.

"Yes, if I can," was the reporter's reply.

"Allow me, please, to get out of the automobile on the side away from the curb, and be good enough to attract the attention of the chauffeur to yourself while I am doing it. Here is a bill," and she pressed something into Hatch's hand. "You may pay the chauffeur a tip for the passenger he didn't know he had."

Hatch agreed in a dazed sort of way, and the automobile came to a stop. He stepped out on the curb, and slammed the door as the chauffeur leaped down from his seat. From the other side came an answering door slam, as if an echo.

Five minutes later Hatch joined Detective Mallory inside. At just that moment the detective was listening to the story of Mrs Dillingham's maid.

"There's nothing missing but the necklace," she explained; "so far, at least, as we have been able to find out. Mrs Dillingham began dressing at about half-past eight o'clock, and I assisted her as usual. I suppose it was half-past nine when she finished. All that time the necklace was in the jewel box on her dressing table. It was the only article of jewelry in the box.

"Well, the butler came up about half-past nine o'clock for his final instructions, and Mrs Dillingham went into the adjoining room to talk to him. It was not more than a minute later when she sent me down to the conservatory for a rose for her hair. She was still talking to him when I returned five minutes later. I put the rose in her hair, and she sent me into her dressing room for her necklace. When I looked into the jewel box, the necklace was gone. I told Mrs Dillingham. The butler heard me. That's all I know of it, except that Mrs Dillingham went into hysterics and fainted, and I telephoned for a doctor."

Detective Mallory regarded the girl coldly; Hatch knew perfectly what was coming. "You are quite sure," asked the detective, "that you did not take the necklace with you when you went down to the conservatory, and pass it to a confederate on the outside."

The sudden pallor of the girl, her abject, cringing fright, answered the question to Hatch's satisfaction even before she opened her lips with a denial. Hatch himself was about to ask a question, when a footman entered.

"Mrs Dillingham will see you in her boudoir," he announced.

From the lips of Mrs Dillingham they heard identically the same story the maid had told. Mrs Dillingham did not suspect anyone of her household.

For half an hour the detective interrogated her; then there came a rap at the door, and a woman entered.

"Why, Dora!" exclaimed Mrs Dillingham

The young woman went straight to her, put her arms about her shoulders protectingly, then turned to glare defiantly at Detective Mallory and Hutchinson Hatch. The reporter gasped – it was the mysterious woman of the automobile. An exclamation was on his lips; but something in her eyes warned him, and he was silent.

When, on the following day, Hutchinson Hatch related the circumstances of the theft of Mrs Dillingham's necklace to Professor Augustus S. F. X. Van Dusen – The Thinking Machine – he did not mention the mysterious woman in the automobile. However curious those incidents in which he and she had figured were, they were inconsequential, and there was nothing to connect them in anyway with the problem in hand. The strange woman's meeting with Mrs Dillingham in the reporter's presence had convinced him that she was an intimate friend.

"Just what time was the theft discovered?" inquired The Thinking Machine.

"Within a few minutes of half-past nine."

"At what time did most of the guests arrive?"

"Between half-past nine and ten."

"Then at half-past nine," continued the scientist, "there could not have been many persons there?"

"Perhaps a dozen," returned the reporter.

"And who were they?"

"Their names, you mean? I don't know."

"Well, find out," directed The Thinking Machine crustily. "If the servants are removed from the case, and there were a dozen other persons in the house, common sense tells us to find out who and what they were. Suppose, Mr Hatch, you had attended that ball and stolen that necklace; what would have been your natural inclination afterward?"

Hatch stared at him blankly for a minute, then smiled whimsically. "You mean how would I have tried to get away with it?" he asked.

"Yes. When would you have left the place?"

"That's rather hard to say," Hatch declared thoughtfully. "But I think I should either have gone before anybody else did, through fear of discovery, or else I should have been one of the last, through excess of caution."

"Then proceed along those lines," instructed The Thinking Machine. "You might almost put that down as a law of criminology. It will enable you in the beginning, therefore, to narrow down the dozen or so guests to the first and last who left."

Deeply pondering this little interjection of psychology into a very material affair, Hatch went his way. In the course of events he saw Mrs Dillingham, who, out of consideration for her guests, flatly refused to give their names.

Luckily for Hatch, the butler didn't feel that way about it at all. This was due partly to the fact that Detective Mallory had given him a miserable half-hour, and partly, perhaps, to the fact that the reporter oiled his greedy palm with a bill of two figures.

"To begin with," said the reporter, "I want to know the names of the first dozen or so persons who arrived here that evening – I mean those who were here when you went up to speak with Mrs Dillingham."

"I might find out, sir. Their cards were laid on the salver as they arrived, and that salver, I think, has remained undisturbed. Therefore, the first dozen cards on it would give you the names you want."

"Now, that's something like," commented the reporter enthusiastically. "And do you remember any person who left the house rather early that evening?"

"No, sir," was the reply. Then suddenly there came a flash of remembrance across the stoical face. "But I remember that one gentleman arrived here twice. It was this way. Mr Hawes Campbell came in about eleven o'clock, and passed by without handing me a card. Then I remembered that he had been here earlier and that I had his card. But I don't recall that anyone went out, and I was at the door all evening except when I was up stairs talking to Mrs Dillingham."

On a bare chance, Hatch went to find Campbell. Inquiry at his two clubs failed to find him, and finally Hatch called at his home.

At the end of five minutes, perhaps, Hatch caught the swish of skirts in the hallway, then the portiéres were thrust aside, and – again he was face to face with the mysterious woman of the automobile.

"My brother isn't here," she said calmly, without the slightest sign of recognition. "Can I do anything for you?"

Her brother! Then she was Miss Campbell, and Mrs Dillingham had called her Dora-Dora Campbell!

"Well-er—" Hatch faltered a little, "it was a personal matter I wanted to see him about."

"I don't know when he will return," Miss Campbell announced.

Hatch stared at her for a moment; he was making up his mind. At last he took the bit in his teeth. "We understand, Miss Campbell," he said at last slowly and emphatically, "that your brother, Hawes Campbell has some information which might be of value in unraveling the mystery surrounding the theft of Mrs Dillingham's necklace."

Miss Campbell dropped into a chair, and unconsciously Hatch assumed the defensive. "Mrs Dillingham is very much annoyed, as you must know," Miss Campbell said, "about the publicity given to this affair; particularly as she is confident that the necklace will be returned within a short time. Her only annoyance, beyond the wide publicity, as I said, is that it has not already been returned."

"Returned?" gasped Hatch.

Miss Campbell shrugged her shoulders. "She knows," she continued, "that the necklace is now in safe hands, that there is no danger of its being lost to her; but the situation is such that she cannot demand its return."

"Mrs Dillingham knows where the necklace is, then?" he asked.

"Yes," replied Miss Campbell.

"Perhaps you know?"

"Perhaps I do," she responded readily. "I can assure you that Mrs Dillingham is going to take the affair out of the hands of the police, because she knows her property is safe – as safe as if it was in your hands, for instance. It is only a question of time when it will be returned."

"Where is the necklace?" Hatch demanded suddenly.

Again Miss Campbell shrugged her shoulders.

"And what does your brother know about the affair?"

"I can't answer that question, of course," was the response.

"Well, why did he go to Mrs Dillingham's early in the evening, then go away, and return about eleven o'clock?" insisted the reporter bluntly.

For the first time there came a change in Miss Campbell's manner, a subtle, indefinable something which the reporter readily saw but to which he could attach no meaning.

"I can't say more than I have said," she replied after a moment. "Believe me," and there was a note of earnestness in her voice, "it would be far better for you to drop the matter, because otherwise you may be placed in-in a ridiculous position."

And that was all – a threat, delicately veiled it is true, but a threat nevertheless. She arose and led the way to the door.

Hatch didn't realize the significance of that remark then, nor did it occur to him that the mysterious affair in the automobile had not been mentioned between them; for here was material, knotty, incoherent, inexplicable material, for The Thinking Machine, and there he took it. Again he told the story; but this time all of it – every incident from the moment he hailed the automobile in front of his office on the night of the robbery until Miss Campbell closed the door.

"Why didn't you tell me all of it before?" demanded The Thinking Machine irritably.

"I couldn't see that the affair in the automobile had any connection with the robbery," explained the reporter.

"Couldn't see!" stormed the eminent man of science. "Couldn't see! Every trivial happening on this whole round earth bears on every other happening, no matter how vast or how disconnected it may seem; the correlation of facts makes a perpetually unbroken chain. In other words, if Mrs Leary hadn't kept a cow, Chicago would not have been destroyed by fire. Couldn't see!"

For an instant The Thinking Machine glared at him; and the change from petulant annoyance to deep abstraction, as that singular brain turned to the problem in hand, was almost visible. It was uncanny. Then the scientist dropped back into his chair with eyes turned upward, and long slender fingers pressed tip to tip. Ten minutes passed, twenty, thirty, and he turned suddenly to the reporter.

"What was the number of that automobile?" he demanded.

Hatch grinned in sheer triumph. Of all the questions he could have anticipated this was the most unlikely, and yet he had the number set down in his notebook where it would ultimately become a voucher in his expense account. He consulted the book.

"Number 869019," he replied.

"Now, find that automobile," directed The Thinking Machine. "It is important that you do so at once."

"You mean that the necklace–" Hatch began breathlessly.

"When you bring the automobile here, I will produce the necklace," declared The Thinking Machine emphatically.

Hatch returned half a dozen hours later with troubled lines in his face.

"Automobile No. 869019 has disappeared, evaporated into air," he declared with some heat. "There was one that night, because I was in it, and the highway commission's records show a private cab license granted to John Kilrain under the number; but it has disappeared."

"Where is Kilrain?" inquired The Thinking Machine.

"I didn't see him; but I saw his wife," explained the reporter. "She didn't know anything about automobile No. 869019, or said she didn't. She said his auto car was–"

"No. 610698," interrupted The Thinking Machine. It was not a question; it was the statement as of one who knew.

Hatch stared from the scientist to the notebook where he had written down the number the woman gave him, and then he looked his utter astonishment.

"Of course, that is the number," continued The Thinking Machine, as if some one had disputed it. "It is past midnight now, and we won't try to find it; but I'll have it here tomorrow at noon. We shall see for ourselves how safely the necklace has been kept."

Detective Mallory entered and glanced about inquiringly. He saw only The Thinking Machine and Hutchinson Hatch.

"I sent for you," explained the scientist, "because in half an hour or so I shall either place the Dillingham necklace in your hands, or turn over to you the man who knows where it is. You may use your own discretion as to whether or not you will prosecute. Under all the circumstances, I believe the case is one for a sanatorium, rather than prison. In other words, the person who took the necklace is not wholly responsible."

"Who is it?" demanded the detective.

"You don't happen to know all the facts in this case," continued The Thinking Machine without heeding the question. "I got them all, only after Mr Hatch, at my suggestion, had located the thief. Originally I began where you left off. I believed you had eliminated the servants, and presumed there was not a burglary. Ultimately this led to Hawes Campbell in a manner which is of no interest to you. Then I got all the facts.

"When Mr Hatch left his office to go to Mrs Dillingham's, he took an automobile which happened to be passing," resumed the scientist. "It was a cab, No. 869019. Inside that cab he found, much to his astonishment, a woman – a young woman in evening dress. She made the surprising statement that the chauffeur didn't know she was there, and that she was not going anywhere – was merely riding around to collect her thoughts. And this was, please remember, about eleven o'clock at night. On its face this incident had no connection with the jewel theft; but by a singular chain of coincidences, subsequently developed, it seemed that Mr Hatch had arrived at the solution of the mystery before he even knew the circumstances of the theft."

Detective Mallory nodded doubtfully. "But how does that connect with the—" he began.

"Subsequent developments establish a direct connection," interrupted The Thinking Machine. "We have the woman in the automobile. We shall presume that she must have had some strong motive for leaving a house at that time of night and doing the apparently purposeless things that she did do. We don't know this motive from these facts – we only know there was a motive.

"Now when you and Mr Hatch were talking to Mrs Dillingham, a woman entered the room. Mr Hatch recognized her immediately as the woman in the automobile. Everything indicated that she was an intimate friend of Mrs Dillingham's. So we pass on to the point where Mr Hatch found that Hawes Campbell arrived at the ball early, went away again, then returned after eleven o'clock. Mr Hatch wanted to know why he left, and went to his home to inquire. Campbell's sister met him there. She was the woman he had met in the automobile. So we have Campbell leaving the ball, immediately after the theft, say, and his sister running away from her home sometime between nine-thirty and eleven, and secreting herself in an automobile.

"Why? I have said, Mr Mallory, that imagination – the ability to bridge gaps temporarily – is the most essential part of the logical mind. Now, if we imagine that Campbell stole the necklace, that he went home, that his sister found it out, that there was some sort of scene which terminated in her flight with the necklace, we account for absolutely every incident preceding and following Mr Hatch's arrival at the Dillingham place.

"I have made inquiries. The Campbells are worth, not thousands, but millions. Therefore, the question. Why should Hawes Campbell steal a necklace? The answer, kleptomania. And again, it was known to the sister, who tried in her own manner to return the stolen property and avoid the scandal. When she was in the automobile, she was trying to collect her thoughts – trying to invent a way to return the necklace. It was the merest chance that Mr Hatch happened to get into that particular vehicle.

"Now, we come to the most difficult part of the problem," and The Thinking Machine dropped back still further into the cavernous depths of his chair. "What would a frightened, perhaps hysterical, woman do with that necklace? From the fact that it has not been returned, we know that she didn't venture into the house with it, and leave it casually in any one of a hundred places where it might have been discovered without danger to herself. Yet everything indicates that she had it while in the cab. The obvious thing which suggests itself is that she hid it in the cab, intending to regain possession of it later and return it. Now, that cab number was 869019. Strangely enough, after Mr Hatch left the cab it seems to have disappeared. The chauffeur, John Kilrain, has another cab number now, 610698 – that is, auto cab No. 869019 was made to disappear by the simple act of turning the number board upside down, giving us 610698."

"Well, by George!" exclaimed Detective Mallory. No mere words would convey the reporter's astonishment; he gasped.

"Now," continued The Thinking Machine after a moment, "there are two reasons, both good, why auto cab number 869019 should have disappeared. The vital one, it seems to me, is that Kilrain discovered the necklace inside and kept it; the other is that he was threatened with arrest by the policeman who took his number for speeding, and to avoid a fine disguised the identity of his cab. There are one or two other possibilities; but if the necklace isn't found in the automobile, I should advise, not arrest, but a close watch on Kilrain, both at his home and in his intercourse with other chauffeurs at the various cab stands."

There was a rap at the door, and Martha appeared. "Did you want an automobile, sir?"

"We'll be right out," returned the scientist.

THE PROBLEM OF THE AUTO CAB 243

And so it came about that The Thinking Machine, Detective Mallory, and Hutchinson Hatch searched the very vitals of auto cab No. 869019, temporarily masquerading as No. 610698, while Kilrain stood by in perturbed amazement. At the end he was allowed to go.

"Remember, please, what I advised you to do," The Thinking Machine reminded Detective Mallory.

With eyes that were heavy with sleep Hutchinson Hatch crawled out of bed and answered the insistent ringing of his telephone. The crabbed voice of The Thinking Machine came over the wire, in a question.

"If Miss Campbell was so anxious to return the necklace that night, she couldn't have done better, could she, than to have handed it to a reporter who was going to the house to investigate the robbery?"

"I don't think so," Hatch replied wonderingly.

"Did you have on your overcoat that night?"

"I had it with me."

"Suppose you go look in the pockets, and–"

Hatch dropped the receiver, already inspired by the suggestion, and dragged his overcoat out of the closet. In the left hand lower pocket was a small package. He opened it with trembling fingers. There before his eyes lay the iridescent, gleaming bauble. It had been in his possession from an hour after it was stolen until this very instant. He rushed back to the telephone.

"I've got it!" he shouted.

"Silly of me not to have thought of it in the first place," came the querulous voice of The Thinking Machine. "Goodnight."

11

THE ROSWELL TIARA

Had it not been for the personal interest of a fellow savant in the case it is hardly likely that the problem of the Roswell tiara would ever have come to the attention of The Thinking Machine. And had the problem not come to his attention it would inevitably have gone to the police. Then there would have been a scandal in high places, a disrupted home and everlasting unhappiness to at least four persons. Perhaps it was an inkling of this latter possibility that led The Thinking Machine to take initial steps in the solution of a mystery which seemed to have only an obvious ending.

When he was first approached in the matter The Thinking Machine was in his small laboratory from which had gone forth truths that shocked and partially readjusted at least three of the exact sciences. His enormous head, with its long yellow hair, bobbed up and down over a little world of chemical apparatus, and the narrow, squint eyes peered with disagreeable satisfaction at a blue flame which spouted from a brazier. Martha, an aged woman who was the scientist's household staff, entered. She was not tall yet she towered commandingly above the slight figure of her eminent master. Professor Van Dusen turned to her impatiently.

"Well? Well?" he demanded shortly.

Martha handed him two cards. On one was the name Charles Wingate Field, and on the other Mrs Richard Watson Roswell. Charles Wingate Field was a name to juggle with in astronomy – The Thinking Machine knew him well; the name of the woman was strange to him.

"The gentleman said it was very important," Martha explained, "and the poor lady was crying."

"What about?" snapped the scientist.

"Lord, sir, I didn't ask her," exclaimed Martha.

"I'll be there in a moment."

A few minutes later The Thinking Machine appeared at the door of the little reception room, which he regarded as a sort of useless glory, and the two persons there arose to meet him. One was a woman apparently of forty-five years, richly gowned, splendid of figure and with a distinct, matured beauty. Her eyes showed she had been weeping but now her tears were dried and she caught herself staring curiously at the pallid face, the keen blue eyes and the long slender hands of the scientist. The other person was Mr Field.

There was an introduction and the scientist motioned them to seats. He himself dropped into a large cushioned chair, and looked from one to the other with a question in his eyes.

"I have been telling Mrs Roswell some of the things you have done, Van Dusen," began Mr Field. "Now I have brought her to you because here is a mystery, a problem, an abstruse problem, and it isn't the kind of thing one cares to take to the police. If you–"

"If Mrs Roswell will tell me about it?" interrupted the scientist. He seemed to withdraw even further into the big chair. With head tilted back, eyes squinting steadily upward and white fingers pressed tip to tip he waited.

"Briefly," said Mrs Roswell, "it has to do with the disappearance of a single small gem from a diamond tiara which I had locked in a vault – a vault of which no living person knew the combination except myself. Because of family reasons I could not go to the police, and—"

"Please begin at the beginning," requested The Thinking Machine. "Remember I know nothing whatever of you or your circumstances."

It was not unnatural that Mrs Roswell should be surprised. Her social reign was supreme, her name was constantly to be seen in the newspapers, her entertainments were gorgeous, her social doings on an elaborate scale. She glanced at Mr Field inquiringly, and he nodded.

"My first husband was Sidney Grantham, an Englishman," she explained. "Seven years ago he left me a widow with one child – a son Arthur – now twenty-two years old and just out of Harvard. Mr Grantham died intestate and his whole fortune together with the family jewels, came to me and my son. The tiara was among these jewels.

"A year ago I was married to Mr Roswell. He, too, is a man of wealth, with one daughter, Jeanette, now nineteen years old. We live on Commonwealth Avenue and while there are many servants I know it impossible—"

"Nothing is impossible, Madam," interposed The Thinking Machine positively. "Don't say that please. It annoys me exceedingly."

Mrs Roswell stared at him a moment then resumed:

"My bed room is on the second floor. Adjoining and connecting with it is the bed room of my step-daughter. This connecting door is always left unlocked because she is timid and nervous. I keep the door from my room into the hall bolted at night and Jeanette keeps the hall door of her room similarly fastened. The windows, too, are always secured at night in both rooms.

"My maid and my daughter's maid both sleep in the servants' quarters. I arranged for this because, as I was about to state, I keep about half a million dollars worth of jewels in my bed room locked in a small vault built into the wall. This little vault opens with a combination. Not one person knows that combination except myself. It so happens that the man who set it is dead.

"Last night, Thursday, I attended a reception and wore the tiara. My daughter remained at home. At four o'clock this morning I returned. The maids had retired; Jeanette was sleeping soundly. I took off the tiara and placed it, with my other jewels, in the vault. I know that the small diamond now missing was in its setting at that time. I locked the vault, shot the bolt and turned the combination. Afterwards I tried the vault door to make certain it was fastened. It was then – then—"

For no apparent reason Mrs Roswell suddenly burst into tears. The two men were silent and The Thinking Machine looked at her uneasily. He was not accustomed to women anyway, and women who wept were hopelessly beyond him.

"Well, well, what happened?" he asked brusquely at last.

"It was perhaps five o'clock when I fell asleep," Mrs Roswell continued after a moment. "About twenty minutes later I was aroused by a scream of 'Jeanette, Jeanette, Jeanette.' Instantly I was fully awake. The screaming was that of a cockatoo which I have kept in my room for many years. It was in its usual place on a perch near the window, and seemed greatly disturbed.

"My first impression was that Jeanette had been in the room. I went into her room and even shook her gently. She was asleep so far as I could ascertain. I returned to my own room and then was amazed to see the vault door standing open. All the jewels and papers from the vault were scattered over the floor. My first thought was of burglars who had been frightened away by the cockatoo. I tried every door and every window in both Jeanette's room and mine. Everything was securely fastened.

"When I picked up the tiara I found that a diamond was missing. It had evidently been torn out of the setting. I searched for it on the floor and inside the vault. I found nothing. Then of course I could only associate its disappearance with some act of – of my step-daughter's. I don't believe the cockatoo would have called her name if she had not been in my room. Certainly the bird could not have opened the vault. Therefore I – I—"

There was a fresh burst of tears and for a long time no one spoke.

"Do you burn a night lamp?" asked The Thinking Machine finally.

"Yes," replied Mrs Roswell.

"Did the bird ever disturb you at any time previous to last night – that is I mean at night?"

"No."

"Has it any habit of speaking the word 'Jeanette.'"

"No. I don't think I ever heard it pronounce the word more than three or four times before. It is stupid and seems to dislike her."

"Was there anything else missing – any letter or paper or jewels?"

"Nothing but the one small stone."

The Thinking Machine took down a volume of an encyclopædia which he studied for a moment.

"Have you any record anywhere of that combination?" he inquired.

"Yes, but it would have been impossi—"

The scientist made a little impatient gesture with his hands.

"Where is this record?"

"The combination begins with the figure three," Mrs Roswell hastened to explain. "I jotted it down in a French copy of 'Les Misérables' which I keep in my room with a few other books. The first number, three, appears on Page 3, the second on Page 33, and the third on Page 333. The combination in full is 3-14-9. No person could possibly associate the numbers in the book with the combination even if they should notice them."

Again there was the quick, impatient gesture of the hands. Mr Field interpreted it aright as annoyance.

"You say your daughter is nervous," The Thinking Machine said. "Is it serious? Is there any somnambulistic tendency that you know of?"

Mrs Roswell flushed a little.

"She has a nervous disorder," she confessed at last. "But I know of no somnambulistic tendency. She has been treated by half a dozen specialists. Two or three times we feared-feared—"

She faltered and stopped. The Thinking Machine squinted at her oddly, then turned his eyes toward the ceiling again.

"I understand," he said. "You feared for her sanity. And she may have the sleep-walking habit without your knowledge?"

"Yes, she may have," faltered Mrs Roswell.

"And now your son. Tell me something about him. He has an allowance, I suppose? Is he inclined to be studious or other wise? Has he any love affair?"

Again Mrs Roswell flushed. Her entire manner resented this connection of her son's name with the affair. She looked inquiringly at Mr Field.

"I don't see—" Mr Field began, remonstratingly.

"My son could have nothing—" Mrs Roswell interrupted.

"Madam, you have presented an abstract problem," broke in The Thinking Machine impatiently. "I presumed you wanted a solution. Of course, if you do not—" and he made as if to arise.

"Please pardon me," said Mrs Roswell quickly, almost tearfully. "My son has an allowance of ten thousand a year; my daughter has the same. My son is inclined to be studious along political lines, while my daughter is interested in charity. He has no love affair except-except a deep attachment for his step-sister. It is rather unfortunate—"

"I know, I know," interrupted the scientist again. "Naturally you object to any affection in that direction because of a fear for the girl's mental condition. May I ask if there is any further prejudice on your part to the girl?"

"Not the slightest," said Mrs Roswell quickly. "I am deeply attached to her. It is only a fear for my son's happiness."

"I presume your son understands your attitude in the matter?"

"I have tried to intimate it to him without saying it openly," she explained. "I don't think he knows how serious her condition has been, and is for that matter."

"Of your knowledge has either your son or the girl ever handled or looked into the book where the combination is written?"

"Not that I know of, or ever heard of."

"Or any of your servants?"

"No."

"Does it happen that you have this tiara with you?"

Mrs Roswell produced it from her hand bag. It was a glittering, glistening thing, a triumph of the jeweller's art, intricate and marvellously delicate in conception yet wonderfully heavy with the dead weight of pure gold. A single splendid diamond of four or five carats blazed at its apex, and radiating from this were strings of smaller stones. One was missing from its setting. The prongs which had held it were almost straight from the force used to pry out the stone. The Thinking Machine studied the gorgeous ornament in silence.

"It is possible for you to clear up this matter without my active interference," he said at last. "You do not want it to become known outside your own family, therefore you must watch for this thief – yourself in person. Take no one into your confidence, least of all your son and step-daughter. Given the same circumstances, the A B C rules of logic – and logic is inevitable – indicate that another may disappear."

Mrs Roswell was frankly startled, and Mr Field leaned forward with eager interest.

"If you see how this second stone disappears," continued The Thinking Machine musingly, without heeding in the slightest the effect of his words on the others, "you will know what became of the first and will be able to recover both."

"If another attempt is to be made," exclaimed Mrs Roswell apprehensively, "would it not be better to send the jewels to a safe deposit? Would I not be in danger myself?"

"It is perfectly possible that if the jewels were removed the vault would be opened just the same," said The Thinking Machine quietly, enigmatically while his visitors stared. "Leave the jewels where they are. You may be assured that you are in no personal danger whatever. If you learn what you seek you need not communicate with me again. If you do not I will personally investigate the matter. On no condition whatever interrupt or attempt to prevent anything that may happen."

Mr Field arose; the interview seemed to be at an end. He had one last question.

"Have you any theory of what actually happened?" he asked. "How was the jewel taken?"

"If I told you you wouldn't believe it," said The Thinking Machine, curtly. "Goodday."

It was on the third day following that Mrs Roswell hurriedly summoned The Thinking Machine to her home. When he arrived she was deeply agitated.

"Another of the small stones has been stolen from the tiara," she told him hurriedly. "The circumstances were identical with those of the first theft, even to the screaming of the cockatoo. I watched as you suggested, have been watching each night but last night was so weary that I fell asleep. The cockatoo awoke me. Why would Jeanette—"

"Let me see the apartments," suggested the scientist. Thus he was ushered into the room which was the centre of the mystery. Again he examined the tiara, then studied the door of the vault. Afterwards he casually picked up and verified the record of the combination, locked and unlocked the vault twice after which he examined the fastenings of the door and the windows. This done he went over and peered inquisitively at the cockatoo on its perch.

The bird was a giant of its species, pure white, with a yellow crest which drooped in exaggerated melancholy. The cockatoo resented the impertinence and had not The Thinking Machine moved quickly would have torn off his spectacles.

A door from another room opened and a girl – Jeanette – entered. She was tall, slender and exquisitely proportioned with a great cloud of ruddy gold hair. Her face was white with the dead white of illness and infinite weariness was in her eyes. She was startled at sight of a stranger.

"I beg your pardon," she said. "I didn't know—" and started to retire.

Professor Van Dusen acknowledged an introduction to her by a glance and a nod then turned quickly and looked at the cockatoo which was quarrelling volubly with crest upraised. Mrs Roswell's attention, too, was attracted by the angry attitude of her pet. She grasped the scientist's arm quickly.

"The bird!" she exclaimed.

"Jeanette, Jeanette, Jeanette," screamed the cockatoo, shrilly. Jeanette dropped wearily into a chair, heeding neither the tense attitude of her step-mother nor the quarrellings of the cockatoo.

"You don't sleep well, Miss Roswell?" asked The Thinking Machine.

"Oh, yes," the girl replied. "I seem to sleep enough, but I am always very tired. And I dream constantly, nearly always my dreams are of the cockatoo. I imagine he calls my name."

Mrs Roswell looked quickly at Professor Van Dusen. He crossed to the girl and examined her pulse.

"Do you read much?" he asked. "Did you ever read this?" and he held up the copy of "Les Misérables."

"I don't read French well enough," she replied. "I have read it in English."

The conversation was desultory for a time and finally The Thinking Machine arose. In the drawing room down stairs he gave Mrs Roswell some instructions which amazed her exceedingly, and went his way.

Jeanette retired about eleven o'clock that night and in an hour was sleeping soundly. But Mrs Roswell was up when the clock struck one. She had previously bolted the doors of the two rooms and fastened the windows. Now she arose from her seat, picked up a small jar from her table, and crept cautiously, even stealthily to the bed whereon Jeanette lay, pale almost as the sheets. The girl's hands were outstretched in an attitude of utter exhaustion. Mrs Roswell bent low over them a moment, then stole back to her own room. Half an hour later she was asleep.

Early next morning Mrs Roswell 'phoned to The Thinking Machine, and they talked for fifteen minutes. She was apparently explaining something and the scientist gave crisp, monosyllabic answers. When the wire was disconnected he called up two other persons on the 'phone. One of them was Dr Henderson, noted alienist; the other was Dr Forrester, a nerve specialist of international repute. To both he said:

"I want to show you the most extraordinary thing you have ever seen."

The dim light of the night lamp cast strange, unexpected shadows, half revealing yet half hiding, the various objects in Mrs Roswell's room. The bed made a great white splotch in the shadows, and the only other conspicuous point was the bright silver dial of the jewel vault. From the utter darkness of Jeanette Roswell's room came the steady, regular breathing of a person asleep; the cockatoo was gone from his perch. Outside was the faint night-throb of a city at rest. In the distance a clock boomed four times.

Finally the stillness was broken by a faint creaking, the tread of a light foot and Jeanette, robed mystically in white, appeared in the door of her room. Her eyes were wide open, staring, her face was chalk-like, her hair tumbled in confusion about her head and here and there was flecked with the glint of the night-light.

The girl paused and from somewhere in the shadow came a quick gasp, instantly stifled. Then, unhearing, she moved slowly but without hesitation across the room to a table whereon lay several books. She stooped over this and when she straightened up again she held "Les Misérables" in her hand. Several times the leaves fluttered through her fingers, and thrice she held the book close to her eyes in the uncertain light, then nodded as if satisfied and carefully replaced it as she had found it.

From the table she went straight toward the silver dial which gleamed a reflection of light. As she went another figure detached itself noiselessly from the shadows and crept toward her from behind. As the girl leaned forward to place her hand on the dial a steady ray of light from an electric bell struck her full in the face. She did not flinch nor by the slightest sign show that she was aware of it. From her face the light travelled to each of her hands in turn.

The dial whirled in her fingers several times and then stopped with a click, the bolt snapped and the vault door opened. Conspicuously in front lay the tiara glittering mockingly. Again from the shadows there came a quick gasp as the girl lifted the regal toy and tumbled it on the floor. Again the gasp was stifled.

With quick moving, nervous hands she dragged the jewels out permitting them to fall. She seemed to be seeking something else, seeking vainly, apparently, for after awhile she rose with a sigh, staring into the vault hopelessly. She stood thus for a

THE ROSWELL TIARA

dozen heart beats, then the low, guarded voice of the second figure was heard—low yet singularly clear of enunciation.

"What is it you seek?"

"The letters," she replied dreamily yet distinctly. There was a pause and she turned suddenly as if to re-enter her room. As she did so the light again flashed in her glassy eyes, and the second figure laid a detaining hand on her arm. She started a little, staggered, her eyes closed suddenly to open again in abject terror as she stared into the face before her. She screamed wildly, piercingly, gazed a moment then sank down fainting.

"Dr Forrester, she needs you now."

It was the calm, unexcited, impersonal voice of The Thinking Machine. He touched a button in the wall and the room was flooded with light. Dr. Forrester and Henderson, suddenly revealed with Mr and Mrs Roswell and Arthur Grantham, came forward and lifted the senseless body. Grantham, too, rushed to her with pained, horror-stricken face. Mrs Roswell dropped limply into a chair; her husband stood beside her helplessly stroking her hair.

"It's all right," said The Thinking Machine. "It's only shock."

Grantham turned on him savagely, impetuously and danger lay in the boyish eyes.

"It's a lie!" he said fiercely. "She didn't steal those diamonds."

"How do you know?" asked The Thinking Machine coldly.

"Because-because I took them myself," the young man blurted. "If I had known there was to be any such trick as this I should never have consented to it."

His mother stared up at him in open eyed wonder.

"How did you remove the jewels from the setting?" asked The Thinking Machine, still quietly.

"I – I did it with my fingers."

"Take out one of these for me," and The Thinking Machine offered him the tiara.

Grantham snatched it from his hand and tugged at it frantically while the others stared, but each jewel remained in its setting. Finally he sank down on the bed beside the still figure of the girl he loved. His face was crimson.

"Your intentions are good, but you're a fool," commented The Thinking Machine tartly. "I know you did not take the jewels – you have proven it yourself – and I may add that Miss Roswell did not take them."

The stupefied look on Grantham's face was reflected in those of his mother and step-father. Drs Forrester and Henderson were busy with the girl heedless of the others.

"Then where are the jewels?" Mrs Roswell demanded.

The Thinking Machine turned and squinted at her with a slight suggestion of irritable reproach in his manner.

"Safe and easily found," he replied impatiently. He lifted the unconscious girl's hand and allowed his fingers to rest on her pulse for a moment, then turned to the medical men. "Would you have believed that somnambulistic sub-consciousness would have taken just this form?" he asked curtly.

"Not unless I had seen it," replied Dr Henderson, frankly.

"It's a remarkable mental condition – remarkable," commented Dr Forrester.

It was a weirdly simple recital of the facts as he had found them that The Thinking Machine told downstairs in the drawing room an hour later. Dawn was breaking over the city, and the faces of those who had waited and watched for just what had happened showed weariness. Yet they listened, listened with all their faculties as the eminent scientist talked. Young Grantham sat white faced and nervous; Jeanette was sleeping quietly upstairs with her maid on watch.

"The problem in itself was not a difficult one," The Thinking Machine began as he lounged in a big chair with eyes upturned. "The unusual, not to say strange features, which seemed to make it more difficult served to simplify it as a matter of fact. When I had all the facts I had the solution in the main. It was adding a fact to a fact to get a result as one might add two and two to get four.

"In the first place burglars were instantly removed as a possibility. They would have taken everything, not one small stone. Then what? Mr Grantham here? His mother assured me that he was quiet and studious of habit, and had an allowance of ten thousand a year. There was no need for him to steal. Then remember always that he no more than anyone else could have entered the rooms. The barred doors excluded the servants too.

"Then we had only you, Mrs Roswell, and your step-daughter. There would have been no motive for you to remove the jewel unless your object was to throw suspicion on the girl. I didn't believe you capable of this. So there was left somnambulism or a wilful act of your step-daughter's. There was no motive for the last—your daughter has ten thousand a year. Then sleep-walking alone remained. Sleep-walking it was. I am speaking now of the opening of the vault."

Grantham leaned forward in his chair gripping its arms fiercely. The mother saw, and one of her white hands was laid gently on his. He glanced at her impatiently then turned to The Thinking Machine. Mr Roswell, the alienist, and the specialist, followed the cold clear logic as if fascinated.

"If somnambulism, then who was the somnambulist?" The Thinking Machine resumed after a moment. "It did not seem to be you, Mrs Roswell. You are not of a nervous temperament; you are a normal healthy woman. If we accept as true your statement that you were aroused in bed by the cockatoo screaming 'Jeanette' we prove that you were not the somnambulist. Your step-daughter? She suffered from a nervous disorder so pronounced that you had fears for her mental condition. With everyone else removed she was the somnambulist. Even the cockatoo said that.

"Now let us see how it would have been possible to open the vault. We admit that no one except yourself knew the combination. But a record of that combination did appear therefore it was possible for some one else to learn it. Your step-daughter does not know that combination when she is in a normal condition. I won't say that she knows it when in the sommambulistic state, but I will say that when in that condition she knows where there is a record of it. How she learned this I don't know. It is not a legitimate part of the problem.

"Be that as it may she was firmly convinced that something she was seeking, something of deep concern to her, was in that vault. It might not have been in the vault but in her abnormal condition she thought it was. She was not after jewels – her every act even tonight showed that. What else? Letters. I knew it was a letter, or letters, before she said so herself. What was in these letters is of no consequence here. You, Mrs Roswell, considered it your duty to hide them – possibly destroy them."

Both husband and son turned on Mrs Roswell inquiringly. She stared from one to the other helplessly, pleadingly.

"The letters contained—" she started to explain.

"Never mind that, it's none of our business," curtly interrupted The Thinking Machine. "If there is a family skeleton, it's yours."

"I won't believe anything against her," burst out Grantham passionately.

"Even with the practical certain knowledge that Miss Roswell did open the vault," The Thinking Machine resumed placidly, "and that she opened it in precisely the manner you saw tonight, I took one more step to prove it. This was after the second stone had disappeared. I instructed Mrs Roswell to place a little strawberry jam on her step-daughter's hands while she was sleeping. If this jam appeared on the book the next time the vault was found open it proved finally and conclusively that Miss Roswell opened it. I chose strawberry jam because it was unusual. I dare say no one who might have a purpose in opening that vault would go around with strawberry jam on his hands. This jam did appear on the book, and then I summoned you, Dr Forrester, and you, Dr Henderson. You know the rest. I may add that Mr Grantham in attempting to take the theft upon himself merely made a fool of himself. No person with bare fingers could have torn out one of the stones."

There was a long pause, and deep silence while the problem as seen by The Thinking Machine was considered in the minds of his hearers. Grantham at last broke the silence.

"Where are the two stones that are missing?"

"Oh yes," said The Thinking Machine easily, as if that trivial point had escaped him. "Mrs Roswell, will you please have the cockatoo brought in?" he asked, and then explained to the others: "I had the bird removed from the room tonight for fear it would interrupt at the wrong moment."

Mrs Roswell arose and gave some instructions to a servant who was waiting outside. He went away and returned later with a startled expression on his graven face.

"The bird is dead, madam," he reported.

"Dead?" repeated Mrs Roswell.

"Good!" said The Thinking Machine rubbing his hands briskly together. "Bring it in anyhow."

"Why, what could have killed it?" asked Mrs Roswell, bewildered.

"Indigestion," replied the scientist. "Here is the thief."

He turned suddenly to the servant who had entered bearing the cockatoo in state on a silver tray.

"Who? I?" gasped the astonished servant.

"No, this fellow," replied The Thinking Machine as he picked up the dead bird. "He had the opportunity; he had the pointed instrument necessary to pry out a stone – note the sharp hooked bill; and he had the strength to do it. Besides all that he confessed a fondness for bright things when he tried to snatch my eyeglasses. He saw Miss Roswell drop the tiara on the floor, its brightness fascinated him. He pried out the stone and swallowed it. It pained him, and he screamed 'Jeanette.' This same thing happened on two occasions. Your encyclopædia will tell you that the cockatoo has more strength in that sharp beak than you could possibly exercise with two fingers unless you had a steel instrument."

Later that day The Thinking Machine sent to Mrs Roswell the two missing diamonds, the glass head of a hat pin and a crystal shoe button which he had recovered from the dead bird. His diagnosis of the case was acute indigestion.

12

PROBLEM OF THE SOUVENIR CARDS

There were three of the post cards. The first one was a vividly colored picture of the Capitol at Washington. It was postmarked, "Philadelphia, November 12, 2:30 p.m." Below the picture, in a small copperplate hand, were these figures and symbols: "I-28-38-4 x 47-30-2 x 21-19-8 x 65-5-3 x 29-32-11 x 40-2-9X."

The second post card was a picture of Park Square, Boston, with the majestic figures of Lincoln and the slave in the foreground. This, too, was postmarked Philadelphia, but the date was November 13. The symbols and figures were unquestionably written by the same hand as those on the first: "II-155-19-9 x 205-2-8 x agree x 228-31-2 x present tense x 235-13-4."

The third card was a colored reproduction of an idyllic bayou near New Orleans. Again the postmark was Philadelphia, but the date was November 14. This card contained only: "III-41-1-9 x 181-15-10 x press."

Professor Augustus S. F. X. Van Dusen – The Thinking Machine – turned and twisted the post cards in his slender fingers while he studied them through squinting, watery, blue eyes. At last he laid them on a table beside him, and sank back into his chair, with long white fingers pressed tip to tip. He was in a receptive mood.

"Well?" he demanded abruptly.

The bearded stranger who had offered the cards for his scrutiny was gazing at the diminutive figure and the drawn, petulant face of the scientist, seemingly in mingled wonder and amusement. It was difficult for him to associate this crabbed little man with those achievements which had placed his name so high in the sciences. After a moment the visitor's gaze wavered a little and dropped.

"My name is William C. Colgate," he began. "Sometime since – four weeks and three days, to be exact – a diamond was stolen from my house in this city, and no trace of it has ever been found. It was one I bought uncut in South Africa five years ago, and its weight is about thirty carats. When cut I imagine it will be eighteen to twenty carats, and it is, as it stands now, worth about forty thousand dollars. You may have read something of the theft in the newspapers?"

"I never read the newspapers," remarked The Thinking Machine.

"Well, in that event," and Colgate smiled, "I can briefly state the facts in the case. I have for several years had in my employment a secretary, Charles Travers. He is about twenty-five years old. Within the last four or five months I have noticed a change in his manner. Where formerly he had been quiet and unassuming, he has, through evil associations I dare say, grown to be a little wild, and, I believe, has lived beyond his income. I took occasion twice to remonstrate with him. The first time he seemed contrite and repentant; the second time he grew angry, and the following day disappeared. The diamond went with him."

"Do you know that?" demanded The Thinking Machine.

"I know it as well as one may know anything," replied Colgate positively. "I doubt if anyone except Travers knew where I kept the jewel. Certainly my servants did not, and certainly my wife and two daughters did not. Besides my wife and daughters have been in Europe for two months. The police seem to be unable to learn anything, so I came to you."

"Just where did you keep the jewel?"

"In a drawer of my desk," was the reply. "Ultimately I had intended to have it cut and present it to my oldest daughter, possibly on the occasion of her marriage. Now—" Colgate waved his hand.

The Thinking Machine sat silent for several minutes. His squint eyes were turned steadily upward and several tiny lines appeared in the domelike brow. "The problem then seems to be merely one of finding your secretary," he stated at last. "The diamond is of course so large that it would be absurd to attempt to dispose of it in its present shape. Travers is an intelligent man; we shall give him credit for realizing this. And yet if it should be cut up into smaller stones its value would dwindle to a tenth part of what it is now. Under those circumstances, would he have it cut up?"

"That is one of the questions which I should like to have answered."

For the second time The Thinking Machine picked up and examined the three post cards. "And what have these to do with it?" he demanded.

"That's another question I should like to have answered," said Colgate. "I can only believe that they in someway bear on the mystery surrounding the disappearance of the gem. Perhaps they give a clue to where it is now."

"This is Travers's handwriting?"

"Yes."

"The cards obviously constitute a cipher of some sort," explained the scientist. "Were you and Travers accustomed to communicating in cipher?"

"Not at all."

"Then why is this in cipher?" demanded The Thinking Machine belligerently. He glared at Colgate much as if he held him to blame.

Colgate shrugged his shoulders.

"Of course," continued the scientist, "I can find out what it means. It is elementary in character, and yet I doubt if, after we know what is in it, it will be particularly illuminating. Still, giving Travers credit for intelligence, I should imagine this to be an offer to return the diamond, probably for a consideration. But why in cipher?"

Colgate did not seem to be able to add to what he had already said, and after a few minutes took his leave, with instructions from The Thinking Machine to return on the following day, after the scientist had had an opportunity to study the post cards. He called at the appointed hour.

"Have you three-volume book of any sort that you read or refer to frequently?"

For some reason Colgate seemed a little startled. It was only momentary, however. "I suppose I have several books of three volumes," he replied.

"No particular one that your secretary would know that you read frequently?" insisted the scientist.

Again some strange impalpable expression flitted across Colgate's face. "No," he said after a moment.

The Thinking Machine arose. "It will be necessary then," he said, "for me to go over your library and see if I can't find the book to which this cipher refers."

"Book?" asked Colgate curiously. "If the cipher has no relation to the diamond, I don't see that—"

"Of course you don't see!" snapped The Thinking Machine. "Come along and let me see."

Colgate seemed a little perturbed by the suggestion. He folded his immaculate gloves over and over as he stared at the inscrutable face before him. "It would be impossible," he said at last, "to find anything in my library just now. As I said, my wife and daughters are abroad, and during their absence I have taken occasion to have my library and one or two other rooms redecorated and refinished. All my books meanwhile are packed away, helter skelter."

The Thinking Machine sat down again and stared at him inquiringly. "Then when your library is in order again you may call," he said tersely. "I can do nothing until I see the books."

"But-but—" stammered Colgate.

"Goodday," said The Thinking Machine curtly.

Colgate went away. It was not till three days later that he reappeared. If one might have judged by his manner, he had achieved something in his absence; yet when he spoke it was in the same exquisitely modulated tone of the first visit.

"The work of redecorating has been completed," he told The Thinking Machine. "My library is again in order, and you may examine it at your leisure. If you care to go now, my carriage is at the door."

The Thinking Machine stared at him for a moment, then picked up his hat. At the door of the Colgate mansion Colgate and the scientist were met by a graven-faced footman, who received their hats and coats in silence. Colgate conducted his guest straight into the library. It was a magnificently appointed place, reflecting in its every detail the splendid purchasing power of money. To this sheer luxury, however, The Thinking Machine was oblivious. His undivided attention was on the book shelves.

From one end of the long room to the other he walked time after time, reading the titles of the books as he passed. There were Dickens, Balzac, Kipling, Stevenson, Thackeray, Zola—all of them. Three or four times he paused to draw out a volume and examine it. Each time he replaced it without a word and continued his search. Colgate stood by, watching him curiously.

The Thinking Machine had just paused to draw out one of the Dumas books when the stolid-faced footman appeared in the door with a telegram.

"Is this for you, sir?" he asked of Colgate.

"Yes," replied Colgate.

He drew out the yellow sheet and permitted the envelope to fall to the floor. The Thinking Machine picked it up with something like eagerness in his manner. It was directed to "William C. Colgate." The scientist looked almost astonished as he turned again to the book shelves.

It was ten minutes later that The Thinking Machine took out three volumes together. These comprised the famous old English novel, "Ten Thousand a Year," a rare and valuable first edition. The leaves of volume 1 fluttered through his fingers until he came to page 28. After a moment he said "Ah!" Then he went on to page 47. He studied that for a moment or more, after which he said "Ah!" once again.

"What is it?" inquired Colgate quickly.

The Thinking Machine turned his cold, squint eyes up into the eager face above him. "It is the key to the cipher," he said.

"What is it? Read it!" commanded Colgate. His clear, alert eyes were fastened on the, to him, meaningless page. He sought vainly there something to account for the scientist's exclamation. But he saw only words – a page of words with no apparent meaning beyond the text of the story. "What is it?" he demanded again, and there was a little glitter in his eye. "Does it say where the diamond is?"

"Considering the fact that I have seen only two words of a possible twenty or thirty, I don't know what it says," declared The Thinking Machine aggressively. "The best I can say now is that with the aid of these books I shall find the diamond."

For half an hour or more the scientist was busy running through the books in an aimless sort of way. Finally he closed the third volume with a snap and stood up.

"Travers says that he will return the gem for ten thousand dollars," he announced.

"Oh, he does, does he?" Colgate's tone was a sneer. Again in his face The Thinking Machine read some subtle quality which brought a slight wrinkle of perplexity to his brow.

"You don't have to pay it, you know," he explained tartly. "I can get it without the ten thousand dollars, of course."

"Well, get it, then!" said Colgate a little impatiently. "I want the diamond, and it is absurd to suppose that I shall pay ten thousand dollars for my own property. Come on! Let's do what is to be done immediately."

"I'll do what is to be done immediately; but I will do it without your assistance," remarked The Thinking Machine. "I shall send for you to-morrow. When you come the diamond will be in my possession. Goodday."

Colgate stared after him blankly as he went out.

The Thinking Machine was talking over the telephone with Hutchinson Hatch, reporter.

"Do you know William C. Colgate by sight?" he demanded.

"Very well," Hatch replied.

"Is he red-headed?"

"No."

"Goodbye."

On the following morning a short advertisement appeared in all the city newspapers. It was simply:

Will give ten thousand dollars. Matter is not in hands of the police. To insure your safety, telephone 1103 Bay and arrange details.

It was only a few minutes past nine o'clock that morning when The Thinking Machine was called to the telephone. For some reason he had difficulty in understanding, possibly due to the spluttering of the receiver. Then he did understand, and sat down for some time, apparently to consider what he had heard. Later he telephoned to Hutchinson Hatch.

"It's about this theft of the Colgate diamond," he explained. "The secretary, Travers, who is wanted for the theft, is now somewhere in the North End, either drunk or drugged, and possibly disguised. I imagine his photograph has been in all the newspapers. I have been talking to him over the telephone, and he is to call me again about eleven o'clock. Go down to the North End near the corner of Hanover and Blank Streets, hire a telephone for the morning, and call me. Remain at the phone from half-past ten until I call you. You are to get Travers. When you get him bring him here. Don't notify the police."

"But will I get him?" asked the reporter.

"If you don't you are stupid," retorted The Thinking Machine.

At five minutes of eleven o'clock the scientist's telephone rang. He was sitting staring at it at the moment, but instead of answering stepped to the door and called Martha, his aged servant.

"Answer the telephone," he directed, "and tell whoever is there that I am not here. Tell them I shall return in ten minutes, and to be sure to call me again."

Martha followed the instructions and hung up the receiver. Instantly The Thinking Machine went to the telephone.

"Can you tell me, please, the number of the telephone which just called me?" he asked quickly. "No, I don't want a connection. Number 34710 North, in a café at Hanover and Blank Streets? Thanks."

A minute later he had Hatch on the wire again. "Travers will call me in five minutes from 34710 North, in a café at Hanover and Blank Streets," he said. "Get him and bring him here as quickly as you can. Goodbye."

So it came about that within less than an hour a cab rushed up to the door, and Hutchinson Hatch, accompanied by a young man, entered. The man was Travers. A week's scrubby beard was on his chin, his face was perfectly pallid; the fever of drink and fear glittered in his eyes. Hatch had to support him to a chair, in which he dropped back limply. The Thinking

Machine scowled down into the young man's face, and was met by a fishy, imbecilic stare in return.

"Are you Mr Travers?" inquired The Thinking Machine.

"That's all right-that's all right," murmured the young man, and overcome by the exertion of speech his head dropped back and in a moment he was sound asleep.

Without apparent compunction The Thinking Machine searched his pockets. After a moment he found what seemed to be a rough rock crystal. He squinted at it closely as he turned and twisted it back and forth in his hand, then passed it to Hatch for inspection.

"That's worth forty thousand dollars," he remarked casually.

"Is this the –"

"It's the Colgate diamond," interrupted The Thinking Machine. "I surmised that he would have it somewhere about him, because he would have no place to hide it. And now for the second man – the brains of the theft. First I shall telephone for Colgate. Look at him when he enters; for I think you will be greatly surprised. And above all, remember to be careful."

Looking deeply into the quiet, squint eyes of the scientist, Hatch read a warning. He understood and nodded. Travers, stupefied, was removed to an adjoining room.

A few minutes later there was a rattle of carriage wheels, the door bell rang, and Colgate entered. Hatch glanced at him, then turned quickly to look out of a window.

"You have the diamond?" burst out Colgate suddenly.

"I said I would have it when you came," retorted The Thinking Machine. "Now for these post cards," and the scientist produced the three cards that had been handed to him at first. "Perhaps you would be interested to know what was really on them?"

"I haven't the slightest curiosity," said Colgate impatiently. "All I want is the diamond. If you will give me that, I think perhaps that will terminate this affair, and there will be no necessity of taking up more of your time."

"Of course you have no desire to prosecute Travers?" asked The Thinking Machine. There was a velvety note in the crabbed voice. Hatch glanced at him.

"I don't think I care to prosecute him," said Colgate steadily.

"I thought perhaps you would not," rejoined The Thinking Machine enigmatically. "But as to these post cards. They constitute what is known as the book cipher. For your information I may state that it is always possible to know a book cipher by the fact that a small number, rarely above twelve or fourteen, always precedes the X; the X merely divides the words. For instance, on the first card we have I-28-38-4; in other words, volume one, page 28, line 38, and the fourth word of that line. Unless one knows or can learn the name of the book which is the basis of the cipher, it is perhaps the most difficult of all. Any ordinary cipher may be solved precisely as Poe solved his great cipher in 'The Gold Bug.'"

"But I am not at all interested—" protested Colgate.

"So really all that was necessary for me to do was to find out what book was the basis of this particular cipher," continued The Thinking Machine to Hatch, without heeding his visitor's remark. "I knew of course it was some book in Mr Colgate's home. The clue to what book was given, either wittingly or unwittingly, by the single I, the two I's and the three I's on the first, second, and third cards. Did these represent volumes? I found a dozen three volume books in Mr Colgate's library, but in each instance there was no connection in the first three or four words which I found in accordance with the numbers given; that is, until I came to 'Ten Thousand a Year.' The first word I found in that was 'will'; the second, page 47, line 30, second word, was 'return'; the third was 'diamond.' So I knew that was the book I wanted. Here is the full meaning of the cipher as it appears on the three cards, as I have transcribed it."

He handed Colgate a slip of paper, on which was written:

Will return diamond for ten thousand. If you agree informed [present tense, i.e., inform] me in daily press.

"This all seems very clever and very curious indeed," commented Colgate; "but really I do not think—"

"The book of Mr Colgate's is a first edition – there is also a first edition in the public library," the scientist went on placidly; "so Travers had no difficulty on that score. We shall admit that the cards were mailed in Philadelphia; perhaps he went there and later returned to this city. The manner in which I got possession of the diamond – by first discovering Travers through an advertisement and then keeping him at the telephone until he was inveigled here by my assistant – is possibly of no interest; it was all very easily done by a prearranged plan with the telephone exchange; so now, Mr. – Mr.—"

"Colgate," his visitor supplied, as if surprised at the hesitancy.

"I mean your real name," said the scientist quietly.

There was a sudden tense silence; Hatch had come a little closer, and was staring at the stranger with keen, inquiring eyes.

"This is not the Mr William C. Colgate you know, Mr Hatch?"

"No."

"Do you happen to have an idea who he is?"

"If I am not mistaken," Hatch replied calmly, "this is a gentleman I have met before on an exceedingly interesting occasion – Mr Bradlee Cunnyngham Leighton."

At the name the erstwhile Colgate turned upon the reporter with a snarl. There was a quick movement of his right hand, and Hatch found himself blinking down the barrel of a revolver, as Leighton slowly moved backward toward the door.

The Thinking Machine moved around behind the aggressor. "Now, Mr Leighton," he said almost pleasantly, "if you don't lower that revolver I'll blow your brains out."

For one instant Leighton hesitated, then glanced back quickly toward the scientist. That diminutive man stood calmly, with his hands in his pockets. Instantly Hatch leaped. There was a quick, sharp struggle, a few muttered curses, and then the discomfited Leighton, in his turn, was gazing down the revolver barrel.

"Won't you gentlemen sit down?" suggested The Thinking Machine.

They were all sitting down when Detective Mallory rushed up from police headquarters. Leighton was farthest from the door. The Thinking Machine sat staring at him with the revolver held in position for quick use.

"Ah, Mr Mallory," he said, without turning his head or glancing back. "This is Mr Bradlee Cunnyngham Leighton. You may have heard of him before?"

"Do you mean the Englishman who brought the Varron necklace to this country?" blurted out the detective.

"The same man of the carrier pigeon case," said Hatch grimly.

"I should like particularly to call your attention to Mr Leighton," continued The Thinking Machine. "He is a man of accomplishments. We know how he distinguished himself by the simple expedient of using carrier pigeons in the Varron necklace affair. In this case, he has risen to greater heights. First – I am assuming some things – he plotted with young Travers to steal the Colgate diamond. In some manner, which is not essential here, Travers got the diamond and sought to profit by the theft alone by negotiating its return for ten thousand dollars. Travers wrote a cipher to Mr Colgate making the proposition – it was possible he knew Mr Colgate would understand his cipher. I shall give Leighton credit for anticipating just this possibility and intercepting the post cards. They meant nothing to him; so – please note this – he came to me as Mr Colgate, knowing that Mr Colgate was in Europe with his family, and sought my assistance in recovering the jewel from his fellow conspirator. The sublime audacity of all these conceptions marks Mr Leighton as little short of a genius in his particular profession.

"Only once was Mr Leighton embarrassed. That was when I told him I should have to visit his library. But he even rose to this necessity brilliantly. He delayed my visit for a day or so, and in some manner, possibly by forgery, secured an entrance to Mr Colgate's home, perhaps as a cousin of the same name. There he received me. Two or three things had happened to arouse a doubt in my mind as to whether he was the real Mr Colgate.

"First was his hesitancy in connection with my visit to the library; then while I was in the house a telegram came for Mr William C. Colgate. A servant asked Mr Leighton in my presence if the telegram was for him. That question would never have been asked if he had been the real William C. Colgate. Then finally I asked Mr Hatch over the phone if William C. Colgate was red-headed. William C. Colgate is not red-headed. This gentleman is, therefore he is not William C. Colgate. I only knew this much. Mr Hatch recognized him as Leighton. He saw him at the time you were all interested in his escape from a Scotland Yard man – Conway, who wanted him for stealing a necklace. That is all, I think."

"But the diamond and Travers?" asked the detective.

"Here is the diamond," said The Thinking Machine, and he produced it from one of his pockets. "Travers is lying on a bed in the next room in a drunken stupor."

13

THE THREE OVERCOATS

Under the influence of that singular feeling of some one being in the room with him, Carroll Garland opened his eyes suddenly from sound sleep. The intuition was correct; there was some one in the room with him – a man whose back was turned. At that particular moment he was examining the clothing Garland had discarded on retiring. Garland raised himself on one elbow, and the bed creaked a little.

"Don't disturb yourself," said the man, without turning, "I'll be through in a minute."

"Through what?" demanded Garland. "My pockets?"

The stranger straightened up and turned toward him. He was a tall, lithe, clean-cut young man, with crisp, curly hair, and a quizzical expression about his eyes and lips. He was in evening dress, and Garland could only admire the manner in which it fitted him. He wore an opera hat, and a light weight Inverness coat.

"I didn't mean to wake you, really," the stranger apologized pleasantly. "I'm sure I didn't make any noise."

"No, I dare say you didn't," replied Garland. "What do you want?"

The stranger picked up an overcoat, which lay across a chair, and deftly, with a penknife, slit the lining on each side. He did something then which Garland couldn't see, after which he carefully folded the coat again, and laid it across the chair. "I have taken what you won at bridge at your club this evening," he remarked. "It will save me the trouble of cashing a check."

Garland gazed at this imperturbable, audacious person with a sort of admiration. "I trust you found the amount correct?" he said sarcastically.

"Yes, thirteen hundred and forty-seven dollars. That will do very nicely, thank you. I am leaving two hundred and some odd dollars of your own."

"Oh, take it all," said Garland magnanimously, "because I am going to make you return it, anyway."

The stranger laughed pleasantly. "I am going now," he said; "but before I go I should like to tell you that you play really an excellent game of bridge, except, perhaps, you are a little reckless on no trumps."

"Thank you," said Garland, and started to get out of bed.

"Now, don't get up!" advised the stranger, still pleasantly. "I have something here in my pocket which I should dislike very much to have to use. But I will use it if necessary."

Garland kept right on getting out of bed. "You are not such a fool as to shoot," he said quietly. "You couldn't get out of this hotel to save your life if you did. It is only half-past eleven o'clock, there are people passing in the halls, and always at this time there are a great many people in the lobby. You would have to go that way. So now I'll trouble you for the money."

The stranger drew a glistening, shining object from his pocket, examined it casually, then went over and stood beside the call button. There was a glitter of determination in his eyes, and the smile had gone from his lips. "I certainly have no intention of returning the money – now," he said. "It would be best for both of us, of course, not to attract anyone's attention."

Garland was coming straight toward him.

"Now, don't do anything foolish," the stranger warned, not unkindly. "You can't reach the call button unless you go over me; you won't shout, because if you do I shall have to use this revolver, and take my chances below. You don't happen to need this money, and I do. It was simply a pick-up for you at the club. If you give an alarm when I go out, it will be disagreeable for me."

Garland stared at him in frank amazement for a moment. The stranger steadily returned the gaze.

"I'll just take one whirl out of you anyhow," declared Garland grimly. "I don't happen to have a gun; but—"

And Garland sent in a vicious right swing, which would have been highly effective had the stranger's head remained stationary. Instead, it ducked suddenly, and a left hand landed jarringly on one of Garland's eyes. Instantly he forgot all about the burglarious intentions of his visitor; it was man to man, and Garland happened to be dexterous in the science of pugilism – Mike Donovan had taught him.

After four blows had been exchanged, Garland became suddenly convinced that the stranger's teacher in the gentle art of bruising was more gifted even than Mike, because, in all the freedom of his pajamas, Garland got in only one blow for two, on a man who was hampered by overcoat and evening dress. A stinging jab to Garland's mouth made him clinch, and in trying to reach the stranger's throat, he forgot all the ethics of the game.

At this close range, the stranger delivered one short arm punch, and as Garland reeled and the world grew dark about him, he recalled the blow as being identical with one which was made famous in Carson City, at the time a world's championship changed hands. Dazzling lights danced before his eyes for a moment, and then all was dark.

The stranger stood looking down at him, planted his opera hat more firmly on his head, drew on his gloves, opened the door, and went out. He sauntered through the lobby carelessly, paused to light a cigar, and disappeared through the revolving doors. At the curb outside, an automobile was waiting. In it sat a veiled woman, and a very much begoggled chauffeur.

"Well?" the woman asked quickly.

The stranger shook his head, climbed in beside her, and the car rushed away.

When Garland recovered consciousness, he had the impression of having experienced a remarkably vivid nightmare. But one look into the mirror at the bulbous black eye, and the absence of thirteen hundred and forty-seven dollars from his pockets, convinced him of the reality of it all. Incidentally he examined the two knife cuts in the overcoat lining, and shook his head in bewilderment.

"What the deuce did he cut those for?" he asked himself.

On the following morning Garland returned the overcoat to its owner, Hal Dickson. There is a freemasonry among roommates at college by which one acknowledges that whatever he owns belongs equally to the other. Garland had exercised certain rights which had accrued to him by reason of this comradeship upon his arrival in the city the day before. He wore then a light weight tan coat, entirely too thin for the extreme cold which set in immediately upon his arrival; so he borrowed a heavier coat, a thick frieze affair, from his old chum, and left his own light coat with him.

"I want to tell you something about this, Hal," he said, and recited in detail the events of the night before. "Now look here where my friend cut your coat," he said in conclusion.

Together they examined the long slits, after which they stared at each other in blank wonderment.

"Send it down to your tailor and have it relined," remarked Garland. "Tell him to send the bill to me."

Dickson continued to stare at the coat lining. "What did he want to cut it for?" he asked.

Garland shook his head. "Give me my own coat," he said; "I've got to go back home at two-thirty, and can manage with this light coat until I get there, and may not have a chance to come here again."

Garland was just about to put on his own coat, when he stopped in fresh amazement. "Well! Look at that!" he exclaimed.

Dickson looked. The lining of the coat was slit wide open on each side, as if with a sharp knife.

Ten minutes later the young men were on their way to police headquarters. Detective Mallory received them. The coats were laid under his official eyes, and he scrutinized them carefully.

Mallory listened, with his feet on his desk, and his cigar clinched in his teeth. "What did the thief look like?" he asked at the end.

"He had every appearance of a gentleman."

"Just like me and you, eh?"

"Well, a little more like me," replied Garland innocently.

"I shall put my men on it at once," said the detective.

Garland caught the two-thirty train for a run of an hour and a half to a small city.

At fifteen minutes before five o'clock Detective Mallory was called to the long distance telephone.

"That Mr Mallory?" came an excited voice. "Well, this is Carroll Garland. Yes, I am at home. Just as soon as I got here I went straight to my room to get a heavier overcoat. I was putting it on, when I found that the lining had been ripped open just like those other two. Now, what does that mean?"

For the first time in his life a question had been asked to which Mallory would confess that he didn't know the answer. He scratched his head thoughtfully, then stopped doing that to tug violently at his bristly moustache. Finally he hung up the receiver with a bang, and went out personally to look into an affair which had not attracted more than passing interest at the time it was reported.

"I can readily understand," Hutchinson Hatch was saying, "why the burglar took the money; but why did he slit the lining of the overcoat?"

The Thinking Machine didn't say.

"Then why did he go to Dickson's room, and slit the lining of an overcoat which Garland left there?"

Still The Thinking Machine was silent.

"And finally why did he go to Garland's home, in another city forty miles away, and slit the lining of an overcoat there?"

Professor Augustus S. F. X. Van Dusen receded still farther into the depths of a huge chair, and sat for a long time with his squint eyes turned upward, and finger tips pressed together. At last he broke the silence. "You have given me every known fact?"

"Everything," the reporter answered.

"There is really no problem in it at all," The Thinking Machine declared, "unless one of the units remains undiscovered. If all are known, the solution is obvious. When the money is returned to Garland, it will definitely prove the only possible hypothesis that may be advanced."

"When the money is returned?" gasped the reporter.

"That is what I said!" snapped the scientist crustily. "If Garland does not care to lose that thirteen hundred and forty-seven dollars, it would not be wise to press the investigation just now. If you will keep in communication with him, and inform me immediately when he receives the money, I shall undertake to close up the affair. Until then it is really not worth attention."

Nearly a week elapsed before there was another development in the mystery – the return of thirteen hundred and forty-seven dollars, by express from Denver. Accompanying the money was an unsigned note of thanks for the use of it, and a line or two which might have been construed into an apology for the stranger's conduct in Garland's room.

The police were astounded; this was against all the rules of the game. Garland was a little more than astounded, and at the same time delighted at the generosity of the thief. It was not possible to develop any fact as to the identity of the intruder from the express records. Obviously the sender had used a fictitious name in Denver. When Hatch explained this point to The Thinking Machine, it was dismissed with a wave of one slender hand.

"It is really of no consequence," declared the scientist. "Garland knows the name of the man who took the money and cut the overcoat."

"But he says he doesn't," Hatch remonstrated.

"There may be circumstances which make it necessary for him to say that," continued the scientist.

"He is prepared to swear that he never saw the man before."

"That might be quite true," was the curt rejoinder; "but I dare say he does know his name. The next time Garland comes to the city, let me know."

"He is here now," the reporter informed him. "He came in today to consult with Detective Mallory about the return of the money."

"That simplifies matters," said the scientist. "We'll see him at once."

Garland was in. Hatch introduced the distinguished man of science, and he came immediately to business.

"Tell me something of your love affairs, Mr Garland," The Thinking Machine began abruptly.

"My love affairs? I have no love affairs at all."

"Oh, I see; married."

Garland gazed straight into the squinting eyes, with a quizzical expression about his mouth. "I don't see that it is absolutely inconsistent for a man to have a love affair and be married," he said smilingly. "There are men, you know, who are in love with their own wives. I happen to be one of these. When you said love affairs, I presumed you meant—"

"There are men," interrupted The Thinking Machine, "who because of being married dare not admit any other entanglements." The aggressive blue eyes were staring straight into Garland's.

After a moment the young man arose, with something like anger in his manner. "I don't happen to be one of them," he said sharply.

The Thinking Machine shrugged his shoulders. "Now, what is the name of the man who robbed you and cut those coats?" he asked.

"I don't know," retorted Garland.

"I know that is what you told the police," said the scientist; "but believe me, it would be best, and possibly save you trouble, for you to give me the name of that man."

"I don't know it," repeated Garland.

The Thinking Machine seemed satisfied on that point, but with his satisfaction came tiny, sinuous lines in his forehead. Hatch knew what that meant.

"You never saw the man before?" asked the scientist after a moment. The aggressiveness had gone from his voice now.

"No, I never saw him before," Garland replied.

"Nor a photograph of him?"

"No, never."

Almost imperceptibly the lines deepened in the brow of The Thinking Machine. His eyes were narrowed down to mere slits, and his thin lips set into a perfectly straight line. Garland studied the grotesque little figure with a curiosity backed by anger. For a long time there was silence, then:

"Mr Garland, how long have you been married?"

"Four years."

The Thinking Machine shook his head and arose. "Please pardon me," he continued, "but what is your financial condition?"

"I am a salaried man; but it is a good salary, twelve thousand a year, quite enough for my wife and self."

"Your married life has been happy?"

"Perfectly."

Again The Thinking Machine shook his head.

Ten minutes later he and Hutchinson Hatch were in the street together.

"He has either lied, or else we have overlooked a unit," volunteered the scientist as they walked on. "Now I can't believe that we missed anything – ergo, he lied, and yet I can't believe that."

"Well, that doesn't leave much," the reporter suggested.

"The next step," the scientist went on, "will be to establish beyond all doubt that he told the truth. I leave that to you. Get his record for the last five years, and inquire particularly about his family life, his club life, and always bear in mind the possibility of another woman in the case. There is a woman – some woman – because she was in the automobile. Of course, the case is inconsequential, since the money has been returned; but I happen to be interested in it, because the return of the money bears out my hypothesis, and other things tend to upset it."

Hatch covered the affair thoroughly. Garland had told the truth, as far as investigation could develop. He so informed the scientist.

"It is singular, very singular," remarked The Thinking Machine, in deep abstraction. "By the inexorable rule of logic we reach a point where we must believe that Garland slit the lining of the coats himself, and had the money sent to him from Denver. When we attempt to find a motive for that, we plunge into absurdities. Two and two always make four, Mr Hatch, not sometimes, but all the time. No problem in arithmetic can be correctly solved, if one figure is missing. There is one figure missing. I'll find it. In your investigation of Garland's career you found out something about his father?"

"Yes. He died several years ago. His name, by the way, was also Carroll Garland."

The Thinking Machine turned suddenly and squinted at the reporter. "Here is our missing unit, Mr Hatch," he said. "Do you happen to know if there were ever any other Carroll Garlands in the family?"

"Years ago, yes. The great-grandfather of the present one was also a Carroll Garland."

The little scientist arose suddenly, paced back and forth half a dozen times, then passed into an adjoining room. Five minutes later he reëntered, with his hat and coat. Accompanied by the reporter, he went straight to one of the fashionable clubs, and sent in a card. After a few minutes' wait a young man appeared.

"My name is Van Dusen," began The Thinking Machine. "I came here to see you about a personal matter. Could we go to some place where we should not be disturbed for a minute?"

The young man led the way into a private parlour and closed the door.

"It's about that compromising letter which you carry there," and The Thinking Machine touched the young man on the breast with one long slender finger.

"Did she send you?"

"No."

"Well, what business is it of yours, then?"

"I do not think that a man of honor – a man of your social position – would care to carry about with him a paper which would not only imperil but might wreck the reputation of a woman who is now another man's wife."

That The Thinking Machine had spoken correctly, Hatch could not doubt from the expression on the other's face.

"Another man's wife," repeated the young man in astonishment. "Since when?"

"A week or so ago. She is now in the West with her husband. He knows of the existence of this document, therefore whatever vengeful spirit you may have had in preserving it is wasted. I would advise you to destroy it."

For a minute or more the young man stared straight into the squint eyes. "If the lady in question should have made such a request of me in person, I should have destroyed it," said the young man; "otherwise I—"

"She makes that request now, through me," the scientist lied glibly.

"Did she ask you to come to me?"

"She makes that request now, through me," repeated the scientist.

Again the young man was silent. Finally he slowly removed his overcoat and laid it across the table. Then from a pocket in the lining, the opening of which was concealed in a seam where the sleeve joined the coat, he removed a letter. A strange expression played about his face, reminiscent, thoughtful, even tender, as he offered it to The Thinking Machine. Instead of accepting it, the scientist struck a match and touched it to the corner. In silence the three men watched it burn.

"It is obvious to the dullest intelligence," said The Thinking Machine to Hutchinson Hatch, "that the man who entered Garland's room at the hotel was not a thief. He went there to open the lining of Garland's overcoat. Why? To find something which he had reason to believe was concealed therein. True, he took some money; but we can readily imagine that he happened to need a large sum at the minute, and took it, intending to return it, as he did.

"When we know that he was not a thief, we know that the thing he sought was in the lining of the coat. It just happened that this particular coat was not Garland's. The thief didn't know that when he cut it; but he had been so certain of finding what he sought that he took pains to see if it was Garland's coat. Instead of Garland's name, he found on a tailor's tab inside the pocket the name of Dickson. If we give him credit for intelligence at all, we must give him credit for imagining how another man's coat came into Garland's possession. Therefore, he went to Dickson's room, found Garland's coat, and ripped that as he did the first. Still nothing. Naturally then, he went to Garland's home and ripped open the third coat.

"All this was obvious. Now we come to the less obvious. What was he after? Money? No. He left money behind him. A jewel? Possibly but improbably, because his was not a mercenary pursuit. Then what? The remainder: some document or letter which was of such importance that he practically risked his life for it. Now, was this letter or document of value to himself, or to some one else?

"At this point logic met an obstacle in the veiled woman who waited in the automobile. Would the man permit the woman to take the chance she was taking with him if the document had been of value only to himself? It seems unlikely. On the other hand, if the document was of value to her, might she not insist on accompanying him?

"What paper was he after? A will or a deed? Perhaps; but would not that have gone into a court of law? A letter? More likely. So what did we have? A man risking his life, prison at least, to recover a letter for a woman near and dear to him. She, perhaps, informed him that the letter was concealed in the lining of Carroll Garland's overcoat. How she knew this does not appear. We can even imagine the woman confessing the existence of a letter by which her character was menaced before she consented to become his wife. In that event everything else is accounted for; no other hypothesis would fit all the circumstances, therefore this must be correct. Obviously the stranger knew the name of the man who had the letter;

therefore it would seem that there could be no mistake. I failed to see at the moment that there might be another Carroll Garland. When I saw that I telephoned to Garland, and he informed me that he had a cousin of the same name who occasionally visited this city and always stopped at the club where we called. You know what happened when we saw this second Carroll Garland. In searching for a Carroll Garland the stranger came across the wrong man and held him up. That is all, I think."

There was a long silence.

"By the way," Hatch inquired suddenly, "what is the name of the strange man and the woman?"

"Why, I don't know," responded The Thinking Machine in surprise.

14

MYSTERY OF THE MAN WHO WAS LOST

I

Here are the facts in the case as they were known in the beginning to Professor Augustus S. F. X. Van Dusen, scientist and logician. After hearing a statement of the problem from the lips of its principal he declared it to be one of the most engaging that had ever come to his attention, and—

But let me begin at the beginning:

The Thinking Machine was in the small laboratory of his modest apartments at two o'clock in the afternoon. Martha, the scientist's only servant, appeared at the door with a puzzled expression on her wrinkled face.

"A gentleman to see you, sir," she said.

"Name?" inquired The Thinking Machine, without turning.

"He-he didn't give it, sir," she stammered.

"I have told you always, Martha, to ask names of callers."

"I did ask his name, sir, and – and he said he didn't know it."

The Thinking Machine was never surprised, yet now he turned on Martha in perplexity and squinted at her fiercely through his thick glasses.

"Don't know his own name?" he repeated. "Dear me! How careless! Show the gentleman into the reception room immediately."

With no more introduction to the problem than this, therefore, The Thinking Machine passed into the other room. A stranger arose and came forward. He was tall, of apparently thirty-five years, clean shaven and had the keen, alert face of a man of affairs. He would have been handsome had it not been for dark rings under the eyes and the unusual white of his face. He was immaculately dressed from top to toe; altogether a man who would attract attention.

For a moment he regarded the scientist curiously; perhaps there was a trace of well-bred astonishment in his manner. He gazed curiously at the enormous head, with its shock of yellow hair, and noted, too, the droop in the thin shoulders. Thus for a moment they stood, face to face, the tall stranger making The Thinking Machine dwarf-like by comparison.

"Well?" asked the scientist.

The stranger turned as if to pace back and forth across the room, then instead dropped into a chair which the scientist indicated.

"I have heard a great deal about you, Professor," he began, in a well-modulated voice, "and at last it occurred to me to come to you for advice. I am in a most remarkable position – and I'm not insane. Don't think that, please. But unless I see some way out of this amazing predicament I shall be. As it is now, my nerves have gone; I am not myself."

"Your story? What is it? How can I help you?"

"I am lost, hopelessly lost," the stranger resumed. "I know neither my home, my business, nor even my name. I know nothing whatever of myself or my life; what it was or what it might have been previous to four weeks ago. I am seeking light on my identity. Now, if there is any fee—"

"Never mind that," the scientist put in, and he squinted steadily into the eyes of the visitor. "What do you know? From the time you remember things tell me all of it."

He sank back into his chair, squinting steadily upward. The stranger arose, paced back and forth across the room several times and then dropped into his chair again.

"It's perfectly incomprehensible," he said. "It's precisely as if I, full grown, had been born into a world of which I knew nothing except its language. The ordinary things, chairs, tables and such things, are perfectly familiar, but who I am, where I came from, why I came – of these I have no idea. I will tell you just as my impressions came to me when I awoke one morning, four weeks ago.

"It was eight or nine o'clock, I suppose. I was in a room. I knew instantly it was a hotel, but had not the faintest idea of how I got there, or of ever having seen the room before. I didn't even know my own clothing when I started to dress. I glanced out of my window; the scene was wholly strange to me.

"For half an hour or so I remained in my room, dressing and wondering what it meant. Then, suddenly, in the midst of my other worries, it came home to me that I didn't known my own name, the place where I lived nor anything about myself. I didn't know what hotel I was in. In terror I looked into a mirror. The face reflected at me was not one I knew. It didn't seem to be the face of a stranger; it was merely not a face that I knew.

"The thing was unbelievable. Then I began a search of my clothing for some trace of my identity. I found nothing whatever that would enlighten me – not a scrap of paper of any kind, no personal or business card."

"Have a watch?" asked The Thinking Machine.

"No."

"Any money?"

"Yes, money," said the stranger. "There was a bundle of more than ten thousand dollars in my pocket, in one-hundred-dollar bills. Whose it is or where it came from I don't know. I have been living on it since, and shall continue to do so, but I don't know if it is mine. I knew it was money when I saw it, but did not recollect ever having seen any previously."

"Any jewelry?"

"These cuff buttons," and the stranger exhibited a pair which he drew from his pocket.

"Go on."

"I finally finished dressing and went down to the office. It was my purpose to find out the name of the hotel and who I was. I knew I could learn some of this from the hotel register without attracting any attention or making anyone think I was insane. I had noted the number of my room. It was twenty-seven.

"I looked over the hotel register casually. I saw I was at the Hotel Yarmouth in Boston. I looked carefully down the pages until I came to the number of my room. Opposite this number was a name – John Doane, but where the name of the city should have been there was only a dash."

"You realize that it is perfectly possible that John Doane is your name?" asked The Thinking Machine.

"Certainly," was the reply. "But I have no recollection of ever having heard it before. This register showed that I had arrived at the hotel the night before – or rather that John Doane had arrived and been assigned to Room 27, and I was the John Doane, presumably. From that moment to this the hotel people have known me as John Doane, as have other people whom I have met during the four weeks since I awoke."

"Did the handwriting recall nothing?"

"Nothing whatever."

"Is it anything like the handwriting you write now?"

"Identical, so far as I can see."

"Did you have any baggage or checks for baggage?"

"No. All I had was the money and this clothing I stand in. Of course, since then I have bought necessities."

Both were silent for a long time and finally the stranger – Doane – arose and began pacing nervously again.

"That a tailor-made suit?" asked the scientist.

"Yes," said Doane, quickly. "I know what you mean. Tailor-made garments have linen strips sewed inside the pockets on which are the names of the manufacturers and the name of the man for whom the clothes were made, together with the date. I looked for those. They had been removed, cut out."

"Ah!" exclaimed The Thinking Machine suddenly. "No laundry marks on your linen either, I suppose?"

"No. It was all perfectly new."

"Name of the maker on it?"

"No. That had been cut out, too."

Doane was pacing back and forth across the reception room; the scientist lay back in his chair.

"Do you know the circumstances of your arrival at the hotel?" he asked at last.

"Yes. I asked, guardedly enough, you may be sure, hinting to the clerk that I had been drunk so as not to make him think I was insane. He said I came in about eleven o'clock at night, without any baggage, paid for my room with a one-hundred-dollar bill, which he changed, registered and went upstairs. I said nothing that he recalls beyond making a request for a room."

"The name Doane is not familiar to you?"

"No."

"You can't recall a wife or children?"

"No."

"Do you speak any foreign language?"

"No."

"Is your mind clear now? Do you remember things?"

"I remember perfectly every incident since I awoke in the hotel," said Doane. "I seem to remember with remarkable clearness, and somehow I attach the gravest importance to the most trivial incidents."

The Thinking Machine arose and motioned to Doane to sit down. He dropped back into a seat wearily. Then the scientist's long, slender fingers ran lightly, deftly through the abundant black hair of his visitor. Finally they passed down from the hair and along the firm jaws; thence they went to the arms, where they pressed upon good, substantial muscles. At last the hands, well shaped and white, were examined minutely. A magnifying glass was used to facilitate this examination. Finally The Thinking Machine stared into the quick-moving, nervous eyes of the stranger.

"Any marks at all on your body?" he asked at last.

"No," Doane responded. "I had thought of that and sought for an hour for some sort of mark. There's nothing – nothing." The eyes glittered a little and finally, in a burst of nervousness, he struggled to his feet. "My God!" he exclaimed. "Is there nothing you can do? What is it all, anyway?"

"Seems to be a remarkable form of aphasia," replied The Thinking Machine. "That's not an uncommon disease among people whose minds and nerves are overwrought. You've simply lost yourself – lost your identity. If it is aphasia, you will recover in time. When, I don't know."

"And meantime?"

"Let me see the money you found."

With trembling hands Doane produced a large roll of bills, principally hundreds, many of them perfectly new. The Thinking Machine examined them minutely, and finally made some memoranda on a slip of paper. The money was then returned to Doane.

"Now, what shall I do?" asked the latter.

"Don't worry," advised the scientist. "I'll do what I can."

"And – tell me who and what I am?"

"Oh, I can find that out all right," remarked The Thinking Machine. "But there's a possibility that you wouldn't recall even if I told you all about yourself."

II

When John Doane of Nowhere – to all practical purposes – left the home of The Thinking Machine he bore instructions of divers kinds. First he was to get a large map of the United States and study it closely, reading over and pronouncing aloud the name of every city, town and village he found. After an hour of this he was to take a city directory and read over the names, pronouncing them aloud as he did so. Then he was to make out a list of the various professions and higher commercial pursuits, and pronounce these. All these things were calculated, obviously, to arouse the sleeping brain. After Doane had gone The Thinking Machine called up Hutchinson Hatch, reporter, on the 'phone.

"Come up immediately," he requested. "There's something that will interest you."

"A mystery?" Hatch inquired, eagerly.

"One of the most engaging problems that has ever come to my attention," replied the scientist.

It was only a question of a few minutes before Hatch was ushered in. He was a living interrogation point, and repressed a rush of questions with a distinct effort. The Thinking Machine finally told what he knew.

"Now it seems to be," said The Thinking Machine, and he emphasized the "seems,"

"it seems to be a case of aphasia. You know, of course, what that is. The man simply doesn't know himself. I examined him closely. I went over his head for a sign of a possible depression, or abnormality. It didn't appear. I examined his muscles. He has biceps of great power, is evidently now or has been athletic. His hands are white, well cared for and have no marks on them. They are not the hands of a man who has ever done physical work. The money in his pocket tends to confirm the fact that he is not of that sphere.

"Then what is he? Lawyer? Banker? Financier? What? He might be either, yet he impressed me as being rather of the business than the professional school. He has a good, square-cut jaw — the jaw of a fighting man — and his poise gives one the impression that whatever he has been doing he has been foremost in it. Being foremost in it, he would naturally drift to a city, a big city. He is typically a city man.

"Now, please, to aid me, communicate with your correspondents in the large cities and find if such a name as John Doane appears in any directory. Is he at home now? Has he a family? All about him."

"Do you believe John Doane is his name?" asked the reporter.

"No reason why it shouldn't be," said The Thinking Machine. "Yet it might not be."

"How about inquiries in this city?"

"He can't well be a local man," was the reply. "He has been wandering about the streets for four weeks, and if he had lived here he would have met some one who knew him."

"But the money?"

"I'll probably be able to locate him through that," said The Thinking Machine. "The matter is not at all clear to me now, but it occurs to me that he is a man of consequence, and that it was possibly necessary for some one to get rid of him for a time."

"Well, if it's plain aphasia, as you say," the reporter put in, "it seems rather difficult to imagine that the attack came at a moment when it was necessary to get rid of him."

"I say it seems like aphasia," said the scientist, crustily, "There are known drugs which will produce the identical effect if properly administered."

"Oh," said Hatch. He was beginning to see.

"There is one drug particularly, made in India, and not unlike hasheesh. In a case of this kind anything is possible. Tomorrow I shall ask you to take Mr Doane down through the financial district, as an experiment. When you go there I want you particularly to get him to the sound of the 'ticker.' It will be an interesting experiment."

The reporter went away and The Thinking Machine sent a telegram to the Blank National Bank of Butte, Montana:

"To whom did you issue hundred-dollar bills, series B, numbering 846380 to 846395 inclusive? Please answer."

It was ten o'clock next day when Hatch called on The Thinking Machine. There he was introduced to John Doane, the man who was lost. The Thinking Machine was asking questions of Mr Doane when Hatch was ushered in.

"Did the map recall nothing?"

"Nothing."

"Montana, Montana, Montana," the scientist repeated monotonously; "think of it. Butte, Montana."

Doane shook his head hopelessly, sadly.

"Cowboy, cowboy. Did you ever see a cowboy?"

Again the head shake.

"Coyote – something like a wolf – coyote. Don't you recall ever having seen one?"

"I'm afraid it's hopeless," remarked the other.

There was a note of more than ordinary irritation in The Thinking Machine's voice when he turned to Hatch.

"Mr Hatch, will you walk through the financial district with Mr Doane?" he asked. "Please go to the places I suggested."

So it came to pass that the reporter and Doane went out together, walking through the crowded, hurrying, bustling financial district. The first place visited was a private room where market quotations were displayed on a blackboard. Mr Doane was interested, but the scene seemed to suggest nothing. He looked upon it all as any stranger might have done. After a time they passed out. Suddenly a man came running toward them – evidently a broker.

"What's the matter?" asked another.

"Montana's copper's gone to smash," was the reply.

"Copper! Copper!" gasped Doane suddenly.

Hatch looked around quickly at his companion. Doane's face was a study. On it was half realization and a deep perplexed wrinkle, a glimmer even of excitement.

"Copper!" he repeated.

"Does the word mean anything to you?" asked Hatch quickly. "Copper – metal, you know."

"Copper, copper, copper," the other repeated. Then, as Hatch looked, the queer expression faded; there came again utter hopelessness.

There are many men with powerful names who operate in the Street—some of them in copper. Hatch led Doane straight to the office of one of these men and there introduced him to a partner in the business.

"We want to talk about copper a little," Hatch explained, still eyeing his companion.

"Do you want to buy or sell?" asked the broker.

"Sell," said Doane suddenly. "Sell, sell, sell copper. That's it – copper."

He turned to Hatch, stared at him dully a moment, a deathly pallor came over his face, then, with upraised hands, fell senseless.

III

Still unconscious, the man of mystery was removed to the home of The Thinking Machine and there stretched out on a sofa. The Thinking Machine was bending over him, this time in his capacity of physician, making an examination. Hatch stood by, looking on curiously.

"I never saw anything like it," Hatch remarked. "He just threw up his hands and collapsed. He hasn't been conscious since."

"It may be that when he comes to he will have recovered his memory, and in that event he will have absolutely no recollection whatever of you and me," explained The Thinking Machine.

Doane moved a little at last, and under a stimulant the color began to creep back into his pallid face.

"Just what was said, Mr Hatch, before he collapsed?" asked the scientist.

Hatch explained, repeating the conversation as he remembered it.

"And he said 'sell,'" mused The Thinking Machine. "In other words, he thinks – or imagines he knows – that copper is to drop. I believe the first remark he heard was that copper had gone to smash – down, I presume that means?"

"Yes," the reporter replied.

Half an hour later John Doane sat up on the couch and looked around the room.

"Ah, Professor," he remarked. "I fainted, didn't I?"

The Thinking Machine was disappointed because his patient had not recovered memory with consciousness. The remark showed that he was still in the same mental condition — the man who was lost.

"Sell copper, sell, sell, sell," repeated The Thinking Machine, commandingly.

"Yes, yes, sell," was the reply.

The reflection of some great mental struggle was on Doane's face; he was seeking to recall something which persistently eluded him.

"Copper, copper," the scientist repeated, and he exhibited a penny.

"Yes, copper," said Doane. "I know. A penny."

"Why did you say sell copper?"

"I don't know," was the weary reply. "It seemed to be an unconscious act entirely. I don't know."

He clasped and unclasped his hands nervously and sat for a long time dully staring at the floor. The fight for memory was a dramatic one.

"It seemed to me," Doane explained after awhile, "that the word copper touched some responsive chord in my memory, then it was lost again. Some time in the past, I think, I must have had something to do with copper."

"Yes," said The Thinking Machine, and he rubbed his slender fingers briskly. "Now you are coming around again."

His remarks were interrupted by the appearance of Martha at the door with a telegram. The Thinking Machine opened it hastily. What he saw perplexed him again.

"Dear me! Most extraordinary!" he exclaimed.

"What is it?" asked Hatch, curiously.

The scientist turned to Doane again.

"Do you happen to remember Preston Bell?" he demanded, emphasizing the name explosively.

"Preston Bell?" the other repeated, and again the mental struggle was apparent on his face. "Preston Bell!"

"Cashier of the Blank National Bank of Butte, Montana?" urged the other, still in an emphatic tone. "Cashier Bell?"

He leaned forward eagerly and watched the face of his patient; Hatch unconsciously did the same. Once there was almost realization, and seeing it The Thinking Machine sought to bring back full memory.

"Bell, cashier, copper," he repeated, time after time.

The flash of realization which had been on Doane's face passed, and there came infinite weariness – the weariness of one who is ill.

"I don't remember," he said at last. "I'm very tired."

"Stretch out there on the couch and go to sleep," advised The Thinking Machine, and he arose to arrange a pillow. "Sleep will do you more good than anything else right now. But before you lie down, let me have, please, a few of those hundred-dollar bills you found."

Doane extended the roll of money, and then slept like a child. It was uncanny to Hatch, who had been a deeply interested spectator.

The Thinking Machine ran over the bills and finally selected fifteen of them – bills that were new and crisp. They were of an issue by the Blank National Bank of Butte, Montana. The Thinking Machine stared at the money closely, then handed it to Hatch.

"Does that look like counterfeit to you?" he asked.

"Counterfeit?" gasped Hatch. "Counterfeit?" he repeated. He took the bills and examined them. "So far as I can see they seem to be good," he went on, "though I have never had enough experience with one-hundred-dollar bills to qualify as an expert."

"Do you know an expert?"

"Yes."

"See him immediately. Take fifteen bills and ask him to pass on them, each and every one. Tell him you have reason – excellent reason – to believe that they are counterfeit. When he gives his opinion come back to me."

Hatch went away with the money in his pocket. Then The Thinking Machine wrote another telegram, addressed to Preston Bell, cashier of the Butte Bank. It was as follows:

"Please send me full details of the manner in which money previously described was lost, with names of all persons who might have had any knowledge of the matter. Highly important to your bank and to justice. Will communicate in detail on receipt of your answer."

Then, while his visitor slept, The Thinking Machine quietly removed his shoes and examined them. He found, almost worn away, the name of the maker. This was subjected to close scrutiny under the magnifying glass, after which The Thinking Machine arose with a perceptible expression of relief on his face.

"Why didn't I think of that before?" he demanded of himself.

Then other telegrams went into the West. One was to a customs shoemaker in Denver, Colorado:

"To what financier or banker have you sold within three months a pair of shoes, Senate brand, calfskin blucher, number eight, D last? Do you know John Doane?"

A second telegram went to the Chief of Police of Denver. It was:

"Please wire if any financier, banker or business man has been out of your city for five weeks or more, presumably on business trip. Do you know John Doane?"

Then The Thinking Machine sat down to wait. At last the door bell rang and Hatch entered.

"Well?" demanded the scientist, impatiently.

"The expert declares those are not counterfeit," said Hatch.

Now The Thinking Machine was surprised. It was shown clearly by the quick lifting of the eyebrows, by a sudden snap of his jaws, by a quick forward movement of the yellow head.

"Well, well, well!" he exclaimed at last. Then again: "Well, well!"

"What is it?"

"See here," and The Thinking Machine took the hundred-dollar bills in his own hands. "These bills, perfectly new and crisp, were issued by the Blank National Bank of Butte, and the fact that they are in proper sequence would indicate that they were issued to one individual at the same time, probably recently. There can be no doubt of that. The numbers run from 846380 to 846395, all series B."

"I see," said Hatch.

"Now read that," and the scientist extended to the reporter the telegram Martha had brought in just before Hatch had gone away. Hatch read this:

"Series B, hundred-dollar bills 846380 to 846395 issued by this bank are not in existence. Were destroyed by fire, together

MYSTERY OF THE MAN WHO WAS LOST 301

with twenty-seven others of the same series. Government has been asked to grant permission to reissue these numbers.

Preston Bell, Cashier."

The reporter looked up with a question in his eyes.

"It means," said The Thinking Machine, "that this man is either a thief or the victim of some sort of financial jugglery."

"In that case is he what he pretends to be – a man who doesn't know himself?" asked the reporter.

"That remains to be seen."

IV

Event followed event with startling rapidity during the next few hours. First came a message from the Chief of Police of Denver. No capitalist or financier of consequence was out of Denver at the moment, so far as his men could ascertain. Longer search might be fruitful. He did not know John Doane. One John Doane in the directory was a teamster.

Then from the Blank National Bank came another telegram signed "Preston Bell, Cashier," reciting the circumstances of the disappearance of the hundred-dollar bills. The Blank National Bank had moved into a new structure; within a week there had been a fire which destroyed it. Several packages of money, including one package of hundred-dollar bills, among them those specified by The Thinking Machine, had been burned. President Harrison of the bank immediately made affidavit to the Government that these bills were left in his office.

The Thinking Machine studied this telegram carefully and from time to time glanced at it while Hatch made his report. This was as to the work of the correspondents who had been seeking John Doane. They found many men of the name and reported at length on each. One by one The Thinking Machine heard the reports, then shook his head.

Finally he reverted again to the telegram, and after consideration sent another – this time to the Chief of Police of Butte. In it he asked these questions:

"Has there ever been any financial trouble in Blank National Bank? Was there an embezzlement or shortage at any time? What is reputation of President Harrison? What is reputation of Cashier Bell? Do you know John Doane?"

In due course of events the answer came. It was brief and to the point. It said:

"Harrison recently embezzled $175,000 and disappeared. Bell's reputation excellent; now out of city. Don't know John Doane. If you have any trace of Harrison, wire quick."

This answer came just after Doane awoke, apparently greatly refreshed, but himself gain – that is, himself in so far as he was still lost. For an hour The Thinking Machine pounded him with questions — questions of all sorts, serious, religious and at times seemingly silly. They apparently aroused no trace of memory, save when the name Preston Bell was mentioned; then there was the strange, puzzled expression on Doane's face.

"Harrison – do you know him?" asked the scientist. "President of the Blank National Bank of Butte?"

There was only an uncomprehending stare for an answer. After a long time of this The Thinking Machine instructed Hatch and Doane to go for a walk. He had still a faint hope that some one might recognize Doane and speak to him. As they wandered aimlessly on two persons spoke to him. One was a man who nodded and passed on.

"Who was that?" asked Hatch quickly. "Do you remember ever having seen him before?"

"Oh, yes," was the reply. "He stops at my hotel. He knows me as Doane."

It was just a few minutes before six o'clock when, walking slowly, they passed a great office building. Coming toward them was a well-dressed, active man of thirty-five years or so. As he approached he removed a cigar from his lips.

"Hello, Harry!" he exclaimed, and reached for Doane's hand.

"Hello," said Doane, but there was no trace of recognition in his voice.

"How's Pittsburg?" asked the stranger.

"Oh, all right, I guess," said Doane, and there came new wrinkles of perplexity in his brow. "Allow me, Mr – Mr – really I have forgotten your name—"

"Manning," laughed the other.

"Mr Hatch, Mr Manning."

The reporter shook hands with Manning eagerly; he saw now a new line of possibilities suddenly revealed. Here was a man who knew Doane as Harry—and then Pittsburg, too.

"Last time I saw you was in Pittsburg, wasn't it?" Manning rattled on, as he led the way into a nearby café. "By George, that was a stiff game that night! Remember that jack full I held? It cost me nineteen hundred dollars," he added, ruefully.

"Yes, I remember," said Doane, but Hatch knew that he did not. And meanwhile a thousand questions were surging through the reporter's brain.

"Poker hands as expensive as that are liable to be long remembered," remarked Hatch, casually. "How long ago was that?"

"Three years, wasn't it, Harry?" asked Manning.

"All of that, I should say," was the reply.

"Twenty hours at the table," said Manning, and again he laughed cheerfully. "I was woozy when we finished."

Inside the café they sought out a table in a corner. No one else was near. When the waiter had gone, Hatch leaned over and looked Doane straight in the eyes.

"Shall I ask some questions?" he inquired.

"Yes, yes," said the other eagerly.

"What – what is it?" asked Manning.

"It's a remarkably strange chain of circumstances," said Hatch, in explanation. "This man whom you call Harry, we know as John Doane. What is his real name? Harry what?"

Manning stared at the reporter for a moment in amazement, then gradually a smile came to his lips.

"What are you trying to do?" he asked. "Is this a joke?"

"No, my God, man, can't you see?" exclaimed Doane, fiercely. "I'm ill, sick, something. I've lost my memory, all of my past. I don't remember anything about myself. What is my name?"

"Well, by George!" exclaimed Manning. "By George! I don't believe I know your full name. Harry – Harry – what?"

He drew from his pocket several letters and half a dozen scraps of paper and ran over them. Then he looked carefully through a worn notebook.

"I don' know," he confessed. "I had your name and address in an old notebook, but I suppose I burned it. I remember, though, I met you in the Lincoln Club in Pittsburg three years ago. I called you Harry because everyone was calling everyone else by his first name. Your last name made no impression on me at all. By George!" he concluded, in a new burst of amazement.

"What were the circumstances, exactly?" asked Hatch.

"I'm a traveling man," Manning explained. "I go everywhere. A friend gave me a card to the Lincoln Club in Pittsburg and I went there. There were five or six of us playing poker, among them Mr – Mr Doane here. I sat at the same table with him for twenty hours or so, but I can't recall his last name to save me. It isn't Doane, I'm positive. I have an excellent memory for faces, and I know you're the man. Don't you remember me?"

"I haven't the slightest recollection of ever having seen you before in my life," was Doane's slow reply. "I have no recollection of ever having been in Pittsburg – no recollection of anything."

"Do you know if Mr Doane is a resident of Pittsburg?" Hatch inquired. "Or was he there as a visitor, as you were?"

"Couldn't tell you to save my life," replied Manning. "Lord, it's amazing, isn't it? You don't remember me? You called me Bill all evening."

The other man shook his head.

"Well, say, is there anything I can do for you?"

"Nothing, thanks," said Doane. "Only tell me my name, and who I am."

"Lord, I don't know."

"What sort of a club is the Lincoln?" asked Hatch.

"It's a sort of a millionaire's club," Manning explained. "Lots of iron men belong to it. I had considerable business with them – that's what took me to Pittsburg."

"And you are absolutely positive this is the man you met there?"

"Why, I know it. I never forget faces; it's my business to remember them."

"Did he say anything about a family?"

"Not that I recall. A man doesn't usually speak of his family at a poker table."

"Do you remember the exact date or the month?"

"I think it was in January or February possibly," was the reply. "It was bitterly cold and the snow was all smoked up. Yes, I'm positive it was in January, three years ago."

After awhile the men separated. Manning was stopping at the Hotel Teutonic and willingly gave his name and permanent address to Hatch, explaining at the same time that he would be in the city for several days and was perfectly willing to help in any way he could. He took also the address of The Thinking Machine.

From the café Hatch and Doane returned to the scientist. They found him with two telegrams spread out on a table before him. Briefly Hatch told the story of the meeting with

Manning, while Doane sank down with his head in his hands. The Thinking Machine listened without comment.

"Here," he said, at the conclusion of the recital, and he offered one of the telegrams to Hatch. "I got the name of a shoemaker from Mr Doane's shoe and wired to him in Denver, asking if he had a record of the sale. This is the answer. Read it aloud."

Hatch did so.

"Shoes such as described made nine weeks ago for Preston Bell, cashier Blank National Bank of Butte. Don't know John Doane."

"Well – what—" Doane began, bewildered.

"It means that you are Preston Bell," said Hatch, emphatically.

"No," said The Thinking Machine, quickly. "It means that there is only a strong probability of it."

The door bell rang. After a moment Martha appeared.

"A lady to see you, sir," she said.

"Her name?"

"Mrs John Doane."

"Gentlemen, kindly step into the next room," requested The Thinking Machine.

Together Hatch and Doane passed through the door. There was an expression of – of – no man may say what – on Doane's face as he went.

"Show her in here, Martha," instructed the scientist.

There was a rustle of silk in the hall, the curtains on the door were pulled apart quickly and a richly gowned woman rushed into the room.

"My husband? Is he here?" she demanded, breathlessly. "I went to the hotel; they said he came here for treatment. Please, please, is he here?"

"A moment, madam," said The Thinking Machine. He stepped to the door through which Hatch and Doane had gone, and said something. One of them appeared in the door. It was Hutchinson Hatch.

"John, John, my darling husband," and the woman flung her arms about Hatch's neck. "Don't you know me?"

With blushing face Hatch looked over her shoulder into the eyes of The Thinking Machine, who stood briskly rubbing his hands. Never before in his long acquaintance with the scientist had Hatch seen him smile.

V

For a time there was silence, broken only by sobs, as the woman clung frantically to Hatch, with her face buried on his shoulder. Then:

"Don't you remember me?" she asked again and again. "Your wife? Don't you remember me?"

Hatch could still see the trace of a smile on the scientist's face, and said nothing.

"You are positive this gentleman is your husband?" inquired The Thinking Machine, finally.

"Oh, I know," the woman sobbed. "Oh, John, don't you remember me?" She drew away a little and looked deeply into the reporter's eyes. "Don't you remember me, John?"

"Can't say that I ever saw you before," said Hatch, truthfully enough. "I – I – fact is—"

"Mr Doane's memory is wholly gone now," explained The Thinking Machine. "Meanwhile, perhaps you would tell me something about him. He is my patient. I am particularly interested."

The voice was soothing; it had lost for the moment its perpetual irritation. The woman sat down beside Hatch. Her face, pretty enough in a bold sort of way, was turned to The Thinking Machine inquiringly. With one hand she stroked that of the reporter.

"Where are you from?" began the scientist. "I mean where is the home of John Doane?"

"In Buffalo," she replied, glibly. "Didn't he even remember that?"

"And what's his business?"

"His health has been bad for some time and recently he gave up active business," said the woman. "Previously he was connected with a bank."

"When did you see him last?"

"Six weeks ago. He left the house one day and I have never heard from him since. I had Pinkerton men searching and at last they reported he was at the Yarmouth Hotel. I came on immediately. And now we shall go back to Buffalo." She turned to Hatch with a languishing glance. "Shall we not, dear?"

"Whatever Professor Van Dusen thinks best," was the equivocal reply.

Slowly the glimmer of amusement was passing out of the squint eyes of The Thinking Machine; as Hatch looked he saw a hardening of the lines of the mouth. There was an explosion coming. He knew it. Yet when the scientist spoke his voice was more velvety than ever.

"Mrs Doane, do you happen to be acquainted with a drug which produces temporary loss of memory?"

She stared at him, but did not lose her self-possession.

"No," she said finally. "Why?"

"You know, of course, that this man is not your husband?"

This time the question had its effect. The woman arose suddenly stared at the two men, and her face went white.

"Not? – not? – what do you mean?"

"I mean," and the voice reassumed its tone of irritation, "I mean that I shall send for the police and give you in their charge unless you tell me the truth about this affair. Is that perfectly clear to you?"

The woman's lips were pressed tightly together. She saw that she had fallen into some sort of a trap; her gloved hands were clenched fiercely; the pallor faded and a flush of anger came.

"Further, for fear you don't quite follow me even now," explained The Thinking Machine, "I will say that I know all about this copper deal of which this so-called John Doane was the victim. I know his condition now. If you tell the truth you may escape prison – if you don't, there is a long term, not only for you, but for your fellow-conspirators. Now will you talk?"

"No," said the woman. She arose as if to go out.

"Never mind that," said The Thinking Machine. "You had better stay where you are. You will be locked up at the proper moment. Mr Hatch, please 'phone for Detective Mallory."

Hatch arose and passed into the adjoining room.

"You tricked me," the woman screamed suddenly, fiercely.

"Yes," the other agreed, complacently. "Next time be sure you know your own husband. Meanwhile where is Harrison?"

"Not another word," was the quick reply.

"Very well," said the scientist, calmly. "Detective Mallory will be here in a few minutes. Meanwhile I'll lock this door."

"You have no right—" the woman began.

Without heeding the remark, The Thinking Machine passed into the adjoining room. There for half an hour he talked earnestly to Hatch and Doane. At the end of that time he sent a telegram to the manager of the Lincoln club in Pittsburg, as follows:

"Does your visitors' book show any man, registered there in the month of January three years ago, whose first name is Harry or Henry? If so, please wire name and description, also name of man whose guest he was."

This telegram was dispatched. A few minutes later the door bell rang and Detective Mallory entered.

"What is it?" he inquired.

"A prisoner for you in the next room," was the reply. "A woman. I charge her with conspiracy to defraud a man who for the present we will call John Doane. That may or may not be his name."

"What do you know about it?" asked the detective.

"A great deal now – more after awhile. I shall tell you then. Meanwhile take this woman. You gentlemen, I should suggest, might go out somewhere this evening. If you drop by afterwards there may be an answer to a few telegrams which will make this matter clear."

Protestingly the mysterious woman was led away by Detective Mallory; and Doane and Hatch followed shortly after. The next act of the Thinking Machine was to write a telegram addressed to Mrs Preston Bell, Butte, Montana. Here it is:

"Your husband suffering temporary mental trouble here. Can you come on immediately? Answer."

When the messenger boy came for the telegram he found a man on the stoop. The Thinking Machine received the telegram, and the man, who gave to Martha the name of Manning, was announced.

"Manning, too," mused the scientist. "Show him in."

"I don't know if you know why I am here," explained Manning.

"Oh, yes," said the scientist. "You have remembered Doane's name. What is it, please?"

Manning was too frankly surprised to answer and only stared at the scientist.

"Yes, that's right," he said finally, and he smiled. "His name is Pillsbury. I recall it now."

"And what made you recall it?"

"I noticed an advertisement in a magazine with the name in large letters. It instantly came to me that that was Doane's real name."

"Thanks," remarked the scientist. "And the woman – who is she?"

"What woman?" asked Manning.

"Never mind, then. I am deeply obliged for your information. I don't suppose you know anything else about it?"

"No," said Manning. He was a little bewildered, and after awhile went away.

For an hour or more The Thinking Machine sat with finger tips pressed together staring at the ceiling. His meditations were interrupted by Martha.

"Another telegram, sir."

The Thinking Machine took it eagerly. It was from the manager of the Lincoln Club in Pittsburg:

"Henry C. Carney, Harry Meltz, Henry Blake, Henry W. Tolman, Harry Pillsbury, Henry Calvert and Henry Louis Smith all visitors to club in month you name. Which do you want to learn more about?"

It took more than an hour for The Thinking Machine to establish long distance connection by 'phone with Pittsburg. When he had finished talking he seemed satisfied.

"Now," he mused. "The answer from Mrs Bell."

It was nearly midnight when that came. Hatch and Doane had returned from a theater and were talking to the scientist when the telegram was brought in.

"Anything important?" asked Doane, anxiously.

"Yes," said the scientist, and he slipped a finger beneath the flap of the envelope. "It's clear now. It was an engaging problem from first to last, and now—"

He opened the telegram and glanced at it; then with bewilderment on his face and mouth slightly open he sank down at the table and leaned forward with his head on his arms. The message fluttered to the table and Hatch read this:

"Man in Boston can't be my husband. He is now in Honolulu. I received cablegram from him today.

"Mrs Preston Bell."

VI

It was thirty-six hours later that the three men met again. The Thinking Machine had abruptly dismissed Hatch and Doane the last time. The reporter knew that something wholly unexpected had happened. He could only conjecture that this had to do with Preston Bell. When the three met again it was in Detective Mallory's office at police headquarters. The mysterious woman who had claimed Doane for her husband was present, as were Mallory, Hatch, Doane and The Thinking Machine.

"Has this woman given any name?" was the scientist's first question.

"Mary Jones," replied the detective, with a grin.

"And address?"

"No."

"Is her picture in the Rogues' Gallery?"

"No. I looked carefully."

"Anybody called to ask about her?"

"A man – yes. That is, he didn't ask about her – he merely asked some general questions, which now we believe were to find out about her."

The Thinking Machine arose and walked over to the woman. She looked up at him defiantly.

"There has been a mistake made, Mr Mallory," said the scientist. "It's my fault entirely. Let this woman go. I am sorry to have done her so grave an injustice."

Instantly the woman was on her feet, her face radiant. A look of disgust crept into Mallory's face.

"I can't let her go now without arraignment," the detective growled. "It ain't regular."

"You must let her go, Mr Mallory," commanded The Thinking Machine, and over the woman's shoulder the detective saw an astonishing thing. The Thinking Machine winked. It was a decided, long, pronounced wink.

"Oh, all right," he said, "but it ain't regular at that."

The woman passed out of the room hurriedly, her silken skirts rustling loudly. She was free again. Immediately she disappeared. The Thinking Machine's entire manner changed.

"Put your best man to follow her," he directed rapidly. "Let him go to her home and arrest the man who is with her as her husband. Then bring them both back here, after searching their rooms for money."

"Why-what – what is all this?" demanded Mallory, amazed.

"The man who inquired for her, who is with her, is wanted for a $175,000 embezzlement in Butte, Montana. Don't let your man lose sight of her."

The detective left the room hurriedly. Ten minutes later he returned to find The Thinking Machine leaning back in his chair with eyes upturned. Hatch and Doane were waiting, both impatiently.

"Now Mr Mallory," said the scientist, "I shall try to make this matter as clear to you as it is to me. By the time I finish I expect your man will be back here with this women and the embezzler. His name is Harrison; I don't know hers. I can't believe she is Mrs Harrison, yet he has, I suppose, a wife. But here's the story. It is the chaining together of fact after fact; a necessary logical sequence to a series of incidents, which are, separately, deeply puzzling."

The detective lighted a cigar and the others disposed themselves comfortably to listen.

"This gentleman came to me," began The Thinking Machine, "with a story of loss of memory. He told me that he knew neither his name, home, occupation, nor anything whatever about himself. At the moment it struck me as a case for a mental expert; still I was interested. It seemed to be a remarkable case of aphasia, and I so regarded it until he told me that he had $10,000 in bills, that he had no watch, that everything which might possibly be of value in establishing his identity had been removed from his clothing. This included even the names of the makers of his linen. That showed intent, deliberation.

"Then I knew it could not be aphasia. That disease strikes a man suddenly as he walks the street, as he sleeps, as he works, but never gives any desire to remove traces of one's identity. On the contrary, a man is still apparently sound mentally — he has merely forgotten something – and usually his first desire is to find out who he is. This gentleman had that desire, and in trying to find some clew he showed a mind capable of grasping at every possible opportunity. Nearly every question I asked had been anticipated. Thus I recognized that he must be a more than usually astute man.

"But if not aphasia, what was it? What caused his condition? A drug? I remembered that there was such a drug in India, not unlike hasheesh. Therefore for the moment I assumed a drug. It gave me a working basis. Then what did I have? A man of striking mentality who was the victim of some sort of plot, who had been drugged until he lost himself, and in that way disposed of. The handwriting might be the same, for handwriting is rarely affected by a mental disorder; it is a physical function.

"So far, so good. I examined his head for a possible accident. Nothing. His hands were white and in no way calloused. Seeking to reconcile the fact that he had been a man of strong mentality, with all other things a financier or banker, occurred to me. The same things might have indicated a lawyer, but the poise of this man, his elaborate care in dress, all these things made me think him the financier rather than the lawyer.

"Then I examined some money he had when he awoke. Fifteen or sixteen of the hundred-dollar bills were new and in sequence. They were issued by a national bank. To whom? The possibilities were that the bank would have a record. I wired, asking about this, and also asked Mr Hatch to have his correspondents make inquiries in various cities for a John Doane. It was not impossible that John Doane was his name. Now I believe it will be safe for me to say that when he registered at the hotel he was drugged, his own name slipped his mind, and he signed John Doane – the first name that came to him. That is not his name.

"While waiting an answer from the bank I tried to arouse his memory by referring to things in the West. It appeared possible that he might have brought the money from the West with him. Then, still with the idea that he was a financier, I sent him to the financial district. There was a result. The word 'copper' aroused him so that he fainted after shouting, 'Sell copper, sell, sell, sell.'

"In a way my estimate of the man was confirmed. He was or had been in a copper deal, selling copper in the market, or planning to do so. I know nothing of the intricacies of the stock market. But there came instantly to me the thought that a man who would faint away in such a case must be vitally interested as well as ill. Thus I had a financier, in a copper deal, drugged as result of a conspiracy. Do you follow me, Mr Mallory?"

"Sure," was the reply.

"At this point I received a telegram from the Butte bank telling me that the hundred-dollar bills I asked about had been burned. This telegram was signed 'Preston Bell, Cashier.' If that were true, the bills this man had were counterfeit. There were no ifs about that. I asked him if he knew Preston Bell. It was the only name of a person to arouse him in any way. A man knows his own name better than anything in the world. Therefore was it his? For a moment I presumed it was.

"Thus the case stood: Preston Bell, cashier of the Butte bank, had been drugged, was the victim of a conspiracy, which was probably a part of some great move in copper. But if this man were Preston Bell, how came the signature there? Part of the office regulation? It happens hundreds of times that a name is so used, particularly on telegrams.

"Well, this man who was lost – Doane, or Preston Bell – went to sleep in my apartments. At that time I believed it fully possible that he was a counterfeiter, as the bills were supposedly burned, and sent Mr Hatch to consult an expert. I also wired for details of the fire loss in Butte and names of persons who had any knowledge of the matter. This done, I removed and examined this gentleman's shoes for the name of the maker. I found it. The shoes were of fine quality, probably made to order for him.

"Remember, at this time I believed this gentleman to be Preston Bell, for reasons I have stated. I wired to the maker or retailer to know if he had a record of a sale of the shoes, describing them in detail, to any financier or banker. I also wired to the Denver police to know if any financier or banker had been away from there for four or five weeks. Then came the somewhat startling information, through Mr Hatch, that the hundred-dollar bills were genuine. That answer meant that Preston Bell – as I had begun to think of him – was as either a thief or the victim of some sort of financial conspiracy."

During the silence which followed every eye was turned on the man who was lost—Doane or Preston Bell. He sat staring straight ahead of him with hands nervously clenched. On his face was written the sign of a desperate mental struggle. He was still trying to recall the past.

"Then," The Thinking Machine resumed, "I heard from the Denver police. There was no leading financier or banker out of the city so far as they could learn hurriedly. It was not conclusive, but it aided me. Also I received another telegram from Butte, signed Preston Bell, telling me the circumstances of the supposed burning of the hundred-dollar bills. It did not show that they were burned at all; it was merely an assumption that they had been. They were last seen in President Harrison's office."

"Harrison, Harrison, Harrison," repeated Doane.

"Vaguely I could see the possibility of something financially wrong in the bank. Possibly Harrison, even Mr Bell here, knew of it. Banks do not apply for permission to reissue bills unless they are positive of the original loss. Yet here were the bills. Obviously some sort of jugglery. I wired to the police of Butte, asking some questions. The answer was that Harrison had embezzled $175,000 and had disappeared. Now I knew he had part of the missing, supposedly burned, bills with him. It was obvious. Was Bell also a thief?

"The same telegram said that Mr Bell's reputation was of the best, and he was out of the city. That confirmed my belief that it was an office rule to sign telegrams with the cashier's name, and further made me positive that this man was Preston Bell. The chain of circumstances was complete. It was two and two — inevitable result, four.

"Now, what was the plot? Something to do with copper, and there was an embezzlement. Then, still seeking a man who knew Bell personally, I sent him out walking with Hatch. I had done so before. Suddenly another figure came into the mystery — a confusing one at the moment. This was a Mr Manning, who knew Doane, or Bell, as Harry – something; met him in Pittsburg three years ago, in the Lincoln Club.

"It was just after Mr Hatch told me of this man that I received a telegram from the shoemaker in Denver. It said that he had made a shoe such as I described within a few months for Preston Bell. I had asked if a sale had been made to a financier or banker; I got the name back by wire.

"At this point a woman appeared to claim John Doane as her husband. With no definite purpose, save general precaution, I asked Mr Hatch to see her first. She imagined he was Doane and embraced him, calling him John. Therefore she was a fraud. She did not know John Doane, or Preston Bell, by sight. Was she acting under the direction of some one else? If so, whose?"

There was as a pause as The Thinking Machine readjusted himself in the chair. After a time he went on:

"There are shades of emotion intuition, call it what you will, so subtle that it is difficult to express them in words. As I had instinctively associated Harrison with Bell's present condition I instinctively associated this woman with Harrison. For not a word of the affair had appeared in a newspaper; only a very few persons knew of it. Was it possible that the stranger Manning was backing the woman in an effort to get the $10,000? That remained to be seen. I questioned the woman; she would say nothing. She is clever, but she blundered badly in claiming Mr Hatch for a husband."

The reporter blushed modestly.

"I asked her flatly about a drug. She was quite calm and her manner indicated that she knew nothing of it. Yet I presume she did. Then I sprung the bombshell, and she saw she had made a mistake. I gave her over to Detective Mallory and she was locked up. This done, I wired to the Lincoln Club in Pittsburg to find out about this mysterious 'Harry' who had come into the case. I was so confident then that I also wired to Mrs Bell in Butte, presuming that there was a Mrs Bell, asking about her husband.

"Then Manning came to see me. I knew he came because he had remembered the name he knew you by," and The Thinking Machine turned to the central figure in this strange entanglement of identity, "although he seemed surprised when I told him as much. He knew you as Harry Pillsbury. I asked him who the woman was. His manner told me that he knew nothing whatever of her. Then it came back to her as an associate of Harrison, your enemy for some reason, and I could see it in no other light. It was her purpose to get hold of you and possibly keep you a prisoner, at least until some gigantic deal in which copper figured was disposed of. That was what I surmised.

"Then another telegram came from the Lincoln Club in Pittsburg. The name of Harry Pillsbury appeared as a visitor in the book in January, three years ago. It was you – Manning is not the sort of man to be mistaken – and then there remained only one point to be solved as I then saw the case. That was an answer from Mrs Preston Bell, if there was a Mrs Bell. She would know where her husband was."

Again there was silence. A thousand things were running through Bell's mind. The story had been told so pointedly, and was so vitally a part of him, that semi-recollection was again on his face.

"That telegram said that Preston Bell was in Honolulu; that the wife had received a cable dispatch that day. Then, frankly, I was puzzled; so puzzled, in fact, that the entire fabric I had constructed seemed to melt away before my eyes. It took me hours to readjust it. I tried it all over in detail, and then the theory which would reconcile every fact in the case was evolved. That theory is right – as right as that two and two make four. It's logic."

It was half an hour later when a detective entered and spoke to Detective Mallory aside.

"Fine!" said Mallory. "Bring 'em in."

Then there reappeared the woman who had been a prisoner and a man of fifty years.

"Harrison!" exclaimed Bell, suddenly. He staggered to his feet with outstretched hands. "Harrison! I know! I know!"

"Good, good, very good," said The Thinking Machine.

Bell's nervously twitching hands were reaching for Harrison's throat when he was pushed aside by Detective Mallory. He stood pallid for a moment, then sank down on the floor in a heap. He was senseless. The Thinking Machine made a hurried examination.

"Good!" he remarked again. "When he recovers he will remember everything except what has happened since he has been in Boston. Meanwhile, Mr Harrison, we know all about the little affair of the drug, the battle for new copper workings in Honolulu, and your partner there has been arrested. Your drug didn't do its work well enough. Have you anything to add?"

The prisoner was silent.

"Did you search his rooms?" asked The Thinking Machine of the detective who had made the double arrest.

"Yes, and found this."

It was a large roll of money. The Thinking Machine ran over it lightly – $70,000 – scanning the numbers of the bills. At last he held forth half a dozen. They were among the twenty-seven reported to have been burned in the bank fire in Butte.

Harrison and the woman were led away. Subsequently it developed that he had been systematically robbing the bank of which he was president for years; was responsible for the fire, at which time he had evidently expected to make a great haul; and that the woman was not his wife. Following his arrest this entire story came out; also the facts of the gigantic copper deal, in which he had rid himself of Bell, who was his partner, and had sent another man to Honolulu in Bell's name to buy up options on some valuable copper property there. This confederate in Honolulu had sent the cable dispatches to the wife in Butte. She accepted them without question.

It was a day or so later that Hatch dropped in to see The Thinking Machine and asked a few questions.

"How did Bell happen to have that $10,000?"

"It was given to him, probably, because it was safer to have him rambling about the country, not knowing who he was as, than to kill him."

"And how did he happen to be here?"

"That question may be answered at the trial."

"And how did it come that Bell was once known as Harry Pillsbury?"

"Bell is a director in United States Steel, I have since learned. There was a secret meeting of this board in Pittsburg three years ago. He went incognito to attend that meeting and was introduced at the Lincoln Club as Harry Pillsbury."

"Oh!" exclaimed Hatch.

15

PROBLEM OF DRESSING ROOM A

It was absolutely impossible. Twenty-five chess masters from the world at large, forgathered in Boston for the annual championships, unanimously declared it impossible, and unanimity on any given point is an unusual mental condition for chess masters. Not one would concede for an instant that it was within the range of human achievement. Some grew red in the face as they argued it, others smiled loftily and were silent; still others dismissed the matter in a word as wholly absurd.

A casual remark by the distinguished scientist and logician, Professor Augustus S. F. X. Van Dusen, provoked the discussion. He had in the past aroused bitter disputes by some chance remark; in fact, had been once a sort of controversial center of the sciences. It had been due to his modest announcement of a startling and unorthodox hypothesis that he had been invited to vacate the chair of philosophy in a great university, later that university had felt honored when he accepted its degree of LLD.

For a score of years educational and scientific institutions of the world had amused themselves by crowding degrees upon him. He had initials that stood for things he couldn't pronounce; degrees from England, Russia, Germany, Italy, Sweden, and Spain. These were expressed recognition of the fact that his was the foremost brain in the sciences. The imprint of his crabbed personality lay heavily on half a dozen of its branches. Finally there came a time when argument was respectfully silent in the face of one of his conclusions.

The remark which had arrayed the chess masters of the world into so formidable and unanimous a dissent was made by Professor Van Dusen in the presence of three other men of standing. One of these, Dr Charles Elbert, happened to be a chess enthusiast.

"Chess is a shameless perversion of the functions of the brain," was Professor Van Dusen's declaration in his perpetually irritated voice. "It is a sheer waste of effort, greater because it is possibly the most difficult of all fixed abstract problems. Of course logic will solve it. Logic will solve any problem; not most of them, but any problem. A thorough understanding of its rules would enable anyone to defeat your greatest chess players. It would be inevitable, just as inevitable as that two and two make four; not sometimes, but always. I don't know chess, because I never do useless things, but I could take a few hours of competent instruction and defeat a man who has devoted his life to it. His mind is cramped; bound down to the logic of chess. Mine is not; mine employs logic in its widest scope."

Dr Elbert shook his head vigorously. "It is impossible." he asserted.

"Nothing is impossible!" snapped the scientist. "The human mind can do anything. It is all we have to lift us above the brute creation. For Heaven's sake, leave us that!"

The aggressive tone, the uncompromising egotism, brought a flush to Dr Elbert's face. Professor Van Dusen affected many persons that way, particularly those fellow-savants who, themselves men of distinction, had ideas of their own. "Do you know the purposes of chess? Its countless combinations?" asked Dr Elbert.

"No," was the crabbed reply; "I know nothing whatever of the game beyond the general purpose, which, I understand, is to move certain pieces in certain directions to stop an opponent from moving his king. Is that correct?"

"Yes," said Dr Elbert slowly; "but I never heard it stated just that way before."

"Then, if that is correct, I maintain that the true logician can defeat the chess expert by the mechanical rules of logic. I'll take a few hours some time, acquaint myself with the moves of the pieces, and defeat you to convince you." Professor Van Dusen glared savagely into the eyes of Dr Elbert.

"Not me!" said Dr Elbert. "You say anyone; you for instance might defeat the greatest chess player. Would you be willing to meet the greatest chess player after you 'acquaint' yourself with the game?"

"Certainly," said the scientist. "I have frequently found it necessary to make a fool of myself to convince people. I'll do it again."

This, then, was the acrimonious beginning of the discussion which aroused chess masters and brought open dissent from eminent men who had not dared for years to dispute any assertion by the distinguished Professor Van Dusen. It was arranged that at the conclusion of the championships Professor Van Dusen should meet the winner. This happened to be Tschaikowsky the Russian who had been chess champion for half a dozen years.

After this expected result of the tournament, Hillsbury, a noted American master, spent a morning with Professor Van Dusen in the latter's modest apartments on Beacon Hill. He left there with a sadly puzzled face. That afternoon Professor Van Dusen met the Russian champion. The newspapers had said a great deal about the affair, and hundreds were present to witness the game.

There was a little murmur of astonishment when Professor Van Dusen appeared. He was slight to the point of childishness, and his thin shoulders seemed to droop beneath the weight of his enormous head. He wore a number eight hat. His brow rose straight and dome-like, and a heavy shock of long yellow hair gave him almost a grotesque appearance. The eyes were narrow slits of blue, squinting eternally through thick glasses; the face was small, clean shaven, and white with the pallor of the student. His lips made a perfectly straight line. His hands were remarkable for their whiteness, their flexibility, and for the length of the slender fingers. Physical development had never entered into the schedule of his fifty years of life.

The Russian smiled as he sat down at the chess table. He felt that he was humoring a crank. The other masters were grouped near by, curiously expectant. Professor Van Dusen began the game, opening with a queen's gambit. At his fifth move, made without the slightest hesitation, the smile left the Russian's face. At the tenth the master's grew tensely eager. The Russian champion was playing for honor now.

Professor Van Dusen's fourteenth move was king's castle to queen's four. "Check," he announced.

After a long study of the board the Russian protected his king with a knight. Professor Van Dusen noted the play, then leaned back in his chair with finger tips pressed together. His eyes left the board and dreamily studied the ceiling. For at least fifteen minutes there was no sound, then:

"Mate in fifteen moves!" he said quietly.

There was a quick gasp of astonishment. It took the practised eyes of the masters several minutes to verify the announcement. But the Russian champion saw and leaned back in his chair, a little white and dazed. He was not astonished; he was helplessly floundering in a maze of incomprehensible things. Suddenly he arose and grasped the slender hand of his conqueror.

"You have never played chess before?" he asked.

"Never."

"*Mon Dieu!* You are not a man; you are a brain–a machine–a thinking machine."

"It's a child's game," said the scientist abruptly. There was no note of exultation in his voice; it was still the irritable, impersonal tone which was habitual.

This, then, was Professor Augustus S. F. X. Van Dusen, Ph. D., LL. D., F. R. S., M. D., etc., etc., etc. This is how he came to be known to the world at large as The Thinking Machine. The Russian's phrase had been applied to the scientist as a title by a newspaper reporter, Hutchinson Hatch. It had stuck.

THE FIRST PROBLEM

That strange, seemingly inexplicable chain of circumstances which had to do with the mysterious disappearance of a famous actress, Irene Wallack, from her dressing room in a Springfield theater in the course of a performance, while the echo of tumultuous appreciation still rang in her ears, was perhaps the first problem which was not purely scientific that The Thinking Machine was ever asked to solve. The scientist's aid was enlisted in this case by Hutchinson Hatch, reporter.

"But I am a scientist, a logician," The Thinking Machine had protested. "I know nothing whatever of crime."

"No one knows that a crime has been committed," the reporter hastened to say.

"There is something far beyond the ordinary in this affair. A woman has disappeared, evaporated into thin air in the hearing, almost in sight, of her friends. The police can make nothing of it. It is a problem for a greater mind than theirs."

Professor Van Dusen waved the newspaper man to a seat and himself sank back into a great cushioned chair in which his diminutive figure seemed even more child-like than it really was.

"Tell me the story," he said petulantly, "All of it."

The enormous yellow head rested against the chair back, the blue eyes squinted steadily upward, the slender fingers were pressed tip to tip. The Thinking Machine was in a receptive mood. Hatch was triumphant; he had had only a vague hope that he could interest this man in an affair which was as bizarre as it was incomprehensible.

"Miss Wallack is thirty years old and beautiful," the reporter began. "As an actress she has won high recognition not only in this country but in England. You may have read something of her in the daily papers, and if—"

"I never read the papers," the other interrupted curtly. "Go on."

"She is unmarried, and as far as anyone knows, had no immediate intention of changing her condition," Hatch resumed, staring curiously at the thin face of the scientist. "I presume she had admirers—most beautiful women of the stage have—but she is one whose life has been perfectly clean, whose record is an open book. I tell you this because it might have a bearing on your conclusion as to a possible reason for her disappearance.

"Now the actual circumstances of that disappearance. Miss Wallack has been playing in Shakespearean repertoire. Last week she was in Springfield. On Saturday night, which concluded her engagement there, she appeared as Rosalind in 'As You Like It.' The house was crowded. She played the first two acts amid great enthusiasm, and this despite the fact that she was suffering intensely from headache to which she was subject at times. After the second act she returned to her dressing room and just before the curtain went up for the third the stage manager called her. She replied that she would be out immediately. There seems no possible shadow of doubt that it was her voice.

"Rosalind does not appear in the third act until the curtain has been up for six minutes. When Miss Wallack's cue came she did not answer it. The stage manager rushed to her door and again called her. There was no answer. Then, fearing that she might have fainted, he went in. She was not there. A hurried search was made without result, and the stage manager finally was compelled to announce to the audience that the sudden illness of the star would make it impossible to finish the performance.

"The curtain was lowered and the search resumed. Every nook and corner back of the footlights was gone over. The stage doorkeeper, William Meegan, had seen no one go out. He and a policeman had been standing at the stage door talking for at least twenty minutes. It is therefore conclusive that Miss Wallack did not leave by that exit. The only other way it was possible to leave the stage was over the footlights. Of course she didn't go that way. Yet no trace of her has been found. Where is she?"

"The windows?" asked The Thinking Machine.

"The stage is below the street level," explained Hatch. "The window of her dressing room, Room A, is small and barred with iron. It opens into an air shaft that goes straight up for ten feet, and that is covered with an iron grating fixed in the granite. The other windows on the stage are not only inaccessible but are also barred with iron. She could not have approached either of these windows without being seen by other members of the company or the stage hands."

"Under the stage?" suggested the scientist.

"Nothing," the reporter went on. "It is a large cemented basement which was vacant. It was searched, because there was of course a chance that Miss Wallack might have become temporarily unbalanced and wandered down there. There was even a search made of the flies—that is the galleries over the stage where the men who work the drop curtains are stationed."

There was silence for a long time. The Thinking Machine twiddled his fingers and continued to stare upward. He had not looked at the reporter. He broke the silence after a time. "How was Miss Wallack dressed at the time of her disappearance?"

"In doublet and hose—that is, tights," the newspaper man responded. "She wears that costume from the second act until practically the end of the play."

"Was all her street clothing in her room?"

"Yes, everything, spread across an unopened trunk of costumes. It was all as if she had left the room to answer her cue—all in order even to an open box of chocolate – cream candy on her table."

"No sign of a struggle, nor any noise heard?"

"No."

"Nor trace of blood?"

"Nothing."

"Her maid? Did she have one?"

"Oh, yes. I neglected to tell you that the maid, Gertrude Manning, had gone home immediately after the first act. She grew suddenly ill and was excused."

The Thinking Machine turned his squint eyes on the reporter for the first time.

"Ill?" he repeated. "What was the matter?"

"That I can't say," replied the reporter.

"Where is she now?"

"I don't know. Everyone forgot all about her in the excitement about Miss Wallack."

"What kind of candy was it?"

"I'm afraid I don't know that either."

"Where was it bought?'"

The reporter shrugged his shoulders; that was something else he didn't know.

The Thinking Machine shot out the questions aggressively, staring meanwhile steadily at Hatch, who squirmed uncomfortably. "Where is the candy now?" demanded the scientist.

Again Hatch shrugged his shoulders.

"How much did Miss Wallack weigh?"

The reporter was willing to guess at this. He had seen her half a dozen times.

"Between a hundred and thirty and a hundred and forty," he ventured.

"Does there happen to be a hypnotist connected with the company?"

"I don't know," Hatch replied.

The Thinking Machine waved his slender hands impatiently; he was annoyed. "It is perfectly absurd, Mr Hatch," he expostulated, "to come to me with only a few facts and ask advice. If you had all the facts I might be able to do something; but this—"

The newspaper man was nettled. In his own profession he was accredited a man of discernment and acumen. He resented the tone, the manner, even the seemingly trivial questions, which the other asked. "I don't see," he began, "that the candy even if it had been poisoned as I imagine you think possible, or a hypnotist could have had anything to do with Miss Wallack's disappearance. Certainly neither poison nor hypnotism would have made her invisible."

"Of course you don't see!" blazed The Thinking Machine. "If you did, you wouldn't have come to me. When did this thing happen?"

"Saturday night, as I said," the reporter informed him a little more humbly. "It closed the engagement in Springfield. Miss Wallack was to have appeared here in Boston tonight."

"When did she disappear—by the clock, I mean?"

"The stage manager's time slip shows that the curtain for the third act went up at nine-forty-one—he spoke to her, say, one minute before, or at nine-forty. The action of the play before she appears in the third act takes six minutes; therefore—"

"In precisely seven minutes a woman, weighing more than 130 pounds, certainly not dressed for the street, disappeared completely from her dressing room. It is now five-eighteen

Monday afternoon. I think we may solve this crime within a few hours."

"Crime?" Hatch repeated eagerly. "Do you imagine there is a crime then?"

Professor Van Dusen didn't heed the question. Instead he rose and paced back and forth across the reception room half a dozen times, his hands behind his back and his eyes cast down. At last he stopped and faced the reporter, who had also risen.

"Miss Wallack's company, I presume, with the baggage, is now in Boston," he said. "See every male member of the company, talk to them and particularly study their eyes. Don't overlook anyone, however humble. Also find out what became of the box of chocolate candy, and if possible how many pieces are out of it. Then report here to me. Miss Wallack's safety may depend upon your speed and accuracy."

Hatch was frankly startled. "How–" he began.

"Don't stop to talk–hurry!" commanded The Thinking Machine. "I will have a cab waiting when you come back. We must get to Springfield."

The newspaper man rushed away to obey orders. He didn't understand them at all. Studying men's eyes was not in his line; but he obeyed nevertheless. An hour and a half later he returned, to be thrust unceremoniously into a waiting cab by The Thinking Machine. The cab rattled away toward South Station, where the two men caught a train, just about to move out for Springfield. Once settled in their seats, the scientist turned to Hatch, who was nearly suffocating with suppressed information.

"Well?" he asked.

"I found out several things," the reporter burst out. "First, Miss Wallack's leading man, Langdon Mason, who has been in love with her for three years, bought the candy at Schuyler's in Springfield early Saturday evening before he went to the theater. He told me so himself rather reluctantly; but I–I made him say it."

"Ah!" exclaimed The Thinking Machine. It was a most unequivocal ejaculation. "How many pieces of candy are out of the box?"

"Only three," explained Hatch. "Miss Wallack's things were packed into the open trunk in her dressing room, the candy with them. I induced the manager—"

"Yes, yes, yes!" interrupted The Thinking Machine impatiently. "What sort of eyes has Mason? What colour?"

"Blue, frank in expression, nothing unusual at all," said the reporter.

"And the others?"

"I didn't quite know what you meant by studying their eyes, so I got a set of photographs. I thought perhaps they might help."

"Excellent, Excellent!" commented The Thinking Machine. He shuffled the pictures through his fingers, stopping now and then to study one, and to read the name printed below. "Is that the leading man?" he asked at last, and handed one to Hatch.

"Yes."

Professor Van Dusen did not speak again. The train pulled into Springfield at nine-twenty. Hatch followed the scientist without a word into a cab.

"Schuyler's candy store," quickly commanded The Thinking Machine. "Hurry."

The cab rushed off through the night. Ten minutes later it stopped before a brilliantly lighted candy store. The Thinking Machine led the way inside and approached the girl behind the chocolate counter.

"Will you please tell me if you remember this man's face?" he asked as he produced Mason's photograph.

"Oh, yes, I remember him," the girl replied. "He's an actor."

"Did he buy a small box of chocolates of you Saturday evening early?" was the next question.

"Yes. I recall it because he seemed to be in a hurry; in fact, I believe he said he was anxious to get to the theater to pack."

"And do you recall that this man ever bought chocolates here?" asked the scientist. He produced another photograph and handed it to the girl. She studied it a moment while Hatch craned his neck, vainly, to see.

"I don't recall that he ever did," the girl answered finally.

The Thinking Machine turned away abruptly and disappeared into a public telephone booth. He remained there for five minutes, then rushed out to the cab again, with Hatch following closely.

"City Hospital!" he commanded.

Again the cab dashed away. Hatch was dumb; there seemed to be nothing to say. The Thinking Machine was plainly pursuing some definite line of inquiry, yet the reporter didn't know what. The case was getting kaleidoscopic. This impression was strengthened when he found himself standing beside The Thinking Machine in City Hospital conversing with the house surgeon, Dr Carlton.

"Is there a Miss Gertrude Manning here?" was the scientist's first question.

"Yes," replied the surgeon. "She was brought here Saturday night, suffering from—"

"Strychnine poisoning, yes, I know," interrupted the other. "Picked up in the street, probably. I am a physician. If she is well enough I should like to ask her a couple of questions."

Dr Carlton agreed, and Professor Van Dusen, still followed faithfully by Hatch, was ushered into the ward where Miss Wallack's maid lay, pallid and weak. The Thinking Machine picked up her hand and his slender finger rested for a minute on her pulse. He nodded and seemed satisfied.

"Miss Manning, can you understand me?" he asked.

The girl nodded weakly.

"How many pieces of the candy did you eat?"

"Two," she replied. She stared into the face above her with dull eyes.

"Did Miss Wallack eat any of it up to the time you left the theatre?"

"No."

If the Thinking Machine had been in a hurry previously, he was racing now. Hatch trailed on dutifully behind, down the stairs, and into the cab, whence Professor Van Dusen shouted a word of thanks to Dr Carlton. This time their destination was the stage door of the theatre from which Miss Wallack had disappeared.

The reporter was muddled. He didn't know anything very clearly except that three pieces of candy were missing from the box. Of these the maid had eaten only two. She had been poisoned. Therefore, it seemed reasonable to suppose that if Miss Wallack had eaten the third piece she also would be poisoned. But poison would not make her invisible. At this point the reporter shook his head hopelessly.

William Meegan, the stage doorkeeper, was easily found.

"Can you inform me, please," began The Thinking Machine, "if Mr Mason left a box of candy with you last Saturday night for Miss Wallack?"

"Yes," Meegan replied good-naturedly. He was amused at the little man. "Miss Wallack hadn't arrived. Mason brought a box of candy for her nearly every night and usually left it here. I put the one Saturday night on the shelf here."

"Did Mr Mason come to the theatre before or after the others on Saturday night?"

"Before," replied Meegan. "He was unusually early, I suppose, to pack."

"And the other members of the company coming in stop here, I imagine, to get their mail?" and the scientist squinted up at the mail box above the shelf.

"Sure, always."

The Thinking Machine drew a long breath. Up to this time there had been little perplexed wrinkles in his brow. Now they disappeared.

"Now, please," he went on, "was any package or box of any kind taken from the stage on Saturday night between nine and eleven o'clock?"

"No," said Meegan positively. "Nothing at all until the company's baggage was removed at midnight."

"Miss Wallack had two trunks in her dressing room?"

"Yes. Two whacking big ones too."

"How do you know?"

"Because I helped put 'em in and helped take 'em out," replied Meegan sharply. "What's it to you?"

Suddenly The Thinking Machine turned and ran out to the cab, with Hatch, his shadow, close behind.

"Drive, drive as fast as you know how to the nearest long-distance telephone!" the scientist instructed the cabby. "A woman's life is at stake."

Half an hour later Professor Van Dusen and Hutchinson Hatch were on a train rushing back to Boston. The Thinking Machine had been in the telephone booth for fifteen minutes. When he came out Hatch had asked several questions, to which the scientist vouchsafed no answer. They were perhaps thirty minutes out of Springfield before the scientist showed any disposition to talk. Then he began, without preliminary, much as he was resuming a former conversation.

"Of course if Miss Wallack didn't leave the stage of the theater she was there," he said. "We will admit that she did not become invisible. The problem therefore was to find her on the stage. The fact that no violence was used against her was conclusively proved by half a dozen instances. No one heard her scream; there was no struggle, no trace of blood. Ergo, we assume in the beginning that she must have consented to the first steps which led to her disappearance. Remember her attire was wholly unsuited to the street.

"Now let us shape a hypothesis which will fit all the circumstances. Miss Wallack had a severe headache. Hypnotic influence will cure headaches. Was there a hypnotist to whom Miss Wallack would have submitted herself? Assume there was. Then would that hypnotist take advantage of his control to place her in a cataleptic condition? Assume a motive and he would. Then, how would he dispose of her?

"From this point questions radiate in all directions. We will confine ourselves to the probable, granting for the moment that this hypothesis, the only one which fits all the circumstances, is correct. Obviously, a hypnotist would not have attempted to get her out of the dressing room. What remains? One of the two trunks in her room.

Hatch gasped. "You mean you think it possible that she was hypnotized and placed in that second trunk, the one that was strapped and locked?" he asked.

"It's the only thing that could have happened," said The Thinking Machine emphatically; "therefore that was just what did happen."

"Why, it's horrible!" exclaimed Hatch. "A live woman in a trunk for forty-eight hours? Even if she was alive then, she must be dead now."

The reporter shuddered a little and gazed curiously at the inscrutable face of his companion. He saw no pity, no horror, there; there was merely the reflection of the workings of a brain.

"It does not necessarily follow that she is dead," explained The Thinking Machine. "If she ate that third piece of candy before she was hypnotized she is probably dead. If it was placed in her mouth after she was in a cataleptic condition the chances are that she is not dead. The candy would not melt and her system could not absorb the poison."

"But she would be suffocated—her bones would be broken by the rough handling of the trunk—there are a hundred possibilities," the reporter suggested.

"A person in a cataleptic condition is singularly impervious to injury," replied the scientist. "There is of course a chance of suffocation, but a great deal of air may enter a trunk."

"And the candy?" Hatch asked.

"Yes, the candy. We know that two pieces of candy nearly killed the maid. Yet Mr Mason admitted having bought it. This admission indicated that this poisoned candy is not the candy he bought. Is Mr Mason a hypnotist? No. He hasn't the eyes. His picture tells me that. We know that Mr Mason did buy candy for Miss Wallack on several occasions. We know that sometimes he left it with the stage doorkeeper. We know that members of the company stopped there for mail. We instantly see that it is possible for one to take away that box and substitute poisoned candy. All the boxes are alike.

"Madness and the cunning of madness lie back of all this. It was a deliberate attempt to murder Miss Wallack, long pondered and due, perhaps, to unrequited or hopeless infatuation. It began with the poisoned candy, and that failing, went to a point immediately following the moment when the stage manager last spoke to the actress. The hypnotist was probably in her room then. You must remember that it would have been possible for him to ease the headache, and at the same time leave Miss Wallack free to play. She might have known this from previous experience."

"Is Miss Wallack still in the trunk?" asked Hatch after a silence.

"No," replied the Thinking Machine. "She is out now, dead or alive—I am inclined to believe alive."

"And the man?"

"I will turn him over to the police in half an hour after we reach Boston."

From South Station the scientist and Hatch were driven immediately to Police Headquarters. Detective Mallory, whom Hatch knew well, received them.

"We got your 'phone from Springfield—" he began.

"Was she dead?" interrupted the scientist.

"No," Mallory replied. "She was unconscious when we took her out of the trunk, but no bones are broken. She is badly bruised. The doctor says she's hypnotized."

"Was the piece of candy taken from her mouth?"

"Sure, a chocolate cream. It hadn't melted."

"I'll come back here in a few minutes and awake her," said The Thinking Machine. "Come with us now, and get the man."

Wonderingly the detective entered the cab and the three were driven to a big hotel a dozen blocks away. Before they entered the lobby The Thinking Machine handed a photograph to Mallory, who studied it under an electric light.

"That man is upstairs with several others," explained the scientist. "Pick him out and get behind him when we enter the room. He may attempt to shoot. Don't touch him until I say so."

In a large room on the fifth floor Manager Stanfeld of the Irene Wallack Company had assembled the men of her support. This was done at the 'phoned request of The Thinking Machine. There were no preliminaries when Professor Van Dusen entered. He squinted comprehensively about him, then went straight to Langdon Mason.

"Were you on the stage in the third act of your play before Miss Wallack was to appear—I mean the play last Saturday night?" he asked.

"I was," Mason replied, "for at least three minutes."

"Mr Stanfeld, is that correct?"

"Yes," replied the manager.

There was a long tense silence broken only by the heavy footsteps of Mallory as he walked toward a distant corner of the room. A faint flush crept into Mason's face as he realized that the questions were almost an accusation. He started to speak, but the steady, impassive voice of The Thinking Machine stopped him.

"Mr Mallory, take your prisoner," it said.

Instantly there was a fierce, frantic struggle, and those present turned to see the detective with his great arms locked about Stanley Wightman, the melancholy Jaques of "As You Like It." The actor's face was distorted, madness blazed in the eyes, and he snarled like a beast at bay. By a sudden movement Mallory threw Wightman and manacled him, then looked up to find The Thinking Machine peering over his shoulder at the prostrate man.

"Yes, he's a hypnotist," the scientist remarked in self-satisfied conclusion. "It always tells in the pupils of the eyes."

This, then, was the beginning and end of the first problem. Miss Wallack was aroused, and told a story almost identical with that of The Thinking Machine. Stanley Wightman, whose brooding over a hopeless love for her made a maniac of him, raves and shrieks the lines of Jaques in the seclusion of a padded cell.

16

THE LEAK

"Really great criminals are never found out, for the simple reason that the greatest crimes – their crimes – are never discovered," remarked Professor Augustus S. F. X. Van Dusen positively. "There is genius in the perpetration of crime, Mr Grayson, just as there must be in its detection, unless it is the shallow work of a bungler. In this latter case there have been instances where even the police have uncovered the truth. But the expert criminal, the man of genius – the professional, I may say – regards as perfect only that crime which does not and cannot be made to appear a crime at all; therefore one that can never under any circumstances involve him, or anyone else."

The financier, J. Morgan Grayson, regarded this wizened little man of science – The Thinking Machine – thoughtfully, through the smoke of his cigar.

"It is a strange psychological fact that the casual criminal glories in his crime beforehand, and from one to ten minutes afterward," The Thinking Machine continued. "For instance, the man who kills for revenge wants the world to know it is his work; but at the end of ten minutes comes fear, and then paradoxically enough, he will seek to hide his crime and protect himself. With fear comes panic, with panic irresponsibility, and then he makes the mistake — hews a pathway which the trained mind follows from motive to a prison cell."

"These are the men who are found out. But there are men of genius, Mr Grayson, professionally engaged in crime. We never hear of them because they are never caught, and we never even suspect them because they make no mistake. Imagine the great brains of history turned to crime. Well, there are today brains as great as any of those of history; there is murder and theft and robbery under our noses that we never dream of. If I, for instance, should become an active criminal — " He paused.

Grayson, with a queer expression on his face, puffed steadily at his cigar.

"I could kill you now, here in this room," The Thinking Machine went on calmly, "and no one would ever know, never even suspect. Why? Because I would make no mistake."

It was not a boast as he said it; it was merely a statement of fact. Grayson appeared to be a little startled. Where there had been only impatient interest in his manner, there was now fascination.

"How would you kill me, for instance?" he inquired curiously.

"With any one of a dozen poisons, with virulent germs, or even with a knife or revolver," replied the scientist placidly. "You see, I know how to use poisons; I know how to inoculate with germs; I know how to produce a suicidal appearance perfectly with either a revolver or knife. And I never make mistakes, Mr Grayson. In the sciences we must be exact — not approximately so, but absolutely so. We must know. It isn't like carpentry. A carpenter may make a trivial mistake in a joint, and it will not weaken his house; but if the scientist makes one mistake, the whole structure tumbles down. We must know. Knowledge is progress. We gain knowledge through observation and logic — inevitable logic. And logic tells us that two and two make four — not sometimes but all the time."

Grayson flicked the ashes off his cigar thoughtfully, and little wrinkles appeared about his eyes as he stared into the drawn, inscrutable face of the scientist. The enormous, straw-yellow head was cushioned against the chair, the squinting, watery blue eyes turned upward, and the slender white fingers at rest, tip to tip. The financier drew a long breath. "I have been informed that you were a remarkable man," he said at last slowly. "I believe it. Quinton Frazer, the banker who gave me the letter of introduction to you, told me how you once solved a remarkable mystery in which – "

"Yes, yes," interrupted the scientist shortly, "the Ralston Bank burglary – I remember."

"So I came to you to enlist your aid in something which is more inexplicable than that," Grayson went on hesitatingly. "I know that no fee I might offer would influence you; yet it is a case which – "

"State it," interrupted The Thinking Machine again.

"It isn't a crime – that is, a crime that can be reached by law," Grayson hurried on, "but it has cost me millions, and – "

For one instant The Thinking Machine lowered his squint eyes to those of his visitor, then raised them again. "Millions!" he repeated. "How many?"

"Six, eight, perhaps ten," was the reply. "Briefly, there is a leak in my office. My plans become known to others almost by the time I have perfected them. My plans are large; I have millions at stake; and the greatest secrecy is absolutely essential. For years I have been able to preserve this secrecy; but half a dozen times in the last eight weeks my plans have become known, and I have been caught. Unless you know the Street, you can't imagine what a tremendous disadvantage it is to have someone know your next move to the minutest detail and, knowing it, defeat you at every turn."

"No, I don't know your world of finance, Mr Grayson," remarked The Thinking Machine. "Give me an instance."

THE LEAK

"Well, take this last case," said the financier earnestly. "Briefly, without technicalities, I had planned to unload the securities of the P., Q. & X. Railway, protecting myself through brokers, and force the outstanding stock down to a price where other brokers, acting for me, could buy far below the actual value. In this way I intended to get complete control of the stock. But my plans became known, and when I began to unload everything was snapped up by the opposition, with the result that instead of gaining control of the road I lost heavily. This same thing has happened, with variations, half a dozen times."

"I presume that is strictly honest?" inquired the scientist mildly.

"Honest?" repeated Grayson. "Certainly – of course."

"I shall not pretend to understand all that," said The Thinking Machine curtly. "It doesn't seem to matter, anyway. You want to know where the leak is. Is that right?"

"Precisely."

"Well, who is in your confidence?"

"No one, except my stenographer."

"Who is he, please?"

"It's a woman – Miss Evelyn Winthrop. She has been in my employ for six years in the same capacity – more than five years before this leak appeared. I trust her absolutely."

"No man knows your business?"

"No," replied the financier grimly. "I learned years ago that no one could keep my secrets as well as I do – there are too many temptations. Therefore, I never mention my plans to anyone – never – to anyone!"

"Except your stenographer," corrected the scientist.

"I work for days, weeks, sometimes months, perfecting plans, and it's all in my head, not on paper – not a scratch of it," explained Grayson. "When I say that she is in my confidence, I mean that she knows my plans only half an hour or less before the machinery is put into motion. For instance, I planned this

P., Q. & X. deal. My brokers didn't know of it; Miss Winthrop never heard of it until twenty minutes before the Stock Exchange opened for business. Then I dictated to her, as I always do, some short letters of instructions to my agents. That is all she knew of it."

"You outlined the plan in those letters?"

"No; they merely told my brokers what to do."

"But a shrewd person, knowing the contents of all those letters, could have learned what you intended to do?"

"Yes; but no one person knew the contents of all the letters. No one broker knew what was in the other letters. Miss Winthrop and I were the only two human beings who knew all that was in them."

The Thinking Machine sat silent for so long that Grayson began to fidget in his chair. "Who was in the room besides you and Miss Winthrop before the letters were sent?" he asked at last.

"No one," responded Grayson emphatically. "For an hour before I dictated those letters, until at least an hour afterward, after my plans had gone to smash, no one entered that room. Only she and I work there."

"But when she finished the letters, she went out?" insisted The Thinking Machine.

"No," declared the financier, "she didn't even leave her desk."

"Or perhaps sent something out – carbon copies of the letters?"

"No."

"Or called up a friend on the telephone?" continued The Thinking Machine quietly.

"Nor that," retorted Grayson.

"Or signaled to someone through the window?"

"No," said the financier again. "She finished the letters, then remained quietly at her desk, reading a book. She hardly moved for two hours."

The Thinking Machine lowered his eyes and glared straight into those of the financier. "Someone listened at the window?" he went on after a moment.

"No. It is sixteen stories up, fronting the street, and there is no fire escape."

"Or the door?"

"If you knew the arrangement of my offices, you would see how utterly impossible that would be, because – "

"Nothing is impossible, Mr Grayson," snapped the scientist abruptly. "It might be improbable, but not impossible. Don't say that – it annoys me exceedingly." He was silent for a moment. Grayson stared at him blankly. "Did either you or she answer a call on the 'phone?"

"No one called; we called no one."

"Any apertures – holes or cracks – in your flooring or walls or ceilings?" demanded the scientist.

"Private detectives whom I had employed looked for such an opening, and there was none," replied Grayson.

Again The Thinking Machine was silent for a long time. Grayson lighted a fresh cigar and settled back in his chair patiently. Faint cobwebby lines began to appear on the dome-like brow of the scientist, and slowly the squint eyes were narrowing.

"The letters you wrote were intercepted?" he suggested at last.

"No," exclaimed Grayson flatly. "Those letters were sent direct to the brokers by a dozen different methods, and every one of them had been delivered by five minutes of ten o'clock, when 'Change begins business. The last one left me at ten minutes of ten."

"Dear me! Dear me!" The Thinking Machine rose and paced the length of the room.

"You don't give me credit for the extraordinary precautions I have taken, particularly in this last P., Q. & X. deal," Grayson continued. "I left positively nothing undone to insure absolute secrecy. And Miss Winthrop, I know, is innocent of any connection with the affair. The private detectives suspected her at first, as you do, and she was watched in and out of my office for weeks. When she was not under my eyes, she was under the eyes of men to whom I had promised an extravagant sum of money if they found the leak. She didn't know it then, and doesn't know it now. I am heartily ashamed of it all, because the investigation proved her absolute loyalty to me. On this last day she was directly under my eyes for two hours; and she didn't make one movement that I didn't note, because the thing meant millions to me. That proved beyond all question that it was no fault of hers. What could I do?"

The Thinking Machine didn't say. He paused at a window, and for minute after minute stood motionless there, with eyes narrowed to mere slits.

"I was on the point of discharging Miss Winthrop," the financier went on, "but her innocence was so thoroughly proved to me by this last affair that it would have been unjust, and so – "

Suddenly the scientist turned upon his visitor. "Do you talk in your sleep?" he demanded.

"No," was the prompt reply. "I had thought of that too. It is beyond all ordinary things, Professor. Yet there is a leak that is costing me millions."

"It comes down to this, Mr Grayson," The Thinking Machine informed him crabbedly. "If only you and Miss Winthrop knew those plans, and no one else, and they did leak, and were not deduced from other things, then either you or she permitted them to leak, intentionally or unintentionally. That is as pure logic as two and two make four; there is no need to argue it."

"Well, of course, I didn't," said Grayson.

"Then Miss Winthrop did," declared The Thinking Machine finally, positively; "unless we credit the opposition, as you call it, with telepathic gifts hitherto unheard of. By the way, you have referred to the other side only as the opposition. Do the same men, the same clique, appear against you all the time, or is it only one man?"

"It's a clique," explained the financier, "with millions back of it, headed by Ralph Matthews, a young man to whom I give credit for being the prime factor against me." His lips were set sternly.

"Why?" demanded the scientist.

"Because every time he sees me he grins," was the reply. Grayson seemed suddenly discomfited.

The Thinking Machine went to a desk, addressed an envelope, folded a sheet of paper, placed it inside, then sealed it. At length he turned back to his visitor. "Is Miss Winthrop at your office now?"

"Yes."

"Let us go there, then."

A few minutes later the eminent financier ushered the eminent scientist into his private office on the Street. The only person there was a young woman – a woman of twenty-six or-seven, perhaps – who turned, saw Grayson, and resumed reading. The financier motioned to a seat. Instead of sitting, however, The Thinking Machine went straight to Miss Winthrop and extended a sealed envelop to her.

"Mr Ralph Matthews asked me to hand you this," he said.

The young woman glanced up into his face frankly, yet with a certain timidity, took the envelope, and turned it curiously in her hand.

"Mr Ralph Matthews," she repeated, as if the name was a strange one. "I don't think I know him."

The Thinking Machine stood staring at her aggressively, as she opened the envelope and drew out the sheet of paper. There was no expression save surprise – bewilderment, rather – to be read on her face.

"Why, it's a blank sheet!" she remarked, puzzled.

The scientist turned suddenly toward Grayson, who had witnessed the incident with frank astonishment in his eyes. "Your telephone a moment, please," he requested.

"Certainly; here," replied Grayson.

"This will do," remarked the scientist.

He leaned forward over the desk where Miss Winthrop sat, still gazing at him in a sort of bewilderment, picked up the receiver, and held it to his ear. A few moments later he was talking to Hutchinson Hatch, reporter.

"I merely wanted to ask you to meet me at my apartment in an hour," said the scientist. "It is very important."

That was all. He hung up the receiver, paused for a moment to admire an exquisitely wrought silver box – a "vanity" box – on Miss Winthrop's desk, beside the telephone, then took a seat beside Grayson and began to discourse almost pleasantly upon the prevailing meteorological conditions. Grayson merely stared; Miss Winthrop continued her reading.

Professor Augustus S. F. X. Van Dusen, distinguished scientist, and Hutchinson Hatch, newspaper reporter, were poking round among the chimney pots and other obstructions on the roof of a skyscraper. Far below them the slumber-enshrouded city was spread out like a panorama, streets dotted brilliantly with lights, and roofs hazily visible through mists of night. Above, the infinite blackness hung like a veil, with starpoints breaking through here and there.

"Here are the wires," Hatch said at last, and he stooped.

The Thinking Machine knelt on the roof beside him, and for several minutes they remained thus in the darkness, with only the glow of a flashlight to indicate their presence. Finally, The Thinking Machine rose.

"That's the wire you want, Mr Hatch," he said. "I'll leave the rest of it to you."

"Are you sure?" asked the reporter.

"I am always sure," was the tart response.

Hatch opened a small handsatchel and removed several queerly wrought tools. These he spread on the roof beside him; then, kneeling again, began his work. For half an hour he labored in the gloom, with only the flashlight to aid him, and then he rose.

"It's all right," he said.

The Thinking Machine examined the work that had been done, grunted his satisfaction, and together they went to the skylight, leaving a thin, insulated wire behind them, stringing along to mark their path. They passed down through the roof and into the darkness of the hall of the upper story. Here the light was extinguished. From far below came the faint echo of a man's footsteps as the watchman passed through the silent, deserted building.

"Be careful!" warned The Thinking Machine.

They went along the hall to a room in the rear, and still the wire trailed behind. At the last door they stopped. The Thinking Machine fumbled with some keys, then opened the way. Here an electric light was on. The room was bare of furniture, the only sign of recent occupancy being a telephone instrument on the wall.

Here The Thinking Machine stopped and stared at the spool of wire which he had permitted to wind off as he walked, and his thin face expressed doubt.

"It wouldn't be safe," he said at last, "to leave the wire exposed as we have left it. True, this floor is not occupied; but someone might pass this way and disturb it. You take the spool, go back to the roof, winding the wire as you go, then swing the spool down to me over the side of the building, so that I can bring it in through the window. That will be best. I will catch it here, and thus there will be nothing to indicate any connection."

Hatch went out quietly and closed the door.

Twice the following day The Thinking Machine spoke to the financier over the telephone. Grayson was in his private office, Miss Winthrop at her desk, when the first call came.

"Be careful in answering my questions," warned The Thinking Machine when Grayson answered. "Do you know how long Miss Winthrop has owned the little silver box which is now on her desk, near the telephone?"

Grayson glanced round involuntarily to where the girl sat idly turning over the leaves of her book. "Yes," he answered, "for seven months. I gave it to her last Christmas."

"Ah!" exclaimed the scientist. "That simplifies matters. Where did you buy it?"

Grayson mentioned the name of a well-known jeweler.

Considerably later in the day The Thinking Machine called Grayson to the telephone again.

"What make of typewriter does she use?" came the querulous voice over the wire.

Grayson named it.

While Grayson sat with deeply perplexed lines in his face, the diminutive scientist called upon Hutchinson Hatch at his office.

"Do you use a typewriter?" demanded The Thinking Machine.

"Yes."

"What kind?"

"Oh, four or five kinds – we have half a dozen different makes in the office."

They passed along through the city room, at that moment practically deserted, until finally the watery blue eyes settled upon a typewriter with the name emblazoned on the front.

"That's it!" exclaimed The Thinking Machine. "Write something on it," he directed Hatch.

Hatch drew up a chair and rolled off several lines of the immortal practice sentence, beginning, "Now is the time for all good men – "

The Thinking Machine sat beside him, squinting across the room in deep abstraction, and listening intently. His head was turned away from the reporter, but his ear was within a few inches of the machine. For half a minute he sat there listening, then shook his head.

"Strike your vowels," he commanded; "first slowly, then rapidly."

Again Hatch obeyed, while the scientist listened. And again he shook his head. Then in turn every make of machine in the office was tested the same way. At the end The Thinking Machine rose and went his way. There was an expression nearly approaching complete bewilderment on his face.

For hour after hour that night The Thinking Machine half lay in a huge chair in his laboratory, with eyes turned uncompromisingly upward, and an expression of complete concentration on his face. There was no change either in his position or his gaze as minute succeeded minute; the brow was deeply wrinkled now, and the thin line of the lips was drawn taut. The tiny clock in the reception room struck ten, eleven, twelve, and finally one. At just half-past one The Thinking Machine rose suddenly.

"Positively I am getting stupid!" he grumbled half aloud. "Of course! Of course! Why couldn't I have thought of that in the first place?..."

So it came about that Grayson did not go to his office on the following morning at the usual time. Instead, he called again upon The Thinking Machine in eager, expectant response to a note which had reached him at his home just before he started to his office.

"Nothing yet," said The Thinking Machine as the financier entered. "But here is something you must do today. At one o'clock," the scientist went on, "you must issue orders for a gigantic deal of some sort; and you must issue them precisely as you have issued them in the past; there must be no variation. Dictate the letters as you have always done to Miss Winthrop – *but don't send them*! When they come to you, keep them until you see me."

"You mean that the deal must be purely imaginative?" inquired the financier.

"Precisely," was the reply. "But make your instructions circumstantial; give them enough detail to make them absolutely logical and convincing."

Grayson asked a dozen questions, answers to which were curtly denied, then went to his office. The Thinking Machine again called Hatch on the telephone.

"I've got it," he announced briefly. "I want the best telegraph operator you know. Bring him along and meet me in the room on the top floor where the telephone is at precisely fifteen minutes before one o'clock today."

"Telegraph operator?" Hatch repeated.

"That's what I said – telegraph operator!" replied the scientist irritably. "Goodbye."

Hatch smiled whimsically at the other end as he heard the receiver banged on the hook – smiled because he knew the eccentric ways of this singular man, whose mind so accurately illuminated every problem to which it was directed. Then he went out to the telegraph room and borrowed the principal operator. They were in the little room on the top floor at precisely fifteen minutes of one.

The operator glanced about in astonishment. The room was still unfurnished, save for the telephone box on the wall. "What do I do?" he asked The Thinking Machine.

"I'll tell you when the time comes," responded the scientist, as he glanced at his watch.

At three minutes of one o'clock he handed a sheet of blank paper to the operator, and gave him final instructions. There was ludicrous mystification on the operator's face; but he obeyed orders, grinning cheerfully at Hatch as he tilted his cigar up to keep the smoke out of his eyes. The Thinking Machine stood impatiently looking on, watch in hand. Hatch didn't know what was happening, but he was interested.

At last the operator heard something. His face became suddenly alert. He continued to listen for a moment, and then came a smile of recognition.

Less than ten minutes after Miss Winthrop had handed over the typewritten letters of instruction to Grayson for signature, and while he still sat turning them over in his hands, the door opened and The Thinking Machine entered. He tossed a folded sheet of paper on the desk before Grayson, and went straight to Miss Winthrop.

"So you did know Mr Ralph Matthews after all?" he inquired.

The girl rose from her desk, and a flash of some subtle emotion passed over her face. "What do you mean, sir?" she demanded.

"You might as well remove the silver box," The Thinking Machine went on mercilessly. "There is no further need of the connection."

Miss Winthrop glanced down at the telephone extension on her desk, and her hand darted toward it. The silver "vanity" box was directly under the receiver, supporting it, so that all weight was removed from the hook, and the line was open. She snatched the box and the receiver dropped back on the hook. The Thinking Machine turned to Grayson.

"It was Miss Winthrop," he said.

"Miss Winthrop!" exclaimed Grayson, "I can't believe it!"

"Read the paper I gave you, Mr Grayson," directed The Thinking Machine coldly. "Perhaps that will enlighten her."

The financier opened the sheet, which had remained folded in his hand, and glanced at what was written there. Slowly he read it aloud: "PEABODY – Sell ten thousand shares L. & W. at

97. McCracken Co. – Sell ten thousand shares L. & W. at 97."
He read on down the list, bewildered. Then gradually, as he realized the import of what he read, there came a hardening of the lines about his mouth.

"I understand, Miss Winthrop," he said at last. "This is the substance of the orders I dictated, and in some way you made them known to persons for whom they were not intended. I don't know how you did it, of course; but I understand that you did do it, so – " He stepped to the door and opened it with grave courtesy. "You may go now."

Miss Winthrop made no plea – merely bowed and went out. Grayson stood staring after her for a moment, then turned to The Thinking Machine and motioned him to a chair. "What happened?" he asked briskly.

"Miss Winthrop is a tremendously clever woman," replied The Thinking Machine. "She neglected to tell you, however, that besides being a stenographer and typist she is also a telegraph operator. She is so expert in each of her lines that she combined the two, if I may say it that way. In other words, in writing on the typewriter, she was clever enough to be able to *give the click of the machine the patterns in the Morse telegraphic code* – so that another telegraph operator at the other end of the 'phone could hear her machine and translate the clicks into words."

Grayson sat staring at him incredulously. "I still don't understand," he said finally. The Thinking Machine rose and went to Miss Winthrop's desk. "Here is an extension telephone with the receiver on the hook. It happens that the little silver box which you gave Miss Winthrop is just tall enough to lift this receiver clear of the hook, and the minute the receiver is off the hook the line is open. When you were at your desk and she was here, you couldn't see this telephone; therefore it was a simple matter for her to lift the receiver, and place the silver box underneath, thus holding the line open permanently. That being true, the sound of the typewriter – *the striking of the keys* – would go over the open wire to whoever was listening at the other end. Then, if the striking of the keys typed out your letters and, by their frequency and pauses, simultaneously tapped out telegraphic code, an outside operator could read your letters at the same moment they were being written. That is all. It required extreme concentration on Miss Winthrop's part to type accurately in Morse rhythms."

"Oh, I see!" exclaimed Grayson.

"When I knew that the leak in your office was not in the usual way," continued The Thinking Machine, "I looked for the unusual. There is nothing very mysterious about it now – it was merely clever."

"Clever!" repeated Grayson, and his jaws snapped. "It is more than that. Why, it's criminal! She should be prosecuted."

"I shouldn't advise that, Mr Grayson," returned the scientist coldly. "If it is honest – merely business – to juggle stocks as you told me you did, this is no more dishonest. And besides, remember that Miss Winthrop is backed by the people who have made millions out of you, and – well, I wouldn't prosecute. It is betrayal of trust, certainly; but – " He rose as if that were all, and started toward the door. "I would advise you, however, to discharge the person who operates your switchboard."

"Was she in the scheme, too?" demanded Grayson. He rushed out of the private office into the main office. At the door he met a clerk coming in.

"Where is Miss Mitchell?" demanded the financier hotly.

"I was just coming to tell you that she went out with Miss Winthrop just now without giving any explanation," replied the clerk.

"Goodday, Mr Grayson," said The Thinking Machine.

The financier nodded his thanks, then stalked back into his room.

In the course of time The Thinking Machine received a check for ten thousand dollars, signed, "J. Morgan Grayson." He glared at it for a little while, then indorsed it in a crabbed hand, *Pay to the Trustees' Home for Crippled Children*, and sent Martha, his housekeeper, out to mail it.

17

THE BROWN COAT

There was no mystery whatever about the identity of the man who, alone and unaided, robbed the Thirteenth National Bank of $109,437 in cash and $1.29 in postage stamps. It was "Mort" Dolan, an expert safe-cracker albeit a young one, and he had made a clean sweep. Nor yet was there any mystery as to his whereabouts. He was safely in a cell at Police Headquarters, having been captured within less than twelve hours after the robbery was discovered.

Dolan had offered no resistance to the officers when he was cornered, and had attempted no denial when questioned by Detective Mallory. He knew he had been caught fairly and squarely and no argument was possible, so he confessed with a glow of pride at a job well done. It was four or five days after his arrest that the matter came to the attention of The Thinking Machine. Then the problem was –

But perhaps it were better to begin at the beginning.

Despite the fact that he was considerably less than thirty years old, "Mort" Dolan was a man for whom the police had a wholesome respect. He had a record, for he had started early. This robbery of the Thirteenth National was his "big" job and was to have been his last. With the proceeds he had intended to take his wife and quietly disappear beneath a full beard and an alias in some place far removed from former haunts. But the mutability of human events is a matter of proverb. While the robbery as a robbery was a thoroughly artistic piece of work and in full accordance with plans which had been worked out to the minutest details months before, he had made one mistake. This was leaving behind him in the bank the can in which the nitroglycerine had been bought. Through this carelessness he had been traced.

Dolan and his wife occupied three poor rooms in a poor tenement house. From the moment the police got a description of the person who bought the explosive they were confident for they knew their men. Therefore four clever men were on watch about the poor tenement. Neither Dolan nor his wife was there then, but from the condition of things in the rooms the police believed that they intended to return so took up positions to watch.

Unsuspecting enough, for his one mistake in the robbery had not occurred to him, Dolan came along just about dusk and started up the five steps to the front door of the tenement. It just happened that he glanced back and saw a head drawn suddenly behind a projecting stoop. But the electric light glared strongly there and Dolan recognized Detective Downey, one of many men who revolved around Detective Mallory within a limited orbit. Dolan paused on the stoop a moment and rolled a cigarette while he thought it over. Perhaps instead of entering, it would be best to stroll on down the street, turn a corner, and make a dash for it. But just at that moment he spied another head in the direction of contemplated flight. That was Detective Blanton.

Deeply thoughtful Dolan smoked half the cigarette and stared blankly in front of him. He knew of a back door opening on an alley. Perhaps the detectives had not thought to guard that! He tossed his cigarette away, entered the house with affected unconcern, and closed the door. Running lightly through the long, unclean hall which extended the full length of the building he flung open the back door. He turned back instantly – just outside he had seen and recognized Detective Cunningham.

Then he had an inspiration! The roof! The building was four stories. He ran up the four flights lightly but rapidly and was half way up the short flight which led to the opening in the roof when he stopped. From above he caught the whiff of a bad cigar, then the measured tread of heavy boots. Another detective! With a sickening depression at his heart Dolan came softly down the stairs again, opened the door of his flat with a latch-key, and entered.

Then and there he sat down to figure it all out. There seemed no escape for him. Every way out was blocked, and it was only a question of time before they would close in on him. He imagined now they were only waiting for his wife's return. He could fight for his freedom of course – even kill one, perhaps two, of the detectives who were waiting for him. But that would only mean his own death. If he tried to run for it past either of the detectives he would get a shot in the back. And besides, murder was repugnant to Dolan's artistic soul. It didn't do any good. But could he warn Isabel, his wife? He feared she would walk into the trap as he had done, and she had had no connection of any sort with the affair.

Then, from a fear that his wife would return, there swiftly came a fear that she would not. He suddenly remembered that it was necessary for him to see her. The police could not connect her with the robbery in any way; they could only hold her for a time and then would be compelled to free her, for her innocence of this particular crime was beyond question. And if he were taken before she returned she would be left penniless;

and that was a thing which Dolan dreaded to contemplate. There was a spark of human tenderness in his heart and in prison it would be comforting to know that she was well cared for. If she would only come now he would tell her where the money –!

For ten minutes Dolan considered the question in all possible lights. A letter telling her where the money was? No. It would inevitably fall into the hands of the police. A cipher? She would never get it. How? How? How? Every moment he expected a clamor at the door which would mean that the police had come for him. They knew he was cornered. Whatever he did must be done quickly. Dolan took a long breath and started to roll another cigarette. With the thin white paper held in his left hand and tobacco bag raised in the other he had an inspiration.

For a little more than an hour after that he was left alone. Finally his quick ear caught the shuffle of stealthy feet in the hall, then came an imperative rap on the door. The police had evidently feared to wait longer. Dolan was leaning over a sewing machine when the summons came. Instinctively his hand closed on his revolver, then he tossed it aside and walked to the door.

"Well?" he demanded.

"Let us in, Dolan," came the reply.

"That you, Downey?" Dolan inquired.

"Yes. Now don't make any mistakes, Mort. There are three of us here and Cunningham is in the alley watching your windows. There's no way out."

For one instant – only an instant – Dolan hesitated. It was not that he was repentant; it was not that he feared prison – it was regret at being caught. He had planned it all so differently, and the little woman would be heart-broken. Finally, with a quick backward glance at the sewing machine, he opened the door. Three revolvers were thrust into his face with unanimity that spoke well for the police opinion of the man. Dolan promptly raised his hands over his head.

"Oh, put down your guns," he expostulated. "I'm not crazy. My gun is over on the couch there."

Detective Downey, by a personal search, corroborated this statement then the revolvers were lowered.

"The chief wants you," he said. "It's about that Thirteenth National Bank robbery."

"All right," said Dolan, calmly, and he held out his hands for the steel nippers.

"Now, Mort," said Downey, ingratiatingly, "you can save us a lot of trouble by telling us where the money is."

"Doubtless I could," was the ambiguous response.

Detective Downey looked at him and understood. Cunningham was called in from the alley. He and Downey remained in the apartment and the other two men led Dolan away. In the natural course of events the prisoner appeared before Detective Mallory at Police Headquarters. They were well acquainted, professionally.

Dolan told everything frankly from the inception of the plan to the actual completion of the crime. The detective sat with his feet on his desk listening. At the end he leaned forward toward the prisoner.

"And where is the money?" he asked.

Dolan paused long enough to roll a cigarette.

"That's my business," he responded, pleasantly.

"You might just as well tell us," insisted Detective Mallory. "We will find it, of course, and it will save us trouble."

"I'll just bet you a hat you don't find it," replied Dolan, and there was a glitter of triumph in his eyes. "On the level, between man and man now I will bet you a hat that you never find that money."

"You're on," replied Detective Mallory. He looked keenly at his prisoner and his prisoner stared back without a quiver. "Did your wife get away with it?"

From the question Dolan surmised that she had not been arrested.

"No," he answered.

"Is it in your flat?"

"Downey and Cunningham are searching now," was the rejoinder. "They will report what they find."

There was silence for several minutes as the two men – officer and prisoner – stared each at the other. When a thief takes refuge in a refusal to answer questions he becomes a difficult subject to handle. There was the "third degree" of course, but Dolan was the kind of man who would only laugh at that; the kind of man from whom anything less than physical torture could not bring a statement if he didn't choose to make it. Detective Mallory was perfectly aware of this dogged trait in his character.

"It's this way, chief," explained Dolan at last. "I robbed the bank, I got the money, and it's now where you will never find it. I did it by myself, and am willing to take my medicine. Nobody helped me. My wife – I know your men waited for her before they took me – my wife knows nothing on earth about it. She had no connection with the thing at all and she can prove it. That's all I'm going to say. You might just as well make up your mind to it."

Detective Mallory's eyes snapped.

"You will tell where that money is," he blustered, "or – or I'll see that you get – "

"Twenty years is the absolute limit," interrupted Dolan quietly. "I expect to get twenty years – that's the worst you can do for me."

The Detective stared at him hard.

"And besides," Dolan went on, "I won't be lonesome when I get where you're going to send me. I've got lots of friends there – been there before. One of the jailers is the best pinochle player I ever met."

Like most men who find themselves balked at the outset Detective Mallory sought to appease his indignation by heaping invective upon the prisoner, by threats, by promises, by wheedling, by bluster. It was all the same, Dolan remained silent. Finally he was led away and locked up.

A few minutes later Downey and Cunningham appeared. One glance told their chief that they could not enlighten him as to the whereabouts of the stolen money.

"Do you have any idea where it is?" he demanded.

"No, but I have a very definite idea where it isn't," replied Downey grimly. "It isn't in that flat. There's not one square inch of it that we didn't go over – not one object there that we didn't tear to pieces looking. It simply isn't there. He hid it somewhere before we got him."

"Well take all the men you want and keep at it," instructed Detective Mallory. "One of you, by the way, had better bring in Dolan's wife. I am fairly certain that she had nothing to do with it but she might know something and I can bluff a woman." Detective Mallory announced that accomplishment as if it were a thing to be proud of. "There's nothing to do now but get the money. Meanwhile I'll see that Dolan isn't permitted to communicate with anybody."

"There is always the chance," suggested Downey, "that a man as clever as Dolan could in a cipher letter, or by a chance remark, inform her where the money is if we assume she doesn't know, and that should be guarded against."

"It will be guarded against," declared Detective Mallory emphatically. "Dolan will not be permitted to see or talk to anyone for the present – not even an attorney. He may weaken later on."

But day succeeded day and Dolan showed no signs of weakening. His wife, meanwhile, had been apprehended and subjected to the "third degree." When this ordeal was over, the net result was that Detective Mallory was convinced that she had had nothing whatever to do with the robbery, and had not the faintest idea where the money was. Half a dozen times

Dolan asked permission to see her or to write to her. Each time the request was curtly refused.

Newspapermen, with and without inspiration, had sought the money vainly; and the police were now seeking to trace the movements of "Mort" Dolan from the moment of the robbery until the moment of his appearance on the steps of the house where he lived. In this way they hoped to get an inkling of where the money had been hidden, for the idea of the money being in the flat had been abandoned. Dolan simply wouldn't say anything. Finally, one day, Hutchinson Hatch, reporter, made an exhaustive search of Dolan's flat, for the fourth time, then went over to police headquarters to talk it over with Mallory. While there President Ashe and two directors of the victimized bank appeared. They were worried.

"Is there any trace of the money?" asked Mr Ashe.

"Not yet," responded Detective Mallory.

"Well, could we talk to Dolan a few minutes?"

"If we didn't get anything out of him you won't," said the detective. "But it won't do any harm. Come along."

Dolan didn't seem particularly glad to see them. He came to the bars of his cell and peered through. It was only when Mr Ashe was introduced to him as the president of the Thirteenth National that he seemed to take any interest in his visitors. This interest took the form of a grin. Mr Ashe evidently had something of importance on his mind and was seeking the happiest method of expression. Once or twice he spoke aside to his companions, and Dolan watched them curiously. At last he turned to the prisoner.

"You admit that you robbed the bank?" he asked.

"There's no need of denying it," replied Dolan.

"Well," and Mr Ashe hesitated a moment, "the board of directors held a meeting this morning, and speaking on their behalf I want to say something. If you will inform us of the whereabouts of the money we will, upon its recovery, exert every effort within our power to have your sentence cut in half. In other words, as I understand it, you have given the police no trouble, you have confessed the crime and this, with the return of the money, would weigh for you when sentence is pronounced. Say the maximum is twenty years, we might be able to get you off with ten if we get the money."

Detective Mallory looked doubtful. He realized, perhaps, the futility of such a promise yet he was silent. The proposition might draw out something on which to proceed.

"Can't see it," said Dolan at last. "It's this way. I'm twenty-seven years old. I'll get twenty years. About two of that'll come off for good behavior, so I'll really get eighteen years. At the end of that time I'll come out with $109,000 odd — rich for life and able to retire at forty-five years. In other words while in prison I'll be working for a good, stiff salary — something really worth while. Very few men are able to retire at forty-five."

Mr Ashe readily realized the trust of this statement. It was the point of view of a man to whom mere prison has few terrors — a man content to remain immured for twenty years for a consideration. He turned and spoke aside to the two directors again.

"But I'll tell you what I *will* do" said Dolan, after a pause. "If you'll fix it so I get only two years, say, I'll give you half the money."

There was silence. Detective Mallory strolled along the corridor beyond the view of the prisoner and summoned President Ashe to his side by a jerk of his head.

"Agree to that," he said. "Perhaps he'll really give up."

"But it wouldn't be possible to arrange it, would it?" asked Mr Ashe.

"Certainly not," said the detective, "but agree to it. Get your money and then we'll nail him anyhow."

Mr Ashe stared at him a moment vaguely indignant at the treachery of the thing, then greed triumphed. He walked back to the cell.

"We'll agree to that, Mr Dolan," he said briskly. "Fix a two years sentence for you in return for half the money."

Dolan smiled a little.

"All right, go ahead," he said. "When sentence of two years is pronounced and a first-class lawyer arranges it for me so that the matter can never be reopened I'll tell you where you can get your half."

"But of course you must tell us that now," said Mr Ashe.

Dolan smiled cheerfully. It was a taunting, insinuating, accusing sort of smile and it informed the bank president that the duplicity contemplated was discovered. Mr Ashe was silent for a moment, then blushed.

"Nothing doing," said Dolan, and he retired into a recess of his cell as if his interest in the matter were at an end.

"But – but we need the money now," stammered Mr Ashe. "It was a large sum and the theft has crippled us considerably."

"All right," said Dolan carelessly. "The sooner I get two years the sooner you get it."

"How could it be – be fixed?"

"I'll leave that to you."

That was all. The bank president and the two directors went out fuming impotently. Mr Ashe paused in Detective Mallory's office long enough for a final word.

"Of course it was brilliant work on the part of the police to capture Dolan," he said caustically, "but it isn't doing us a particle of good. All I see now is that we lose a hundred and nine thousand dollars."

"It looks very much like it," assented the detective, "unless we find it."

"Well, why *don't* you find it?"

Detective Mallory had to give it up.

A HUMAN PROBLEM

"What did Dolan do with the money?" Hutchinson Hatch was asking of Professor Augustus S. F. X. Van Dusen – The Thinking Machine. "It isn't in the flat. Everything indicates that it was hidden somewhere else."

"And Dolan's wife?" inquired The Thinking Machine in his perpetually irritated voice. "It seems conclusive that she had no idea where it is?"

"She has been put through the 'third degree,'" explained the reporter, "and if she had known she would probably have told."

"Is she living in the flat now?"

"No. She is stopping with her sister. The flat is under lock and key. Mallory has the key. He has shown the utmost care in everything he has done. Dolan has not been permitted to write to or see his wife for fear he would let her know some way where the money is; he has not been permitted to communicate with anybody at all, not even a lawyer. He did see President Ashe and two directors of the bank but naturally he wouldn't give them a message for his wife."

The Thinking Machine was silent. For five, ten, twenty minutes he sat with long, slender fingers pressed tip to tip, squinting unblinkingly at the ceiling. Hatch waited patiently.

"Of course," said the scientist at last, "$109,000, even in large bills would make a considerable bundle and would be extremely difficult to hide in a place that has been gone over so often. We may suppose, therefore, that it isn't in the flat. What have the detectives learned as to Dolan's whereabouts after the robbery and before he was taken?"

"Nothing," replied Hatch, "nothing, absolutely. He seemed to disappear off the earth for a time. That time, I suppose, was when he was disposing of the money. His plans were evidently well laid."

"It would be possible of course, by the simple rules of logic, to sit still here and ultimately locate the money," remarked The Thinking Machine musingly, "but it would take a long time. We might begin, for instance, with the idea that he contemplated flight. When? By rail or steamer? The answers to those questions would, in a way, enlighten us as to the probable location of the money, because, remember, it would have to be placed where it was readily accessible in case of flight. But the process would be a long one. Perhaps it would be best to make Dolan tell us where he hid it."

"It would if he would tell," agreed the reporter, "but he is reticent to a degree that is maddening when the money is mentioned."

"Naturally," remarked the scientist. "That really doesn't matter. I have no doubt he will inform me."

So Hatch and The Thinking Machine called upon Detective Mallory. They found him in deep abstraction. He glanced up at the intrusion with an appearance, almost, of relief. He knew intuitively what it was.

"If you can find out where that money is, professor," he declared emphatically, "I'll – I'll – well you can't."

The Thinking Machine squinted into the official eyes thoughtfully and the corners of his straight mouth were drawn down disapprovingly.

"I think perhaps there has been a little too much caution here, Mr Mallory," he said. "I have no doubt Dolan will inform me as to where the money is. As I understand it his wife is practically without means?"

"Yes," was the reply. "She is living with her sister."

"And he has asked several times to be permitted to write to or see her?"

"Yes, dozens of times."

"Well, now suppose you do let him see her," suggested The Thinking Machine.

"Lord, that's just what he wants," blurted the detective. "If he ever sees her I know he will, in some way, by something he says, by a gesture, or a look, inform her where the money is. As it is now I know she doesn't know where it is."

"Well, if he informs her won't he also inform us?" demanded The Thinking Machine tartly. "If Dolan wants to convey knowledge of the whereabouts of the money to his wife let him talk to her – let him give her the information. I dare say if she is clever enough to interpret a word as a clue to where the money is I am too."

The detective thought that over. He knew this crabbed little scientist with the enormous head of old; and he knew, too, some of the amazing results he had achieved by methods wholly unlike those of the police. But in this case he was frankly in doubt.

"This way," The Thinking Machine continued. "Get the wife here, let her pass Dolan's cell and speak to him so that he will know that it is her, then let her carry on a conversation with him while she is beyond his sight. Have a stenographer, without the knowledge of either, take down just what is said, word for word. Give me a transcript of the conversation, and hold the wife on some pretext until I can study it a little. If he gives her a clue I'll get the money."

There was not the slightest trace of egotism in the irritable tone. It seemed merely a statement of fact. Detective Mallory, looking at the wizened face of the logician, was doubtfully hopeful and at last he consented to the experiment. The wife was sent for and came eagerly, a stenographer was placed in the cell adjoining Dolan, and the wife was led along the corridor. As she paused in front of Dolan's cell he started toward her with an exclamation. Then she was led on a little way out of his sight.

With face pressed close against the bars Dolan glowered out upon Detective Mallory and Hatch. An expression of awful ferocity leapt into his eyes.

"What're you doing with her?" he demanded.

"Mort, Mort," she called.

"Belle, is it you?" he asked in turn.

"They told me you wanted to talk to me," explained the wife. She was panting fiercely as she struggled to shake off the hands which held her beyond his reach.

"What sort of a game is this, Mallory?" demanded the prisoner.

"You've wanted to talk to her," Mallory replied, "now go ahead. You may talk, but you must not see her."

"Oh, that's it, eh?" snarled Dolan. "What did you bring her here for then? Is she under arrest?"

"Mort, Mort," came his wife's voice again. "They won't let me come where I can see you."

There was utter silence for a moment. Hatch was overpowered by a feeling that he was intruding upon a family tragedy, and tiptoed beyond reach of Dolan's roving eyes to where The Thinking Machine was sitting on a stool, twiddling his fingers. After a moment the detective joined them.

"Belle?" called Dolan again. It was almost a whisper.

"Don't say anything, Mort," she panted. "Cunningham and Blanton are holding me – the others are listening."

"I don't want to say anything," said Dolan easily. "I did want to see you. I wanted to know if you are getting along all right. Are you still at the flat?" "No, at my sister's," was the reply. "I have no money – I can't stay at the flat."

"You know they're going to send me away?"

"Yes," and there was almost a sob in the voice. "I – I know it."

"That I'll get the limit – twenty years?"

"Yes."

"Can you – get along?" asked Dolan solicitously. "Is there anything you can do for yourself?"

"I will do something," was the reply. "Oh, Mort, Mort, why – "

"Oh never mind that," he interrupted impatiently. "It doesn't do any good to regret things. It isn't what I planned for, little girl, but it's here so – so I'll meet it. I'll get the good behavior allowance – that'll save two years, and then –"

There was a menace in the tone which was not lost upon the listeners.

"Eighteen years," he heard her moan.

For one instant Dolan's lips were pressed tightly together and in that instant he had a regret – regret that he had not killed Blanton and Cunningham rather than submit to capture. He shook off his anger with an effort.

"I don't know if they'll permit me ever to see you," he said, desperately, "as long as I refuse to tell where the money is hidden, and I know they'll never permit me to write to you for fear I'll tell you where it is. So I suppose the goodby'll be like this. I'm sorry, little girl."

He heard her weeping and hurled himself against the bars in a passion; it passed after a moment. He must not forget that she was penniless, and the money – that vast fortune-!

"There's one thing you must do for me, Belle," he said after a moment, more calmly. "This sort of thing doesn't do any good. Brace up, little girl, and wait – wait for me. Eighteen years is not forever, we're both young, and – but never mind that. I wish you would please go up to the flat and – do you remember my heavy, brown coat?"

"Yes, the old one?" she asked.

"That's it," he answered. "It's cold here in this cell. Will you please go up to the flat when they let you loose and sew up that tear under the right arm and send it to me here? It's probably the last favor I'll ask of you for a long time so will you do it this afternoon?"

"Yes," she answered, tearfully.

"The rip is under the right arm, and be certain to sew it up," said Dolan again. "Perhaps, when I am tried, I shall have a chance to see you and – "

The Thinking Machine arose and stretched himself a little.

"That's all that's necessary, Mr Mallory," he said. "Have her held until I tell you to release her."

Mallory made a motion to Cunningham and Blanton and the woman was led away, screaming. Hatch shuddered a little, and Dolan, not understanding, flung himself against the bars of his cell like a caged animal.

"Clever, aren't you?" he snarled as he caught sight of Detective Mallory. "Thought I'd try to tell her where it was, but I didn't and you never will know where it is — not in a thousand years."

Accompanied by The Thinking Machine and Hatch, the detective went back to his private office. All were silent but the detective glanced from time to time into the eyes of the scientist.

"Now, Mr Hatch, we have the whereabouts of the money settled," said The Thinking Machine, quietly. "Please go at once to the flat and bring the brown coat Dolan mentioned. I dare say the secret of the hidden money is somewhere in that coat."

"But two of my men have already searched that coat," protested the detective.

"That doesn't make the least difference," snapped the scientist.

The reporter went without a word. Half an hour later he returned with the brown coat. It was a commonplace-looking garment, badly worn and in sad need of repair not only in the rip under the arm but in other places. When he saw it The Thinking Machine nodded his head abruptly as if it were just what he had expected.

"The money can't be in that and I'll bet my head on it," declared Detective Mallory, flatly. "There isn't room for it."

The Thinking Machine gave him a glance in which there was a touch of pity.

"We know," he said, "that the money isn't in this coat. But can't you see that it is perfectly possible that a slip of paper on which Dolan has written down the hiding place of the money can be hidden in it somewhere? Can't you see that he asked for this coat – which is not as good a one as the one he is wearing now – in order to attract his wife's attention to it? Can't you see it is the one definite thing that he mentioned when he knew that in all probability he would not be permitted to see his wife again, at least for a long time?"

Then, seam by seam, the brown coat was ripped to pieces. Each piece in turn was submitted to the sharpest scrutiny. Nothing resulted. Detective Mallory frankly regarded it all as wasted effort and when there remained nothing of the coat save strips of cloth and lining he was inclined to be triumphant. The Thinking Machine was merely thoughtful.

"It went further back than that," the scientist mused, and tiny wrinkles appeared in the dome-like brow. "Ah! Mr Hatch please go back to the flat, look in the machine drawers, or work basket, and you will find a spool of brown thread. Bring it to me."

"Spool of brown thread?" repeated the detective in amazement. "Have you been through the place?"

"No."

"How do you know there's a spool of brown thread there, then?"

"I know it because Mr Hatch will bring it back to me," snapped The Thinking Machine. "I know it by the simplest, most rudimentary rules of logic."

Hatch went out again. In half an hour he returned with a spool of brown thread. The Thinking Machine's white fingers seized upon it eagerly, and his watery, squint eyes examined it. A portion of it had been used – the spool was only half gone. But he noted – and as he did his eyes reflected a glitter of triumph – he noted that the paper cap on each end was still in place.

"Now, Mr Mallory," he said, "I'll demonstrate to you that in Dolan the police are dealing with a man far beyond the ordinary bank thief. In his way he is a genius. Look here!"

With a penknife he ripped off the paper caps and looked through the hole of the spool. For an instant his face showed blank amazement. Then he put the spool down on the table and squinted at it for a moment in absolute silence.

"It must be here," he said at last. "It must be, else why did he – of course!"

With quick fingers he began to unwind the thread. Yard after yard it rolled off in his hand, and finally in the mass of brown on the spool appeared a white strip. In another instant The Thinking Machine held in his hand a tiny, thin sheet of paper – a cigarette paper. It had been wound around the spool and the thread wound over it so smoothly that it was impossible to see that it had ever been removed.

The detective and Hatch were leaning over his shoulder watching him curiously. The tiny paper unfolded – something was written on it. Slowly The Thinking Machine deciphered it.

"47 Causeway Street, basement, tenth flagstone from northeast corner."

And there the money was found – $109,000. The house was unoccupied and within easy reach of a wharf from which a European bound steamer sailed. Within half an hour of sailing time it would have been an easy matter for Dolan to have recovered it all and that without in the least exciting the suspicion of those who might be watching him. For a saloon next door opened into an alley behind, and a broken window in the basement gave quick access to the treasure.

"Dolan reasoned," The Thinking Machine explained, "that even if he was never permitted to see his wife she would probably use that thread and in time find the directions for recovering the money. Further he argued that the police would never suspect that a spool contained the secret for which they sought so long. His conversation with his wife, today, was merely to draw her attention to something which would require her to use the spool of brown thread. The brown coat was all that he could think of. And that's all I think."

Dolan was a sadly surprised man when news of the recovery of the money was broken to him. But a certain quaint philosophy didn't desert him. He gazed at Detective Mallory incredulously as the story was told and at the end went over and sat down on his cell cot.

"Well, chief," he said, "I didn't think it was in you. That makes me owe you a hat."

Love Golden Age crime fiction? Have you checked out the full yellowback range?

From Locked door mysteries to blind detectives through first women detectives, the yellowback reissues is one of the largest selections of classic crime fictions, in the original format with a modern clean easy read page layout. A sampling below.

For more details and a full list of titles:
visit https://www.hachetteindia.com/home/yellowbacks

H. Rider Haggard
MR. MEESON'S WILL

Melville Davisson Post
MASTER OF MYSTERIES
THE COMPLETE UNCLE ABNER COLLECTION

Jack London
THE ASSASSINATION BUREAU LTD.

Baroness Orczy
THE SKIN O' MY TOOTH

Earl Derr Biggers
SEVEN KEYS TO BALDPATE

Horace Walpole
THE CASTLE OF OTRANTO
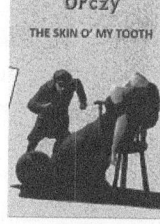

Sexton Blake
THE SEXTON BLAKE COLLECTION VOLUME 1

Francis Beeding
THE HOUSE OF DR. EDWARDES

A. E. W. Mason
AT THE VILLA ROSE

Fergus Hume
THE MILLIONAIRE MYSTERY

Donald Henderson
A VOICE LIKE VELVET

Richard Hallas
YOU PLAY THE BLACK AND THE RED COMES UP

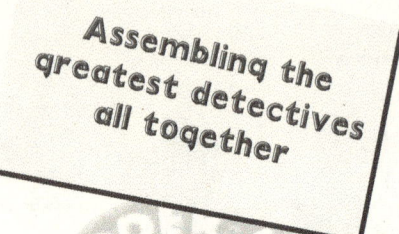

Assembling the greatest detectives all together

Covering the full range and history of detective fiction.
From Zadig, *The Moonstone*, and Dupin through Sherlock Holmes, Loveday Brooke, Montague Egg, Lord Peter Wimsey, *The Thinking Machine*, Father Brown down to Solar Pons.

For more details and a full list of titles:
visit https://www.hachetteindia.com/home/yellowbacks

WELCOME BACK TO THE GOLDEN AGE